To Kill a Tsar

Also by New Academia Publishing

RUSSIAN FUTURISM: A History, by Vladimir Markov

WORDS IN REVOLUTION: Russian Futurist Manifestoes 1912-1928
A. Lawton and H. Eagle, eds., trs.

MOSCOW BELIEVES IN TEARS: Russians and Their Movies, by Louis Menashe

IMAGING RUSSIA 2000: Film and Facts, by Anna Lawton

BEFORE THE FALL: Soviet Cinema in the Gorbachev Years, by Anna Lawton

WE'RE FROM JAZZ: Festschrift in Honor of Nicholas V. Galichenko
Megan Swift and Serhy Yekelchyk, eds.

*NEW PERSPECTIVES ON SOVIETIZATION IN CENTRAL AND EASTERN
EUROPE AFTER WORLD WAR II*, Balázs Apor, Péter Apor and E. A. Rees, eds.

*THE INNER ADVERSARY: The Struggle against Philistinism as the Moral Mission
of the Russian Intelligentsia*, by Timo Vihavainen

RED ATTACK WHITE RESISTANCE, by Peter Kenez

RED ADVANCE WHITE DEFEAT, by Peter Kenez

ASPECTS OF BALKAN CULTURE: Social, Political, and Literary Perceptions
by Jelena Milojković-Djurić

*SLAVIC THINKERS OR THE CREATION OF POLITIES: Intellectual History and
Political Thought in Central Europe and the Balkans in the 19th Century*
by Josette Baer

Fiction

ON THE WAY TO RED SQUARE, by Julieta Almeida Rodrigues

Memoirs

*THROUGH DARK DAYS AND WHITE NIGHTS: Four Decades Observing a
Changing Russia*, by Naomi F. Collins

JOURNEYS THROUGH VANISHING WORLDS, by Abraham Brumberg

www.newacademia.com

To Kill a Tsar

by G.K. George

ILLUSTRATIONS by

George O. Linabury

NEW ACADEMIA PUBLISHING · SCARITH

Washington, DC

Printed in the United States of America

Library of Congress Control Number: 2010929809
ISBN 978-0-9844062-7-2 paperback (alk. paper)

 An imprint of new Academia Publishing
P.O. Box 27420, Washington, DC 20038-7420

 NEW ACADEMIA PUBLISHING   www.newacademia.com
info@newacademia.com

To the memory of the real G.K. George,
master story teller

ACKNOWLEDGEMENTS

The author and the illustrator are equally indebted to their grandfather, G.K. George, for his wondrous tales of far-off times and exotic places that inspired their choice of careers. The author would like to thank many people for their encouragement along the way but especially Marjorie Mandelstam Balzer, Ben Eklof, Felicia Eth, Adlele Lindenmeyr, Alexei Miller, Monty Montee, Saul Morson, Alexander Riasanovsky and Edith Finton Rieber. I am deeply grateful to Marsha Siefert for her critical acumen, technical assistance and above all, for Irina, the Swan.

Prologue

He slept fitfully even though he was exhausted. He was not accustomed to working with his hands. Every evening he examined his blisters and broken nails. These fingers, he thought, should be turning pages of a book, not mixing cement and hauling bricks. There were worse things happening to him. He felt a tremor pass through his body. The fumes from the dynamite were poisoning his lungs. The spasms came more often now, rattling his thin ribs like a broken shutter. He was spitting blood too, but that was the consumption. Most of the time he lay in a stupefied state afraid to turn his face into the pillow with its smell of death. He stared at the scratches on the wall beside his bed. No one would know what they meant even if they had been noticed. And who would come down to this dank cellar? Every morning he woke feeling an obsessive need to recalculate the charge. He was sure now that he had enough dynamite to blow the imperial dining room sky high and kill everyone in it. He glanced at the ceiling. It was right above him. They would come in together the tsar and Prince Alexander of Battenburg. It had taken him some trouble to find out just when they would step into his little dynamite trap. He had squeezed the information out of the guards with the excuse that he did not want to disturb the reception by hammering from below. Soon his work would be over. He no longer thought of himself as Stepan Khalturin, but only as an instrument of the People's Will. How many times had they tried to kill the tsar? How many men and women had they lost in the process? But soon the hunt would be over; he kept repeating the words to give himself courage. It was a month since he had begun to build the bomb. With one blow he would avenge centuries of tsarist brutality. The tsars and their henchmen had been the first to resort to terror. Ivan the Terrible had created a secret police – the *oprichniki*; now they called themselves the Gendarmes. They were the most dangerous of them all. Clever bastards, inventing the idea of the double agent, employing psychological techniques of interrogation. Who had ever heard of these things before? Even the Sûreté in Paris could learn from them. For once Russia was in advance of Europe! But they were not clever enough. They failed to destroy the organization; the martyrs were replaced; the cadres seemed immortal. Long ago they sowed the wind. Now Alexander II would reap the whirlwind. Funny how the Holy Scripture had it right. Well, there were plenty of regicides in the Old Testament.

He took pride that the Exec-Com had assigned him the task. It had been his idea to masquerade as an ordinary workman repairing the basement rooms of the Winter Palace. So easy to convince the guards to let him to spend the night in this wretched hole. Proof of his devotion to the throne!

He stared into the darkness waiting for the hallucinations to begin. They arose from the miasma of the dynamite fumes; he had read about the danger but he had no choice but to conceal the sticks under his pillow and the mattress. The visions took the same shape every time. Childhood memories were the worst. He could have been no more than five years old when he first saw a convoy of exiles. They had passed through the market square of his village on the long road to Siberia. He remembered standing beside his father, squeezing his hand in terror. Over the years the images had blurred, but the horror remained. Weren't the men bound to one another with manacles? They seemed to be shuffling through some kind of soft stuff that splashed and darkened their leg wrappings. Was it mud or snow? He couldn't tell now. So long ago. A chill seeped into his body and he drew the worn blanket up to his chin. They said that the tsar also slept on an army cot and ate a frugal breakfast. To hell with him! Let him enjoy the last night of his stoic imposture.

Suddenly, he sat bolt upright, straining his ears. A muffled sound overhead—boots coming and going. Had they discovered him? Impossible. He had left no traces, made no mistakes. No one, not even members of the Exec-Com knew his plans. He had insisted on that. There had been too many betrayals, too many attempts foiled by double agents. A solitary assassin was the only guarantee of success. The boots retreated. He sank back on his pillow. They must have been inspecting the dining hall for the last time.

Far away in the city he heard the faint tolling of church bells. He recognized the sound. The big bells of St Isaac's Cathedral. The wind must have shifted off the Gulf of Finland. It was time to get up. Mechanically, he counted the seconds, allowing himself the luxury of two more minutes, then he swung his legs over the side of the cot. He felt the iron frame cut into his thighs. Everything gave him pain. He struggled to his feet. His jacket flapped open and the odor stung his nostrils. Sweat and the odor of dynamite. Would he ever get rid of it? The rash on his side had become an open sore. That too he knew had come from the sticks of dynamite rubbing against his ribs as he had trudged daily across the Alexander Bridge from the Vyborg side to the Palace. How careless they were. The back entrances weren't even patrolled. Inside the guards were used to him and waved him by without a search. But each time he passed them he could feel the tension mounting. His leg muscles tightened up, his nerves stretched to the breaking point. There were days he felt like screaming out loud. He feared most losing his will power; it was the only strength he had left. He imagined himself fainting from the fumes and the rot in his lungs, of spilling the sticks of dynamite at the feet of a Grenadier officer. What would he say then?

"Sorry, Your Honor, just a few necessary repairs, just removing the tsar from the Palace grounds."

He laughed soundlessly, and a spasm of coughing doubled him over. He splashed water from the iron pot onto his face and chest, soaking his shirt. He moistened his cracked lips, swallowing a few drops. He had finished his ablutions for the day. It would take time to set the charge, check the fuses. He began to work, listening for the tolling of the bells that would sound the death knell for the tsar.

One decision remained. He thought about it whenever he took a rest. Would he stay with the bomb and perish with his August Master? Wasn't that the only way to make certain? He had to be sure the imperial party had entered the dining room. The prospect of death did not frighten him. But he was tempted by the alternative.

He wanted to live long enough to see the whole rotten structure collapse once the linchpin had been removed. He yearned to share the joy of liberation with his comrades. He would gladly die a martyr if that was required, but only after he had savored Liberty, the magic word that spurred him on.

He bent over his task. His mind was clear, alert; the fatigue was gone, the phantoms dispersed. He packed the last of the dynamite sticks into the chest, a hundred pounds of it. Zheliabov and the others had protested. "Why do you need so much dynamite?" they wanted to know. "Whatever your purpose, you've more than enough." Again he had insisted. He had built a colossal mine; it was a work of art, he mused, ready to detonate. The church bells summoned him to set the charge—and leave.

When he stepped outside the guards paid no attention to him. They were smoking and quarreling about something. He bowed obsequiously as he never failed to do. He left the Palace for the last time, his legs trembling so hard he was afraid they would give way. He breathed in the cold fall air and a sense of relief flooded over him. He seemed to float across the Winter Palace Square past the Alexander Column under the Triumphal Arch. He hardly felt the pavement under his feet. He turned and waited with folded arms. In a few minutes Zheliabov was there beside him, his fiery red beard wafting in the breeze off the Neva. Khaturin thought of him as the indomitable leader. But he had not shared his secret preparations even with him. They did not look at one another. After a few minutes Khalturin slowly nodded. There was no more to be said.

The explosion rocked the west wing of the Palace, shattering hundreds of windows along the Palace facade and in the Army Chief of Staff building across the Square. A column of dense, black smoke rose into the air as if from a funeral pyre. Stepan Khalturin found himself running with frantic energy not in the direction of safety but toward the heart of danger, irresistibly attracted by the sight of the devastation he had wrought. He did not hear Zheliabov shout at him. All around him people were running, coming from nowhere and everywhere, jostling him, enfolding him in a protective envelope, Cossacks, passers-by, tradesmen, soldiers. As if by an unspoken command they came to an abrupt halt facing a gaping hole torn in the facade of the Palace and stood dumbly as if they were lined up on a parade ground or along the path of a funeral procession. Khalturin felt gripped by an almost unbearable excitement. The crowd was breathing in unison like some multi-headed creature. A collective sigh swept over it as the portal of the Palace opened and the Court Chamberlain, Count Adlerberg, staggered onto the porch. Several officers rushed to support him but he waved them aside.

"By the Grace of God, the tsar is unhurt. A divine intervention... he was delayed by the Prince...a few moments earlier...." The Count collapsed. Several voices shouted, "Hurrah!" Stepan Khalturin turned his face away from the recumbent form of Count Adlerberg and slowly walked back across the deserted Winter Palace Square into the city.

Winter Palace Square, St. Petersburg

Chapter One

Inspector Vasiliev, Vasili Vasilievich to his acquaintances, Vasya to his friends, entered police headquarters with a sense of foreboding. He had just solved the murder of the merchant Boldreyev. But something else was bothering him. True, the chief wasn't happy about the outcome. To hell with him. So the murderer was a titled noble rather than the shop assistant. They didn't like to send nobles to Siberia. Who cared if a shop assistant got shipped off? No it wasn't the Boldreyev case but the reports of the attempt on the tsar's life.

"Hey, Vasya! How goes it?" Two detectives lounging on a leather sofa broke into his thoughts. He nodded and gave a half-smile showing his crooked teeth and without a word closed the door to his office

"What's eating our Count today. He broke the Boldreyev case."

"Right, but he also broke the chief's heart." They laughed.

"I still can figure him out, I mean Vasya, after all these years. Why in God's name did he give it all up for this?" He gestured vaguely. The drab yellow paint was beginning to peel from the walls; scratched wooden tables and worn out chairs were scattered throughout the lounge.

"Forget it. That's a mystery you'll never solve. Nobody knows why except maybe Serov, and he'll never tell. I figure by this time Vasya could have been a Colonel in the Guards, or a Titular Counselor in one of those cushy Petersburg offices. That is, if he'd stayed in service."

"Did you ever ask him about it? Why he joined the police? Hell, he graduated from the Page Corps. A decorated veteran. All the right contacts. To give it all up. It doesn't make sense."

"Once he gave me a little lecture. All about his debt to the people. Christ, he sounded like one of those intellectuals. Mooning over the peasants."

"Well, you've got to remember. His mother was one, a peasant I mean."

"Yes, but papa was Count Vorontsov."

"Peasant blood is thicker."

"You really think that?"

"Got a better explanation?"

"No. Still, to give up being a Colonel in the Guards..."

"You and I weren't cut out to make such sacrifices." They laughed again, stood up, shook hands and went to their desks.

Vasiliev slumped into his chair and began to skim the newspapers on his desk. They all carried the same story. Reported it the same way. "By the grace of God, His Imperial Majesty, Alexander Nikolaevich, narrowly escaped death at the hands of murderous revolutionaries who would turn Russia into a charnel house." So much for Katkov in the *Russian News*. And then all the tripe about standing firm in the face of terrorist threats. Nothing about the lapse in security; nothing about the failure to make an arrest. But you could hardly expect journalists to take on the Gendarmes.

Sergeant Serov knocked softly before coming in. He took a few steps into the office and stopped, hesitating. A glance at Vasiliev was enough to warn him. He decided to occupy himself with the samovar and wait for whatever was coming. It would be something out of the ordinary. He knew all about that look. It was familiar to him since childhood when they were playmates in his mother's village. That was before Vasya went off to the Page Corps and returned as Vasili Vasilievich, an accomplished young gentleman. Well, not quite or at least not always one. That look of his; yes, it was all about what Vasiliev like to call unfairness in the world. He had tried to explain this to Serov more than once. Serov would nod in agreement. But to a man like himself, born a serf, life had to be taken as it was. There was no sense breaking your head over fairness. But Vasiliev was a fair man. That was why Serov felt bound to him, not as a slave or a serf, forced to submit to a master in the old type of bondage but as a man acting of his own free will.

"Sergeant, how do you explain the easy access?" Vasiliev accepted a glass of tea from Serov along with a small dish of jam as he swept the papers from his desk.

Serov knew immediately this was not a question he was expected to answer. Access to what ? By whom? He glanced at the papers on the floor. He did not set much stock in newspapers. Vasiliev would tell him in time what he had to know. Serov gave a noncommittal grunt and returned to the samovar.

"The man was working there for days, perhaps weeks. Smuggling in sticks of dynamite, for God's sake. And no one checked his documents? No one wondered why he was working alone? All of this after four previous attempts on the tsar. Remember the derailed train, and all the rest. The Gendarmes are supposed to be on top of these things. Just ask them. They'll tell you. On top of everything. Listen Serov, how do these things happen?"

Serov felt that now he was expected to make some response. "A clever lot, the revolutionaries. Maybe a wee bit more clever than the Gendarmes, if you see my meanin'." It was safe he knew to slander the Gendarmes. Vasiliev had always shown his dislike for the secret police. "The boys in blue" he called them. But Vasiliev did not rise to the bait.

"It looks like Zheliabov's work." Vasiliev sipped his tea and gazed hard at the papers lying in a heap on the floor. "Damned elusive, that man." Vasiliev drank his tea quietly, thinking about how it all had started.

Almost two years had passed since the revolutionary organization called the Land and Liberty Party had split into two wings. The moderates called themselves *Cherny peredel*, Black Partition or the Partition of the Land. A catchy phrase, that. What they meant by it was the redistribution of Russia's rich black earth among the peasants. No compensation for the landlords, of course. But they weren't killers. They believed in propaganda. Hoped to spread socialism among the peasants by preaching to them. Well, it was naïve. Really rather harmless despite the babbling of the Gendarmes. Zheliabov on the other hand was a different piece of work. He had split off from them, formed a terrorist faction. Called themselves the People's Will. They set their sights on the tsar, quite literally. They still believed that if they could kill him the whole creaky edifice of the Russian autocracy would collapse. Vasiliev wondered how much of this Serov knew.

"Smacks of Rousseau," he blurted out.

Serov's head jerked up.

"Sorry, my friend. You quit listening to my lessons before we got to Rousseau."

"There was work to be done on your papa's estate, Vasili Vasilievich. The bailiff wasn't none too happy about my shirkin' my duties. He'd shout at me. 'What's all this rubbish about history lessons?' I can tell you, he came down hard on me. My ears still ache at night from the boxin' he gave me."

Vasiliev laughed. "Come on, Sergeant that was twenty years ago."

"Right, permanent damage it was."

"All right, so we'll begin where I left off. Rousseau was a French philo…, a French writer, eighteenth century. He had an idea about 'the General Will', that's what he called it. All the people would exercise power for the common good."

"Sounds a fine idea to me."

"Of course, it does, 'sounds like' that is. But there are some problems. You see Zheliabov claims to speaks for all the people and then goes hunting for the tsar."

"He didn't asked us in the village about that."

"Not exactly. But you remember how the students came to village in the summer of '74 preaching socialism."

"Wet behind the ears, they was. Pretty silly, some of 'em. Well-meanin' enough, I guess. We listened politely. Some laughed in their faces. A few rascals turned 'em in to the police. It was their hands, you see, all white and soft. So who was goin' to do the work under this socialism?"

"Well, Zheliabov thought much the same about going to the people. Peasants were too ignorant. So he pushed the idea of terror. All the naïve, nice, gentle types with the soft hands took the name Partition of the Land. Doesn't have the same ring as People's Will, right?"

"No, but sounds another good idea. If you're still askin' my opinion."

Vasiliev burst into laughter. Serov loved to provoke that effect. The full-throated tenor voice. It recalled the old days. How they used to sing peasant songs together, he and Vasya. There always seemed to be a balalaika player strumming in the background. But that too stopped when he went away to the Corps.

"I'll have to watch you, Sergeant. Before long you'll be joining up, calling for land and liberty."

Serov was tempted to say, not unless you do. Instead he gave another grunt and added for the sake of good manners. "Aye, that's what they used to call themselves, I remember now. Land and Liberty."

"Right. And now they've parted ways, the terrorists in the People Will and the preachers in the Partition of the Land. There's your history lesson for the day. It still doesn't help us clear up what happened at the Winter Palace."

Serov put down his glass and began picking up the scattered papers.

"Well, God's in heaven and Petersburg's far away."

"And it's none of our damn business either. I had my chance to join the boys in blue. I don't regret not taking it." Serov knew the reason for this and for the other mysteries that baffled the detectives in the lounge. But he would have been hard put to state it in so many words. It all had something to do with Vasiliev's mama; his youth spent half in the village and half in the manor house. Then there were the books people would bring him wrapped in strange looking paper and written in foreign tongues. Now they were all crammed into his office. There were many other things that Serov had glimpsed but hadn't fully understood about Vasiliev's life. He thought that maybe now Vasiliev would speak of Irina. After all she was one of the revolutionaries now. Probably not a terrorist, but still an illegal. Serov waited, but was disappointed.

"Be a good fellow will you and clip the papers for me. I'll file them later. Right now I have to finish up the report on the Boldreyev case. The chief has been snapping at me more than usual. Didn't care much for the way things turned out."

Serov tried to find the right words to get him talking about her. But he couldn't think of them. Vasiliev turned back to his desk, pulled out sheaf of foolscap and began scribbling.

He was moving in the right direction, Serov thought, but then he stopped in his tracks. He'd done it before, not too long ago. Was this getting to be a habit? He hoped not for she was part of his life too.

They worked quietly side by side, the only sounds being the scratching of the quill, the snipping of scissors and the bubbling of the samovar. Occasionally, Serov would pause to read an article, quietly moving his lips, or Vasiliev would lift his head, sometimes for longer than it might have taken to find the right word. Each time Serov waited expectantly, but he was not rewarded.

Vasiliev wrote swiftly but he was distracted by thoughts that had nothing to do with the Boldreyev case. Serov knew him only too well. Once he had mentioned the revolutionaries he would start thinking about Irina.

Serov was right; Vasiliev kept wondering about her and her dangerous new life. She must have gone from Land and Liberty to the Partition of the Land, he thought. He couldn't imagine her as a terrorist. No question, she must have split from Zheliabov and his gang. Still, he never understood why she had joined the revolutionaries in the first place. Why, oh why had she done it? The question haunted him. Sure, it was the same question they always asked about him, whispered behind his back. Everyone from his father to his teachers and friends in the Pages. Why or why did you do it? Top of the class, son of a Count. All right, illegitimate, but no one cared so much about that. A brilliant career. Was it a whim they wondered?

He sighed and selected another sheet of foolscap, numbered it and started on the second half of his report. He cursed under his breath. He needed to concentrate all his thoughts on the case. A small error could cost him the conviction. The evidence was clear. But they had to be made to see it. Thank God for the jury system. In the old days there wouldn't have been a chance to convict a nobleman. Not on forensic evidence. Then he caught himself. Old days, Hell. The jury reform was less than twenty years old. And the prosecutor was a tough relic of the old days. Another skeptic like the chief. Doubted that a noblemen could commit murder except in a duel.

He set down his pen again. Serov watched him carefully, but

then turned away. Vasiliev read over what he had written. Vague images waited for him at the end of every paragraph. They were too polite to break into the flow of his prose. But they would not disappear.

On papa's estate, they were inseparable, he remembered. The three of them, he, Irina and her brother. Where were they always rushing off to? He couldn't remember. But there was another image. It was all too clear some days, like this one. He was standing on her veranda holding out her brother's sword. The sword of a dead hero. Brought back from the Turkish war. Her look of great sadness, no tears. He had trouble holding back his own. A year later she vanished. There were a few traces. He followed them until the trail went cold. Then the rumors came. The sources were not reliable. But the end of the story was always the same. She had joined the nihilists, revolutionaries, call them what you will. He could see no connection with her brother's death on the battlefield. What was eating at her that she wouldn't share with him? He didn't tell her family about the rumors. Perhaps they still didn't know the truth. He couldn't be sure. One thing was clear to him. They too were hiding something behind their public face of grief over the disappearance of their daughter. He caught a glimpse of it in the repressed anger of her father, a Colonel in the Guards. A happy family destroyed. It seemed to happen more and more in Russia these days, he reflected. He had no sympathy for the old patriarchal ways. But the path to whatever lay in the future was not going to be easy.

He moved on to the third section of his report. Irina's image was fading. He bid her another farewell. Too much romantic poetry, he thought. It's a problem. Being a literate bachelor. Too much Pushkin, perhaps. But then again could one ever have too much Pushkin? He would better spend his time with Dostoevsky. There was a man who understood the criminal mind. Reading him might be too much like taking home a case file. But he had to admit that Dostoevsky knew a hell of a lot more about the criminal mind than his colleagues lounging out in the corridor.

A loud knock startled him. The door opened a crack and a hand slipped in waving a telegram. A screechy voice sang out: "The capital calls, Vasili Vasilievich. You are a favored son." Serov snatched the message, fighting the temptation to slam the door before the fingers withdrew. But he resisted and handed Vasiliev the coded message.

"Ivan has written. He's coming to Moscow and wants to consult. We know what that means. He's going to try to drag me somewhere I don't especially want to go."

"Where might that be?" asked Serov with as much sarcasm as he dared.

"You know perfectly well, my friend. Attempt on tsar, followed by message from Ivan to consult; the Iron Colonel in action. Damn it, he won't leave me alone happily hunting murderers in Moscow. He's lonely up there in Piter, the high world of politics. He wants company. Well, he's not going to get it, old friend or not."

Serov was gazing out the window at a rook that had settled on the sill, and he began to whistle softly.

"Whistle as you will, Sergeant. Only a summons from the tsar is going to make me budge. My holidays are coming up next week. You know where I'll be. Off to the Urals to hunt. And once I'm gone they won't find me for a month. That's why I never tell you exactly where I'm going. You'll never have to lie for me. Never have to choose between betraying me or getting yourself cashiered."

Une chambre separée for two men was unusual, but the owners of the Yar were nothing if not discreet. Ivan's high rank was a sure guarantee that the utmost discretion would be observed. After coffee had been served there would be no further interruption. As Vasiliev expected Ivan had prepared the ground carefully. He led off with the latest court gossip about the tsar's scandalous liaison with Ekaterina Dolgorukaya. The former lady in waiting to the recently deceased tsaritsa would soon become his wife. "Morganatic marriage, of course. She'll be called Princess Yurovskaya." Then he laid out the news about the latest plans for reform. Loris-Melikov, the Minister of Interior—Ivan was now calling him the dictator of the heart—had just about persuaded the tsar to call a consultative assembly. He hoped to rally public opinion against the revolutionaries. "A big gamble" was Ivan's verdict, "but better than a constitution."

"You see, *mon vieux*, our agents tell us that people are afraid to take sides. They won't condemn the revolutionaries. But they won't line up with them either. Fence-sitters. Here's what's hard to believe. The attempts on the tsar's life haven't won him any sympathy. We have to convince the doubters. And that is what Loris-Melikov, our dictator of the heart, has in mind. There are lots of rumors about a constitution. All nonsense. What he's proposing is an elective assembly of wise men. We have some you know. The point is to get them to advise the tsar on what needs to be done to win over the public."

Vasiliev toyed with his dessert fork. He was tempted to lick off the last traces of chocolate. But this was not done in polite society, and Ivan was polite to his finger tips. He replaced the fork on his plate and gazed wistfully at the last éclair. This too would have to be sacrificed to good taste and left for the waiters to demolish in the kitchen.

"Half measures," he growled, less concerned about a constitution at that moment than the éclair.

Ivan looked shocked. "What do you mean? Anything more radical would never pass the ministers."

"So, to Hell with the ministers. Alexander Nikolaevich is the autocrat, isn't he? His father would never have hesitated. Do what he had to and the ministers could go to Hell."

"Those were the old days, Vasya." There was a pause. Maybe there were some good things about the old days, Vasiliev thought. But no. He was being petulant.

Ivan guessed the time had come to make his approach. Vasiliev was like some hundred-gun frigate; you had to get under the range of his cannons before you could board.

"Listen, Vasya, all this brings me to the business at hand. I need your help to be my man in Moscow."

"Ah ha! Now I have to sing for my dinner. In that case I am going to have this last éclair. Where do you think they get their chocolate, from Belgium?"

Ivan leaned forward in what Vasiliev recognized as his best conspiratorial manner. Was it copied from some cheap melodrama at the Malyi Theater? These bureaucrats needed some modern stage direction.

"There are rumors that the revolutionaries are planning some outrage in Moscow at the opening of the season. A special detachment of Gendarmes has been designated to mount guard at the early balls, especially at the big aristocratic houses."

"Good," Vasiliev managed to mutter between bites. He swallowed hard. "It's the business of the boys in blue. But why would the terrorists switch targets from the tsar to the aristos. Doesn't make sense."

"The theory is that an attack on the nobility would further undermine confidence in the reform, you know, as a way of dealing with the subversion"

Vasiliev couldn't help smiling. He loved that evasion, the subversion. Such a delicate way of portraying the bombers. Made them sound like nasty writers.

"So you want me to dust off my old dancing shoes? Not a chance, Ivan. It's not my kind of job. Besides I'm off on holiday and I've earned it after the Boldreyev case. I bruised some noble egos. I would not be a welcome guest in the big houses, let me assure you."

"Nonsense, Vasili." Vasiliev noted the sterner tone. Ivan might start calling him Vasili Vasilievich soon, or, God forbid, Inspector Vasiliev. Then things could get heated and more official than he wanted.

"Before you accuse me of stupidity in addition to talking nonsense, let me tell you something, Ivan. With all due respect, one lonely police Inspector nosing around the big Moscow houses is not going to impress or dissuade any bomber worth his salt. I don't even know the cast of characters. The boys in blue have been studying these madmen for years. They know their moods and modus operandi. I'd be like a white crow in a pine forest."

"The point is, Vasili (so things hadn't gotten that much worse) that you've got it all upside down. It is precisely the Gendarmes who are the white crows. They stand out in any crowd. You know that. Whereas you…. You have that great repertoire of disguises. You can just melt into the background of any place you go. I've seen you…or rather I've not seen you in action. Once in a merchant's bazaar, another time at a peasant *skhod*. I knew damn well that you were there. I still couldn't pick you out. And neither will the revolutionaries. As for the holidays. We'll double your time off…

"It won't do. The hunting season will be over. It may be my last chance to get Burya."

"God in heaven, does hunting down that damn bear mean more to you than…"

"…than going off on a wild goose chase. Yes! Rumors about some kind of outrage. Hell, that could mean anything. Imagine me showing up at Prince Bagration's or anybody else's ball in some outlandish disguise. First thing some eager Gendarme would arrest me. The whole idea is ludicrous."

Later Vasiliev remembered with some chagrin his remark about Prince Bagration's ball. Well, how could he have known? And would it have made a difference if he had been there?

Chapter Two

A cool breeze sprang up early in the evening of the first ball of the fall season in 1880. Prince Bagration's Moscow manor house was a blaze of light. The guests were reassured by the sight of the police who seemed to be everywhere, directing traffic, patrolling the neighboring streets, scanning the faces of the passers-by. Glimpses of sky blue cloth could be seen under grey coats.

In the labyrinth of narrow streets between Arbat and Prechistenka a broken-down hack lurched over the uneven paving stones. The colorless figure of the cabby blended with the cab and horse as if they were all stamped from the same worn out press. The mare was slightly lame in her left foreleg, and there was a running sore on her flank where the bent wooden shaft chafed her raw flesh. When she stumbled over a badly patched stretch of Old Stables Road where it crossed Sivka Gully, the hack shuddered from top to bottom. A muffled pounding from inside roused the cabby from his stupor. Cursing under his breath he pulled savagely at the reins. The mare quivered and veered to the right down Gagarin Lane.

"For Christ's sake, he nearly turned us over, what the Hell is he up to?"

"Relax, Marko, a few potholes aren't going to kill us. It's likely to get rougher by the time we're finished."

Marko impatiently jerked open the curtain on his side and peered into the Street of the Dead. The lamps were barely visible through the streaked and dirty windows of the hack. The street was deserted. In the dim light the two-story, old-fashioned houses also appeared to be lifeless which was, he reflected, a bad joke. He pulled the curtain closed, plunging them into darkness.

"We're coming up on the Church of the Assumption of the Tombs," he muttered. "We'll be there in a few minutes, Magician." He rubbed his knuckles against the rough cloth of his coat.

"Don't be so nervous. We're not out to assassinate the tsar."

"Thank God for that. The whole point...," Marko bit his lip.

"The whole point of this little adventure, my dear friend, is to prevent such a stupidity."

"You really believe that, don't you? I mean in the depths of your soul."

"My soul! God, Marko, I have no soul. None of us does. Don't you get it yet? Sometimes I wonder why you went underground. It was an accident, wasn't it?"

"What do you mean by that?"

"You got thrown out of university by chance. That's what you told me."

"That's not fair. I was arrested. There was a demonstration...."

"By chance, Marko, by chance. Your friends dragged you in and pushed you into the first row. The rector recognized you, so out went Marko."

"You really are a swine, Magician. I agreed to go with you on this crazy adventure and you pay me back with insults."

Magician reached over and patted Marko on the knee.

"Just teasing old man. Of course you're a real comrade."

They fell silent. Marko hated it when Magician played his little games. What right did he have to question motives? Who knew anything about his past? He never explained why he had left university and gone underground. Maybe that too was by chance. There had been some vague talk about his distributing illegal literature and preaching socialism to the peasants. That had been six years ago, in the mad summer of '74. Marko envied him, if it were true. But had anyone actually seen Magician in the villages, going to the people? Marko had never met an eye witness. Had he been there or not? He dare not ask. A real magician he was. When you thought you had a fix on him, he pulled a disappearing act. Still, Marko thought he had one trump. He knew Magician's real identity. That was something to keep in reserve.

Tonight, at least, Marko was sure he would prove his value to the cause. No one knew the back streets of Moscow better. He had worked out a system of signals to guide the cab through every twist and turn. He reached up and tapped the roof of the cab three times. The cabby shifted his weight and the nag slowed to a shambling gait.

Finding the mansion was easy. But he had no idea how Magician would get inside. He had been so damn vague about it all. He was vague about everything. He talked about it as if it were a promenade. The trouble was they could end up getting arrested.

"You'll take about half an hour?"

"Hey, it's a promenade, remember? It can't be timed to the second." Magician fidgeted with the coil of rope by his side. Now he would tell his little story, a fairy tale of sorts. But he was sure it would be enough to reassure old nervous Marko. The main thing was to prevent Marko from telling tales, or worse running to the Exec-Com, creating a scandal. That could unravel the whole thing.

"Listen, Marko, I'm going to let you in on the real reason for the promenade. I'm sorry I didn't tell you up to now. But I know your generous spirit. You might have said something to Swan. Maybe just a slip the tongue. But she must be kept in the dark. Hey, without you I couldn't carry it off. You're the key to success."

Marko knew he was being flattered. But he half believed Magician. He sounded sincere for a change. What annoyed him was the way Magician slurred his r's when he pronounced his name— Ma'ko. A Petersburg affectation. Besides, Marko disliked his own pseudonym. He hadn't picked it. He hated it in fact. It wasn't Russian enough. The comrades had begun to call him "Marko the Serb" once they discovered that his father had volunteered to fight the Turks in '76. They had heard that he was something of a local hero to the Bosnian rebels. Dear Papa, he wouldn't have liked it either, this Serbian nickname for a revolutionary son. On his better days Marko thought his looks might have inspired the idea. His coal black hair and deep set, dark eyes. He tried to make it work for him. He even grew a fierce-looking moustache. But it ended in humiliation. The Exec-Com had ordered him to shave it off.

"No need, better to keep your secrets to yourself."

"Who's talking about secrets? Listen, Marko..."

"No, you listen. You dreamed up this promenade. Remember. I had my doubts. I still do. But you were very persuasive. I'm here, aren't I? Just keep in mind that I'm not happy about it."

"God, you are touchy." Had he gone too far? Old Marko was all right, just a bit obtuse. But there was no sense offending him, not now when he needed him. Misleading Marko was risky. Lying to the committee later on would be worse. All right, he thought, no fairy tale for old Marko. Besides, he had his own devils to contend with, devils beyond their imagination.

"The tricky part will be scaling the fence and crossing the gardens. I'll have to avoid the rose beds." He chuckled but there was no response from Marko. "All right, all right, I'll be serious, a properly professional revolutionary. On the ground floor of the west wing the window will be unlocked. We can be sure of that. You know, the downstairs maid, what's her name? Lisa, She's trustworthy. Hey, she's even a little in love with me, eh Marko?" He glanced at Marko again. Nothing. Staring straight ahead, thick lips tightly contracted. The devil take him.

"If there's a problem Lisa will leave a lighted candle on the table. But there's no need to expect trouble. The servants will be swamped with work in the kitchens. Working their arses off, preparing meals for a hundred guests. The lackeys will be busy as hell running around, unloading the coaches, leading them back into the park. The cream of Moscow's parasitic class will pile into the east wing. They'll be gorging themselves, gambling and flirting, dancing and otherwise engaging in those socially productive activities for which they are famous and despised. How am I doing, Marko? Literary enough for you?"

Marko sat unmoving, silent.

"All this leaves me a clear field. I slip into the storage room. I make sure there is no lighted candle flickering in the corner. I tiptoe down the passageway. It leads me to the service staircase. See how carefully I move. Ready to disappear if anyone pops up unexpectedly. Just like a real Magician, eh? At the top of the stairs I turn right and then left. At the third...no, wait a minute the second door isn't it?"

"For God's sake get it right, it's the second door."

"Bravo, Marko, you're awake after all."

"A mistake would ruin us."

"Don't be a fool. I've been over the course a dozen times in my head. Second door, three taps. Repeat the signal. The young prince opens the door and *voilà!*"

"So, say half an hour."

"And I say that's your timing, not mine."

"The committee instructed...."

"Mother of God, Marko, the committee is not breaking into the mansion of Prince Alexander Ivanovich Bagration, grandson of Russia's most famous General and adversary of the great Bonaparte. A hundred of Moscow's most worthy nobles are milling about under the protection of the secret police. Who's more frightened the cops or the nobles? I don't know and don't care. They're both terrified that Zheliabov and company will blow them all to kingdom come. Besides, our princeling may have to be coaxed."

The nag shuffled to a halt in the dark lane but the cab kept swaying, buffeted by the wind that was now blowing strongly from the northeast. Marko felt slightly queasy as if he were on board a small boat drifting aimlessly. The swaying motion, the musty odor of frayed curtains stirred old fears. His nerves finally gave way.

"Listen," he whispered, frantically pulling on Magician's sleeve. "We can still get a message to Swan. She could pick up the letters without causing any suspicion. She'll be mixing with the crowd...."

"Are you crazy? She has her own assignment. She has no idea that we'll be here tonight. She'll never know if you keep your mouth shut. Security above all, Marko. Must keep the promenades separate. Besides, young Bagration trusts no one but me."

He pried loose Marko's fingers, one by one.

"Maybe we're both fools. The place will be filled with army officers, swarming with security people...."

"Is this Marko, the daring revolutionary speaking? Get hold of yourself. The setup is perfect. The noise, confusion, the orchestra playing full blast. The cops will be too busy peering down the bodices of all those lovelies. They won't take notice of anything else. This is the best chance to get at the boy. How many times do I have to repeat? He's rarely allowed out of the house by himself. He's terrified of his father. He can't make a move without his permission. What do you want to do? Are we going to sit here all night and have one of our interminable Russian discussions? Damn it, I'm getting out of here."

Magician wrenched open the door and hurled himself out of the cab. He felt a tug at his shoulder. He whirled ready to strike out at Marko. But it was only the coil of rope that had caught on the metal handle as the door slammed shut. Magician pulled free and scampered across the cobbled pavement toward a high iron fence barely visible in the gloom.

Marko fell back against the cushions. The threadbare upholstery ripped open under the force of his weight, releasing a coiled spring that jabbed him in the back. He lunged forward banging his head against the paneling. The old man on the box scratched his head. Was that a signal? He couldn't remember it as part of the system. What to do? He opened his mouth, gulped down a draught of cold air and was seized by a paroxysm of coughing.

"God, it's enough to wake the...," Marko caught himself and pounded on the roof of the cab. The cabby gripped the edge of his seat and retched. The nag moved forward. Marko impatiently tugged the curtain aside again. His hands felt clammy. He was barely able to make out the figure of Magician moving in the deep shadows. He had thrown the rope high on the iron palisade to catch the sharp points at the top. Marko remembered how their golden tips had sparkled in the light of day. The dim figure of Magician seemed to be dancing at the foot of the fence. Then he doubled over as the cab passed him. Marko seized hold of the cab door. It was so cold he thought his flesh would freeze to the metal.

He was seized by a moment of panic; should I help or leave him? He stared at the door handle. His muffler slipped down revealing a smooth shaven face, dark eyes staring wildly, the face of a frightened young man. Papa's words came back to him in a rush. "You are children, amateurs, playing with people's lives." Marko felt the tears welling up and cursed his weakness. His father's voice was drowned out by others. Magician mocking him, Swan scolding him gently. He thought of her somewhere out there in the dark, moving toward Bagration's without knowing about their promenade, their little conspiracy within a conspiracy.

He collapsed against the torn cushion as the cab turned a corner into Prechistenka Street where it suddenly swerved in order to avoid colliding with a troika bearing down on them. Marko pressed his face against the window. He recognized the matched Orlov bays and the armorial crest of Count Ushakov, the deputy minister of interior. He felt the panic rising again. They had almost collided with Swan's target.

Marko lost all sense of caution, staring dumbly at the oncoming traffic. His eyes locked with those of a young woman in a small horse drawn trap. It had come up behind Ushakov's troika. He pulled back into a corner, cringing. He touched his exposed face. Swan must have recognized him. He buried his face in his hands.

The Ushakov coach had followed the inner boulevard that divided the Earth City from the White City, the outer districts from the center of Moscow. Throughout most of the journey the two passengers did not exchange a word. The count appeared to be dozing. His delicately modeled head was inclined to one side, the mass of curled, silver hair rested against the silk cushion. His tapered fingers were folded primly on his lap. He had perfected this languorous pose over many years. It was part of his repertoire of practiced deception. Through his half-closed eyes he had been studying his wife with ironic detachment.

The Countess was seated beside him, her white silk ball gown spilling over his knees. It seemed to him that she was preoccupied by something besides her appearance. If so it was a rare moment. He racked his brain for anything unusual that had happened earlier during her elaborate toilette, something that would explain the strange look of concentration on her features. She was still beautiful, he reminded himself. A pity she could no longer hope for a portrait painter to do her justice. There were no Russian artists worthy of the task. The Englishmen Reynolds and Gainsborough were long dead. Perhaps only a living mask would satisfy her, an exact imprint of her features in soft clay. But then the pale color would be missing. Damn it! What could she be pondering for so long? The Count found himself uncomfortably interested.

She was not, for once, toying with her hooded cloak. Her fingers were not stroking the blue fox trim in that sensual way that drove him to distraction. She had not uttered a word of complaint about the coachman's handling of the Orlov bays. She had yet to drop as single cutting remark about their hosts, the Bagrations, or any of the other guests who would, depending on their rank and title, bow and scrape or shower her with compliments—the beauty of her gown, her coiffure, her jewels. Yet most of them would hardly spare him a word. He could only expect a grudging acknowledgement of his existence despite the fact that he outranked them all. In the past he had courted their approval. Now their indifference meant nothing to him. Unfortunately, Elena was still part of that world.

He methodically went over her good points. Her smooth, lofty forehead, delicate cheek bones, Slavic rather than Tatar, her refined nose embellished with flaring nostrils to lend a touch of passion, the small but full lips about which he thought much. She was cut like a flawless diamond. A banality, he mused, but also perhaps a problem. All her lines were etched too sharply. In old age they would accentuate her shrewish disposition. Now she looked merely petulant.

He also took note of her heightened color. Not from cosmetics, he knew. Her good taste dictated no more than a tinge of rouge on her lips. Nothing could be allowed to detract from her much envied translucent skin.

He began to feel discomfort from a faint stirring of desire in his loins. He was too old for that sort of thing and his britches were too tight. But he could not tear his eyes away from her. For a moment she reminded him of the desirable woman he had courted, fought over, bedded and then married, not an unusual sequence among men of his class. But in her case he had surprised himself.

They entered Prechistenka Street where the newly installed kerosene lamps cast shadows on her face. Should he tell her they had been installed to illumine every line of her crystalline profile? She wouldn't appreciate the compliment, not coming from him.

"I'm delighted to see that the drive pleases you, my dear." He could not resist breaking in on her reverie or whatever it was.

Her lips trembled. It was her imitation of a disdainful smile.

"One ceases to complain about lost causes," she drawled in her normal tone of affected weariness. But he knew he had startled her. Since when could he boast of having surprised her in her private thoughts?

"Street repairs can transform a hopeless situation," he turned slightly to study her expression.

"Please Dmitri, spare me your lecture on public improvements. The next thing you'll be telling me about your sewer projects." She simulated a shiver.

"Arkady will be going back to the village soon enough." He nodded toward the front of the coach. "Then you'll regret not having him. He is the best coachman in Moscow."

"I believe you have told me that before," she said dryly. "I fear his departure will be one of the saddest days in your life."

"Not quite, my dear." The Count's voice dropped to a whisper.

"Oh, you are not going...."

"No my little pigeon no more lectures or regrets I assure you. Quite the contrary.I was just about to compliment you. I have never seen you more ravishing."

"Really, Dmitri, you are becoming quite intolerable."

She was pouting now, an expression he had begun to observe among the court ladies in waiting. It must be the latest rage, to pout. His excitement subsided. His eyes narrowed again. His mind wandered to the papers lying on his desk. The long columns of figures and dry accounts of the governors general added up to one conclusion. The peasants were falling more deeply into misery. They were still loyal, but only God knew how long that would last. It had been almost twenty years since the serfs were freed, but their life had not improved. They were growing in numbers, pressing against the land. The land, always the land. They thought more land would solve all their problems. They believed it was rightfully theirs. So far they had not listened to the siren calls of the revolutionaries for land and liberty. But for how long ?

The Count took out a small enamel box embossed with a portrait of the tsar in his coronation robes. He inhaled a pinch of snuff. The Countess was too absorbed in her reverie to complain. Ushakov was so distracted that he did not notice this extraordinary lapse on her part.

Land and Liberty! He moved his hand in an involuntary gesture of dismissal. And who would run this peasant Utopia? The beardless youths and young girls who had gone to the people? He couldn't recall without a shiver how they had quit the universities or been expelled in the mad summer of '74. He had read the police reports. How they had run around in their peasant dress, preaching socialism! What did they know of taxation and finance, of legal practices and administrative law, of raising and maintaining an army, or negotiating a treaty? He caught himself rehearsing his righteous indignation. The problem was that Russia needed more than police repression to stop them. The peasantry would listen to their natural leaders. If only the tsar would grant the nobles a voice in governing. He would have to start with a consultative body. That was the way to win over men of good will. An assembly of the land would break down the tsar's isolation. There was no time to lose. The terrorists were closing in, hunting Alexander Nikolaevich like a wild animal.

The Count's thoughts turned to his report. What was he doing going off to a ball at the house of his old enemy? He should be closeted in his study. This was the critical moment. In Petersburg the forces of reform were gathering around Loris-Melikov. The two of them worked well together, though they were an odd match, the tough, Armenian military hero and the aristocratic Russian bureaucrat. Yes, a critical moment. He would have to make his excuses early tonight.

And what of dear Elena? He had no choice but to leave her to dance the last mazurka. The thought of being alone in his own house became very agreeable to him.

The Ushakov coach began its wide turn into the Bagration drive when a cab lurched out of the Street of the Dead and cut across its path. Arkady swerved, uttering a string of mother curses. The incident had ruined a perfect trip. Now the Countess would be in one of her moods.

The major domo of the Bagration household watched the incident standing on the top step of the entrance. A Georgian from the mountains he had been trained since childhood to watch for unusual movements, the fall of a pebble from an outcropping of rock that might betray the presence of a concealed rifleman, the stirring of reeds in a pond where no wind blew. In Moscow there were other kinds of signs, but they too could reveal hidden foes. Nothing was accidental until proven so. He shifted his attention from the hack to the Ushakov coach. He reflected, not for the first time, on the custom peculiar to Russian nobles of dressing up their coachmen. This one was wearing a bright blue coat, they called it an *armiak*, and a frilly lace cap. The major domo approved of his graceful movements as he swung down from the box and in the same fluid motion opened the door and bowed as low as his paunch would allow.

Recognizing the armorial bearings the major domo quickly descended the steps. He extended his hand to the Countess who swept by Arkady as though he had ceased to exist.

"My apologies, Your Excellency, the fool almost ran us down," Arkady blurted out. But the Countess had reached the portico before the words were out of his mouth. The Count descended more slowly. He was smiling.

"A near miss, Your Excellency, it could have been a serious matter. I swear to you he came straight at us, out of the Dead. I had to swerve."

Ushakov placed his hand on Arkady's shoulder.

"A brilliant maneuver, my dear fellow. I saw it all, still don't miss much, you know. We hardly felt a ripple."

Arkady bowed, feeling the leather belt cut into his belly. His eyes followed the Count mounting the steps. A good master. Hearing the clatter of a light trap behind him, he jumped back onto his box and turned the bays into the wide courtyard behind the mansion.

The trap drawn by an Arabian mare had passed along the quiet back streets of Zamoskvorechie, the district south of the river where the great merchant families had their mansions. It crossed onto Big Yakimanka Street and then cut across Kaluzhskaya Square before turning west along the old Crimean Rampart that had once formed an earthen wall of defense against Tatar raids from the south. It traversed the Crimean Bridge and then headed directly for Prechistenka Street. But the driver suddenly turned down a quiet lane, slowed the mare to a walk, and brought the trap to a complete halt. The two women passengers fell silent. The driver checked the light traffic that passed them. There was no indication that they were being followed. After a few moments the trap started up again and made another turn.

"Does he really have to be so conspiratorial?" the younger of the two women asked softly.

"It's out of habit, Swan. It's good to have these kinds of habits as you must learn." The other woman smoothed the wrinkles in her brown cloth dress, but fixed her bulging eyes on the woman she had called Swan.

"Please don't patronize me, Norka. I'm not a novice at this sort of thing. But excessive caution can also look suspicious."

Swan wondered how a woman who looked like a mole had become known to her comrades as Norka, "the mink". It was hard to imagine her even clothed in mink. She immediately reproached herself for the thought. There was more to worry about than Norka's appearance. It was her own dress that concerned her. She had tried her best with what she had left of a gentlewoman's wardrobe. She worried whether it would measure up to the exacting standards of Moscow society. She touched her hair, swept up and held in place by two jeweled combs. At least they were in fashion. But what else was?

"As for being nervous, what do you expect? I'm an uninvited guest at an opening ball of the new season and I look ten years out of date. The dress may seem elegant to you but the last time it saw service was when my mother wore it at a reception in Paris for Emperor Napoleon III. Just look at this high waist and the lace at the wrists and throat. And the only jewels I still own are this child's pearl necklace. The gloves? Belgian lace, slightly discolored from lying at the bottom of a trunk for twenty years, thank you. At least my shoes match. God knows where Magician got them, from one of his aristocratic conquests no doubt. They even fit."

Norka shrugged. "You don't expect me to understand these things. I didn't have the advantage of noble birth."

"You're just as fortunate. I keep trying to forget the past. Now they want me to reenter it."

"Your family knew the Count, at least that's what you told us."

"And Magician confirmed it, remember that. But it has been a long time since he has seen me. I was still a girl. Our families drifted apart. Such things happen. But I'm sure that the Ushakovs do not know that mama and papa live abroad for most of the year. Still we're taking a chance. Suppose he has heard that I left the family, vanished?"

Norka heard the catch in her voice. "Is it still hard for you to admit that?'

"Don't be foolish, Norka. It's just a question of getting myself in the right state of mind. I'm trying to become a proper young lady again. It takes more than putting on a fine dress to carry it off."

"I'm sorry, I did not mean to offend you." Norka reached out to touch her comrade's sleeve. She had given Irina her pseudonym, Swan –*Lebedeva*. Her beautiful neck arched like a premiere ballerina. No one suspected the rest, what she was really thinking. After all Lebedeva was a common Russian name. Norka's fingers brushed Swan's wrist. But Irina, had turned away to stare at the traffic. Norka quickly withdrew her hand. What had possessed her? To touch…She bit her lips and ran her fingers through her brown hair. It was cut short in the nihilist style. No, she thought, they would never mistake me for a child of the nobility.

For several minutes they sat quietly listening to the regular rhythm of the wheels.

"I've rehearsed the conversation with him a dozen times in my head. But I don't seem to be able to catch the right tone." Swan tossed her head and mimicked her mother's high-pitched voice: "How do you do, monsieur le Comte. You haven't seen me in ten years, but tell me about your plans for a constitution."

"This is no time to joke, still less to joke badly."

"But it is, Norka, or else I'll go to pieces. We may have staked too much on this meeting. Even if I get past the introduction, the pleasantries, what are the chances that he will listen to me? If he does there is so little time to act. Our dear comrades in the People's Will have lost their reason. Ever since Khalturin's bombing. Oh what's the use. They boast of how ruthless they are, how tough-minded. But they are hopeless romantics, worse still, utopians, especially Zheliabov. They think they can topple the whole empire by seizing the right lever. As if Russia were nothing more than a heavy stone blocking the road to universal progress."

Norka grunted in agreement. Yes, they had chosen well. Swan had the passion and the style to carry it off if anyone could. Expecting too much? They had no choice, really. Terror was not working, would never work. Somehow they had to persuade the liberals to move faster or face disaster. This lovely girl could make the difference. But it had been crazy to want to touch her. At all cost she had to mask her feelings. She clenched her fists.

The first kerosene lamp on Prechistenka came into view, casting strong shadows.

"Let's put the best face on it. I won't be able to get him to tell me everything, but it will be a start. The main thing is to arrange another meeting. That is where the Countess fits in. I shall have to please her as well. I remember her as a conceited ornament."

Norka nodded her head but said nothing.

Suddenly, Swan sat bolt upright and pressed her handkerchief against her mouth, repressing a cry. Norka's body went rigid. She plunged her right hand into her overcoat pocket, clutching the butt of her Browning revolver.

"What is it?" Her bulging eyes squinted at the passing shadows.

"A cab, it passed so close it startled me." Swan could not control her voice from shaking. "Ghostly, wretched," she muttered. One glance had been enough for her to recognize the familiar face of Marko pressed against the window. A chill ran through her. What in God's name was he doing here?

Norka grunted again but kept a firm grip on the Browning until the trap slowed to turn into the circular drive of the Bagration mansion.

"We'll be back in four hours and wait in the courtyard until you call for us."

Swan drew a deep breath, threw off her fur and lightly stepped out of the trap. She immediately caught sight of Count Ushakov standing under an iron lantern suspended from the roof of the portico. The years had been kind to him, she thought, the hair more silver but still thick and curly. He was engaged in an animated conversation with a tall officer wearing the pale blue uniform of the Gendarmes, a general judging by the high epaulets. She hesitated only a fraction of a moment and then tripped up the staircase breathlessly accosting the Count.

"Dmitri Andreevich," she cried with all the girlish enthusiasm she could summon up. She stopped just short of embracing him. She caught the look of amusement on the face of the General and the confusion of the Count whose eyebrows shot up in surprise. He bowed graciously wondering who this little treasure might be.

"Ah, I knew it! You don't remember me, and yet you used to bring me the finest confections in Moscow." He could see she was pretending to be hurt. Then she burst into laughter and that brought a look of recognition into his eyes.

"Irisha! You...well, what a splendid young lady you've become. And your parents?" The Count glanced at the trap as it disappeared around the corner of the house.

"They are still at Como. You know how mama despises the cold and the heat." She went off into peals of laughter, relieved to hear him chuckle in return.

"My dear Irisha, may I still call you by that name? Let me present you to General Grigory Alexandrovich Shuev, a very important man especially in these difficult times."

Shuev bent his large domed head over the girl's gloved hand.

"Grigory Alexandrovich is responsible for our safety, my dear. He is the real power in His Majesty's Third Section. Foreigners call it our secret police, but it is no secret that they are very good at hunting terrorists." He turned to Shuev who seemed to have trouble releasing her hand. The policeman thought of himself as a fine judge of character and summed up Swan as a fledgling hardly out of the paternal nest, innocent, even naive yet already possessing the allure of a mature woman. And modest, he added to the list, unlike many young women including his own daughter. Too bad the Count had blurted out his rank and responsibilities. It might intimidate her. That would be a bad beginning. Shuev turned down the corners of his mouth. Swan thought it was an ugly gesture.

"The Davidovs were my neighbors during the best years of my life, yes, Grisha, the happiest. And some of my happiest moments were spent with my dear little Irisha."

Shuev smiled which Swan decided did not improve things, while his eyes swept the drive and the in-coming coaches. She assumed he was not searching for her parents but for signs of trouble. Apparently satisfied that his men were well placed in the courtyard and along the perimeter of the iron fence, he offered her his arm. Would her comrades believe her? She could hardly believe it herself, that Irina Nikolaevna Davidova, alias Swan, a revolutionary of the Partition of the Land, was entering the mansion of Moscow's most distinguished noble family escorted by the Deputy Minister of Interior and the Assistant Director of the Third Section of His Imperial Majesty's Chancery.

Swan had long prepared herself for this moment, but she had almost forgotten what it was like. The blaze of light from the cut glass chandeliers imported from Murano, the women in decolleté gowns of white and pastel silks, their bosoms held high by brightly colored sashes, the men in black dress coats or else wearing the uniforms of the Hussars or the Guards, one more gaudy than the next. The inner staircase was lined by lackeys wearing the black and white livery of the Prince and holding silver candelabras each one fitted with five black candles. Carpets from the Caucasus and Persia were casually thrown over the marble stairs. Where the flight of steps divided, curving to the right and left, Swan saw her own figure reflected in the tall mirrors set in gold frames of entwined acanthus leaves. A bit of fluff, she thought, suspended between two pillars of state.

In the reception hall windows from floor to ceiling reflected a thousand lights from the masses of black and white candles held by free standing candelabra. The famous Bagration parquet floors, laid down a century before by house serfs, glistened under a high polish. In the ballroom beyond a string orchestra was playing arias from Italian operas. Shuev steered them off to the side avoiding a plump woman in a heavy brocade gown of vaguely oriental style.

"Is that the Princess Bagration?" Swan whispered to Ushakov.

"Yes, Irisha, later, we'll find her after the crush."

But Swan kept her eyes fixed on the Princess while wondering all the time when Countess Ushakova would appear. She was surprised how the guests greeted the Princess with the deference due her rank, but then passing quickly on as if they were embarrassed to remain in her company. Through the open doors Swan could see the grand ballroom. To the right and left smaller rooms tables had been set for cards and a buffet supper had been laid. The food was arrayed on an enormous, hollow, circular table covered with white damask table cloths. Silver bowls and platters were heaped high with mounds of osetra, sevruga and beluga caviar. She could hardly take it all in. A whole poached salmon and smoked sturgeon from the Caspian, chicken in the Georgian style, drowned in walnut sauce, trays of *lavash* bread, bottles and carafes of Georgian wines and Armenian brandies, tropical fruit—how long had it been since she had seen a pineapple? It had all been shipped to Moscow from the south, the Count told her, on specially commissioned steamers of the Volga-Mercury Line.

Swan looked back at the Princess as the stream of guests parted around her. Then a ripple passed through the company. The Countess Ushakova had entered the hall from the dressing rooms. She still creates a sensation, mused the Count. There were murmurs all around them, "how lovely she is." The Countess ignored everyone as she hurried across the room to embrace the Princess. "The public performance begins", the Count murmured.

"What is that, Dmitri?" asked Shuev, not removing his eyes from Irisha.

The Princess appeared to cling to the Countess. Elena did not break away although she disliked public displays of affection between women. The Count turned away from the scene and dropped Irisha's arm, but Swan led Shuev toward the two women. He seemed satisfied to go wherever she wanted. They were close enough now to hear the Countess who spoke in a stage whisper.

"Your gown is exquisite, *chère amie*. The cut of the bodice is enough to drive men mad, *de vrai chic parisien*."

The Princess blushed, her fingers tightening their grip on the folds of the Countess' gown. Swan marveled at the change in the mood of the guests. As if they had been waiting for a secret signal, they swarmed around the two women, chattering gaily. The Princess had become the center of attention. Elena then detached herself and passed on into the ballroom with the effortless ease of a woman supremely confident of the effect she was making.

Swan steered Shuev back to the Count.

"I've never seen Princess Bagration before. Papa said she was always hidden from view."

"Yes, well Bagration, that is the Prince, still keeps to the old, half-Asiatic traditions."

"Ah, Dmitri, you are too harsh. I think the Princess herself dislikes our Russian routs. She surrounds herself with servants from the south. I think her major-domo, splendid type though he is, disapproves of us all."

"She is strangely beautiful," said Swan.

"Unfortunately the exotic Caucasian beauty, like the Mediterranean, fades quickly" replied the Count. Then he added to himself, but it retains its warmth which cannot always be said of the northern type.

The Countess surveyed the hall hoping that Bagration would delay his appearance until later. Perhaps he has learned some self-control she reflected. He should have stayed in the mountains where life suited his savage nature. She had seen enough of his violent side to last her for a lifetime, but it was necessary to settle accounts with him one last time.

As she entered the ballroom the musicians exchanged glances and launched into a new waltz by Tchaikovsky that was all the rage. She took it as a tribute. They knew she would stay until they had played their last chord. A group of young Guards officers rushed to her side. They were laughing as they drew a circle around her, pleading for a place on her dance card.

"You can't have promised a single favor yet," exclaimed a hussar resplendent in his peacock green uniform with white frogging slashed with gold braid. "We've had you under observation since you arrived. No one else came near you."

The Countess assumed an expression of mock astonishment, as though she had not expected the onslaught, although it was always the same everywhere. Then she joined the laughter and dangled her dance card in front of them. The name of Prince Bagration appeared three times in a row.

"Impossible," they shouted, "The Prince no longer dances."

"But what can I do, gentlemen? That doesn't seem to matter to him."

They roared their disapproval in unison and a dozen hands reached for hers. As their fingers brushed hers she felt a familiar tingling sensation in the small of her back. Her card was rapidly filled out. But her "band of heroes" as she called them did not disperse. They escorted her across the ballroom. Those who watched compared her progress to a treasure train moving under guard across the steppe.

"So, the Countess has already made off with the pride of the army," Shuev lisped in his Petersburg affectation.

The Count shrugged."This time they may have marched too quickly, Grisha. They should have reconnoitered a bit. There are some charming prizes here this evening." He beamed at his Irisha.

"But the Countess is the most fascinating woman in Moscow." Irina gave him what she hoped was her innocent smile.

"Perhaps only the most beautiful," Shuev bent over her hand.

"If she were a man, she would be a Russian Murat."

"My dear!" the Count exclaimed. He had never thought of his wife as the Russian counterpart of a Napoleonic cavalry leader.

"You forget, as a child I saw her ride. She has no fear."

"True enough, dear girl, she has no fear."

"And she would look splendid in a cavalry jacket, her waist, slim as a boy's."

"I can't deny that either."

Shuev felt he was being left out. His eyes followed the white gown of the Countess as she cut a swath through the darker uniforms.

"Interesting," he said, "I've always believed, if you don't mind my saying so, Mitya, that your wife also has the kind of intelligence a man might envy. As Irina Nikolaevna says, she has the impetuosity of a Napoleonic cavalry officer. I dare say we could use her in our service."

"You are both right," the Count replied following Shuev's gaze. "The Countess has the instincts of a hunter."

Irina was impatient for Shuev to join the dancers so she could be alone with the Count. But she realized that her protective cover of girlish modestly and flirtatious banter had succeeded only too well. Shuev refused to leave her side until she had promised him all the mazurkas. His polished dome gleamed as he again bent over her gloved hand. Still, he lingered until Princesses Bagration waddled up to them.

"Grisha, you cannot keep this treasure to yourself," She extended her bejeweled fingers to Shuev. "*Mais qui est-ce qu'elle? Viens ici ma cherie.*" She took Swan with her other hand as if she were about to join her two guests together. Swan wondered whether this too was a Georgian custom. She felt a strange emotion, the shadow of a premonition. The princess stared at her for an instant as if trying to convey a message then took Shuev's arm and moved away.

"I need your protection tonight, Grisha." She laughed but Swan saw the fear in her eyes.

Swan guided the Count into the next room where the lackeys were setting up the tables for games of Boston. The Count nodded at his acquaintances, but made no effort to leave her. Did it occur to him, she wondered, how odd it was that she preferred his company to that of the young officers who kept glancing enviously in their direction.

"You didn't give us your opinion of the Princess, Irisha. What do you think?"

"She doesn't seem to be happy. I thought she looked frightened."

"So you noticed too, and yet you have never seen her before. Well, I dare say everyone these days is a little nervous, especially at these big affairs. All foolishness, of course, but the ladies have become terrified that the revolutionaries will start tossing bombs into their drawing rooms. Just the other day one of them whispered to me, 'But Count if they can blow up the tsar's dining room!'"

"Terrible," she paused. "They are misguided people, I mean most of the young radicals, aren't they?"

"Dear girl, even as a child you had more sense than the silly young things around you. Where did your mother find those playmates of yours, I wonder? Misguided is the word. That is just what they are, misguided. Their heads are filled with all kinds of nonsense. Imagine them wandering around the countryside, living with peasants when they know nothing of village life. They never understood the peasants. And their hair, wild like a pony's. Their clothing, disgusting, those coarse linen blouses."

They stood under an archway leading into the ballroom. The Count folded his arms and watched his wife flash by in the arms of a Grenadier officer.

"But who is to guide them?" the Count went on. "Not their professors. Most of them are armchair revolutionaries themselves. They preach materialism. Turgenev was right about them. They are nihilists, believe in nothing. They find the truth in dissecting frogs. Their parents? The aristocracy is no better. They subscribe to the thick journals, read banned literature from France so that they can gossip about forbidden things. The authorities? We may be most at fault. All around me," the Count gestured at the game room where bearded men wearing brightly colored decorations studied their cards, "the guardians of public order cannot see any difference between students and bomb throwers. It is one thing, Irisha, to scribble manifestoes and smuggle literature into your bed at night. It is quite another to conspire against the life of the tsar. You have to admit that, don't you? If you treat them all the same way you turn the scribblers into terrorists."

She recalled all the awkward openings she had thought up and discarded. Here was the Count driving the conversation just where she wanted it to go. She could only ruin it by saying too much.

"I can see that now when you explain it,"

"You know when I was young," he patted her hand," we all read Mirabeau, well, to be frank with you even Danton. A few desperados looked into the furnace of Robespierre. But that did not turn us into bomb throwers. Today they read Chernyshevsky and work themselves up into a fever of excitement about the millennium. You smile, but believe me that is what they do. It's a fever. But wait! Let me tell you what I think. It's rubbish what they read, but it isn't dangerous. Unfortunately, my friends in the police think differently. Imagine! They are convinced that reading about Chernyshevsky's utopian sewing circles turns a normal human being into a savage. Now, I'm not talking about the real criminals, the Khalturins, the Zheliabovs. They are the terrorists. They are beyond the pale of civilization."

"If only the students could hear you, Dmitri Andreevich, they would be astonished. Someone so high in government putting things so clearly. If someone like you could talk to them, reason with them. They might be brought back to their senses. A voice of reason, a kindly voice. That's what they need. But the government tells them nothing. All they hear are rumors." Swan hoped she was not laying it on too thick.

"Yes, Irisha, there is too much secrecy. Besides, I must tell you, the government is divided." The Count took her arm and led her away from the card players toward an empty table in a corner.

"My old friend Grisha, you just met him, does not agree with me. I think he humors me because his uncle and I attended the Lycée together. Grisha lacks subtlety in politics, quite unlike his uncle.

He ends all our discussions the same way: 'Crush them, Mitya,' he shouts at me. 'Stamp them out like vermin. Radicals, revolutionaries, they're all the same.' There are times when I despair."

"There must be someone on your side, Dmitri Andreevich. You are not alone, are you?"

"Not tonight." The Count wrinkled his nose at her the way he used to when he held a sweet behind his back. Swan laughed in order to conceal her rising excitement.

"You mean they are all your enemies," her eyes darted around the room.

"Exactly, that is why I keep you at my side," he grinned at her. "But perhaps you should be with the younger crowd." He waved his hand in the direction of the dancers beyond the archway.

"But surely there's someone among the leaders who values your opinion. Isn't General Loris-Melikov behind you?" She felt she was forcing the pace but could no longer hold back.

"Good girl. So you keep up with politics in far off Como. Yes, a brave man, and the tsar has given him immense power. Of course he lacks polish; they make fun of his Armenian accent at court. But a man of action, a veteran of the Turkish War, you know. He has great plans."

Irina snapped open her purse and taking out a faded lace handkerchief dabbed the beads of perspiration on her upper lip.

"They say he is preparing a constitution."

"Mmmm, yes." A movement in the ballroom caught the Count's attention. "Bagration has finally made his appearance. There's no way of avoiding him now. I'll have to say a few words, but you can be spared that pleasure for the moment, Aren't they striking up a mazurka?"

Out of the corner of her eye Swan noticed that Shuev was bearing down on her. He bowed deeply, offered his arm with the urgency of a command and led her triumphantly into the ballroom.

Chapter Three

The strains of the same mazurka reached Magician as he lowered himself into the darkened storage room. The candle on the table was firm and cold to his touch. The wick, he smiled to himself, was virginal. He tore open the buttons on his high collar, peeled off his Russian tunic and flung it on the floor. He loosened the knotted rope around his waist and kicked off his nankeen trousers. He slid his hands down his chest fingering the silken fabric of the dress suit he wore underneath, making sure that the crease had held up. He wondered what Marko would make of his quick change.

He felt a surge of excitement as he tugged his cravat into place. "Now into high society," he muttered to himself and eased open the door to the corridor.

He made his way along the passageway that led through the servants' quarters. Without turning his head, he passed the staircase that led to the upper floors and headed toward the sounds of the music. Behind him a door opened and closed followed by a rush of air that wafted the odor of seared lamb down the corridor. They're preparing shish kebab, he thought, and why not? I'm in the house of a Georgian prince. He heard a heavy step behind him. Someone had stumbled into the passage. If they stopped him he would say that he had gotten lost. That's what he would say. No need to be worried, he was properly dressed. They would recognize his educated voice, his manners. He was the guest of young Prince Bagration. We were in school together, the Nobles Pension, you know. Go ask him or better bring him to me. I got lost you see in this grand house. He heard a gasp behind him. Was it of surprise or fear? And then the sound of heavy boots retreating in the opposite direction. He hurried along feeling a twinge in his stomach.

The footsteps died away. He stopped to listen. Nothing now but the faint strains of the Prince's orchestra. He recognized the melody, the waltz from Tchaikovsky's newest opera, Eugene Onegin. A good omen, he thought; after all Onegin was the first of them, the superfluous man. Hadn't he paved the way for revolutionaries like himself?

The hardwood floor gave way to carpeting. His fingers closed around an antique brass doorknob as cold to the touch as the cab handle in the Street of the Dead. He threw open the door. At the opposite end of the room another door slammed shut, cutting off loud males voices and leaving clouds of cigar smoke to drift up toward the ceiling.

He was in the Prince's library. The music sounded as if it were coming from the next room or perhaps just beyond. He tried to imagine the grand ballroom and he felt his heart quicken. He tried to steady his nerves by fixing his eyes on every object in the library as if to commit it all to memory. The warm tones of the wooden paneling, the high bookcases lining the walls interrupted by spaces filled with etchings of mountainous country, the Caucasus, of course. He recognized the outlines of Mount Elbruz and remembered his first sight of it on a frigid winter day. He admired the cut glass brandy decanter, letting his fingers briefly caress the stopper before dropping his hand. He would need his wits about him. He went over to the bookcase where he stood for several minutes, running his fingers over the leather bindings. He pulled down a volume of Pushkin's verse.

"Why not keep to the theme of the evening," he said half aloud. He turned to the opening stanzas of Eugene Onegin and skimmed the lines he knew by heart. The orchestra had shifted back to mazurkas. He sat down at the oaken desk and propped the book up against a bronze figure of a mounted Cossack. A Lancerey wasn't it? The tall German clock in the corner showed half an hour to midnight. He wondered how long he would have to wait. He was sorry in a way for Marko fidgeting in the broken down coach. He had left him quite literally in the dark. Magician smiled to himself. If Marko thought making contact with the princeling was risky what would he think about what I have in mind? It would make his thick black hair stand on. So what if it were madness. It would only take him a few minutes to do what he had to do; then his conscience would be free for the rest of his life. Or so he promised himself.

He stared at the door across the room and wondered whether he would have the courage to turn the handle and casually walk into a world he had only read about. Would they take him immediately for the imposter he was? Not alone he couldn't do it. But then how? He felt paralyzed. Suddenly he knew he had to look as though he belonged there, perform another magic trick, turn into a young, languishing nobleman. He would have to look preoccupied, immersed in some work of the mind as if he were indifferent to the attractions of *le bel monde*. That's one lesson the Exec-Com never taught us, he mused. How does a revolutionary look natural in the study of a prince? Tossing the book aside, he searched the desk drawers for a sheet of foolscap and began to copy verses from memory to steady his nerves. He no longer heard the ticking of the German clock. Then without warning, two men dressed in the uniform of hussar officers in the Life Guards burst into the room.

"We beg your pardon," they bowed, "we have disturbed the scholar in his lair."

Magician nodded, "Good evening, gentlemen. You've come just in time. I'm stuck on this one rhyme," he slapped the paper and stood up to shake hands.

"Imagine," said one of them, "with all the beautiful ladies at his beck and call this one sits brooding like Onegin."

They went directly to the sideboard and poured three brandies, handing one to Magician. He inhaled its bouquet.

"My God, it's the real thing, a genuine Napoleon, must predate the fire of 1812."

The hussars raised their glass: "To your scribbling!"

"Just some light verse, it came over me during the waltz."

"You see! I was right, Onegin brooding."

"No, you've got it wrong, Lensky was the poet. Onegin shot him, don't you remember?" They laughed and gulped down the brandy.

"Listen, Mitya, how much of your Pushkin do you remember?"

"Well, Shura, how about this from his dirty little verses, the stuff that never sees the printer's shop." Mitya began to recite an erotic poem that circulated throughout the barracks. He was a real *basso profundo*. When he faltered Shura took over, Magician chiming in from time to time so they ended in perfect unison. Shura raised the empty decanter to the light.

"Time to rejoin the ladies. Coming along, poet?"

They linked arms and squeezed through the doorway. Magician thought it was a brilliant entrance.

Swan clutched the Count's coat begging him not to leave her. "There is so much we haven't talked about, Dmitri Andreevich. You remember our autumn walks in the Zvenigorod forest, the linden trees scattering their leaves in your garden and the mushroom expeditions. Remember, remember how Mama always brought home the poisonous ones?"

"No, you really haven't changed. How is it possible not to change in our times?"

"And there is the important matter, you know," she raised herself on her toes so she could whisper in his ear, "the new constitution."

"Hush," he wagged his finger at her. "If you want to talk politics, this is not the time. You must come to see me when I'll be receiving at home. But come early, before dinner around three in the afternoon. Then there will be only the two of us, just like the happier days."

She pressed his hand to her cheek and released him. She felt a pang as she saw his eyes grow moist. How painful, she thought, to return to the old life. For a moment her thoughts were confused, weakening her revolutionary discipline. Were there still some decent men at the head of the country or was the whole structure rotten?

The Count too was beginning to wonder. Irina had quite turned his head. Were there more like her? Had he given up too easily on Russia's youth? Perhaps he had lost touch. He belonged to Pushkin's generation, a different world. She might be his guide to the new generation. He suddenly felt a burst of energy. It was time to shake free of the Bagrations and their empty life. Too bad Elena was so much a part of it. Time to get back to serious work.

The Count lifted Irina's hand to his lips. "*Au revoir* my child. You have quite restored my spirits." He threw back his head and, with an air of defiance, strode out of the ballroom, glancing neither left nor right. Irina had a sudden impulse to run after him, take hold of his arm and insist that he take her home. Had she gone soft in the head? She repeatedly the word mechanically, Home! Home! It no longer existed for her. That was the problem wasn't it? Her parents' house on Arbat, darkened behind iron shutters, not a servant in sight, leaves swirling up an empty drive. Home! The word was an obscenity. Her childhood memories had been blotted out by the terrible day in June. She could still feel the hot sun, the wind blowing her hair as she galloped down the military road to surprise Papa on his name day. He stood in front of the barracks, handsome as he always was in the colonel's uniform, handsome for the last time in her eyes. She had reined in when she saw the gauntlet, the soldiers in a double line, wielding their sticks, beating again and again until she lost count, the young private, Boris—she knew them all by name—until his back had been reduced to a red pulp. Only later had she learned that he had been sent off to a labor battalion and then mustered out, a cripple who could no longer even work in the fields. And what for?

Her face burning with shame she had ridden away only later confronting Papa. She would never forget the astonished look on his face and then the cruel expression that distorted his features. His harsh words still resounded in her head: "You understand nothing of the army, the need for iron discipline to control these half savage peasant boys. One man punished on the parade ground means a hundred saved on the battlefield," he ranted at her, his voice filled with contempt. Afterwards she began to ask questions of the officers. How evasive they were until in a tipsy moment one of them had blurted out the truth. Papa was a martinet, much feared, "a regular Arakcheev" he stuttered. The name was unfamiliar to her. She asked more questions, began to read. Arakcheev, the most hated man in the old army! Her Papa, so kindly to his sickly wife, so tender with his Irisha, was being compared by his own officers to the brutal taskmaster Alexander I had set over the army of heroes that had defeated Napoleon. How could she have grown up in his household and not have known all this? The question made her frantic. She could not stand to have him touch her. He changed tactics, tried to be reasonable, then lectured her, scolded her, and finally ignored her. She could not share the terrible secret with her ailing mother. She was unable to study, to read, to think. The bloody image sprang at her from every page of a book and from every corner of the house. If she had not met Magician she would have gone out of her mind. Whatever his faults she would always be grateful to him, forgive him his pretentious posing, his worst sins for lifting her out of the pit of despair and giving her a vision of a new Russia.

The Count paused to exchange a word with the major domo. Was Ushakov any different from Papa? Twenty years ago he too had owned serfs, ordered them beaten or sent into exile at a whim, perhaps even claimed the right of the first night with a serf bride? And now he was toying with the idea of a constitution for Russia. What drove him to it? Repentance, a sense of religious mission, the need to make Russia strong again? Or was it only another way of currying favor, sucking up to the tsar who seemed ready to complete the business left unfinished by the emancipation and create some kind of assembly of the land as in the old days?

Swan was shaken out of her reverie by a loud orchestral chord summoning the company to a quadrille. As the dancers moved into place they screened the Count from her sight so that she did not immediately see him advancing toward her. She raised her hand to her throat. Why had he come back? Had someone betrayed her?

"J'ai oublié mes devoirs. Je dois faire mes adieux à la princesse." Why was he speaking French to her? "She is resting in the Georgian Room." Irina hesitated. It was all right then, her heart stopped pounding. She moved to take his arm when she glanced over his shoulder at the dancers. What she saw drove all thoughts of the constitution out of her head.

Magician had broken into the five-figure dance opposite Countess Ushakova, brushing aside her partner, an elderly gentleman with side-whiskers in the style of the tsar. His pince-nez went spinning to the floor where it was ground under the boots of the dancers. Someone dragged him away. Swan registered the shock on the faces around her. She bit her lip until she tasted blood. The Count had turned away without noticing what was happening. Swan felt powerless to follow him. She could not tear her eyes away from the face of the Countess whose lips had twisted into a contemptuous grimace.

The intricate dance figure propelled the Countess toward Magician. They glided past Swan who heard the Countess hiss between clenched teeth, "imbecile!" His smile crumpled and he averted his head as if he had been slapped. For an instant they drew within a few inches of one another so that their breaths intermingled before the music forced them apart. Their features seemed distorted, twisted almost beyond recognition. Swan felt stricken, helpless. She shuddered at the terrible danger closing in on them. A display of raw passion in this tightly regulated world could not long escape the attention of the most casual observer to say nothing of the trained eye of a policeman.

Shuev chose this moment to approach Swan surveying the room with his penetrating gaze. She knew she had to distract him but the words would not come. She pivoted on her heel, forcing him to turn his back on the dancers in order to meet her eyes.

"I hope the Count has not been boring you with his abstract theories." She heard nothing in his voice to suggest that he was aware of what was happening. But she knew it was just a matter of time before his eyes like those of a gyre falcon's would fix on the ridiculous figure of her comrade in arms. She struggled to give Shuev her full attention but heard only bits and pieces of what he was saying.

"...a grandee of the old school, almost too much of a gentleman to survive politics in our day...." Shuev rambled on, his gaze taking in the card players in the adjoining room, alert to the slightest sign of danger, a sudden commotion, a raised voice, an overturned chair that might signal a terrorist attempt. She felt a sudden impulse to laugh hysterically. It was all taking place within a few feet right behind his back and the great policeman hadn't a clue. She got herself under control. The main thing was to keep him distracted. He had asked a question, but what was it? He was talking about the Count again.

"He was held up to us as a model since childhood," she blurted out. Shuev seemed not to have heard.

"This whole business of winning over public opinion is really too naive. Do you know Mitya has convinced himself that he can isolate the terrorists and disarm them morally?"

Irina risked a glance over Shuev's shoulder. The Countess had cast an imploring look to someone outside the circle of dancers. Shuev shrugged and his epaulets blocked her view.

"And he wouldn't even be here tonight if the Countess hadn't dragged him...even regards me as an adversary."

The Countess felt trapped in the geometry of the quadrille. The music relentlessly brought them face to face where she was compelled to endure the familiar smirk on his lips.

"Your arrogance is insufferable," she spat out at him as he whirled and bowed. He too remembered that expression of hers, the fury in her eyes that would have aroused the old Count for certain.

"Madame doubted my ardor," he rapped out in return.

Swan watched his movements become disjointed as if he were about to lose control. She knew how to read his emotions and what she saw was humiliation giving way to anger. She cursed him inwardly for his adolescent passions. He was going to wreck everything they had struggled to achieve. She had been so close. An open scandal would turn the Count into a figure of fun here in the midst of his enemies. She herself was in danger of being exposed as Magician's accomplice, a nihilist. Oh how they loved that word! But she kept Papa's lessons in mind: "It's ruin for a soldier to run from a fight," he had said. Anyway, she had nowhere to run. Only one thing was sure to her. She was not going to sacrifice herself to save him. If he had not brought the danger on himself, yes, then she would have risked everything to save him, but not for this stupidity. He had broken discipline when the fate of the country hung in the balance.

"...they must be stamped out...." She heard more shreds of Shuev's monologue.

"...the fate of Russia hangs in the balance...." She was startled. It was if he had been reading her mind but had reversed her meaning. It broke the spell. Hadn't she thought of the simple solution because it was so conventionally feminine? She passed her hand over her forehead and seized the sleeve of his tunic.

"Why what's the matter. You look unwell. I'm terribly sorry all this political talk has upset you, frightened you. How thoughtless of me. Please forgive me." She felt the gentle pressure on her wrist.

"Perhaps if we could sit down. It seems that I've gotten overly excited." She leaned on his arm as they moved away from the dancers. As they passed out of the ballroom she caught a glimpse of a large figure striding across the floor toward the orchestra.

Prince Bagration, who until then had been a shadowy presence at his own ball, suddenly materialized at the side of the conductor. He gave a whispered order and the orchestra cut off the quadrille. Without missing a beat it glided into the waltz from Onegin.

The Prince whirled, strode back through the broken figure of the quadrille and with scarcely a bow claimed his first dance with the Countess. The dancers scattered in all directions as he maneuvered her away from the forlorn young man abandoned in the middle of the half-empty dance floor.

The guests murmured their approval. At a distance they seemed perfectly matched. He was thirty years her senior but he still retained his youthful figure, his broad shoulders tapering to a narrow waist, his muscular legs carrying them both with precision and lightness. Up close the contrast could not have been greater. The Countess had seen it all before, the noble features fallen into ruin, the puffy cheeks, the drooping eyelids masking two gray green orbs dull with dissipation. A light film of his wife's rouge barely covered the rash on his forehead. She tried to avoid inhaling his foul breath. He was rotting away from the inside. She saw him now as a doomed man.

"Your attraction to odd members of the species continues to amaze me, my dear Countess."

"And your formality of address continues to amuse me." She averted her face.

"Who is he and what is he doing here?" His lips were curved into a smile but he gripped her waist with such violence that she almost cried out.

"I cannot be expected to answer for all your guests. A deranged young man. There are so many of them these days. God knows from what sinkhole he emerged, but this is hardly the time for one of your jealous rages, *mon ami. Après tout, nous avons des choses sérieux à discuter, n'est-ce pas?*"

The Prince nodded curtly in the direction of a footman who had kept his eyes riveted on his master. A series of hand signals flashed across the room. Lackeys scurried to extinguish the candles in the largest candelabra plunging the room into semi-darkness. An orchestra crescendo drowned out the cries of alarm.

"Clear the floor," the Prince's voice resounded throughout the hall. The guests formed into small groups chattering in anticipation of a spectacle for which the House of Bagration had become notorious. There was a commotion in one of the side rooms. Four figures dressed in the costumes of the Greben Cossacks burst into the hall and catapulted into the center of the dance floor. Bandoleers of cartridges gleamed on their breasts, black lambs' wool caps perched on their shaven heads. They held their swords overhead, flashing in the candlelight. Their wild cries and the pounding of their heavy boots on the parquet floor sent a tremor through the crowd.

"Hurrah, the Terek Sword Dance!" shouted the Russian officers, clapping their hands and stamping in unison until the entire hall was vibrating like an enormous drum.

Swan had lost sight of Magician in the half shadows. As the Cossacks leaped past her she caught a glimpse of him pushing his way through clusters of guests, muttering his apologies. She watched with horror as two lackeys seized him from behind, but he broke loose and hurled himself into a knot of officers. She made her way through the ranks of cheering guests. Shuev was nowhere to be seen. The Count too had disappeared. As she hurried through the doorway and across the reception room into the vestibule she could hear the thud of boots behind her as the Caucasian swordsmen brought their dance to a climax. It occurred to her that only in Russia would an aristocrat mount such a primitive display.

For a moment she lost her bearings. The candles were burning low, the black wax dripping over the silver candelabra spattered the carpets. There was no one in sight. On impulse she slipped into the shadowed recess of the central staircase. She had only a vague sense of why she felt the need to conceal herself as if she were the one being hunted. She heard them before she saw them, Bagration and the Countess, rushing past her up the stairs that led to the private apartments on the floor above. An instant later the Count emerged from the door to the Georgian Room and raised his head to catch a glimpse of heavy boots, silver slippers and pale white stockings before they disappeared from sight. Turning slowly like a wounded animal he placed his hand on the door jamb for support, then staggered back into the arms of the major domo who half dragged, half carried him back into the Georgian Room. Swan smothered a cry and started forward, but then drew back as another figure scampered into the vestibule and bounded up the stairs. When he reached the top he appeared to hesitate. Swan broke cover and moved quickly to the foot of the staircase just in time to see Magician throw open an ornately carved oak door and vanish from sight.

She waited until she was sure no one was pursuing Magician and then mounted the stairs. At the top the oaken door stood ajar She grasped the massive antique handle and pushing hard swung the heavy door wide open. She entered a long gallery where old fashioned gilded candelabra cast a flickering light over rows of military standards hanging from the walls. Trophies and arms from the campaign of 1812 were arranged to give the impression of an abandoned battlefield. In the gloom at the far end Prince Bagration hovered above her. His piercing glance cut through the darkness. She was startled for an instant until she realized that it was only a life size portrait; it was not of the Prince but his grandfather, the General of Infantry, Peter Ivanovich Bagration, who had crossed swords with Napoleon.

The air stirred as though a door had closed somewhere in the depths of the mansion. The draft brought to life the banners of Borodino. Gutted candles at the far end flickered and went out. She walked past row after row of display cases crammed with uniforms, high shakos of the Grenadiers, scarred shell casings, unsheathed bayonets, broken drums. Above them hung pairs of crossed sabers and faded miniatures of Russian heroes. She recognized some of them from stories her father had told her in childhood; there was General Kutuzov, Denisov, the Partisan leader, Prince Dolgorukov, yes and Arakcheev too. All the vainglories of war that Papa had drummed into her young head.

"Romantic rubbish," she whispered as if to suppress the rush of blood to her cheeks. The strings of the orchestra below could barely be heard. But another fainter sound reached her, or was she imagining things? A low cry, briefly sustained. Whether it was human or not, man, woman or child she could not tell.

She pressed her forehead against cold glass and found herself staring into a display case lined with plush velvet that bore the deep imprint of some ancient weapon that was no longer in its place.

"You certainly took your time tearing yourself away from the party. God, I'm half frozen waiting in the courtyard with no one but a wretched yardman and his dog for company. I'm sure you enjoyed yourself for all your nervousness. Well, why so silent? I deserve to know what happened. You can't deprive me of that. The committee will have no objection. After all, I'm one of them. So, is there a constitution in the making or are we just wasting our time?"

Swan had prepared carefully for what she knew would be an uncomfortable interrogation. Her head fell back against the cushions, her eyes closed. She listened to the wheels of the trap roll over the Crimean Bridge. Somehow she would have to cover the gaps in her story. She had not decided what to do about Magician. And there was Shuev. How much should she reveal about him? She was afraid the committee would see a chance to turn her into an agent, a role she despised. Discipline and self-sacrifice, it was harder than she had expected. Magician was in clear violation. And what about Marko? He must have been in on the scheme, whatever it was. If the two of them, and now she as the third were all holding back something, then what could they expect from others in the movement. Give up the personal life; it was easy enough to say. But there were some things you could not reveal to anybody else, not even for the cause.

"Well, Irina?" The fact that Norka had blurted out her real name revealed the level of her annoyance.

"The contact was good. We need another meeting. The Count is wedded to reform. Loris-Melikov is backing him. The tsar is leaning in their direction, but there is strong opposition from the police and others in the ministries. The Count makes the distinction between propagandists and terrorists. Others are not so discriminating. I'm not sure about a constitution. It may only be a step in that direction, an assembly of the land."

"What! A *zemskii sobor*! Christ, the last one met more than two hundred years ago."

"True, but remember that in France the calling of the Estates General after a hundred years touched off a revolution."

"Not likely to happen in Russia with its crew of drunken priests and ignorant land owners."

"Anyway, the Count invited me to meet again, his place this time. It will be a good chance...."

"More waiting," Norka cut in. "Every day we lose makes it harder for us. The comrades might not wait, you know, even if we prove we're right."

"The leaders of the People's Will don't care what we do. Nothing will convince Zheliabov or Khalturin to sign a truce. They're determined to kill the tsar. But we can win over the some of the more reasonable people. I thought you believed in that?"

Norka jammed her hands deep into the pockets of her shabby coat, fondling the Browning. She did believe, but she was getting impatient too.

"Of course, of course, we are right. Terror gets us nowhere."

Swan stole a glance at Norka. What did this change in tone mean? Were they all getting corrupted?

Norka kept pressing for more details as if she wasn't sure that Swan was experienced enough to see all the implications of what she had seen and been told.

"Tell me more about the general, Shuev wasn't it. I've heard of him. They call him the Schoolmaster or something like that. Seems he is bright but pedantic. He could be useful if you cultivated him."

"What do you want me to do, sleep with him?"

Norka looked shocked. Swan barely listened to her protests. They went on too long and sounded insincere.

"I'm exhausted, Norka, let's sign our own truce. We are both behaving badly. We'll go over it all again when the committee meets. They may take a more detached view of it all. We're too closely involved. And that will give me time to think it through again, to remember the details you want. The brain just won't work any longer."

Norka grunted and slouched down in the cushions, determined to show that she was not happy with the outcome.

Swan tried to recall how she had made her way back down

the stairs and into the courtyard. She felt the evening had left her holding too many loose ends. How did Magician get to know the Countess, and what was he after confronting her like a disgruntled lover? What finally became of him? And what was the secret between Bagration and the Countess? They too acted like a pair of lovers. The whole Bagration household seemed screwed up to the breaking point. Frightened faces, strange looks, police and revolutionaries running around the ballroom like a French farce. She was tempted to burst out laughing again. And what would Norka make of that? Discipline, discipline, she repeated the mantra. She was not her father's daughter for nothing, she mused. It was just discipline in a different cause. She had carried out her assignment well, perhaps too well with Shuev. It would not do to have a general in the Gendarmes pursuing her for romantic purposes. Or would it? The melody of the last mazurka kept interrupting her thoughts.

The nag refused to go on. Fatigue and hunger brought it to a halt in the middle of the Street of the Dead. The coachman lifted his head. He could smell the snow coming.

Marko sat motionless, grinding his teeth together to keep them from chattering. Was it the cold or were his nerves giving way again? He wondered why these thoughts came over him so frequently now. He tried to recall how the Irina looked, posed regally in that smart trap with her hair swept up, exposing the line of her long neck, her trademark. Hadn't it been Magician who named her Swan? But for him it was the glossy auburn hair that set her apart. From the first he had realized that it would be impossible to treat her like an ordinary comrade. It was stupid how he teased her, but it was the only way he could mask his feelings. How clumsy she must have thought him. But his thoughts of Swan were not enough to keep out the fear. He never should have allowed himself to agree to this madcap adventure. It wasn't the first time either that Magician had led him into a false position. His honeyed words sounded hollow in the chill of the early morning.

Marko was beginning to wonder whether the incriminating letters existed at all. The idea had caught his fancy at first. Magician had made it all sound so plausible; getting the letters, blackmailing Bagration for the money they needed for a hectograph to print their leaflets. And if he didn't pay up they would publish the letters and ruin the reputation of one of the worst reactionaries at court. Either way the Partition of the Land would win. The trouble with this expedition was that Magician liked to play the man of mystery, never sharing his innermost thoughts. Marko thought he would be just as happy on the stage, acting the revolutionary. Maybe that's what he was doing, God forbid. You never knew what he was really up to. All that false bravado, just like tonight. Maybe Magician had confided in Swan. Marko thought he might try to sound her out in the spirit of comradely relations. It would be a good way to establish himself on a new footing with her. The idea comforted him.

The long wait and the cold made him drowsy. He was nodding when the door was wrenched open and Magician jumped into the cab, rocking it violently. He was pounding on the roof shouting, "Why the Hell aren't we moving?"

Marko stared at him wide-eyed. "Christ, you frightened me half to death. I've been frozen waiting for you. Do you have the letters?"

Magician continued to beat his fists against the roof until the worn out covering ripped down the middle. The whip cracked for the first time. The nag put one hoof painfully in front of another so and they inched forward. Magician slumped back in his seat.

"Is someone pursuing us?" cried Marko, suddenly aware of how absurd their getaway must appear; a limping horse, a bent, gray figure on the box, a dilapidated cab with its torn roof and broken springs, bearing two scared revolutionaries from the scene of their exploits.

"Well, even a blind cripple could catch us now," Magician was laughing hysterically.

"The letters...,"bleated Marko.

"Go to Hell with your letters. I had them in my hands. I was reading them; we were interrupted. I barely made it out of there."

Marko cursed under his breath. "Mad, mad. The whole thing was ridiculous. We are ridiculous. God, what children we are." Wasn't that the verdict of his father? It was then that he noticed that Magician was wearing patent leather pumps.

For many years Count Ushakov's coachman, Arkady, had taken pleasure in driving the troika down the best streets of Moscow, showing off the matched bays from the Orlov stud. Prechistenka at night was one of his favorite routes. Drawn up in classical order, the mansions of the Moscow nobility had been built of granite in the eighteenth century by French and Italian architects. When wooden Moscow had burned down in 1812, the stone buildings had survived. He didn't have to see the facades; he knew every cornice and column by heart. In a hundred conversations he had squeezed out of his fellow coachmen the histories of the great families that lived behind those solid walls. When the Count took him to St. Petersburg he would remind the puffed up cabbies there that this quarter of Moscow rivaled anything they had in the north. Arkady repeated it to all who would hear; the true heart of Russia beats in Moscow. Petersburg or Piter as they liked to call it reminded him of the countess; it had the same cold, fragile beauty.

Prechistenka Street, Moscow

As for the churches in Piter, there was nothing of old Russia about them either; they couldn't compare with the ancient Moscow churches and the monasteries, the Simonovsky, Novospassky, Novo-Devichy, Donskoi. Spread round the city like a necklace of precious stones they were. Each one a great walled fortress built to defend against the Tatar raids. And lying beyond them the churches of the Golden Ring, towns he had visited as a youth working as a hired hand. That was long before the Count, bless his soul, had freed him from the shackles of serfdom. He loved the heartland. And who could love Piter with its geometry of straight streets and huge empty squares, as if laid out by a carpenter's measure. Moscow's twisting streets and lanes revealed the unexpected at every turn, protected against the summer sun by a green canopy of shade trees lining the curbs, not like Piter where the avenues were too broad and buildings too close. Why Peter's city didn't even have any city walls to defend it from Russia's enemies, no fortresses like the kremlins in Moscow and the Upper Volga towns that had held off the Tatars. In Piter the canals bred swarms of mosquitoes and the autumn fogs turned the solid buildings into ghostly shapes. Yes, Piter was the proper setting for the Countess all right.

At Prechistenka Gate he guided the horses north and maneuvered around the potholes. "We'll cradle her all the way home," he tried to reassure himself. But he felt uneasy. The night had been filled with strange forebodings. He was upset by his encounter with the house demon scurrying along the corridor of Prince Bagration's mansion, and the arrogance of the lackeys there, bringing round the coach from the back court without his knowledge. It was against all custom.

Just as they reached Arbat Square the clouds broke. Bright moonlight flooded over the sky-blue cupola and golden cross of the Antipevsky Church nestled among a cluster of low wooden houses. It was a good sign. Arkady crossed himself and murmured encouragement to the bays. Within minutes they turned into Povarskaya Street past a line of noble houses at the west end of the street where the formal gardens surpassed even those on Prechistenka.

Arkady slowed the horses to a walk before wheeling into the long drive that led to a large structure of Finnish granite. It was dark except for the lights burning in the upstairs library. Arkady shook his head. The master was a very devil for work, he was. But it was risky letting a high-spirited filly like the Countess prance about while he bent over his papers even if it was for the good of the motherland. God spare him, he was a good master.

Count Ushakov raised his eyes from a thick sheaf of documents. He pulled out his watch, another precious gift from the hands of the tsar himself. It was four o'clock. He snapped the silver lid shut and opened a file labeled "Commission for the Study of Worker Grievances in the Putilov Factory. Report of Findings. Section 1. Possible Violations of Paragraphs 27, 30b and 42 of the law of September 4, 1874." His hands shook. He raised his arm and held it out straight in front of him staring at the fingers as if willing them to stop trembling.

His eyes slid back to the page. He forced his mind to concentrate on the wavy lines of the copyist's script. The words did not connect with one another. He went back over the sentence again. It was no use. He could not get rid of image that ran through his head like a brush fire—the flash of the Countess' white stockings at the head of the stairs. He sat back and folded his hands, listening intently. He heard Arkady climb down from the coach box, apply the wheel brake and set his riding whip back in its socket, then silence.

Arkady patted the outer bay on her flank, sighed deeply and stepped up to the door of the coach. He automatically assumed his most humble pose. He dared not raise his eyes for fear of offending her. For a moment he hesitated. There was no movement inside the coach, no rustling of the silk gown. He felt compelled to peer into the dark interior, but there was no sign of the Countess. How could she have vanished? Had some demon of the night had spirited her away? Panic-stricken he wrenched open the door and saw nothing after that.

An explosion blinded him, hurling him back against one of the stucco pillars that supported the balcony over the main entrance. He was dead before the back of his skull was shattered by the impact. His lace trimmed cap fluttered to the ground where the wind lifted and turned it over and over down the entire length of the drive.

Count Ushakov rose from his desk and rushed to the window. He parted the heavy drapes. The Orlov bays had bolted, dragging the remnants of his shattered carriage through the open gate into the street. In the circle of light thrown by the two lamps flanking the portico Ushakov thought he saw sprawled in the drive a shimmering mass of white silk enveloped in the fur of a wild animal.

Chapter Four

Even in death the Countess commanded the attention of Moscow society. But not all the mourners had danced attendance on her. Scattered throughout the cemetery of the Donskoi Monastery several dozen police agents succeeded in being obvious in their attempt to be inconspicuous. Swan felt safe gliding between her escorts, Count Ushakov and General Shuev. Like Shuev's men she scanned the crowd for a familiar face and took comfort from the fact that she recognized no one. At least Magician had not taken complete leave of his senses.

As the ceremony unfolded she could not help but compare the solemn movements of the Metropolitan of Moscow as he conducted the graveside service with the flailing arms of Bagration's *chef d'orchestre*. What a great distance between the sacred and profane and how alien they both seemed to her.

Under a brilliant autumn sun the procession moved past the Church of Our Lady of the Don resplendent in its fresh coat of red paint with white trim, the scalloped forms piled round a delicate drum supporting the deep blue cupola. Swan had to shade her eyes from the glare reflected from the white crenellations crowning the blood red walls of the monastery.

A slight pressure from the Count's hand reminded her how quickly his old feelings for her had returned. At first she had been surprised that except for herself and Shuev he walked alone through the crowd of mourners. Only a few older men approached him, bowed and uttered conventional words of sympathy. But hadn't it been the same at the ball? She shot angry looks at them all, but then was annoyed at herself. She was allowing her own feelings to get in the way of her mission. And things had not moved forward at all. The Count had emptied his mind of politics.

"Today they are also burying Arkady in the village. You remember the place don't you Irisha? The little white fence, the wooden crosses, on the hillside overlooking the stream. He said he was going back to the village to spend the last years." The Count turned away from the mound of earth that was all but hidden under masses of flowers. His glance wandered over the gravestones of Russia's poets and came to rest on Chaadayev's.

"Our official madman. You know the story?"

She nodded, but he did not look at her.

"Perhaps one day they will declare me to be officially mad"

She squeezed his arm but made no reply. It was hard to read his mood. A faint odor of incense was suspended in the air, an odor she loathed. They walked on toward the coaches.

Shuev was dissatisfied with the placement of his men and drifted off muttering his apologies. The Count hesitated and then went into the Church of Our Lady of the Don. Swan remained outside. She watched Shuev make his rounds. Heads turned; it appeared that he was much admired by the ladies.

Ushakov was gone a few minutes. When he came back his features were set.

"We must be going, my dear."

"Shouldn't we wait for Grisha?" How easily she had slipped into the habit of using his name.

"He said to go ahead. He feels personally responsible for the surveillance. And he has a theory about people who kill. Something about their wanting to make sure their victims are buried."

"Does he have any suspicions? I don't understand. And what about the Prince? Did you see him?"

"No, he sent a message, the big bouquet of white flowers. What kind are they? I never knew the names of flowers."

The coach passed through the brick arch of the Holy Gates of the monastery surmounted by the church of Our Lady of Tikhvin.

"The main thing, Dmitri Andreevich, is not to lose sight of your life's work. It is terribly important for all Russia. It will be your memorial to the Countess and Arkady. The people will be eternally grateful. You are completing the work of the Emancipation."

The Churches of Our Lady of Tikhvin and Our Lady of the Don, Moscow

The Count nodded gravely. "You are right, Irisha. But her death makes my task more difficult. I cannot grieve deeply, you must know that. We lived in different worlds. She abhorred politics. I mean the real world of politics. Oh, she was ambitious enough. But she craved the excitement of the chase, of conquering society, being received at court. In the beginning she thought I might become a Russian Disraeli. You smile! She read his novels, dreamed that I would do for Alexander Nikolaevich what he was doing for Queen Victoria. She urged me to persuade the tsar to revive Catherine's Greek Project. Her friends must have put that crazy idea into her head. Ushakov, liberator of the Balkan Slavs! Well, we saw how it turned out at Berlin. We got our fingers burned by *der alte Jude.* That's what Prince Bismarck called Disraeli you know. He admired the old Jew, and why not. He cheated us out of victory, cut us down to size, the old Jew did, and grabbed Cyprus for his trouble. How is it the English always get rewarded for not fighting?"

The Count remembered how angry the tsar was when Shuvalov came back from Berlin, having given up so much won with Russian blood. But how did he get off on that tangent? Elena, yes, Elena it was who imagined he could do better, for her sake no less.

"As for me, I became for Elena, *der alte russisch* and there was no admiration there. But I think she had given up on me long before that. Public works and constitutional reform were too boring for her. She wanted an empire builder."

"Forgive me, Dmitri Andreevich, but Russia needs to build from the inside now."

"Again, you are right," the Count became animated. "The trouble is that her death has given my enemies a stick to beat me with. Even Grisha is convinced that the People's Will is to blame for her death. He thinks the terrorists have switched tactics and are turning their bomb throwers loose on the nobility, or else what is worse, are aiming to kill me. Oh, not worse. I am not worried about myself. No, no! If the government and the educated public believe that I am the target then they will reject reform as a sign of weakness. They will give up on the idea that reforms can disarm the radicals. We will lose all chance of winning over sensible people who want to save Russia from civil war."

"But that makes no sense."

"It does if you accept their assumptions."

"Not even then. If the terrorists had really wanted to kill you, they would have made an attempt when you left the ball early by yourself. They don't make mistakes like that. And why should they go after the Countess? She was not in the inner circle at court. At least, so I have heard. You should not underestimate public opinion, Dmitri Andreevich."

The Count bent his head toward her. He liked this girl, her quick mind, her common sense. Perhaps the gloomy predictions about Russia's youth were wrong.

"The police mentality is too convoluted," Swan said. "Our dear Grisha is gracious and high-minded but he does not understand the terrorists. The People's Will do not go in for subtlety. They have no interest in influencing opinion. They have one purpose, to kill the tsar. Anyway, why should they want to throw bombs at you when you are working for the good of the people?"

"Thank you my dear. We think much alike. But how do the people know what we think, you and I? The government is a victim of its own secrecy. We have kept the public in ignorance for too long. It was the same twenty years ago. We made the mistake of hiding the truth from the peasants. They did not know what to expect from the Emancipation. They thought they were getting all the land and were disappointed. Now they are bitter. And who can blame them?"

Swan moistened her lips. She had rehearsed the speech, now she had to deliver it.

"Dmitri Andreevich, you must forgive me for speaking frankly. I want to help you. You may think that I am only a naive girl, inexperienced in the ways of the world, ignorant of high politics. But you once told me that I was intelligent, so I beg you to listen to me as you would to a man, to a trusted adviser. The one thing I do know something about is the mood of young people."

She paused waiting for him to interrupt, but he had turned in his seat and was listening intently.

"You are right to want to let the people know about the plans for reform. It is the only way to stop the rumors and gossip, to win over the public, especially the students. They will rally to the throne. Remember 1861 when even Herzen praised the tsar? 'O Galilean, thou hast triumphed!' is what he said. If we could only believe that His Majesty has restored his faith in reform. To many he is still the tsar-liberator. I remember as a child how the peasants came to Papa. It was the whole village led by the elders. They crowded round the veranda. The elders mumbled a few words and the people went down on their knees, thanking Papa for their land and Liberty. They did not understand that the landowners would keep most of the land for themselves, or that they would have to pay for their small parcels scattered over the fields. You have heard their words, 'we are yours but the land is ours.' This is their faith, as strong as their belief in God, perhaps stronger. They crave the land, Dmitri Andreevich, and some day they will take it by force if it is not given to them."

They were crossing over the Crimean Bridge, bringing back once again memories of the night she wished she could relive.

"The government must move in this direction. It must break up the big estates."

"Wait a moment, my dear, you are running ahead of us. Redistribute the land? This is going too far right now. We are only talking about an assembly."

"Of course the nobles must get their Liberty too, their political Liberty. They should have the same rights as the English gentry, then they will begin to behave like them. Bring them into the government, let them share power and they will forget their attachment to the land. They are bad cultivators anyhow. If the tsar would issue a constitution; the word is magical, Dmitri Andreevich, magical."

Ushakov was at a loss for words. If only Elena had been like this. Perhaps she was, long ago. He quickly dismissed the idea. Elena's passion had been nothing more than sensuality. But it was useless to deny that is what attracted him in the first place. Was Tolstoy right? Did a man really have to lose his lust in order to become wise?

The horses slowed to a walk and turned into the circular drive of the Ushakov mansion. They listened to the crunch of the wheels on the pebble drive and fell silent.

"So this is how the youth think. Well, let's discuss it with tea, my little radical." Swan was not pleased to hear the ironic tone in his voice. Had she lost her advantage? Perhaps she was naive and inexperienced.

The footman bowed them into the drawing room and softly closed the doors. Swan perched on the edge of the divan, running her fingers over the velvet armrest. The room was furnished in the style of the First Empire, greens and gold, also favored by Papa.

The Count folded his hands in his lap. She watched his every move, trying to decide whether she had offended him.

"The problem is more complex than simply letting the public know of our plans." He began in a respectful tone as if to reassure her that he was going to treat her seriously. "You must understand there is a great deal of opposition to reform, even to our modest plans, within the ministries and court. People are afraid that an assembly will plunge Russia into a swamp of partisan politics, that the country will be torn apart if the autocratic power is weakened. They tell us to look what happened to the United States of America with its Civil War. This is the way they like to frighten us. Now after the killing of the countess they will claim that the terrorists are striking out at the nobility, General Loris-Melikov already fears this. He has called me to the capital to review out policies. If he is wavering, then we are truly lost. So, let's be practical, Irisha. For the moment there can be no thought of redistributing the land. What I need now is arguments, evidence, or promise of evidence that the Gendarmes are wrong, that Elena was not blown up by terrorists."

There was a light tapping at the door. A young woman entered carrying a silver Danish tea service. Swan recognized it as a gift to the Count's grandfather from Empress Catherine. But it was the girl who caught her attention. She filled the room with a delicate fragrance that made Swan catch her breath. It was French and expensive. The dress was made of fine cloth and closely fitted her full figure. Her hands showed no sign of rough work. Had she been the Countess' personal maid? Then why was she serving tea? She was facing Swan but her profile was reflected in the mirror over the mantelpiece. A lock of her fine spun golden hair fell over her forehead she bent to adjust the samovar. The resemblance to the Countess was eerily striking.

The Count stared at the lumps of sugar dissolving in the boiling water. He slowly raised his eyes. The look on his face startled Swan and set her teacup jingling on the saucer. The Count quickly averted his gaze but not before the girl had intercepted it. Swan watched the smile play on her lips.

The Count nodded abruptly, the fire in his eyes died out. The girl left the room undulating her hips just enough to be provocative. The Count continued to stir his tea long after the sugar had dissolved. Swan sipped her tea, saying nothing for several minutes. Whatever this meant she could not let it distract her. She calculated that the time had come to test the idea that she had been pondering for days. He couldn't say it wasn't practical.

"We have a chance, Dmitri Andreevich, to convince General Loris-Melikov that you are right."

The Count avoided her eyes. "What is this you are saying, Irina?" It was a slight change, dropping his affectionate name for her, but it almost made her lose heart.

"What is this chance you speak of?" he repeated.

"An independent investigation."

He shook his head and with great deliberation put down his

spoon. He had not yet started to drink his tea.

"Independent, you mean outside the police?" He chuckled briefly. "This is not England, my dear. We have no Sherlock Holmes." The spoon was back in his cup stirring aimlessly.

"Yes, independent. It must be carried out by someone who is not under the thumb of the Third Section, someone who is respected as a professional, who cannot be corrupted or bullied to drop the case, a man who will uncover the truth."

It had been her idea from the beginning. But it had taken hours to persuade the others. Norka had presided over the meeting, sitting at the desk with her loaded revolver within reach. Marko and Magician were crowded together on the sofa that sagged under their weight. The last member of the committee, Letchik, known as the Healer, a medical student who had recently joined them stood by the window, as the watcher. He and Marko had immediately supported her. Magician looking distracted said nothing constructive. Norka shrugged and wagged her head as she always did when someone else proposed a fresh idea. It had been agreed unanimously, because she chose to interpret Magician's wan smile as a vote in favor, to make the approach to the Count.

The Count set down his spoon again. Had he been too abrupt?

"Splendid, Irisha, you find him and I will add him to my staff. We'll make him a state secretary. Such men are not easy to find in Russia these days."

"There is one such man. He does not hold a high rank; he is only a detective Inspector. But he is incorruptible, a bulldog when he sinks his teeth into a case or a criminal. He also has the imagination of an artist. He is a virtuoso, Dmitri Andreevich. He refuses to be bound by rules and conventions."

"Must rules always be binding, my dear?"

"Don't be offended, Dmitri Andreevich, but you know how our clerks scribble away, buried in paper. Wasn't Gogol right about them? And the police, how they antagonize people with their officious ways."

"All right, all right, who is this paragon of virtue?"

"You know him, I think, or have heard of him. It is Vasiliev."

"Oh my goodness! Vasiliev, our intrepid Vasili Vasilievich, illegitimate son of Count Vorontsov. Well, my dear you are full of surprises. Let's see what we can recall about your candidate for saint-hood. To begin with an able detective, good war record, all the right decorations, mentioned in dispatches twice by the Grand Duke no less. A staff officer on the Danube if I'm not mistaken. Has excellent contacts but lots of enemies, though mainly of the right sort." The Count rubbed his chin.

"I believe he also served under General Loris-Melikov on a spe-cial mission in the Caucasus during the storming of Kars. Perhaps the General would remember him," Swan added quietly.

"Good lord! You've thought it all out, haven't you? Astonish-ing. But you have to admit that he does have the reputation of being eccentric. After all, he passed up a promising career in the Guards to become a lowly detective. No one could figure that out. Lives a bachelor's life, but has no famous love affairs. Also strange."

Irina was determined not to tell all her secrets. She had prob-ably said too much already to the comrades. It was another of those things that you didn't share with anyone.

"You may be right. Yes, it's just possible that you may be right. Even eccentricity has its advantages. Still, it's bound to be risky. The Gendarmes won't like it a bit. Grisha might raise objections, but I can handle him."

She watched the Count's eyes brightened for the first time since the night of the ball when he recognized her on the steps of the Bagration mansion.

"I wonder whether General Loris-Melikov would approve."

Chapter Five

Ushakov caught the night express to Petersburg to arrive early for his appointment with Loris-Melikov. The Nikolaevsky Line had been built for comfort; the slow speed of the train and the gentle gradient produced a soothing effect on Count Ushakov, lulling him into a deep sleep. Suddenly, the crash of hail against the windows startled him out of restless dreams in which he kept confusing Elena with somebody else. He was still unsettled when he was ushered into the office of the Minister. General Loris-Melikov did not bother to greet the Count but instead pointed to sheets of newspaper scattered over his desk.

"Well, Count, what do you think of that?"

Ushakov was not offended by the General's brusque manner. Others at court might have been, but he had made it his business to study Loris-Melikov's humors and mannerisms. The General had been a field officer most of his life; he was used to giving orders not paying compliments.

Ushakov glanced at the paper. It looked as though it had been chewed over. Obviously, the editorial in the *Moscow Gazette* by Katkov had gotten under the General's skin. So much the better.

"A clumsy piece of journalism, Your Excellency, and far off the mark."

"Well, you're taking it calmly enough, I must say that...," the General broke off and lowered his voice; "...terribly sorry, my dear fellow, your loss, the shock, my condolences, awful thing. How are you holding up?"

"Your presence was felt in Moscow." The Count bowed recalling the enormous wreath sent from the Ministry, towering over the grave like a protective shield. It was not necessary to say anything more; the General disliked effusive outbursts.

"Of course it's clumsy, vulgar journalism," the General hurried on as if the Count's grief caused him embarrassment, "but it sows panic at court. You've heard the rumors that the tsar is displeased with me. Nonsense of course, nothing further from the truth. But those closest to him, I'm talking about the ones he meets in his daily routine, the aides-de-camp, ladies in waiting, yes, the ladies above all, are running scared."

"Then we must reassure them"

"How in God's name? You've read this slander. Katkov's rag calls it an indiscriminate attack on the aristocracy. The weasel's exact words. Read this, "Concessions in the face of terror are a failure of nerve." It's all rubbish. Has he forgotten that they tried to kill me too? That did not stop us from trying to move ahead. And we have made progress, Count. We have won over some of the fence sitters, or we had up to now. The next few months are crucial, absolutely crucial. Hotheads like Katkov could ruin everything. The idiot calls for massive repression. Who are we to repress massively? The first person on my list is that chatterbox. We'll shut down his rag for inciting disloyalty, spreading panic."

The Count patiently observed Loris-Melikov work himself up into his Armenian fury, as his aides called it. He was pacing up and down in front of the tall windows overlooking the Palace Square. He came to an abrupt halt, leaned on a polished marble sill and peered into the autumn mist that enveloped the city. His deep-set eyes swept the square but he found no comfort in what they saw. In the center of the vast amphitheater the Alexander Column, a monolith of Finnish granite stood guard. Barely visible at the far end of the square a Cossack detail cantered under the Alexander Arch. The same thought came back to him again and again. I've commanded twenty thousand men down there, maneuvered them with a precision that cannot be matched in all of Europe. But the entire army might not be enough now to save my emperor.

He whirled to face the count.

"The leeches clinging to the emperor are beginning to whine

about the dangers, afraid now of their own skins. The reforms are in serious trouble, Count. The emperor is not afraid of death, you know. He is a brave man, a Roman stoic, faces personal danger without turning a hair. But he's good-hearted, yes, I fear at times even softhearted. He'll give in to their bleating if he hears it going on long enough. It's all around him. I'm worried, Count, really worried this time."

What worried the Count was the change that had come over Loris-Melikov. The tic on the right side of his face that had not been there a few months before, the swelling under the eyes, the nervous gestures, all recent signs of stress. A year ago he was still in the field, celebrated as the hero of Kars, the great Turkish fortress he had besieged and stormed. His Armenian countrymen had acclaimed him as the savior of their race. For centuries no one had done more to unite them in one Christian state even if it was not their own but rather part of the Russian Empire. Even, Disraeli had not been able to take that away from us at Berlin, the Count mused.

Since then Ushakov had studied his habits, how he lived like a soldier on bivouac. He had no ambitions to be a minister hemmed in by protocol, drowned in paper, serving time in stuffy committee rooms. But his emperor had entrusted him with virtually unlimited powers to exterminate the subversion, their euphemism for terror, and protect the throne. The Count remembered the day when in the Council of Ministers Loris-Melikov, calm and eloquent for a change, had beaten down the doubters, the skeptics and the fainthearted; he recalled his exact words: "With one hand I will crush the terrorists and with the other win over the public to assume their civic responsibilities." They were right to call his government a dictatorship of the heart. But the effort had cost him dearly.

The General irritably rubbed the tic.

"You know my strengths, Count. I am a soldier. I speak plainly. I have no patience with officers in peacock feathers. Sometimes the emperor himself thinks I am too blunt and reminds me with his exquisite politeness that I should be more attentive to the sensibilities of the high born. All right, I accept his reproaches. I rely on you for advice; you know how to handle the high born. What in God's name does one say to them now?" It was clear that he did not expect an answer.

The General turned his attention again to the activity on the Palace Square. He studied the Cossack horsemen below him, making their rounds. He had completely reorganized the security measures after Khalturin had dynamited the imperial dining room killing a dozen men, wounding fifty others. The General knew them all, good lads struck down by one of their own people, a Russian not a Turk. Khalturin, the worst of the fanatics, posing as a workman, smuggling in dynamite. Reports said the guards thought it was sugar. Absurd! The very thought of it infuriated him. What kind of security lets a man like that have free reign below the emperor's living quarters. Suppose Khalturin had done the job right? As it was he had bungled the attempt, blew up the basement rooms, punched a hole in the facade and hardly damaged the dining room above. Thank God, the Emperor had been delayed, but the explosion had shaken a whole wing of the palace, a moral victory for the terrorists if nothing more.

Ushakov cleared his throat, but Loris-Melikov ignored him pursuing his own thoughts. One great fear obsessed him, that another Khalturin would penetrate the heart of his defenses. Most of all he feared Zheliabov, reputedly the mastermind behind every attempt so far. The Palace was a security nightmare. Fifteen hundred rooms stretching out half a mile along the Neva embankment. He had stationed sentries at all the entrances, but as a soldier he knew each post was vulnerable to deception, infiltration or assault. He made the rounds whenever he could, never satisfied with the reports of his subordinates. There was hardly a moment he felt at ease living in this pile of stone. Like everything else in the city it was outsized, too grand, built as if it were always necessary for Russia to outdo the rest of Europe. Passing from room to room he caught himself relaxing, dropping his guard. At times he felt the energy drain out of him and seep down the long corridors with their endless vistas. Wherever he turned another suite of rooms opened up, drawing him deeper into the maze.

It was no mystery to him why the emperor choose to live a Spartan life in private; why he slept on an army cot in a sparsely furnished room, bathed in cold water, believing that iron self-discipline was the only protection against the enervating atmosphere of the place. Loris-Melikov repeated a dozen times a day the formula that kept him going: "Keep to the routine but vary the schedule." In a way it was like campaigning, and this too was a war.

"It used to be the Turks," he found himself speaking out loud, "but now it's our own people who are the enemy."

The Count waited for the fury to pass. He had been idly turning the crumpled pages of the *Moscow Gazette*. The General finally tore himself away from the window.

"You realize, Count, how impossible it is to turn the Palace into an armed camp. The Emperor forbids me to close the public galleries, says we cannot turn away foreign tourists for fear of undermining confidence in the stability of the Empire with all the consequences for our bonds on the London Exchange. I am grateful for one thing. The imperial apartments are far removed from the public rooms. And I have covered the approaches with a network of guards. Every day I wrack my brains, trying to anticipate the worst. One has only to remember Khalturin. Still, I cannot make the Emperor a prisoner in his own house."

"Your Excellency has taken every possible precaution. Inside the Palace the Emperor is safe. But we have to check the moral rot that Katkov and others are spreading outside. His is a powerful voice and the court is listening. His friends crawl through every crack in the ministries. There are even leaks to him from the Council of Ministers informing him of our confidential discussions. And he has allies among the Gendarmes where the rank and file are restless; the officers complain we have clipped their wings."

"I shall punish any case of insubordination." Loris-Melikov was aroused again. "I will not permit petty squabbling. The whole purpose of placing you in charge of the reorganization was to put an end to inter-service rivalry. You must not spare them, Count. You know you have my full confidence."

Ushakov bowed, sensing an opening.

"You ask me how to deal with the court. They have to be convinced that Katkov is wrong, that the nobility is not in imminent danger. It will not be easy to do, but it isn't impossible. The main thing is to tread softly."

"Don't' worry, I won't trample them to death," Loris-Melikov muttered angrily. "Agreed we are in a ticklish position and cannot afford to be too hasty. But my God, man, we must take action. In half an hour the Council of Ministers meets. The Emperor will preside today, and I will have to defend myself. Give me something, anything to gain time." In his excitement the General's Armenian accent had become more audible, and Ushakov could not help but fear the effect that a rain of sibilants would have on the ears of the Russian nationalists in the Council.

Ushakov took a deep breath and moved to the center of the room.

"Today, you may report to the Council that the Gendarmes had bungled the investigation of my wife's death. I have just finished reading their report and I can assure you that their methods were slip-shod. They hardly conducted any investigation; they assumed from the outset that the terrorists were to blame. They refused to consider any other possibility."

Ushakov noted with satisfaction that his timing was perfect; he had the General's full attention. Loris-Melikov stared with astonishment at his deputy. "If not the terrorists, who then?"

"I do not know, Your Excellency. But I am prepared to accept any verdict, even one that causes me personal embarrassment, as long as it is the truth."

"I should never underestimate you, Count. You are a loyal and resourceful servant of the state. You want me to be careful, but now it is you who are taking a big risk. Even if you sacrificed your honor, they would accuse you of ulterior motives, or worse, of doing my bidding for political reasons. Your offer is admirable, but it lacks any basis in fact, as you yourself have just admitted. Is that all you have to offer me?"

"No, Your Excellency, there is more to be said. Your objections are well founded so we must overcome them. I propose that you authorize a special investigation to be conducted outside the jurisdiction of the Secret Department for Combating Revolutionary Activity."

"Go on, Count, this interests me."

"You can assure the Emperor and the ministers that you are taking the matter under your personal supervision. You will have to tell them that you are not entirely satisfied with the report of the Gendarmes. But you can soften your criticism by saying that fresh evidence has come to light, evidence that you are not free to reveal. You may wish to add that you are entrusting the inquiry to a reliable source that must remain anonymous for security reasons. I already have someone in mind for the job. He is discreet, energetic and intelligent. His record is spotless. Most important he is fiercely independent. He has a reputation for using unorthodox methods, but that too may be to our advantage. My inquiries have convinced me that he is the best detective in our service. I am speaking of course of Vasiliev, Vasili Vasilievich."

"Ah Count," sighed the General, "long odds to match the high stakes. Unorthodox you say, more like eccentric."

Ushakov smiled to himself. Hadn't this been his first reaction to Irina's suggestion? What was it about the man?

"If you like, your Excellency, call him eccentric. But look at our choices. Over the past few years the regular police have been demoralized. We have not finished weeding out the dead wood. There are plenty of unreliable men in the ranks. We cannot count any longer on the Gendarmes. They have invested too much in the campaign against terror to take an objective view of things. Besides, the top ranks dislike me intensely because you have authorized me to bring them under control. Only my old friend Grisha Shuev tolerates me and he thinks I am half mad."

Ushakov paused, not sure how far he should press this line of argument. His rivalry with the Gendarmes had reached a critical point. The problem was that they saw every violent crime as the work of terrorists. Their obsession threatened to undermine public confidence in reform. Loris-Melikov was backing him, but even he had to admit that their record in hunting down revolutionaries was impressive.

"The Gendarmes have scored some notable successes, but they are too closely linked to Your Excellency's enemies. One of the most dangerous has just replaced me as the Minister of Post and Telegraphs. That gives him access to the mails, the best source for tapping the mood of the country. I know the game. We need men of integrity to read other people's letters. There are too many temptations for intrigue and blackmail. I have good reason to believe he is the conduit to Katkov, another source of leaks that has caused us so much trouble."

"He's the next man on my list to get rid of, but I have to catch him red-handed and he's been very careful."

"I'm afraid we cannot afford to wait until that happens. This is why we have to work outside official channels, to by pass the flow of correspondence, reports and memos that would give the game away. Vasiliev is our man. He's always been willing to play a lone hand. Think about him for a moment. As the natural son of Count Vorontsov he has access to the best houses. But his mother was a peasant girl, and he has the popular touch. He is as much at home in the village as in the drawing room. There's a good chance he will have to pass through both. Your Excellency will remember that he graduated from the Page Corps at the head of his class. Knew his classical languages but also played the flute. Because of that his classmates called him Fritz after Frederick the Great. Brilliant war record." Ushakov had saved that for the last. He slipped a folder onto the edge of the desk.

"I know all this," Loris-Melikov toyed with the pages of the file. "His diplomatic skills are well known. The Grand Duke appreciated them. He probably did as much as anyone to restore morale after the first Plevna. Still, he is known to have rather advanced ideas on the peasant question. Some call him a Red. If he makes a mistake, Count, the Gendarmes will skin him alive. We would not be able to save him."

"In that case, we will have to sacrifice him. He will be told that he is expendable. I don't think it will deter him."

For a few moments neither man spoke. Through the tall windows the Alexander Column was no longer visible in the fog. There was a soft tapping at the door. An orderly's head peered in, announcing in a hushed voice that the Council of Ministers was assembling. Loris-Melikov waved him away and grasped Ushakov with both hands.

"Proceed, and God be with you."

As Ushakov hurried past a knot of high-ranking officials in the anteroom he wondered whether he had done the right thing. The truth might ruin his career. Dear, foolish Elena, he thought, even in dying you create difficulties for me.

Chapter Six

The telegrapher reined in his horse at the edge of the clearing where two men regarded him with curiosity. One, crouched over a pair of hunter bitches, was a Komi tribesman in traditional dress. Leaning against a fallen oak was a white man who looked in the eyes of the telegrapher, more like a figure out of a Fennimore Cooper novel than an Inspector of His Majesty Police. His beard was luxurious but untrimmed; there were a few streaks of gray in his sandy hair, but he could not have been more than forty. He wore a worn leather jacket with fringes and homespun linen trousers. Nothing except the rifle he cradled in his arm gave any sign that he was a nobleman. The telegrapher had never seen anything like the gun. But the stories that circulated in the district about this man claimed that it was an English model, a Martini-Henry carbine. Such weapons did not end up in the hands of local woodsmen.

"Major Vasiliev?" his voice was not as firm as he intended.

The white man gestured vaguely. The telegrapher dismounted, and giving the tribesman a wide berth, he approached Vasiliev with the message extended in his hand. At the touch of their fingers Vasiliev felt the calluses.

"So the telegrapher himself had shown up. And who is minding the office?"

The man stepped back in alarm. Were the stories true then about his supernatural powers?

"Well, what is it now, a war or a revolution that sends them after me."

"Your Honor?"

Vasiliev was prepared to make a further deduction that this was a humorless man. The detective brushed back a lock of hair from his eyes. The gesture appeared almost feminine, but if the telegrapher had exercised his own powers of observation he would have seen that the fingers were stubby and muscular, the knuckles prominent, the hands of a boxer.

His smile showing a row of crooked teeth reassured the telegrapher. There was something in the man's bearing that reminded him of his commanding office in the last war. He straightened his shoulders.

Vasiliev ran his eyes over the telegram and his smile faded.

Assassination of Countess Ushakova has
greatly alarmed society. Emperor personally
concerned. Your presence urgently required
Come with all haste.

It was dated October 23, 1880 and signed by Lt. General Loris-Melikov, Minister of Interior.

Vasiliev folded the paper, tucked it inside his jacket and tossed the envelope in the campfire at his feet. He glanced at the sky to the west bathed in a reddish glow where columns of fiery clouds were burning themselves into gray ash.

"Too late to set out now. We'll wait until dawn. You will have to share our quarters for the night. But we can promise you a good meal, rousted grouse, isn't that right, Borka?" The Komi guide nodded and muttered a few words in his own language, bringing the smile back to Vasiliev's face.

"Borka doubts whether you'll like his cooking. He is too modest. You won't find better grouse anywhere else. It was something to do with the herbs, of course, but also the basting, you see. He refuses to share the recipe, the only secret he keeps from me."

The Komi's knife flashed over the plumage of the dead grouse. He nodded and spoke again but this time in heavily accented but correct Russian. "You know many great things, Vasili Vasilievich. What is the harm of keeping from you one small thing."

Vasiliev leaned his carbine against the oak and began to build up the fire. The sun had touched the crest of the foothills of the

Ural to their east and an unusual radiance suffused the sky. Vasiliev threw back his head and let his mind go slack. Ural sunsets were like Borka's grouse; they had no parallel anywhere else. Then there would be the sudden coolness, as if it had been hovering impatiently over the tops of the ancient firs, waiting to descend on them. As the light died the gloom of the forest sprang into the sky like a wild animal. It was always like that in the Urals, from daylight to darkness without dusk to modulate the passage of time. Wolves began to bay in the distance. The telegrapher felt a chill and he huddled close to the fire. They ate in silence.

After the grouse, Borka set out bowls of honey mixed with nuts. The telegrapher was surprised to see Vasiliev lick his fingers just like a peasant,

"Borka, there isn't a French chef in Piter who can hold a candle to you, no not even at Dominique's. You could make a fortune there in no time. The grouse alone would make you famous. I'd recommend you to the right people, warn you off the sharp dealers. In no time you would save enough to come back, buy yourself a good herd, say twenty, twenty-five head, and spend the rest of your life watching it multiply. What do you say?"

Borka acted as though he had heard nothing of this before. But it was always the same on the last night. This time it had come too early. The message had brought evil news. The hunt was over for another year.

"Not until we finish the big hunt, Vasili Vasilievich. Then perhaps I will go with you. First we have to end the life of the great one."

Vasiliev tossed another log on the fire. "They call him the great one in these parts, but I call him *Burya*, the Storm. It suits his temper better. He's a bear, but not your ordinary Ural variety, mind you. This fellow is enormous, perhaps seven feet standing if we can judge by his tracks. A renegade from Siberia it seems who has wandered off course and liked what he found. No competition here. He terrifies the peasants, raids their livestock. The local gentry have given up trying to kill him, and that leaves it up to us."

The night sounds were growing louder, but the baying of the wolves was fainter as they moved off in another direction.

"We've been after him for seven years and only once did we

catch sight of him plunging through the undergrowth. There was no clear shot. Borka says I will never kill him because that will end the grouse banquets. I say we never will because Borka insists we must kill him courteously. That's important to the Komi, you see. Perhaps we are both right. I would miss the grouse, and Burya, damn him, has earned a death with dignity."

Borka fed his dogs with scraps from the grouse and puzzled over why Vasiliev was talking so freely with this stranger. Perhaps he did not wish to think about the message and what it meant for him.

"Burya is more clever than most of the criminals I have known. Thank God he isn't human—though some people believe he is a werebear—or we would have a mastermind on our hands. One time we were certain we had him trapped. We had a pack of dogs with us, though Borka wasn't happy about that, thought it gave us too great an advantage. Nothing of the sort! The old rogue led us right into the Mokhovoe Swamp. We lost two dogs and were lucky to get out of it ourselves."

Borka silently collected the metal plates, scraped them and went off to wash them in a nearby stream. Then he packed them into the knapsacks. How well he tells it all, he thought. But soon he will leave, another year will pass. Would he ever get to Petersburg and see the White Tsar? He handed his sheepskin to the telegrapher, an unwelcome guest, but a guest nonetheless. Besides he had the dogs who pressed up against him. They stretched out by the fire.

Vasiliev hadn't let the telegram ruin his last grouse meal of the season. But the printed words came back to him now. There was something ominous about them. Not much to go on, but enough to make him uneasy. An assassination that alarmed society and concerned the Emperor had all the earmarks of a political crime. That was out of his range. He had always steered clear of that sort of thing, kept turning down offers to join the secret police. Their methods were bad enough, but their way of looking at things appalled him. Persecuting journalists and exiling poets was not his idea of criminal justice. It was something of a family tradition, on his father's side of course, to despise the secret police. It was one of the few things that drew him close to the old Count who had drummed into his head from the moment he could understand such things, and probably even before then, that he, Vasili or Vasya as was called as a boy, had come into the world ten years to the day that Pushkin passed out of it on January 29, 1837. It had been D'Anthes' bullet that killed him, and it had been a fair duel. But the old Count was sure that the secret police had driven Pushkin to that bloody field of honor.

Vasiliev rolled over on his back to stare at the thick stream of the Milky Way. The fragment of Pushkin's last, unfinished poem came back to him.

I have ripened for eternity
And the torrent of my days
Has slowed...

Why summon him, a regular criminal investigator on holiday four hundred miles from Moscow a fortnight after the outrage had taken place? His views were well known. He had joined the Criminal Investigation Department when everyone predicted a brilliant career for him in the Guards, the Foreign Ministry or even the Gendarmes. What had they said? "If you get bored you can always retire from the service, take up the flute again, read your books and manage one of your father's estates." His friends thought him crazy when he told them of his choice. His father had raised an eyebrow, his most eloquent comment on important matters, but said nothing. Vasiliev always believed that the old man admired the rebelliousness of his beloved bastard, his son of the soil, as he half-mockingly called him.

What did he know about Ushakova? A famous beauty. Unsavory stories clung to her skirts. Her husband had the reputation of a reformer, not in good odor with his subordinates, the Gendarmes. They said he was close to Loris-Melikov. All that was to the good. But even decent men had recourse to shady tricks when their career or honor was at stake. He had no desire to be dragged into a test of wills between reformers and diehards. In a political crime, justice was always the next victim.

He awoke just before dawn to the smell of fresh pike being broiled over the fire. At breakfast everyone was absorbed in his own thoughts and hardly a word passed among them until the telegrapher had been sent on his way. Vasiliev watched the horseman disappear into the forest and thought how someone in Moscow had been lazy. It was always the same. A secret message coded in the Ministry was entrusted to a young provincial telegrapher who could easily have been bribed to reveal the contents. Everywhere the imperial chain of command tapered off to a frayed and rotting rope.

They talked it over and decided to avoid the easier route down the broad Kama River to the old Tatar city of Kazan and then back up the Volga on a steamer to Nizhny Novgorod where he would take the train to Moscow. It would cost Vasiliev an extra day. They chose the more direct but rugged overland trail to the headwaters of the Big Kokshaga. From there they could paddle downstream to the small river station of Marinsky Posad in time to catch the steamer that called there once a week. Before they broke camp Vasiliev handed the Martini-Henry to Borka.

"Keep it for me, old friend. I go to seek a different game," is all he said. Borka's eyes glistened, but Vasiliev withdrew his hand before Borka could bring it to his lips.

They traveled south through wild and deserted country where the firs gave way to a mixed forest of poplar, aspens and silver birch. The summer had been abnormally wet. There had been no big fires in the fall, and the new growth was luxuriant. But the swamps and bogs had crept out from their ancient beds and the two men had to make several wide detours. They quickened the pace. The forest gave way to large clearings where grain had recently been harvested, and the villagers came out to greet them with bread and salt. The Big Kokshaga proved more difficult to navigate than they expected. The water was high in its channel and arching branches of trees that covered the stream like a filigree canopy swept down within a few feet of the surface forcing them to ship oars and slide to the bottom of their flat hulled *lodka* as they passed underneath. The river opened up and the forest retreated. They caught glimpses of peasant huts clustered on shore. From a distance they looked prosperous with their brightly painted wooden shutters and gables, encircled by green fences that were hidden under a mass of fall flowers. But Vasiliev knew that behind the facades there was much sickness and misery.

A few days later they floated into the Volga. It spread out before them like an inland sea. Swollen by the heavy rains it had overflowed its low right bank and flooded the plains as far as they could see. Vasiliev had always felt the pulse of excitement at the sight, but now there was only the dull sensation of loss and the feeling that the great river marked the end of his freedom.

Chapter Seven

A police barouch stood at dockside of the river port of Nizhny Novgorod. A small group of Gendarmes preening in their sky blue uniforms strolled along the wharf. The officers fondled their sabers but failed to look casual as they scrutinized the passengers coming down the gangway. The merchants and their wives bowed and scraped. The officers ignored them. The third class, debarking last of all, gave them a wide berth. Cabbies shouted and cursed. A song sprang up as the stevedores began to unload bundles of hides. The Gendarmes grew fretful.

"Damned annoying," an officer muttered to no one in particular. A sergeant shrugged and signaled his men to form up. There was nothing more that could be done until the next steamer docked in two days. They would have to wait.

The crowd on the wharf gradually thinned out. The commanding officer stepped back as one of the crew, a rough looking man in a shabby blouse and frayed trousers, brushed by him. The man positively reeked of some kind of tanning substance. Even his face looked like coarse leather. Over his shoulder he had slung an oddly shaped canvas bag. No one would have suspected that the bag carried a man's arm severed just below the shoulder and packed in ice.

The deck hand mounted the steep hill leading to the inner town. He stopped at the first intersection, removed his cap and scratched his head. He turned to look for some time at the paddle steamer being unloaded. The Gendarmes piled into their barouche and drove off. He spat in their direction and resumed walking up the steep path, giving a good imitation of a sailor's rolling gait.

He shifted the bag to his left shoulder and felt the moisture seeping through the canvas. He had not decided how much to tell Ivan. It all depended on how much Ivan was prepared to tell him. He glanced up at the yellow and red houses of Nizhnyi. Traffic was picking up as he approached Alexander Nevsky Street. He passed in front of a pharmacy and caught his reflection in the plate glass. Not bad for a quick improvisation. Foma would be pleased. The stubble and dark stain on his face, his hair chopped off and the smell. Yes, that was real enough. It was often the smell that turned their eyes away so you could get away with a hasty disguise. Foma again, always right. It had been a nice touch to keep his right shoulder hitched up as if it had been broken and badly set. He had not forgotten his lessons. But then again he had sat at the feet of a master, a master unknown to the rest of the world. If Foma had been born a free man he would have grown rich and famous in the Imperial Theater. No matter. He died happy, satisfied with his life, though God knows why. Until he was an old man he had belonged to the old Count, had lived on the Vorontsov estate near Kolomenskoe most of his life. After the serfs were freed he had been too old and sick to start a new life. In his prime he had taught Vasili everything he knew.

A shop assistant darted out of the doorway to the pharmacy and glared at him. Vasiliev hoisted the bag higher on his shoulder and moved on. Ahead he could hear the dull rumble of carts and wagons. It was the time of the annual fair. He had already passed a few hawkers and soon it would be hard to get through the press. The crowd would swallow him up. But he needed time to think before he met Ivan. Too much had happened on the steamer that puzzled him. It wasn't too hard for a poor man to find a quiet place in a town like Nizhny. A tea house stood on the next corner, its weathered sign proclaiming the generic type, TRAKTIR. In England, he recalled, even the most wretched pub had a name, but a traktir was not a pub and Nizhny was not Bristol. He ducked his head to enter and sat by the window watching the flow of people, studying the faces. He was not worried about the Gendarmes or even plain-clothes men if they had sent any of those as well. It would be easy to pick them up in this crowd of Russian craftsmen, Tatar merchants, Kirghiz horse traders. Vasiliev sipped his hot, strong tea and thought about Foma.

His first memories were of Foma reciting folktales or singing epic songs and accompanying himself on the *gusli*. He knew thousands of verses by heart. It was only later that Vasiliev learned that his mother had secretly made Foma his godfather. The old Count knew nothing about it and Vasili's official godfather was a Vorontsov, a distant uncle from whom he had learned nothing. Foma had no children and even as a boy Vasili understood he was the heir to Foma's art as well as the Vorontsov estates. And which was worth more?

Foma had taught him slowly, watching for signs of impatience or boredom. He needn't have worried. When was it? Was he five or six when they began foraging in the woods, gathering roots and flower pods, tapping the sugar maples, scraping the birch bark, picking up reddish clay by the river. Foma made a game of it. Back in his *izba* he showed Vasili how to pound and mixed different ingredients into natural cosmetics. The result would have astonished a Moscow pharmacist. So many talents in Russia where you least expected them, hidden in plain view.

They sat side by side in the dark, smoky hut applying the makeup by the light of a candle. Vasiliev recalled how Foma had told him that one day he might have to do it in the dark and he had been right. But he probably hadn't been thinking about the fo'c'sle of a Volga steamer.

First a game and then a test. "Let's see how you look in the sunlight, eh?"

Next came instructions in body movements. They would sit for hours and study the field hands. "See how that one uses the scythe, and the other, over there, he's cheating as he mows." Foma had invented a few simple exercises to strengthen the leg and arm muscles. "No, No!" Foma would reprove him gently. "A merchant would never walk that way. Look, watch." He insisted that Vasili learn to imitate young women. "There's nothing wrong with that, as long as you remember who you are. Did you know that in the olden times women were not permitted to act, so it was left to the men? Now, practice the mincing steps again." Vasili had felt embarrassed but it did it.

Foma was wise. He had waited until Vasili's voice broke before he initiated him into the world of mimicry. Foma gave him his first singing lessons, taught him how to control his breathing and give his voice color. New games. Copying the speech of the servants and the Count's innumerable relatives who swarmed over the estate.

"Now we go for the highest level," Foma had announced one day, "the regional accents." He spoke little about his past, but it seemed that he had roamed the country as an *otkhodnik*, a seasonal worker traveling, with the Count's permission, from the grimy industrial towns of the central region to the Black Sea ports, sending back half his wages as his cash payment to the estate. He mastered the local speech patterns and proverbs, salting it all away in his prodigious memory. Years later, when Vasiliev was a student, he found that plenty of Foma's proverbs could not be found in the standard collection by Dahl.

As the time approached for Vasili to enroll in the Page Corps he began to notice that Foma parceled out his secrets more grudgingly. He often wondered if the old man was fearful of losing his child and heir. The day before he left Foma took him on a last walk in the woods. The old man was limping badly and he said little. Suddenly, he stopped and squinted up at his godson. His words were engraved in Vasiliev's memory. "Aye, lad if you had stayed with me a few more years...." Then his voice broke."Well, never mind, if God's will casts you down, the doors of the Imperial Theater will always be open for you. You have the makings of a great one. Yes, the makings of a Shchepkin."

Was God's will about to cast him down? Vasiliev wondered.

Vasiliev ordered a second glass of tea, swallowed it and left the traktir with a group of trading peasants. He wandered down a narrow lane and doubled back along a parallel side street. He was sure no one had picked him up at the wharf but it was best to get back into the right habits. The trackers who had been waiting for him at Marinsky Posad were amateurs. What puzzled him was that there seemed to be two kinds, the thug and the student. It was pretty clear they were working at cross-purposes.

He stood for a long time under a shed where they were selling rawhides. He might as well be consistent; he smelled enough like a tanner. No one showed any interest in him. He surveyed the hotel for a while and then circled it before entering the delivery entry. He climbed a service staircase and went down a carpeted corridor. He knocked loudly.

"So you gave them the slip," Ivan chuckled and embraced him. But Vasiliev could tell that his old friend was not entirely pleased. "Well, you look a fine wreck. And the odor. Good God, did you have to carry it that far?"

A samovar was bubbling on the table. Vasiliev poured himself a glass and inhaled.

"Darjeeling, Ivan. Been shopping at the bazaar?"

Ivan had put on weight since he had last seen him. Too many buffets and banquets, the mark of a successful man. Always the favorite of ministers, brilliant but self-effacing, ambitious but never ruthless, a shrewd judge of men, but hopeless with women. He was reputed to have no enemies, his only real weakness. Never tortured by self-doubt, he had acquired the sobriquet the iron colonel. Knowing him as he had for years, Vasiliev had already concluded that Ivan would listen to him patiently, nod his fine head, cluck in sympathy and then insist that he take the assignment.

"A good trip?"

"If you like excitement."

Ivan smiled gamely on. It was going to be tougher than he thought. Vasiliev was already bristling. Ivan motioned him to a chair. Vasiliev dumped his bag on the floor.

"Trouble?"

"We'll get to that later. Why the dramatic summons? What's so special about the Ushakova case?" Vasiliev hesitated for dramatic effect. "I'd like to know if only to compare your version to what I've heard so far."

Ivan struggled to keep his smile from fading altogether. It was always this way with Vasiliev. He would never advance beyond Inspector. Yet Ivan could not help but like him. He was after all the best there was.

"I've gone to the trouble of getting you a copy of the Gendarme's report, such as it is. You won't like it any more than I do. But it's all we've got. We need to have the job done right, even if it means starting from the beginning. Listen I'm sorry about your holidays."

Vasiliev pushed the bag against the wall. Was this all he was going to get? Did they think it would satisfy him? Wouldn't they ever learn it wasn't just about giving orders? No doubt Ivan had been told, "Tell him as little as possible, but get him to come aboard." He would have to pry the rest out of Ivan.

"I want to know what I'm getting into, Ivan. We've just met and I already sniff a rotten fish head. First of all, why call me in? It seems this is no ordinary homicide, but I am just an ordinary detective in..."

"Not so ordinary, Vasya."

"...in the Criminal Investigation Department. I've no experience with political cases. Why not rely on the specialists. We have plenty of them. They are not incompetent, you know, whatever else one may think of them. Right now what you say makes no sense to me. There has to be more to it."

"It's a delicate matter, you know, dealing with the murder of a minister's wife. We need someone who is discreet. You have a reputation for that sort of thing. The Plevna case was political, wasn't it?"

"That was a fluke. It didn't start out that way. I was on the ground. It was wartime and there wasn't anyone else to handle it. Sorry, Ivan, I want more."

Ivan took out a cigarette from his tunic pocket, lit it and inhaled.

"All right, you'll find out sooner or later anyhow." Ivan avoided Vasiliev's eyes and exhaled a cloud of smoke that drifted between them. "I'm not supposed to tell you anything more than that, just offer my help. But I know I can trust you...." Ivan stopped himself. He did not want to overdo it, not with Vasiliev.

"The reason we've called in an ordinary detective is that this may in fact be an ordinary crime. The Gendarmes don't think so, but it's in their interest not to think so. Their investigation was so slipshod we think they are covering up."

"And it is in your interest, Ivan, to prove that it is not a political crime, or at least not a terrorist attack."

Ivan tapped his ash on the floor and took another drag on his cigarette. Pretty soon I won't be able to see behind that smoke screen, Vasiliev mused.

"You may not know what is involved here, Vasya."

"Please tell me."

"The stakes are high, very high. Ushakova's murder has put a heavy strain on everyone. Loris-Melikov's position has been shaken. The court is lining up against him. As long as the tsar was the target, society shrugged and went about its business. I tell you it was sickening to watch. The Emperor's popularity isn't what it used to be. Surely you know that. It's been true ever since he began his affair with Dolgorukaya. But when he married her the court was scandalized. It was too soon after the death of the Empress. But he was so infatuated he couldn't wait."

Vasiliev nodded and said nothing. There had been rumors, but it was useful to get confirmation from somebody on the inside.

"What you may not know, Vasya, is that the heir, Alexander Alexandrovich, has turned against his father. He always idolized the Empress and despised Dolgorukaya. He was beside himself when he saw her take his mother's place. So, he has become vulnerable to intrigue. As you might expect there are people who see a chance to use the occasion for their own purposes."

"Naturally," muttered Vasiliev. He knew the type only too well. His father had compared them to slimy toads sucking up to the grandees like himself, spending their lives scheming to destroy one another. And the old Count wondered why his son kept as far away from court as he could.

"The reactionaries have hitched their wagon to Alexander Alexandrovich. They are spreading rumors that Loris-Melikov is preparing a constitution. It's all rubbish of course, as anyone who knows the man realizes. But Loris is surrounded by liberal hot heads who are being spurred on by some of the university professors. And let us not forget the students. So it's easy to tar him with the same brush. Then along comes the Ushakova killing and it plays right into the hands of the reactionaries, scares the whole aristocracy. They see themselves as the next targets. Some influential people have begged the Emperor to delay the reforms. Now that they are worried about their own skins, they are beating the drums for repression. Katkov fans the flames."

"And if the Emperor doesn't go along with them?"

"I don't know, Vasya, but I tell you that I'm frightened."

"You don't mean...you're not worried about a coup are you?"

"There have been stranger things in our history."

"I see. So I stand between the throne and disaster?" Vasiliev stood up, placed his empty glass on the table and folded his hands behind his back. "All I have to do is prove that Ushakova was murdered by a disappointed lover, or would that not set well with the Count?"

"For God's sake!"

"How about this, then; the murder was a provocation by police reactionaries to discredit the reforms, save their ass and get their own men to cover up."

Ivan winced. "I don't understand are you serious? Where...?"

"Just another theory making the rounds, Ivan."

It was time, thought Ivan, to push a little harder. He would not take more of this.

"Vasili, the Council of Ministers has authorized me to assign you to the case. You will report directly to me. I'll be your liaison to the security services. The Moscow Chief of Police will continue to be your nominal superior, but that is only for the sake of form. We can put any number of men at your disposal."

"Will you accept my findings, Ivan, if they do not match your theories?"

"I give you my word of honor, Vasya, that we will not interfere in any way. We will accept your report. We don't need you to cover up for us, my friend. We could do that ourselves."

It was clear to Vasiliev that he could not contradict Ivan without insulting him. There were only two alternatives—accept or resign. For a moment he thought about it.

Ivan's cigarette had gone out in his mouth. He thought about the last few days spent in this provincial town, bored by the company he had to keep, by the conversation at table about stock prices and shipping schedules. Even the dinner with the Gendarmes had been a relief. Now his old friend Vasiliev was putting on one of his petulant performances. Well, he knew how to appeal to his sense of honor and duty even better to his sympathy for the innocent victim. Why had he made such a clumsy start? Was he losing his touch? Vasiliev was partly to blame. He had thrown him way off by his bizarre appearance, a real scarecrow. Christ, why the elaborate disguise?

"I have to admit that it's a strange case, Vasya. Even bystanders get hurt."

Vasiliev seemed far away but something in Ivan's tone wrenched him back to the drab hotel room now thick with smoke.

"What's that?"

"The telegrapher, you know the fellow who carried the message?" Ivan paused to glance at Vasiliev. He didn't like the look that was coming into his eyes. "Well, you didn't know him personally did you? They found him dead on the trail the morning after he set out to find you. It seems that bear of yours got hold of him, mauled him pretty badly."

Vasiliev swore under his breath. "So that's how they found out."

"I don't understand, *mon vieux*. Do you have to be so mysterious?"

Vasiliev went to the samovar again and made a strong tea. He almost scalded his hand with the boiling water. He stared at the dark leaves at the bottom of the glass.

"The disguise, Ivan, I didn't get rigged out like this to play games with the Gendarmes. I was just trying not to get myself killed. As you see I succeeded. Somebody gave it a good try. On the steamer it was, and they bungled it. I thought it best to make myself less conspicuous for the rest of the trip. The captain was quite an accommodating fellow. I persuaded him to let me sign on as a deck hand. So I had to look the part."

"My God! A deck hand!" Ivan shook his head but knew better than to interrupt. Typical Vasiliev. You thought to surprise him and he trumped you. Ivan also took refuge in the samovar.

Ivan's reaction angered Vasiliev.

"Hard to imagine, isn't it, mingling with the dark people. Do you have any idea what they are like, Ivan, the river crews, the navvies, stevedores? Let me tell you. We call them ignorant and depraved, but they accepted me. Probably saved my life. And do you know how I was able to win their trust? By reading to them at night. *Ivanhoe*, Ivan, imagine. One of them, the boiler man I think, had an old translation. Pretty battered it was. But no one could read except the cook who had gotten so astigmatic he couldn't see the print any more. But they wouldn't give up the book."

Ivan set his face against the outburst. He knew he was in for one of Vasiliev's sermons as they called them.

"Down in the stinking foc'sl'e they used to crowd around me at night, so damned beat they could hardly keep their eyes open. And they listened like children. No, that's wrong, like men who no longer wanted to be children. And they permitted no interruptions. Only once was the rule broken. It was the third night. The moon had broken through a dark patch of clouds, and a cry came up from the watch. 'Exiles!'"

"The men rose silently, went topside and lined the rail. On the starboard side a tug was towing a barge, painted dirty red like the rest. But this one had a different cargo, not grain, Ivan, but men. An iron cage covered the deck. Inside dark shapes were pressed against the bars. They made no sound. And our men standing at the rail were quiet too. When the two boats drew parallel our men took off their caps. I remember the smell of burning oil just then. If you closed your eyes you might have thought you were in church."

Vasiliev had let his tea grow cold. Ivan had forgotten to light up again. Outside the rumble of traffic could be heard. The samovar bubbled contently.

"Russia is a sad country, Vasya. We are trying to change that. There are moments when I think we do not have enough time to do it all. Even the best of us work at cross-purposes. Everything worthwhile takes too long."

Ivan was staring at the floor where a pool of water was beginning to form around Vasiliev's canvas bag. Vasiliev caught his eye and without a word he picked up the bag and set it down at Ivan's feet. He pulled up his right trouser leg, unstrapped a sheath knife and cut the twine, releasing a disagreeable smell. Ivan started back, striking the edge of the desk.

"An arm, Ivan. Another trophy of the hunt. But this belonged to one of the hunters. He came aboard at Marinsky Posad, Actually there were two of them waiting for us, Borka and me. But they hadn't trailed us, I'm sure of that. They must have ambushed the messenger, tortured him for information and then made it look like an animal had killed him. Poor fellow, he couldn't have told them much, only that we were headed for the river. They must have had horses. Maybe there were more than two. Others might have gone up to Kazan. All they had to do was watch the boats."

"This looks bad, an operation that needed men, planning. But you see what it means."

"I'm not sure what it means, just yet. It gets more complicated, Ivan, so let me give you as much as I know. The two thugs boarded with me. They had the look of town peasants, burly, bearded chaps with thick hair parted down the middle and plastered flat with greasy stuff that smell like lard. Cheap woolen coats belted around the middle and good soft leather boots. I didn't like the looks of them from the first; chalk it up to a policeman's instinct or my suspicious nature. So I took precautions. When they jumped me on deck the first night I was ready for them. At dinner I sat with two hussars, recruited them with a story about escape convicts. We set a little trap…"

Ivan had taken out a linen handkerchief and was holding it over his mouth.

"Sorry, *mon vieux*, I forgot, you've never been on a battlefield."

Vasiliev picked up the bag and glanced at the inner door. Ivan nodded and Vasiliev pushed the bag into the next room and threw open the window.

"No need to prolong this. When they rushed me the officers took them from the rear. They panicked and vaulted the railing, the big one, name of Petya jumped clear. The other one moved more slowly. One of my friends cut him with his cavalry saber, sheared off his arm like a joint of lamb. Poor devil toppled over the side and cracked his skull open on the rail of the lower deck, then rolled into the water. We never found him but fished out his arm. They'll have a police launch dragging the area for the rest of him."

"And the other man, Petya, you say?"

"Disappeared. We lowered a boat, searched the nearest bank; it was only fifty meters away but it was thick with reeds. A dark night. We had lanterns but never caught sight of him."

"How will the story get out?"

"The story I told the hussars and the captain was the same. I was on the trail of cattle thieves. They seemed convinced. The captain let me write the report and he signed it without a word."

"Good. And the disguise?" Ivan knew better than to ask why he had brought the arm. Vasiliev had a weakness for dramatics. Or was it just that Russians tend to excess when attacked?

"I wasn't sure they were alone. In any case there was another contact, a student"

"What! This is incredible. But maybe not. We seemed to have turned over a stone, and I don't like what's underneath it."

Chapter Eight

"Listen, Ivan, you are always a good host, but you're forgetting your manners. I am famished and all you give me is tea. Are you trying to starve me into submission?"

"My dear fellow, I apologize. I've ordered...but your story... well, yes, let's dine right away. Here, in this other room. Everything has been prepared."

There was a steaming tureen of *solyanka* soup followed by sturgeon *shashlik*, buckwheat kasha, a bottle of Haut Brion '75, a *macedoine* of fresh fruit and *petits fours*. They observed their rule of no serious talk at table and so they reminisced about the war, holidays together on the Black Sea coast.

Ivan's servant cleared and set down a bottle of Armenian brandy. Ivan raised his glass "In honor of our good Loris-Melikov."

"My goodness Ivan, your loyalty knows no boundaries. Why there was a time when only Courvoisier would do."

"I've corrupted you enough for the day, Vasya. Now, I want the rest of your adventure on the Volga."

"Well, my new found popularity puzzles me. No sooner was I settled on board than a student type introduced himself, no beating around the bush with him. He knew who I was, claimed to have read about my exploits and so forth. He began to spout some nonsense about Lombroso of all things. He said Lombroso was weak on the social problem, too psychological. We batted that back and forth for a while. Then he switched to the Sokhovo-Kobylin case and it was clear that I had some kind of budding nihilist on my hands. He was taking the line that no one in a frock coat would ever be punished for a violent crime. I agreed with him in principle but had to tell him about the Boldreyev case. So we agreed to have dinner and continue the conversation. But he never turned up that evening. Turns out that he had an accident, fell down the forward companionway, or so he said when I paid him a visit the next morning in his cabin."

Vasiliev held out his glass and Ivan refilled it.

"But you're going to tell me that it wasn't an accident."

"Right. Now here is the interesting part. I had to squeeze it out of him. He didn't just tumble down the companionway. He was pushed by the same Petya who tried to kill me. The student, called himself Iuri, said that he first ran into Petya several years before when the tradesmen on Hunter's Row broke up a demonstration against university officials and beat some of the students badly. Petya had been dressed in a butcher's smock but Iuri claimed no one on the Row had ever seen him before, that he was just a hired thug. When he spotted him on board, he lost his head and began to curse him. Petya just picked him up and tossed him down the companionway, could have broken his neck. His story was pretty muddled. Finally he told me what he really wanted, but I had to coax it out of him.

"I accused him of being a student radical, a revolutionary. He got terribly excited, said he didn't believe in terror, that it was a blind alley. Now listen to this, Ivan. He said the real purpose for coming aboard was to warn me that the secret police would do everything to block my investigation of the Ushakova case. He said that he and his companions were committed to non-violent change. They wanted to help me solve the crime."

Ivan gasped. "How the Hell did they even know you were on the case? That part about the secret police is ridiculous. So this Iuri is the source of this crazy idea that the murder was their work, a deliberate provocation on their part. No, I can't believe it. They have their own ideas, but to interfere with an order of the Minister of Interior. No, it's crazy. This Iuri may have been an imposter. God knows what his game is."

"Whatever his game, Ivan, my appointment was not a well guarded secret. You'll have to admit." Vasiliev added dryly.

"So, where is this Iuri now?"

Vasiliev had made up his mind to lie on this one. He trusted Ivan but there would be reports and no matter how confidential they could easily be seen by the wrong eyes. He wanted to save Iuri for himself. He had seen to his transfer to a zemstvo hospital. Borka would be waiting for him when he was discharged. There might be a file on him, if he was arrested in the student demonstration. He would get Serov to work on running down Petya. Suddenly, he realized he had made up his mind to take the Ushakova case. He didn't like being intimidated or manipulated. And besides they should never have tried to blame Burya for a murderous attack; it was out of character.

"He gave us the slip somewhere between Kazan and Nizhny. Down in the foc's'le I couldn't keep an eye on him. But we'll pick him up somewhere, and Petya too. They have one thing in common. They are both amateurs."

"So, you'll take the Ushakova case?"

"Ivan you have lost none of your subtlety. You probably could get me to sign up at my mother's funeral." He ran his fingers through his hair. "But I imagine that you do not want me to show up like this on the Moscow train. Is it possible to wash up here?"

Ivan was pleased with himself. It had been a stroke of genius on his part to play on Vasiliev's sympathy for the telegrapher, the innocent victim. He was always vulnerable on that score. If you could get him to believe that he was serving the common folk... From then on it had been easy. Vasiliev was meek as a hermit.

Ivan could hear the splashing of water in the next room. He rummaged in his tunic for a cigarette. Had he really smoked them all? It had not been an easy interview, but Ushakov would be pleased. Ivan had ceased to wonder whether that was all that mattered to him any longer. Vasili had not even complained about the travel arrangements, though they had worried Ivan. Now he would win points with the Gendarmes as well. They would have Vasili to themselves all the way to Moscow. Shuev had insisted on bringing along his deputy, Van der Fleet, not one of Ivan's favorites. But the man had a talent for turning revolutionaries into double agents.

Through the thin partition he heard a tin cup knocking against a porcelain basin. He had made the right preparations, ordering the food, all Vasili's favorite dishes, engaging the barber. He knew what

Vasili would look like after emerging from the wilds. There wasn't much they could do about his hair. But having brought the dress uniform would help some.

"Sorry, Your Honor," the barber had nicked his chin, but Vasiliev scarcely noticed. He was just grateful the man wasn't a chatterbox. There had only been the clucking of the tongue as he tried to repair the damage Vasiliev had inflicted on his hair. He was thinking about the telegrapher. The local police were fools. Burya would never have attacked a man on horseback except under extreme provocation and never on a well traveled trail. Besides, all signs pointed to the bear having already left the area. The murder had angered him but he was also annoyed that they had tried to frame Burya. Borka would understand that.

The door swung open and Ivan appeared on the threshold, his face all smiles. "You look splendid, *mon vieux*, quite presentable at court. Here is Perrin to take us down."

A stocky man with wavy white hair peered out from behind Ivan's sturdy back. He was twirling a pince-nez and bowing.

"Bon jour, cher monsieur. Je m'excuse de vous déranger, mais le train part en quinze minutes."

"Just enough time to make an unhurried departure, eh, Vasili? Monsieur Perrin, you have been very good to us."

"Ah monsieur le colonel, for a friend and stockholder in La Grande Société one is delighted to give service."

The main waiting room was crowded with trading peasants carrying heavy burlap bags on their shoulders. At the first bell they surged toward the third class carriages, battling one another for a good seat, or just any seat on the hard wooden benches. Through the open doors to the storage rooms Vasiliev caught a glimpse of packets of tea shipped in from Kiakhta on the Chinese frontier and pyramids of hides from the lower Volga, bales of cotton from Ferghana.

They stepped onto an empty stretch of platform that had been cordoned off. Two railroad guards snapped to attention.

"We are taking extra precautions now," Perrin whispered.

A Gendarme posted at the entrance to a sleek iron-gray parlor car saluted smartly.

"An armored car!" exclaimed Vasiliev.

Ivan touched him lightly on the shoulder. "I'll leave you in good hands, *cher ami*. Whatever you need we can provide it. You have my personal cipher. Use it. The decoding is done in my office by my aide. No leaks, I assure you." He winked at Vasiliev and wrapping his cape around himself he strode rapidly down the platform.

A uniformed conductor with gold braid on his hatband escorted Vasiliev and Perrin into a sumptuous suite fitted with upholstered armchairs, a drum table covered with drinks and *zakuski*. A large map of the empire stretched over one wall. A formal portrait of the imperial family done early in the reign of Alexander Nikolaevich faced it on the other side. Two men sat smoking on the divan. Vasiliev's heart sank when he recognized them.

So the Headmaster himself had come. The familiar blue eyes, aquiline nose and thin, bloodless lips. Behind the bulbous forehead lay a keen but dogmatic intellect. His subordinates had nick named him well. Shuev rose to greet him and waved a hand carelessly at the slim, erect figure beside him.

"You are acquainted with Van der Fleet, of course," he was speaking in French.

"Of course," Vasiliev replied in Russian. Van der Fleet bowed amiably. Vasiliev had last seen him before the war, was it four or five years ago? Van der Fleet had changed little, his skin drawn tightly over a fine bone structure, a pencil thin moustache etched into his upper lips, his expressionless blue eyes—was the color *de rigueur* with the Gendarmes? His sky blue uniform was beautifully tailored to show off his narrow waist. Vasiliev had always been suspicious that he wore a corset. On the breast of his tunic he wore several decorations, but none of them for service in the war. Vasiliev wondered whether the man had ever been under fire.

"Our host, Perrin, has provided us with a little refreshment. Would you care for a brandy, Vasiliev?" The label proclaimed Courvoisier, no Armenian brandy here.

"Of course", Vasiliev repeated in the same flat tone.

Perrin cleared his throat. These moody Russians made him uneasy.

Vasiliev abruptly turned to Perrin. "Tell me, Monsieur, what are your security arrangements for the special trains?" He spoke French effortlessly with a Parisian accent. He was only being polite;

Perrin had not learned much Russian in ten years of service on the railroads. "I mean those for carrying exalted personages. You must have tightened up a bit since the Moscow incident."

It was now the turn of the Headmaster to feel uncomfortable. Almost a year had gone by but the image of the wreck was still vivid in Shuev's mind. The engine and three cars of the imperial train had been sprawled grotesquely down the embankment of the Southern Line, not more than fifty kilometers from Moscow. When he had first caught sight of it from a distance his mouth had gone dry from fear. A few minutes later a sense of relief had flooded over him. He almost had broken out laughing at what he saw. The ground was covered with watermelons, hundreds of them, spilling over the line and down the embankment. Peasants were swarming over the site, picking up the undamaged ones, wolfing down pieces of the smashed ones. The People's Will had struck again, but this time they had dynamited the wrong train. The decoy had confused them and an ordinary train carrying the tsar had already passed over the explosive device. Moscow lost nothing more serious than a week's supply of watermelons. The terrorists had been ingenious; Shuev had to give them that. He had personally led the search party, bursting into the cottage where they uncovered a tunnel fifty meters long leading from the basement to the tracks. A fire burned in the grate and the food on the table was still warm, but there was no trace of the terrorists. It had been the worst day in Shuev's life.

It had also been a blot on the Gendarmes' record. Like the Khalturin bombing it was a subject they did not like to discuss. Shuev thought it tactless of Vasili to have alluded to the incident. But Perrin was not rattled.

"There are ten armed guards from the railroad police on every train, and two sentries stationed at each trestle. The army is giving us some help too. The line is patrolled by the hussars of the Life Guards."

Vasili nodded. "Yes, I know the unit; it's a good one. You've taken all the right precautions, it seems to me."

"Security will be even tighter for the trip of Her Royal Highness, Grand Duchess Maria Alexandrovna," Perrin concluded. He was beginning to like this Vasiliev.

"One last thing. How many people know the details of your arrangements?"

"Only myself, the chairman of the board of directors and the commanders of the security detachments, that is outside the ministries of course."

"The ministries Monsieur Perrin? Ah, the ministries. But they are sieves for confidential information."

Shuev looked stunned. Van der Fleet smiled thinly.

Vasiliev ignored them. "What a pity, Monsieur. It would be better if no one except the commanders were informed. Confidential messages have a habit of going astray these days." Vasiliev sipped his brandy. He judged the Armenian no less good. "Let me give you an example. As the result of an intercepted telegram I have been followed ever since I left the Viatka district. So someone is leaking information from the Ministry of Interior, or perhaps Posts and Telegraph."

"Wait a moment, Vasili Vasilievich," Shuev protested, "Why blame the ministries. There are other possibilities."

"Really, Grigory Alexandrovich? Not in this case, I'm afraid. Sorry to shock you but the leak is probably coming from a rather high level."

"How can you say that?"

"It's really quite simple. The message originated in the office of General Loris-Melikov himself. The message was not coded because I have no access to codes and would not have been able to read it. The only person outside who knew of its contents was the clerk at the local station. And he told no one before delivering it."

"Are you sure?"

"The message was sealed and there was no sign of tampering. But even assuming that I could have been fooled, there are other circumstances that prove my case. A duplicate of the message must have fallen into the hands of certain people after the telegrapher had left his post to deliver the original. Otherwise they would simply have followed him to our camp and slaughtered us in our sleep. But they were late in picking up his trail. They missed us. And that is why they found it necessary to torture and murder him."

"What are you saying?" Shuev was now visibly upset. Van der Fleet kept his eyes fixed on Vasiliev but gave no sign of reacting.

Shuev turned to his deputy, "Kolya, I have heard nothing of this. I do not understand."

"Nor I, perhaps Vasiliev will enlighten us now." Van der Fleet too had shifted to Russian.

"The messenger's body was found on the trail leading back to the station. The head was badly damaged as though mauled by a wild beast. According to the local police it was the work of a legendary bear that roams the area. That is impossible for many reasons. I've hunted the animal for years; I know its habits and migratory pattern. When the messenger was killed the bear was no longer in the vicinity. So you see, Grigory Alexandrovich, the messenger was murdered by those who had intercepted the telegram, or most probably their agents. They arrived on the scene too late to catch us but they followed his trail. It looks like they tried to force him to tell where we were headed, but the poor fellow did not know. We never told him. They probably disfigured him to conceal the evidence of torture. They finally caught up with me, probably riding hard overland while we went by the water route to Marinsky Posad. Two of them attacked me on board the steamer. Thanks to your hussars, Monsieur Perrin, we evened the score."

Shuev could hardly contain his agitation "Astonishing, I find it hard to believe. It sounds like an adventure story."

"Yes, Grigory Alexandrovich, only too true. But life in Russia these days resembles an adventure story, don't you think?"

"It doesn't surprise me, Grisha." Vasiliev noticed how Van der Fleet adopted just the right tone of deference while contradicting his superior. "After all, the terrorists have penetrated our defenses in other places as well. Enterprising chaps."

"You assume terrorists, then."

"It seems logical, doesn't it? Who else could it have been? You see, Vasili Vasilievich, the terrorists have switched tactics recently. Perhaps that is why you have been called in. So it is important that you know this. They are trying to sow panic everywhere. The assassination of Countess Ushakova was just the beginning. They may have intended to kill her husband, we don't know. Just imagine the effect if they had succeeded in killing Russia's most eminent detective?"

Vasiliev bowed politely. "You flatter me, Nikolai Sergeevich. But it is flattery. The revolutionaries haven't the men to spare for diversionary operations, especially after your successful operations against them. You have deprived them of some of their best men. And they have more ambitious aims."

"I fear that you still don't have the full picture, Vasili Vasilievich. The situation is more complex than you think. That is why we are here, to help you understand what has been going on. The Populists, as they call themselves, have split into two camps. Those who advocate terror have adopted the name People's Will. Rather grandiloquent, don't you think? Khalturin is one of them, but a man called Andrei Zheliabov is the real leader, a former serf with a bit of schooling. You see how dangerous it is to educate the lower classes above their station?

"The other wing goes by the name of Repartition of the Land Some of them cling to the old name of the unified movement before the split, Land and Liberty. They claim to be pacifists, but we are not deceived. Their propaganda among the peasants is just as dangerous to the state order. Besides they have not broken relations with the People's Will. We've heard that they even borrow money from them. It may surprise you to know that we have infiltrated the terrorist section of the People's Will, slipped into the wolf's lair you might say. You see, two can play at that game. In the long run we will win because we are stronger, steadier, smarter. We also have moral authority on our side."

How many times had Van der Fleet rehearsed this speech, Vasiliev wondered? It sounded so pat.

"Perhaps Vasili Vasilievich would appreciate an example or two," Shuev put in.

"Of course, Grisha. Let's take the case of Goldenberg, one of the top men in the People's Will. Last year a colleague and I persuaded him to cooperate. When I say persuaded don't imagine that we use crude methods, threats or beatings. No, it is a matter of applying psychological pressure, a new method unknown to the police in Western countries. Before he lost his head Goldenberg passed on valuable information about his old comrades, plans, codes, safe houses, the lot. But then his conscience began to trouble him. Our doctors call it a spiritual crisis." Van der Fleet pronounced the words with disdain. "You know these intellectuals, they're fanatics, sometimes foolhardy but ultimately unstable. They collect all sorts of rubbish in their heads, like a sewer grating. He hanged himself in his cell."

Vasiliev showed no reaction, but Perrin gave a slight shudder. Vasiliev doubted that the Sûreté Nationale was a kinder, gentler force. Perhaps Perrin had been in Russia too long.

"Strangely enough," Van der Fleet went on after a short pause, "we had less success penetrating the top levels of the other wing, the Repartition. It would be a great advantage if we could; then we would be able to play one faction against the other. You understand?"

Van der Fleet leaned forward from the waist and for a moment Vasiliev thought he might break in half. If the body had its own language, his was speaking volumes.

"We didn't give you a chance to finish your story. Is it not possible that a member of the Repartition has already tried to make contact with you?"

"It would be my duty to report it, if they had, isn't that so?"

"Quite right," Shuev seemed content to let Van der Fleet take the lead; there was no sense antagonizing Vasiliev at this stage.

Perrin glanced nervously at his watch, relieved that he could now decently take his leave.

"*Bon voyage, messieurs.* You will not be disturbed during your voyage unless you ring. Dinner will be served at your pleasure."

Almost imperceptibly the train quivered and glided out of the station. It was bound to be a long trip, Vasiliev mused, possibly the longest of his life.

"Perhaps we could review the preliminary investigation," he began.

Shuev handed him a sheaf of papers. It was the same report that Ivan had let him read, but Vasiliev knew better than to say so. He skimmed the eight hand-written pages while Shuev tapped his boot noiselessly on the carpet. There was no sense pretending that there was anything in it that required close study.

"Not much to go on, just a narrative of events and a lot of speculation. Have you any suspects?"

"We've made a dozen arrests, all known revolutionaries or sympathizers, eh Kolya?" Van der Fleet was too absorbed in his brandy glass to answer.

"I see. Was this a routine sweep or did you collect more evidence than is documented here…" Vasiliev slapped the papers against his thigh…"that point to one or more individuals?"

"What do you mean by evidence, Vasili Vasilievich? They are all associated in one way or another with the People's Will or the other faction, what is it called, Kolya?"

"Repartition of the Land, or Land and Liberty."

"Yes, right, ridiculous names, damned nihilists, all of them."

"No real suspects, then, so far." Vasiliev muttered. Shuev looked offended.

"Was an autopsy performed?"

"The deputy minister opposed a violation of his wife's remains. Besides the cause of death was clear enough."

"What about the coachman?"

Shuev look blankly at Vasiliev.

"The report mentions that a coachman was also killed in the blast."

This time Shuev expressed his annoyance. "Precisely, killed in the blast. No need for an autopsy."

"No? Then what can you tell me about the explosive device?"

"The terrorists have been using either dynamite or small amounts of nitroglycerin."

"And in this case?"

"Presumably dynamite."

"But you are not certain."

"I am certain that the explosion killed the wife of the deputy Minister of Interior."

"Witnesses? Any unusual movement in the street, cabs parked, loiterers, that sort of thing?"

"The servants were asleep. At four o'clock in the morning, Vasili Vasilievich; no one was promenading in the streets, if that's what you mean." Shuev seemed to have lost interest in the matter.

"But the report states that the Count heard the explosion and rushed to the window of his study. There is no mention of what he saw."

"He saw the body of his wife. That was enough of a shock."

Vasiliev glanced out the window at the pine and birch forest. The trees hurtled by as though fleeing his life forever.

"Tell me, Grigory Alexandrovich, has the Bagration household been questioned? No mention of it here."

"What an odd idea. The assassination took place at Usha-kov's."

"True, but the killer or killers might have had a confederate among the servants at Bagration's. Might help explain the timing of the attack."

"You may wish to interrogate the servants," Shuev sniffed his brandy. "I observed nothing out of the ordinary there."

Vasiliev straightened up in his armchair. "You were a guest at Bagration's that night? The report does not mention that."

"Careful, Grisha," Van der Fleet had come to life again, "You may end up as Vasiliev's star witness."

"I can think of no more reliable witness," Vasiliev parried.

"Bravo Vasiliev! But it is my duty to warn General Shuev against taking the stand."

Shuev glanced uneasily at both men. Memories of the Davidova girl, Irina, came back in a rush. "Well, what is it you wish to know?"

"Let us begin with the Countess. Do you recall seeing her at any time during the evening. I would be grateful if you could remember everything about her, the way she behaved, her companions, well, I don't have to remind you what I am after, Grigory Alexandrovich, you are a trained observer."

"Excuse me once again," Van der Fleet broke it, "but really, Vasili Vasilievich, you are starting off on the wrong foot. Wouldn't it be better to save your interrogation for the suspects?"

"We each have our methods, Nikolai Sergeevich."

This time it was Shuev who signaled his subordinate for silence. Vasiliev felt as though he were seated on a wooden school bench. The Headmaster was about to give a lesson in total recall.

"The Count and Countess arrived together at approximately 10:30. I noticed their coach almost collided with a lower class droshky just before entering the drive. The Countess may have been upset by this. She jumped out of the coach and rushed into the house with a fixed look on her face. She scarcely greeted me. The Count stepped down more deliberately, as is his custom, exchanged a few friendly words with his coachman and joined me on the porch. We went in together. The Countess was quickly surrounded by a group of admirers, hussars mainly."

"Which regiment?"

"The Third, I believe."

"Please go on. Everything you say is very helpful."

"You see, I am leaving nothing out! Well, I wouldn't be surprised if the Countess had her entire card filled out within minutes. Every time I caught a glimpse of her she was in motion, yes, a study in perpetual motion." The image seemed to please him.

"Even Prince Bagration came out of retirement to waltz with her. In fact, he brought the quadrille to a stop, right in the middle if you please, and claimed her as his partner."

Shuev paused for more encouragement.

"You paint a vivid picture, Grigory Alexandrovich."

Shuev was enjoying himself now, searching his memory for the smallest detail with which to impress Vasiliev.

"The Prince had prepared a special entertainment, the Terek Sword Dance, a little flamboyant for my taste, but he has always been attracted to the exotic. This was already after midnight. I didn't see it because I had gone off to say a few words to the Princess, in the Georgian Room. Come to think of it I never saw the Countess alive again."

"You returned to the ballroom, later?"

"Yes, shortly after the Sword Dance was over."

"And she was no longer in perpetual motion, as you so neatly put it. So she must have left during the Sword Dance. Seems like she vanished while everyone was distracted, doesn't it?"

"What are you implying, Vasili Vasilievich?" Vasiliev was getting tired of Van der Fleet popping into the conversation. Like Punch, he couldn't keep off stage.

"I never imply things, Nikolai Sergeevich, but I do not believe in coincidence either." He turned in his chair.

"When did you leave the ball, Grigory Alexandrovich?"

"About three o'clock."

Van der Fleet rose to refill their glasses from a sideboard behind Vasiliev.

"So the Countess was absent from the ballroom for over two hours, nearer three, between the time she had her last waltz with the Prince and the time she left. When was that, three thirty, quarter to four? It's a short coach ride from Prechistenka to Povarskaya, unless they took a detour. Of course, that is quite possible too. And the Count when did he leave?"

"Early, shortly after the Sword Dance. It was curious...."

A discreet tapping, the parlor door opened and the dining steward appeared brandishing three menus. Vasiliev looked up in surprise. Perrin had promised no interruptions, unless they rang. Then he noticed the bell pull over the sideboard.

"Are you ready to order your Excellencies? This evening I can offer you smoked salmon rolls filled with caviar whipped cream, a turtle soup, chicken *po kievskii*, a mushroom pie and an almond-raspberry torte."

"We haven't eaten all day", exclaimed Van der Fleet.

Vasiliev could hardly contradict his hosts but the prospect of a second feast of these proportions might put him out of action for a week. Possibly that was the aim.

Van der Fleet made a great fuss over the wine declaring that they would stay in Burgundy all evening. "To begin a Chambolle-Musigny, then to accompany the chicken a Chambertin and closing with a Chablis, but attention my good fellow only if it is dry as flint, *un grand cru*, say Valmurs, no? then Bougros."

Van der Fleet waved away the menus.

"Shall we adjourn to the dining saloon car? Over dinner we can discuss more pleasant matters. The new season has opened at the Marinsky. Petipa has become the toast of Petersburg. I'd be delighted to bring you up to date."

"With pleasure, Nikolai Sergeevich, but what was this curious incident, Grigory Alexandrovich?"

"Nothing really, nothing to do with the Countess."

"Yet it struck you all the same."

Van der Fleet had his hand on the door handle, but Shuev was not ready to surrender his podium.

"Yes, well, while I was in the Georgian Room, the Count came in to say his good-byes, left the room, and then he seemed to have had some kind of attack or fit, I didn't see it, but the next thing I knew the major domo was helping him back into the room, half carrying him. Of course, the Princess made a great fuss over him, called for smelling salts, the whole thing, you know. But the Count is a tough bird and he was back on his feet in five, ten minutes. Pale, but moving under his own steam. I offered to accompany him, we are old friends, you know. But he refused, very stern he was. The funny thing is that when he walked out of the Georgian Room he turned to the left. But that would have taken him in the opposite direction from the entrance, toward the interior of the house. Well, we know that he got home all right. I don't know why I should be telling you all this. But you wanted details and now you have them."

"Thank you very much, Grigory Alexandrovich. You have given me a perfect sense of the occasion. You must forgive me," he added turning to Van der Fleet. "You mentioned Petipa. I fear I am a frustrated regisseur. I like my *mis en scène*."

"It is a pleasant way to work, my dear fellow. I wish we could all afford the same luxury. So, we will leave you to rest. Dinner in an hour? *À toute à l'heure*."

Vasiliev moved to the window feeling degraded by the game of cat and mouse with Van der Fleet. Outside the forest was broken up by stretches of open field covered with stubble. Along the tracks as far as the eye could see a ragged file of peasants trudged through the dust. Some carried burlap sacks on their backs. Others had slung pouches over their shoulder. They clasped wooden staves. From the look of them they were mendicants or pilgrims, tramping from village to village, begging a crust "in Christ's name." Others were probably migrants in search of work, now that the harvest was over, following the rails as the most direct route to the cities.

Vasiliev thought of the young radical, Iuri, or whatever his name was and youths like him, their heads swimming with ideals of uplifting the peasants by preaching socialism in the villages. He thought too of the terrorists who were tossing bombs in the name of the same people, and finally of the tsar who twenty years ago had freed the serfs but still regarded the peasants as helpless children. And what of the peasants themselves, roaming over a vast and hungry countryside? How well did anyone really understand them? He thought of his mother and her friends. The train flashed by the marching men, but none of them raised his head to catch a glimpse of the brightly blue colored engine clattering down the track heading west.

Chapter Nine

Swan arrived first for the meeting. Recently, she was taking more precautions, staying only a few nights in any one place, avoiding the main thoroughfares, eating in lower class traktirs and never the same one twice in succession. She had learned a great deal from old friends in the People's Will about conspiratorial methods, but the habits were becoming second nature. Mounting the stairs to the safe room, she stepped over the broken wooden planks and wondered whether the coming of socialism would transform the house porter into an honest man. On the second floor she turned down a dim corridor and passed several doors, checking to see if the torn scrap of paper was still in place. She retraced her steps, slipped the key into the lock and hesitated feeling the same peculiar sensation, not of fear, but of revulsion. The door swung open on a large, sparsely furnished room. Broad strips of discolored wallpaper hung down like unrolled parchment scrolls. Several flimsy chairs, a lumpy couch and a long wooden table stained by an accumulation of unknown liquids were distributed around the circumference of the room, leaving an open space in the center. A threadbare rug drained of all color covered only a few meters of the wood plank floor. Above the table pinned to the wall hung a faded lithograph of Nikolai Chernyshevsky, his deep-set eyes staring into another world. On the dust covered window ledge an open lavender parasol rested on its points like a ballerina on an empty stage.

She closed the door and sighed. She hadn't counted on such a strong reaction, too many caviar canapés and mazurkas lately. Angry with herself she crossed to the window and watched the passers-by. Above the dingy store fronts, hand painted signs stared back at her. She glanced farther down the street where an artisan's trade was advertised by the facsimile of a boot hanging beside an oversize pair of scissors. There were no loiters, no suspicious signs of activity. The parasol could stay where it was, *en point*; the all clear signal. She glanced distastefully at the couch and pulled a chair from the wall. It scraped the boards with a plaintive cry. She sat down, folded her hands in her lap and stared at a large stain under the lithograph. The chair wobbled beneath her.

She had no sense of time. Once she heard footsteps shuffle past the door and then continue down the stairs. How much later did she hear the rapping out of the code followed by the metallic click of the key? She had no idea but the sound startled her. She regained her composure before she had to face him. Marko stepped quickly inside, his eyes shifting furtively in that exaggerated conspiratorial manner of his that she detested. He nodded and half bowed to her. The effect was unintentionally comic. He edged along the wall toward the window, and stood to the side peering down into the street. Satisfied by the innocent behavior of the few passers-by, he slumped down on the couch and ran his hands through his hair in a gesture familiar to her as a sign of despair. But it was always hard to tell with Marko how serious this was to be taken.

"The operation did not go as expected?"

"No, not as expected."

She waited.

"We made contact as planned, or rather Magician did. We didn't know exactly where he would embark. Our friend in Posts and Telegraph told us only one of the river stations between Marinsky Posad and Kazan. So we split up, the three of us. As it happened Vasiliev boarded at Marinsky Posad. That was Magician's assignment."

"And why have you come and not he? I assume the answer to that is going to be long and complex, so please begin."

Marko puffed out his cheeks and exhaled.

"Listen, Swan, these things are not handled easily. Don't judge us before you know...."

"No one is judging, Marko. I am just waiting to know what happened."

"Yes, well I had this all from Magician. You see, he is in a hospital run by the zemstvo in Kozmodemiansk." He was alarmed by the look on Swan's face and raised his hand. "Don't jump to conclusions; he is not badly hurt, just a concussion, a few cuts, bruises. It's not important how we got there, Letchik and I, but we, or rather Letchik, made sure that there is nothing to worry about, I mean about his condition, that is his physical well-being."

"I take it that is a delicate way of saying nothing about his mental state."

"Please, Swan, no, I'm trying to reassure you. He just has to rest. But he told us everything."

"I very much doubt that, Marko. But what did he tell you, for heaven's sake."

"Right. He explained how he got Vasiliev to talk to him, something about Lombroso. You know how Magician is obsessed by him, carries around *L'uomo deliquente* in his pocket."

"My God, leave it up to him to take the most round about approach. Does he think we intend to conduct a university seminar with Vasiliev?"

"Wait a moment, I may not get all of this just the way he explained it, but it made sense, at least when he said it," Marko finished weakly.

"Go on."

Marko expected her to be skeptical, but her words cut into him and he grew more confused. He jumped to his feet.

"Right. Well, they had a discussion about crime and that was good, I mean, he piqued Vasiliev's interest, so it was easy to get him to have dinner, but it didn't happen."

"Marko, can you tell me in plain words how Magician was injured?"

"Right. He lost his footing and fell down a companionway. So Vasiliev came to see him the next morning. It was too bad because Magician was bandaged up and lying down in a wretched third class cabin, you know; that put him at a disadvantage. Too bad it was the only conversation they had. After that Vasiliev seems to have disappeared."

Swan resigned herself to hearing him out and promised herself no more interruptions. That would only lead to Marko's further confusion.

"Magician made it clear to Vasiliev who we were, I mean, whom he represented. Disabused the Inspector of the idea that we were terrorists, said that we reject it on principle, or rather because history has proven it is a blind alley, 'Just read Gibbon,' he told the Inspector. A nice touch, eh! He meant that killing one Roman emperor led to a worse tyrant taking his place. No different in Russia. So, he distanced himself from Zasulich, Khalturin and Zheliabov, explained how the split came about and how our old comrades spat on us and called us village lovers because we have contempt for their bombs and daggers. Magician must have been very convincing, you know; he had all the details at his fingertips. Told Vasiliev that the reason for the split was Soloviev's attempt on the tsar's life and then Kravchinsky's assassination of Mezentsev. Well, of course who would mourn the head of the Third Section, not us. But the killing made that pig Kravchinsky into a hero."

It was no longer clear to Swan what was Magician and what was Marko in this recital. But she as determined to hold her tongue. He would get to the point at last.

"So what good is a hero who flees abroad? And what do we get in place of Mezentsev? Why Drenteln, who also gets himself shot but recovers and turns deportation to Siberia into a real system. So Vasiliev knew this, of course, but Magician is showing him what a different path we follow. Did Vasiliev know, for example, that after Ushakova was killed, the police swept up forty *derevenshchiki*, village propagandists, who had nothing to do with Ushakova or terror? Vasiliev did not. Then he told Vasiliev about the meeting near Voronezh, when the terrorists broke away from us to create the People's Will. It was all news to Vasiliev. According to Magician there was no doubt that Vasiliev was showing signs of sympathy. Then he warned Vasiliev that the murder of Ushakova was a provocation by the police to discredit all of us, to cover socialism with all kinds of dirt. That's just the way he put it, cover socialism with all kinds of dirt."

"Wait a minute, Marko. There was nothing in our instructions to you that Ushakova was murdered as a provocation. That is sheer speculation, and you know it. We planned to offer our help to Vasiliev not present him with unproven allegations." Her chair was wobbling wildly now and she stood up abruptly knocking it over with a crash. They stared with horror at the fallen chair. Had they given themselves away? They listened for steps in the corridor, but all they could hear was scratching in the walls. Marko had the sense of being back on the Street of the Dead with his father's reproaches ringing in his ears. Were they really just amateurs?

Marko took a deep breath. "I'm sorry to upset you. Perhaps I didn't get it right, what he said."

"That is one thing I am sure you did get right. I can't understand why Magician keeps complicating our task."

"I don't understand what you mean."

"Listen, Marko, I did not say anything to the committee, not even to Norka, about your escapade at Bagration's. The time wasn't right. The aim was to make contact with Vasiliev not to spread false theories. I am beginning to wonder about the whole Bagration episode now. I thought Magician was just being foolish, but I am beginning to wonder whether he and you as well were not involved in something unsavory. I don't like it, and you will now tell me what you were doing at Bagration's"

"Bagration's," Marko repeated stupidly.

"I think it would be easier to tell me than to face charges in the Exec-Com."

"You are taking a great deal on yourself, Irina Nikolaevna."

"I believe it was you who took on a great deal. I am trying to help you because Magician is an old comrade and I do not wish to see him destroyed. But what you did was dangerous and stupid. The place was swarming with security people. And what was the purpose of that ridiculous appearance on the ballroom floor."

"I don't understand you, Irin...Swan," Marko uttered a forced laugh. "I am not in the habit of attending gentry balls; you see I do not dance..." Marko stopped short. He had suddenly remembered that Magician was wearing patent leather shoes.

"Oh, my God." he moaned.

"So your memory is improving. Let me help it along. You and Magician arrived at Bagration's about ten o'clock in a hack drawn by a wretched beast. You arranged to drop him off and pick him up later, no? He gained entrance to the house by some kind of ruse. In the middle of a quadrille, Magician appeared on the dance floor in a rumpled dress suit and confronted Countess Ushakova..."

"Impossible!" Marko blurted out. He could not keep still and kept pacing the room running his hands through his thick black hair. "I had nothing to do with that, Irina Nikolaevna. I swear it... he's mad. He told me nothing. You know I was against it from the beginning. I let myself be persuaded...you know how he is...."

"Just calm down, Marko and tell the story in sequence, leaving nothing out"

Marko began haltingly. It had been Magician's idea in the first place. He had been wracking his brains for a scheme to raise money for the movement. He was enraged that the People's Will had carried out robberies to fill their party treasury. It wasn't the fact that they had violated the law that bothered him, but that the money might have belonged to a poor widow or pensioner who would lose everything. A couple of months ago the solution just dropped into his hands. It was a great piece of luck. He had struck up an acquaintance with young Prince Bagration at one of those literary evenings in Moscow. He was a strange looking boy, always tugging at a gold crucifix around his neck, never looking you in the face, but Magician courted him, won his trust. They met at different public events, a concert, a lecture and always managed to steal a few minutes together, talking. They exchanged books. The boy was reading a lot of religious tracts and, of course, Dostoevsky and Leskov. Magician did not feed him any propaganda. The talk became more personal, less abstract. The young Prince, it turned out was in awe of his father, feared him actually. The Prince had been one of the old Caucasus hands from the fifties, the ones who hung around the Viceroy. The gilded youth, they called them. According to the son his father had been a regular Childe Harold, wrote romantic poetry, disappeared into the hills for weeks on end, riding and hunting with the mountaineers. That was after his first wife died, the boy's real mother. Marko couldn't recall all the stories. But Bagration got into a number of scrapes with the native women until finally the Viceroy intervened, married him off to a Dadian, Georgian aristocracy. This tamed the Prince for a while. But after the old Viceroy left, Bagration moved up the bureaucratic ladder and began to prey on the local Russian women. His wife was so fearful of losing him that she raised no objections. The boy said that he heard rumors that she even selected his father's mistresses. This is what turned the young Prince against her. Bagration couldn't be easily managed, it turned out. One of his affairs led to a rivalry with a high ranking official. The new Viceroy, the tsar's own brother, Grand Duke Mikhail Nikolaevich, had to send him packing back to Moscow in order to avoid a big scandal. All of this came out in an exchange of love letters between Bagration and his paramour. The young Prince found the letters and read them. It had cost him a great deal to tell a stranger all this, but Magician immediately saw the possibilities. Over the years Bagration had become an intimate of the heir to the throne, Alexander Alexandrovich, and hoped for a high post under the next reign. If Magician could get hold of the letters, he could extort money from the Prince, feed the movement and then when the time came publish them to discredit or destroy one of the next tsar's leading advisers.

"But Marko, a love affair, long ago, the Prince might just have laughed it off."

"There was something else, Swan." Marko was standing in the center of the room, hands clasped behind his back staring at the lithograph.

"Magician found out from young Bagration that someone else was already blackmailing the Prince. And there was written proof of this too, a second set of letters. So, Magician decided to join the party, as he put it. When he told me all this, it seemed believable. Now, I can't be sure, but Magician convinced me that the only way to get the letters was to get to the boy inside the house. The ball seemed to offer the perfect cover. He got to know one of the servants on her day off and, well you know how he was. She agreed to help. That's all, honestly."

"So, breaking into the ballroom was not part of the plan."

"No. No. Do you think I am mad too? I still don't see...well he wore his street clothes, except for the patent leather shoes. But I only saw them afterwards. I didn't understand what that meant. I just wanted to get out of there. What was he up to?"

"Did he get the letters?"

"No, he said that he was interrupted while reading them and had to make a run for it."

"Did you believe him?"

"What else could I do?" Markov extended his hands to her. A despondent look came over him.

"Do you think Magician has betrayed us? Is he working for the other side?"

"Other side? There are many sides in this struggle, Marko. If you mean the police, no, I think not. But it may be just as bad. Magician may be working for himself, and he may drag us all down with him."

After a short pause, she continued.

"Tell me whether he ever talked to you about Countess Ushakova."

"You don't think he is mixed up in killings, for God's sake."

Swan shook her head. "Just tell me."

"Nothing, he never mentioned her name."

Swan was pursuing her own thoughts. All she had were pieces of a puzzle that did not fit. Wasn't Count Ushakov also posted to the Caucasus when Bagration was in service there? Was it possible the Countess was the object of a rivalry between Bagration and Ushakov? She recalled the Prince's dramatic appearance at the ball, the way he swept the Countess into the waltz as if to break her loose from Magician's grip. What was the connection between the Countess and Magician? Three men infatuated with the same woman? Not impossible, not if you thought about her the way men did.

Swan's features composed themselves into a look of grave serenity that made Marko's throat go dry. He tried to imagine her in a ball gown; her auburn braid combed out allowing her hair to fall loosely on her shoulders, a tint of rouge on her lips. He pressed his fist to his mouth.

"Irina Nikolaevna...," he said softly.

Swan whirled on him, recognizing the tone in his voice, the look on his face that betrayed him. She advanced a few steps toward him forcing him to retreat.

"What arrangements did you make to have Magician moved?"

"Listen, Irina Nikolaevna, you must forgive me, my mistakes, I'm sorry. I should have consulted you. But there is something else. You and Magician..."

"Don't play the fool, Marko." Did it always have to end like this? She was breathing more rapidly now, her breasts rising and falling, the coarse blouse rubbing against her body. She dressed purposefully, to make herself as unattractive as possible. She wore worn leather shoes buttoned up to the ankles, the ugliest she could find. Her face was scrubbed and her hands were dry and rough. Her hair was her only indulgence. She had drawn the line at cutting it short like Norka and the others. She refused to sacrifice it. She did not believe the movement aimed at eliminating all one's individuality. It was to fulfill the human personality, to free it of convention, false values and frivolous thoughts. She would not disfigure herself. Was the price too high? Could she never be an ordinary comrade to any of them, even to Norka?

"Damn you, Marko, tell me the arrangements," she rasped in a voice he had never heard from her. His face went slack as if it had been struck. He fell back onto the couch.

"The arrangements...he said he would stay in the hospital until he felt strong enough to make his way back to Moscow. He would be careful. Vasiliev might have put him under surveillance. He will find a place to stay in the Tatar quarter and leave us a message at the Taganka traktir."

"Good. Then we'll call a meeting of the group. I cannot protect you any more. In the meantime, we'll take turns visiting the traktir, alternate afternoons and evenings. I will take the first shift, then you and Letchik. Norka can come in when she likes."

Swan went to the window and stood there for a long time. Then she turned and without a glance at Marko, who sat huddled in a corner of the couch, she walked out. He sat dumbly until the room grew too dark to see the opposite wall. Then he rose and stepped to the window. A few drops of water had spattered the windowpane, the cobblestones were wet, but it was no longer raining. He moved his head from side to side, his eyes sliding mechanically over dark objects in the street, registering nothing. He stroked his chin and realized he had not shaved. Perhaps he disgusted her. His fingers dropped to the edge of the parasol and he ran his fingers over the soft silk fabric.

Chapter Ten

From Moscow's four hundred churches a thousand copper bells rang out in waves of discordant sound. Startled flocks of rooks flew up into a cloudless sky the color of faded Gendarme uniforms. Vasiliev stopped short bringing Shuev and Van der Fleet to an abrupt halt. They were standing under the low-pitched roof of the Nizhegorod Station in the east end of the city. They stared at him, puzzled. At the end of the platform a crowd had gathered around one of the second class carriages. Almost everyone carried a bouquet of fall field flowers, reds and blues mixing with green pine boughs. Young men in students' uniforms were surrounded by family and admirers. From time to time a shout went up and then laughter. Vasiliev recalled how two years before youths like these would have been in uniform going off to fight the Turks. Puffs of black smoke were rising from the engine and a second warning bell sounded.

Suddenly there was a sharp report followed by screams. "My God, they're bombing the station." Another cloud of black smoke swirled up from the track on the other side of the train. Bunches of flowers fell to the platform, the knots of well wishers dissolved in panic, people were running toward the officers. Vasiliev noticed a short stocky woman with closely cropped brown hair brush by him and run into the reception hall. Van der Fleet and Shuev had drawn their side arms and were trotting toward the column of smoke that billowed out over the locomotive. Vasiliev took a hesitant step or two behind Shuev but then hesitated. It couldn't have been a bomb. The sound was all wrong, and the smoke looked more like burning gunpowder than a real fire.

A firm hand gripped his forearm and a gentle voice spoke close to his ear.

"Vasili Vasilievich, there is something urgent I must say to you. Please take my arm and come with me."

It had been a long time, but Vasiliev knew her at once.

Van der Fleet and Shuev had come up alongside the locomotive where two railroad guards with leveled rifles peered into the dense smoke. The engineer was calling to them from his cab.

"It's nothing serious, but have a look. I don't think we've been hit. I don't see any flames out there."

Swan did not relax her hold on him. "Quickly we have only a little time."

Vasiliev could not have said why but he took her arm and allowed himself to be led out of the station, pushing through the crowd to a waiting cab.

"You are not afraid of their following us?" he asked as he helped her into the cab.

"Shuev's barouche will not be waiting for him at the appointed place..."

Vasiliev took a moment to study her face more intently, his hand resting on the handle of the coach door. The first thought that came into his head was a frivolous one. A young girl does mature into a woman. He had to laugh at himself. His crooked smile was just the way she remembered it.

"...but he is not going to give us the whole day."

He swung himself into the cab as it started forward. He could have sworn that buried under the driver's felt hat was a woman. Swan scanned the traffic as they maneuvered out of the mass of vehicles leaving the station. Vasiliev was content to observe her out of the corner of his eye.

They sped through the noisy east end. Beyond the outer ring new construction, mainly railroad workshops and factories, relentlessly pushed out the city limits; they were swallowing up the empty fields, smoking monsters of brick and iron with insatiable appetites. Every year, it seemed, new, untidy industrial towns were springing up on the outskirts. Sprawling in every direction, they lacked the most elementary conveniences of paving, lighting and sewers. They were known to Vasiliev as pestholes of drunkenness and crime, impossible to police.

The cabby was not very experienced. They cut in and out of the heavy traffic, barely avoiding collisions with on-coming vehicles, while occasionally bouncing against the curb. At one point they were severely jolted and his arm brushed hers. He murmured an apology but she did not reply. They passed the Pokrovsky Monastery and crossed Pustaia Street. The cab slowed in one of the side streets off Taganka Square.

"I need your word that you will say nothing of our conversation."

"You have it."

She turned for the first time during the ride and fixed him with her level stare. He remembered again how disconcerting it could be, even when she was hardly more than a child.

"There's no sense trying to deceive you. It would be futile in any case. It's risky for both of us to talk at all. But it would be safer to continue where we cannot be interrupted. I have to ask your solemn promise again;we, it's the fashion these days to say we all the time, and we have decided already to trust you."

"Don't worry. I'll not betray your confidence unless...well you know my limits as I expect I know yours. What is it then, you want to take me to a safe room?"

She nodded.

"Won't that cause you difficulties, my uniform and all."

"The yard porter will be in the corner tavern."

"And a chance meeting in the corridor?"

"You are looking for a certain Marmeladov," she said with the slightest trace of a smile. He couldn't help tossing his head and laughing. "And they say you people have lost your sense of humor."

Swan struck the roof of the cab three times and they moved forward again.

"There is such a name on the door of a vacant room, though not ours."

They walked through an empty courtyard and climbed to the second floor, avoiding the broken planks. The unframed lithograph of Chernyshevsky suspended over the table struck him as a bit of bravado.

She had taken off her long gray cloak and sat primly on a wooden chair. Like everything else in the room, it did not seem very stable or permanent. She had decided not to shock him with her new identity so she dressed as he might have remembered her. Her gray silk dress cinched tightly at the waist revealed her full form. He knew right away that the cameo brooch at her throat was a likeness of Antigone. A gift from her brother on her fourteen birthday. The dress, hadn't it been her mother's?

She motioned him to the battered couch where he sat dutifully on the edge and pulled off his gloves.

"You have been approached before, but for our part the contact was a failure. Not entirely his fault. Besides there is new information. The Gendarmes do not intend to give you any help. They may even put up obstacles. Possibly they have something worse in mind."

"Ah yes, your man already revealed their most secret conspiracy, blowing up the Countess as a provocation. Do you swallow that?"

"It was his own view, not shared by the rest of us. But the fact remains that the Gendarmes, for whatever reason, are dead set against your investigation. Perhaps they fear being exposed as incompetent..."

"Unlikely."

"...or else they have too much invested in the theory of the terrorist."

"More probably."

"Besides, your own chief is not too happy about your assignment. He is a nasty little careerist. You know that. Besides, he's terrified of the responsibility. The investigation could blow up in his face. How much do you think you can count on him?"

"You portray me as a lonely knight."

"No, you have Serov, and you make a good team. But...."

"Of course, you remember Serov."

"How could I forget him? After all he saved me from serious injury, perhaps from being killed."

"Yes."

"And you never forgave yourself for having been absent that day."

Vasiliev shrugged. "Perhaps not."

"That's all ancient history. Right now, the odds are against you. It is simply a matter of arithmetic which counts, wouldn't you agree, even in solving crimes. You are strong, but the others are more numerous, and in many ways stronger."

"This sounds like a little sermon I just heard from our Gendarme friends. 'They are weaker, we are stronger' and so forth. But tell me who are these others?"

"The security forces and the People's Will, neither of them interested in the truth, or else more interested in other things, like power."

"Am I caught in the middle, between two fires?"

"Yes," Swan ignored Vasiliev's irony," but so are we."

Vasiliev glanced at Chernyshevsky's stern face.

"A broad middle then."

He felt the sudden impulse to take her hands in his and say, Irushka, this is quite mad. But he knew that this would insult her, and besides the madness of Russia in 1880 was not something either of them could easily escape.

He stood up and walked to the window.

"It's only one of our people on watch."

He looked down at the parasol.

"A simple signal, but effective. When it's open...well you get the point."

He frowned and muttered, "Go on."

"We are offering our help because we have, for the moment, the same goals. We do not believe this was a terrorist attack. There is nothing coming out of the People's Will that would suggest that. We still have friends there who would tell us about a shift in tactics. But we have no way of convincing the authorities. We are hoping that you can prove to them that we are right."

"And if it turns out differently?"

"We are so certain that we are willing to take the chance."

"And what are our common goals?"

"The truth by itself is not important to us, as it is to you. But the Gendarmes are using the terrorist theory to discredit the reformers in the government. We believe that if the reformers succeed, if Russia gets a constitution and civil rights, then we will be able to spread legal propaganda and win over the educated public and the more intelligent peasants to a program of socialism."

Vasiliev sighed deeply. "So your goal is socialism and mine is justice. Are they really the same?"

"Some other time we can debate this. Right now my purpose in spiriting you away from Shuev and company is to offer an alliance, a strange alliance, but a good one. We do not need to do anything that will compromise one other. We do not intend to interfere with your investigation. You can rely on us to supply the foot soldiers, the watchers, the errand runners. That will free you and Serov for more important tasks. We know our limitations. But we are very good at operating clandestinely. After all we have survived the manhunts so far. Now it will be our turn to help you conduct one. You mention a broad middle, a bit disdainfully I thought. Well the real danger for Russia is that the middle disappears and the extremes are left to fight it out. We are still close enough to reach out and touch. If it comes to civil war then each of us will have to choose the lesser of two evils. I am not sure that it will be easy to make the distinction."

"Your sources in the People's Will may be reliable. But did you ever consider the possibility of a splinter group breaking off from them, just like the People's Will did from Land and Liberty?"

"Doesn't every crime bear a trade mark? That's what you used to tell me years ago. This one has none of the trademarks of a terrorist attack. Not even of a lone wolf. I don't expect you to believe me. You always had to convince yourself of everything. It's better that way. We have only negative evidence. We do not know who killed her and her coachman. Only you can find this out."

"I appreciate your confidence," the words sounded wooden in his ears, "but you will have to give me time to think. I've hardly begun... Irina you are asking nothing...and offering a great deal. But years have passed, you know. You have become an illegal, much has changed. I have to rely on a trust that...."

She interrupted him again. "You have only to rely on the logic of the situation. No trust is involved, only logic."

"I remember your friend saying something of the sort."

"If you have to think in terms of trust, then consider what I have risked in bringing you here. Remember, it is just as long ago for me as for you."

"Of course," he said. But what was a vacant room with a lithograph of Chernyshevsky? They could have a dozen places like this one.

"Of course," he repeated, "this has cost you a great deal."

"If you agree, I want you to come with me to see Ushakov as soon as possible."

"You are in touch with him? He can't know of course what you've become. Well, you should have told me this before. It changes everything."

"Perhaps I should have also told you that it was my idea to bring you onto the case, and I convinced him. But you will see for yourself when we meet."

"You have already arranged it?"

"There's no telling how long I can keep up this double game, playing sweet little Irisha one day and slipping into the underground the next. The important thing now is to get you to believe me, take up our offer and then I will vanish from the scene forever as Irisha."

"We can do it whenever you wish. But my Gendarme guardians will wonder where I've disappeared. It's been half an hour and I will need a good excuse."

"I realize that our plan is a long shot as the English say. It's from their game of golf, isn't it? It used to be a favorite phrase of yours."

She was always clever. How clever was she being now?

"So what does your watcher say?" He was pulling on his gloves, and spoke in English. "Is the coast clear?"

She smiled for the first time and walked across the room. She waited until he had turned his back to insert a slip of paper into the doorjamb. They rode in silence until they spotted a likhach, one of Moscow's fast cabs that would take him to police headquarters. On impulse he took her hand and pressed it before leaping out of the cab.

She sank back against the cushions and listened to the thumping of her heart. "Romantic rubbish," she quoted herself.

Her cab circled the ring and stopped in front of Ushakov's mansion. The curtains had been drawn in all the front windows. She hurried up the steps and raised the brass knocker which seemed to descend with terrifying force. There was a long pause as the echo resounded in the hall. At last a liveried footman opened and bowed deeply.

"Good day, Irina Nikolaevna. Count Ushakov presents his regards. He regrets that he has been called away suddenly to the capital on urgent business of state. He begs your forgiveness and instructed me to say that he would be pleased to receive Inspector Vasiliev in Petersburg when the convenient occasion arises."

The words rang hollow in Swan's ears. Urgent business of state was understandable, but "when the convenient occasion arises" was ominous in its cavalier vagueness. She walked slowly down Povarskaya until the cab stopped for her. Norka looked slightly ridiculous in her felt hat perched on the cabby's box, but Swan hardly noticed.

Chapter Eleven

Vasiliev's likhach pulled up by the newly erected Pushkin statue opposite police headquarters. The poet was finally on pedestal, Vasiliev mused, but why was his head drooping wearily. Was he mourning for Russia? Or was he merely brooding over Moscow where he had met the woman who had sealed his fate?

Pushkin Monument, Moscow

Van der Fleet and Shuev were standing on the bottom steps leading to headquarters, each one striking an attitude, no doubt for his benefit. Van der Fleet, ramrod straight, legs spread apart, had hooked his thumbs in his belt, a vacuous smile playing over his thin lips. Shuev bent slightly forward like many tall men approaching middle age, hands clasped behind his back, tapping the ground with a polished black boot.

"What did I tell you, Grisha. Vasiliev was not trying to give us the slip. And it would take more than a harmless charge of gunpowder to frighten him."

Shuev frowned as if on cue, his bulbous forehead shining even in the dull light of early morning.

"Sorry we lost touch with one another. I dodged round the rear of the train to cut off that escape route and picked up a false trail. It looked like a diversion, don't you agree?" It was the best he could think of, but Van der Fleet would not let it pass.

"A trick? Perhaps, but we never found out, did we, who was playing it or on whom?"

"The others will be waiting, Vasili Vasilievich, men with little time to waste." The Headmaster began to irritate Vasiliev with his hectoring tone; but after all, he thought, that's what earned Shuev his sobriquet.

The two Gendarmes fell in on either side of Vasiliev and marched him up the steps. For an instant he had the uncanny sensation of being under arrest. They passed rows of clerks bent over their desks, scribbling furiously. In the outer corridor two of Vasiliev's colleagues nodded morosely and walked on without a word. He was not particularly surprised by the absence of the good-humored banter that normally greeted him. The chief must have passed the word around that their Count's Petersburg connections had finally paid off, lifting him above the ranks of ordinary mortals. As if by prearranged signal the door to the chief's office swung open. They entered in single file, Van der Fleet and Shuev pushing ahead and taking their places at the long table where five men were already seated. Vasiliev remained standing as if facing a board of inquiry.

The chief shuffled papers on his desk and looked around as if expecting to be prompted. He was the kind of man, Vasiliev reflected, who bullied his subordinates and fawned on his superiors of whom there were a number seated round the table. Vasiliev knew most of them, the public prosecutor with Dundreary whiskers who had built a reputation on reciting long Ciceronian quotations in Latin to uncomprehending juries. Next to him, a representative of the Ministry of Justice, a tight-lipped, pasty-faced young man who already wore the Order of St. Anna in his buttonhole. An assistant to the governor-general of Moscow, a sour faced general who rested his bleary eyes by sleeping through committee meetings, was just about to nod off when Vasiliev and his escorts entered the room. An aide de camp from court gave no sign of having any special characteristics at all, a cipher. Vasiliev immediately noted that there was no representative from Ushakov's ministry. He had the impression that he was already cast in the role of the sacrificial lamb.

Vasiliev glanced up at the portrait of Alexander II. The colorful uniform of the Life Guards he was wearing did nothing to dispel the tsar's gloomy expression. Like Pushkin on his pedestal, the tsar also seemed unhappy at how things had turned out.

The chief was rambling on but only a few disjointed words reached Vasiliev; "... security forces at your disposal...the emperor's personal concern...the fate of the empire...." Stock phrases, he had heard them all a hundred times, though the last one seemed to be in great favor these days. He studied the wooden faces in front of him. The guardians of law and order. If Alexander had to rely solely on them, then his chances for survival were fast diminishing. The ordeal lasted no more than ten minutes.

Vasiliev closed the door of his office and surveyed the disorder around him. The overstuffed bookshelves were constantly threatening to collapse. Rows of cardboard files burst with clippings on criminal cases in half a dozen European languages. Tacked to the sides of the bookcases were three unframed wood block prints. The portraits were arranged in chronological order beginning with Lomonosov, Russia's first polymath. Next came Denis Vonvizin, the eighteenth century satirist, and lastly, General Suvorov, an autograph inscribed in a faded hand to Vasiliev's grandfather. A man likes to think that he has something of his heroes in himself.

His desk was an heirloom of a different sort. It had been carved out of a single block of oak by a serf artisan a century before. Its polished surface was now covered with what looked like official files.

Vasiliev glanced at them and then out the window where the first flakes of snow were turning lazily in the air. The thought that perhaps he had escaped an early blizzard in the Urals was no consolation. Serov's familiar knock on the door interrupted his thoughts.

"I'd like to welcome you back, Vasili Vasilievich. But I know you'd rather be somewhere else."

"Ah, Serov, what a relief to see a human face for a change. What is all this, now?" Vasiliev waved his hand over the accumulation of paper. "It looks like enough reading to keep us unhappily busy for a month. Is there anything worthwhile here?"

"Them on the left are dossiers of the suspects they've hauled in. That's what the captain in sky blue with the ramrod up his ass called them when he dumped them here. To your right, beggin' your pardon, that smaller heap are the lads still at large; those wanted for questionin', is how Mr.Spic and Span put it to me."

"And you've probably been through most of it."

"Just the once over lightly, Vasili Vasilievich."

How ironic, Vasiliev thought, that Irina was one of the few people who understood his relationship to Serov. It baffled the chief and most of the detectives. Together they violated all the fine distinctions of rank and class that they observed around them. It went back to their childhood. Serov, the son of a serf family owned by the old Count Vorontsov, had been Vasiliev's playmate and closest friend. A visitor to the estate from England told the old Count he had seen things like this in the American South before the war between children of slaves and masters, but it changed completely when they grew up. With Serov and Vasiliev it also changed but as the old Count put it, "in the Russian way."

When Vasiliev entered the force he brought Serov with him, not as an orderly, but as a Sergeant although it was never clear just how he had obtained that rank. He had never held a lower rank, and it was correctly assumed by everyone that he would never be promoted either. There were rumors that it had been his service with Vasiliev in the Russo-Turkish War that fixed the rules. Stories circulated about how they had taken turns saving one another's life, stories that never got into official reports.

Some on the force were unhappy about Serov's uncouth manners and the strong traces of peasant speech which he seemed determined to preserve despite Vasiliev's best efforts to smooth out the last of the rough edges. There were times when Vasiliev was sure that Serov enjoyed annoying his betters. When they were youngsters Serov had submitted willingly enough to Vasiliev's instructions on how to read and write until he reached a certain level of proficiency, set by an inner mechanism, and then he lost interest. Vasiliev had also taught him how to shoot and box. But Serov balked at learning to fence or master any other form of gentlemen's sport. He had acquired some skill in the arts of disguise and mimicry but refused to impersonate anyone above a certain social station, another limit he set himself. After a while Vasiliev realized that his father had been right, their friendship had changed but in the Russian way.

"Serov, I don't need more paper to read. A glass of strong tea would be perfect and a taste of your mother's gooseberry preserve, assuming of course that she still remembers my weakness."

Serov rolled his eyes comically. "As it turns out, Vasili Vasiliev-ich, mama sent along a jar of gooseberries, and another of apple jelly. Made from Antonovkas, your favorites. They've been very good this year."

Serov busied himself brewing a strong *zavarka* of Chinese leaves in a Gzhel pot. Vasiliev sat back in his chair and watched Serov perform his ritual with as much simple elegance as if it were a Japanese tea ceremony. When Serov decided the leaves had steeped long enough, he spooned a small quantity of the *zavarka* into a glass set in a silver holder and slowly added boiling water from the samovar. He then produced a fresh lemon, cut off several thin slices and placed them on a dish together with two cubes of hard sugar suitable for being held between the teeth as the tea was sipped. He handed Vasiliev the silver holder and the plate. He opened a china pot, scooped out a spoonful of pale brown jelly and set it down on Vasiliev's desk. He clicked his heels and saluted as Vasiliev shook his head, laughing and clapping his hands. It was Serov's turn to watch Vasiliev inhale the bouquet of the jelly, savor a portion on the tip of the spoon, swallow a mouthful off scalding tea and smack his lips as though he were savoring a Bordeaux *grand cru*, which in a way he was, knowing that his every word and gesture would be reported in loving detail to Serov's mother. He remembered her as a diminutive but sturdy woman who used to tell them tales of the firebird while they watched her spin wool shirts on hot summer afternoons. Vasiliev frowned, raised his head and fixed Serov with a mock serious look: "Exactly as I remembered it." He flashed a quick smile revealing his crooked teeth. Serov responded by adopting a parade rest position. It was all part of the ritual. They both laughed like schoolboys. Serov turned back to the samovar while Vasiliev began to leaf through the dossiers, sipping tea and spooning up apple jelly for the next hour, until his eye caught a familiar face. Staring up at him with a quizzical expression, Iuri Tarashkin looked much younger, perhaps because of the unkempt blond beard that covered the lower part of his face. Without raising his eyes from the page Vasiliev handed Serov his glass for a refill and began to read the Gendarmes' personnel file No. 1292.

Born in the village of Osholovo, Semenov district, Nizhny Novgorod Province; son of a parish priest, educated at home until age fourteen when he entered the Nizhny Novgorod Seminary; graduated with a certificate of merit in Greek and Latin, (this was underlined by the examining magistrate as a sign of approbation); passed entrance examination to the Juridical Faculty of Moscow University; received a warning for political activity in his second year; expelled in his third year for participating in student disorders; served as a volunteer elementary teacher in the Semenov district zemstvo school; reprimanded for insubordination to school Inspector; arrested for harboring a fugitive and sentenced to exile in a line regiment in the Caucasus with deprivation of civil rights; served in Russo-Turkish War in non-combat role as regimental clerk; amnestied but not permitted to reside in the two capitals; returned to Osholovo to teach; reportedly involved with populist agitators in the district; member of the Land and Liberty Party, later joining the Repartition of the Land faction; personal relations with Count and Countess Ushakova through their interest in the local educational system; present whereabouts unknown; wanted for questioning in connection with explosion of a mine on the Nizhny to Moscow railroad; revolutionary pseudonym *Volshebnik*, Magician.

"Here is our young agitator, Sergeant. Let me tell you how I ran into him, or rather how he waylaid me." Vasiliev loosened the collar of his tunic and gave Serov a full account of the events on the Volga. Serov punctuated Vasiliev's monologue with hums, grunts and low whistles and an accompaniment of rolling eyes and raised eyebrows, interpreted by Vasiliev as Serov at his most eloquent. It was only when Vasiliev told him about his meeting with Irina, that Serov fell silent.

"As I see it, there are three problems with this case right from the beginning. The trail is cold, memories are fading and too many people want to solve it in their own interest. This includes our superior officers, all of them. They're going to lean heavily on anyone who works with us. Their story will be the same: 'it would be best to look for this and ignore that.' I trust only you and Borka. If we can believe Irina, her people might give us some help, but it will be risky to rely on them as well. Tarashkin seems unstable. I don't doubt that Irina is sincere, even though her politics are something else." Vasiliev had decided to say nothing about Ivan for the moment, His old friend moved in exalted circles where the temptations of power might prove irresistible. Vasiliev felt badly that he had already consigned Ivan to the camp of the doubtful.

"If you can believe it, I've already been told several times that the outcome of this case might decide the fate of the empire." Serov whistled again. "Three men is slim weight in that balance, beggin' your pardon."

"I know. The odds seem ridiculous. Can't be helped.We'll work separately this time. You have two assignments. First, find out what you can about the daily routine of the Ushakov household, how the downstairs looks at the upstairs, what the gossip is among the tradesmen, you know the drill. Every household has its secrets and I want you to sniff them out."

Serov pursed his lips as if to whistle again, but no sound came forth. "I'm not sure about the last, Vasili Vasilievich, secrets bein' what they are."

"Don't underestimate yourself. I've seen your broom sweep clean. Next, you'll do the Row. Still know people down there, don't you? Good, you'll be looking for one of the men who jumped me on the steamer. He's called Petya. A giant, over a hundred kilos, in his mid-thirties, clipped beard, greasy black hair parted down the middle, arms like a blacksmith, but very quick on his feet. The lobe of his left ear is missing, bad teeth and a nose that has taken more than a few punches. No surname or passport number to go with that charming mug of his. He and his friend boarded the steamer late. Someone slipped up or was bribed let them on without checking papers."

"Lots like him on the Row. They pick 'em out of the same hat." Serov scratched his cheek. "I'll do my best, Vasili Vasilievich. Anything is better than strainin' my eyes over that toil." He jerked his head toward the pile of dossiers.

"Bedtime reading. I'll be working from the top down at Ushakovs. We'll compare notes. Then we'll do the Bagrations and find out whether reality matches any of the theories in the field. What should we call them? Provocation, passion or terrorism? Who knows, maybe an explosive mixture of all three?"

Chapter Twelve

The old police stable was in a decaying section of the northern suburbs of Moscow, beyond the ring. Vasiliev arrived in a police cab; it was to be an official visit then. He requested torches from the caretaker who led him to the carcass of Ushakov's coach. The Gendarmes had apparently stripped off the panels and floorboards, but Vasiliev was surprised to see less damage to the exterior than he expected from their report. It looked to him as though the blast had taken place inside the carriage blowing out one door, smashing the left rear wheel but leaving the right hand side of the carriage intact. The irregular pattern of perforations in the silk cushions and along the panel of the right hand door suggested to him the effects of a small bomb, but he could find no shell fragments. He concluded they must have passed right through the wooden frame. Curious, he thought to himself. Shuev had insisted the terrorists used only dynamite and nitroglycerine packed inside thin tin cylinders.

Placing one torch in a wall sprocket and holding another high over his head, Vasiliev went over the interior surface of the coach and the panels lying on the ground but found no traces of blood. "Tidy fellows, these Gendarmes", he muttered to himself. He looked around for the caretaker, called his name but heard only an echo and the scurrying of rats. Holding his torch high he made his way toward the interior of the stables. A maze of empty stalls and corridors, still smelling of horse droppings and rotten oats, seemed to stretch out in all directions. It would be no easy task to find the old man who had wandered off. In some places gaps in the roof of the stables allowed the sun to filter in, casting jagged shadows.

Vasiliev caught glimpses of the sagging walls and underfoot he could feel straw covered floorboards give under his weight. Drafts blowing through cracks in the walls and ceiling rustled the straw. Vasiliev moved deeper into the building where it became darker. He had ceased to shout for the old man, but something about the place drew him on. Suddenly it became darker; his torch flickered and threatened to go out. A gust of cooler air touched his face.

He turned to listen to a sound like water running down the walls, or was it feet he heard splashing through puddles? Surely the stable rats were not that big. He extinguished his torch and made his way down a side corridor, trailing his fingers over the damp wood until he felt a rusty hinge. He stood motionless for a few moments, flattened against the wall, straining his ears. Nothing now except the creaks and groans of an old structure protesting against the autumn wind. He heard his own light breathing too, but no running feet, rats or otherwise.

Vasiliev groped for the latch and flung open the door. Another gust of wind blew past him rushing down the corridor. For an instant he imagined the spirits of dead cavalry mounts sighing for their lost riders. He shook himself. Outside he could see the police cab standing at the edge of the drive, the figure of the driver nodding over his reins. Why so jumpy? he asked himself. Just an old stables, a quiet street stretching into the countryside, and cold blasts of air from the east. Not long enough on holiday to calm the nerves. Or was it the incident on the steamer that had put him on guard? Then he looked to his left and saw the likhach, one of Moscow's fast cabs drawn by two excellent horses, standing empty on the road back to the city. He could not help asking himself what a likhach was doing in these open fields. Unless they were in constant use, normally on the great boulevards where they were in great demand, they could not pay for themselves, and there was no chance of picking up a fare out here. Vasiliev climbed into his cab and ordered the driver to wait. Some moments passed but no one appeared no cabby and no passengers. Strange. The old buildings sat mute in the sunlight. A few cottages were scattered beyond the fields, but the landscape was empty of any living thing. Vasiliev thought about what he might tell Serov; he would call it the mystery of the unemployed likhach. He smiled to himself. Why does everything have to be significant? It was a question he frequently asked himself in the middle of a case. He signaled the driver and they set off for the Ushakov mansion. He thought about the condition of the Ushakov carriage; that constituted the real puzzle.

As the police cab turned onto the ring, Vasiliev caught sight of a likhach coming up fast behind them.

"Take a sharp left on Malaya Bronnaya," he shouted, "and pull up to the curb."

As they crossed the intersection a uniformed policeman on duty saluted the cab and Vasiliev signaled him to meet them around the corner. The driver neatly executed the turn but pulled up so abruptly that Vasiliev was nearly thrown to the floor. He barely recovered his balance and reached for the door handle when the likhach was almost on top of them. The policeman broke into a run, raising his whistle to his lips. Vasiliev wrenched open the door and leaped out, gripping his service revolver. He immediately recognized the porcine eyes of the likhach driver, it was Petya.

Vasiliev waved his revolver and shouted.

Petya jerked the reins. His two horses reared, blocking Vasiliev from taking a clear shot. He stumbled back into the wheel of his cab and barely escaped being crushed by the iron-shod hooves descending on him. His revolver was knocked from his hand and went skittering along the pavement out of reach. Trapped between the rearing horses and the police cab he fell to the ground and rolled under the likhach a searing pain shooting through his arm where the hooves had grazed him. He heard a woman's voice scream, a shrill blast from the policeman's whistle, more shouts and curses. He snatched his arm away from the wheels of the likhach as the horses lunged forward under Petya's whip. Reaching up Vasiliev seized hold of the undercarriage but the pain forced him to let go and he dropped back on the pavement, feeling as though his chest was being crushed. He imagined it would feel like this in the embrace of Burya. In his last minute of consciousness he wondered whether Borka would think his death undignified for a police Inspector.

Steps rapidly approaching, strong arms lifting him, noise everywhere around him, a ringing in his ear. "Leave me alone...get the cab...." He tasted blood as he spat out the orders. The policeman had unbuttoned his holster but realized that a shot was too risky in the crowded thoroughfare. Vasiliev turned on his driver who had jumped down and rushed to his side.

"What the Hell are you doing? Get back up on top. You idiot." The policeman was holding Vasiliev around the waist; someone else to his left helped to support him. Vasiliev recognized the constable.

"Vasili Vasilievich, Your Honor, you've had a nasty fall, you're cut."

Vasiliev forced his trademark smile, fought down his nausea and gripped the policeman by the shoulder.

"Good man, Karpov, just give me a hand for a minute, I'll be all right, then back to your post." Vasiliev winced as he hauled himself into the police cab.

The likhach had a long lead, and the horses were very fast. Pedestrians scattered in all directions as it bore down on them, the police cab lurching in pursuit. At the corner of Big Kozikhinskaya Street the likhach cut to the right and vanished in the rabbit warren of alleys and lanes between the outer and inner boulevards. The chase was over in a few minutes. Vasiliev realized there was no chance now of overtaking the likhach. He slumped back against the cushions furious with himself for having let Petya slip through his fingers a second time, swearing that he would never doubt his intuition again. His forearm was beginning to swell, his uniform was ripped and filthy, and there was blood on the front of his tunic and trousers. He couldn't show up at Ushakovs looking like a battle casualty. Another day wasted. Irritably he jabbed the shoulder of his driver: "Home," he shouted, not even trying to resist the black rage. How in Hell did they know he was going to the stables? He had not been under surveillance, he was sure of it. But there must have been a leak in the department, possibly through the dispatcher. More evidence of an effective network of information but one that used a thug like Petya to carry out the dirty work. Why, he asked himself would a first class organization employ a second rate operative? No more jokes about unsolved mysteries. Someone was determined to have his head.

His arm was stiff the following day when he drove up to the Ushakov mansion where the footman relayed the message that the

Count had been delayed in the capital by urgent business. Orders had been left for Vasiliev to examine the grounds and, if necessary — the caution was not missed by Vasiliev — to question the servants. He reminded himself that in Russia even the pursuit of criminals followed a leisurely pace. He examined every foot of the circular drive but found no traces of an explosion. Here too everything had been tidied up. The stucco columns supporting the portico showed signs of recent repairs. Vasiliev ignored the expression of disapproval on the footman's face as he gouged fresh holes in the plaster with his hunting knife. He extracted several small pellets and rolled them between his fingers before wrapping them in cloth and stuffing them inside his tunic. He observed that the low bushes bordering the drive were thickest in the area closest to the building and tall enough to have concealed a man. It was just possible that a bomb could have been thrown from behind this screen into the carriage. But the angle looked wrong to him. The coachman must have been facing the carriage door when the blast occurred or else he had already opened it. The terrorist, if that is what he was, would have had to have lobbed the bomb high in the air over the coachman's head so that it fell on an almost perpendicular line. An unlikely scenario. And then there was the problem of the escape route.

Ushakov had clearly stated that he had rushed to the window right after he heard the blast but had seen no one. The footman had insisted that within seconds after he heard the explosion he had rushed out onto the porch only to see the Orlov bays dragging the broken carriage down the drive, the body of Arkady stretched out at the foot of the portico and the countess sprawled in the drive. But no trace of the bomber. Where had he disappeared to?

"Are there any other entrances to the grounds?"

"The north gate is always chained shut, Your Honor," the footman replied, slightly inclining his head as if eager to please.

Vasiliev circled the perimeter of the garden. An agile man might have scaled the wrought iron fence surmounted by sharp points but not without the aid of a rope. Vasiliev found no traces of a scaling operation, no lofty trees overhanging the fence, no sign of shrubbery having been disturbed at its base. It did not take a genius, Vasiliev reflected, to figure out that an experienced terrorist could not have chosen a worse place to carry out an attack than the Ushakov drive. Why would the killer take the risk of entering the grounds at all when he could have stationed himself at the gate and tossed his bomb as the carriage slowed to make its turn into the drive? That way he could have made his escape down one of the side streets or jumped into a waiting cab. The People's Will planned carefully. This was another amateur job if the attack had taken place as the Gendarmes had reported.

Vasiliev instructed the footman to have the servants brought into the drawing room one by one. The Gendarmes had already interrogated them but he considered their report to be useless. He took each one back over the events of the night of the murder. Later he would compare notes with Serov who would be getting a different perspective. He was polite and attentive but learned nothing new of importance. Two footmen agreed that they had secured the doors to the north side of the house. They made their last rounds at eleven and again at one when they routinely checked the ground floor windows. There was no sign of a forced entry. All of the servants but one had been in the Count's service for years, most of them for a generation and were married to one another.

When Arkady's widow entered the room Vasiliev sensed by the alert look in her eyes and the slow deliberate movement of her swaying body that she was eager to tell him something. Had the Gendarmes picked up the signs? He doubted it. There was no mention of her testimony in their report. She quickly assured Vasiliev that she and her husband worshipped the Count. Arkady would willingly have given up his life, if need be, to save the Count's life. But a word here and a hesitation there suggested to Vasiliev that Arkady's relations with the Countess were more complex, inspired more perhaps by a sense of awe or even fear rather than devotion.

"The Count was less exacting in his requirements than the Countess, perhaps?"

"I wouldn't be saying that, Your Honor."

"More tolerant then?"

"It may be."

"Forgiving?"

"That he was."

"Did the Countess often return alone from balls?"

"There was times when she did and times when she didn't."

"But the Count was tolerant in this as well?"

"Aye."

"And when the Countess was alone in the coach, did she give her own instructions?"

"What do you mean, sir?"

"Well, did she make any special requests, give orders about his driving?"

"Arkady Arkadievich was a good coachman, sir."

"Of course, he had a reputation of being one of the best, but his best might have been different for his master and his mistress, each in his or her own fashion, if you catch my meaning."

She thought for a moment. "Aye, she had her own ways of doin' things."

"How so?"

"The Countess liked to drive fast but smooth like, she did, no sudden stops and starts. 'If you take a deep breath, she'll know it,' Arkady used to say. 'So once you're on your way, God save you from a pothole or a fast turn in the road. But if He don't hear your prayers then there's nothing but to keep goin'.' That's what he used to say."

"On the night when your good man was taken from you, he drove them together to Prince Bagration's, is that correct?" She nodded. Vasiliev felt sure now she wanted to tell him something. He had to be careful not to frighten her. "Then he brought the Count back alone, isn't that so?" She nodded again this time more eagerly. "Did you have a chance to speak with Arkady then? Did he come in?"

"Yes, sir. He stopped at the kitchen for a glass. It didn't harm his driving but kept him warm, you know."

"And did he tell you anything that seemed, odd, you know, unusual about the ride, either coming or going?" She stared at him, uncertain how to answer. Vasiliev tried again. He leaned back in his chair and fiddled with a plate on the table. "You were close. He must have enjoyed telling you about his drives around Moscow, the things he saw. After all you were cooped up here all day and he was all over the city. You looked forward to his coming back and listening to his stories."

She rubbed her eyes on her sleeve. "The Lord did not grant us children, so we kept close; that's the way it was. And Arkady, he liked to talk about driving around Moscow. It was strange, him being a villager, how he liked the city."

"What did he tell you that night?"

"He stood right by me in the kitchen, my work was done, his blue armiak over his arm like he had all the time in the world. He wasn't in no hurry to go back. The Countess never was an early return when she was out alone. We chatted about this and that." She stopped and squeezed her palms together, staring at the floor.

"Please, sir, Arkady was a good man, he's done nothin' wrong in his life."

"Nothing wrong, I know that. No need to be afraid of me. You might be surprised to know that your Arkady and I had something in common. I too come from the village. My mother, you see. As a boy I knew many people like your Arkady, solid, God-fearing, and keen. Men who saw much and said little. But to you he must have told everything. If he said something that has been worrying your mind. You can trust me well enough. I promise you what you say will stay locked in my heart. You'll feel the better for it." Vasiliev had gradually lapsed into the accents of the village.

She lowered her eyes and crossed herself. For a moment she was silent. Then as if she had digested what Vasiliev had said she began in a low voice. "Arkady was a brave man, fought the Turks, did you know? Won a George's Cross. That night—he told me standin' in the kitchen, he was— there was strange things about, frightening things. It all started in the Prince's kitchen. That's where the coachmen waited for the masters. The cooks treated them well. That's why the Prince's household was well thought of by the coachmen. Arkady leaves his place by the hearth. You know, for a moment, has to go out in the hall," she blushed. "On the way back he gets lost in the back of the house. Goin' down a dark passage he runs into a house demon all in black except for a gold crown and passin' so fast he left a wind behind him."

"And did the demon speak, cry out?"

"No, and he was gone before Arkady could grab him. Not afraid for himself, but for the Count who was somewhere in the house and might have come to harm 'cause of the demon. Then a boy came into the kitchen and told him the Count was ready to leave. He went into the courtyard to fetch the carriage, to bring the Count home. They told him they'd brought up the carriage to the front. Arkady got angry because none was to touch the Orlov bays but for him. They was something special in horseflesh you know. And when he got back to the coach the Count was already inside. That was strange too as Arkady was always there to help him, not that the Count was feeble or anything but just, well, it was his duty. So he said how sorry he was and the Count said a few words so quiet like that Arkady could scarcely hear. But up onto his box he got. They came back without any trouble. The trouble came later."

"What about the other coachmen, did they see the house demon? They say meeting a house demon is a bad sign."

"No, but Arkady was not one to make things up. He got mad at the others with their stories and gossip, so he didn't say a word about the demon."

"You're right, Arkady was a serious man. Sounds like he didn't like gossip as you say. Did he ever tell you what kind of gossip made him mad? Funny how gossip sometimes helps me in my work. Not that I believe gossip but you'd be surprised. It lets me understand how people think."

She was swaying from side to side so that the chair creaked under her weight. She had rolled her handkerchief into a ball and was staring straight at Vasiliev.

"He didn't like the teasing."

"Well they couldn't have teased him about you or himself, or even the Count. So what was left?"

"It was her again."

"The Countess. Well, don't worry, I've heard rumors too, but how much can you believe? Of course, coachmen see a lot and they talk with one another, isn't that true?"

"But they was hard men and Arkady didn't like some of the talk, dirty it was, and he'd tell them to stop and they would 'cause they were afraid of his fists."

"But there you were together, standing in the kitchen, he with his armiak over his arm, just warming up from a glass and the heat of the stove and you with your work done, talking as he always did, sharing with you and he was telling you about the gossip, the gossip about the Countess."

"No need for him to do that, for I knew the stories as well as him." She shook her head.

Vasiliev thought it was time to prompt her. "The rumors I heard were that the Countess liked dancing and staying late at balls even coming home alone, and there's nothing wrong with that is there?"

"There was that and other things that needn't be concerning us."

Vasiliev pressed her to explain but she no longer looked at him, fixing her eyes on some distant point where he could not reach her. He hoped that the Count appreciated her loyalty, but then again did the nobility ever understand her kind of devotion?

As he watched her leave she paused at the door and cast a look of unmistakable hatred at a striking young woman who brushed past her. The butler introduced her as the Countess's personal maid. Vasiliev was startled by her resemblance to the portrait of the Countess suspended over the mantle piece, the same coils of blonde hair piled high on her head, the high cheek bones and delicately modeled nose, the small mouth but full lips. They could have been sisters. As soon as she was seated she pulled out a lace handkerchief and daubed her eyes. Vasiliev turned away from her, fixing his eyes on the portrait as if it demanded his full attention. He started off with simple questions that he hoped would put her at ease. Suddenly he turned his full gaze on her and caught her staring boldly at him above her crumpled handkerchief. It was an old trick, he had to admit, but one that worked for him with less sophisticated types. Or was this one just very sure of herself?

"Do you know how closely you resemble the Countess, my dear?"

The girl bent her head. "You did not know her, she was truly beautiful."

Vasiliev was beginning to get annoyed at her coquettish manner, the way she shrugged her shoulders and tilted her head as if she were playing the part of a noblewoman in a provincial theater. She would have done better to have had Foma as a teacher. She said her name was Nasya and that she was the child of house servants at the Ushakov country estate in Semenov district. Another fledgling from the same nest of gentlefolk.

"I have to ask some indiscreet questions. You understand I am trying to track down the man who murdered your mistress. You helped her get ready for the ball at Prince Bagration's?" She dipped her head again, but Vasiliev perceived the wariness that had come over her features. "Good", he went on, "then you are the best person to tell me about her mood. Did she show any signs of worry, or was she excited by the prospect of another ball?"

"The Countess lived for excitement. She was the most alive person I have ever known."

"So I understand. But people who show their emotions so openly find it difficult to hide what they are feeling. I have spoken to others who saw her that night, and I want to know whether you saw the same things they did."

"What did they see?"

"Different people see different things. I need to borrow your eyes and fill out a more complete picture than I have."

The girl paused, moving her lips as if composing her answer.

"The Countess was the same as always. She asked me to lay out her white satin gown and matching shoes with the tiny gold buckles. She wore her triple necklace of pearls which the Count had given her."

"You disappoint me, Nasya, I thought you would be a more observant girl."

"What do you mean? I'm not making up anything. The Countess was always," she paused searching for the right word, "poised," and when it came out it sounded as if she had never spoken it before in her life. More play-acting?

"You can't help her or me if you keep dodging the truth, unless of course you have something to hide and that would not be good for you or your future in this house." Vasiliev had promised himself not to bully her, but she irritated him and he recalled the look Arkady's widow had shot in her direction.

"You have no..." she began, bit her lip and shrank back, her fingers doing something with the fringes of the cushions.

"No what? No right? I have the right of a special investigator authorized by the Minister of Interior with the support of the Emperor. But perhaps you have reason to believe you are protected by some higher power?"

Her eyes darted about the room as she muttered "No, no," her nails now digging into the arms of her chair.

"Good. Now tell me whether the Countess enjoyed dressing you up in her own finery."

He noticed with satisfaction that his guess had struck home by the look of real fear that came over her features. No fake dramatics now.

"I would imagine that having a lovely look alike as a personal maid would have tempted her...well, to see herself in the flesh, as it were, rather than as a pale reflection in her bedroom mirror. I can imagine too how she might have encouraged you to model her clothes for her, an innocent enough pastime I should think." He was smiling and made a gesture as if dismissing the whole idea as a lark.

"The Countess always treated me with respect."

"No one is suggesting anything different. But you haven't answered my questions. Did she take pleasure from dressing you?"

"Yes." The answer came meekly.

"And did she give you her gowns when she tired of wearing them?"

"Sometimes."

"And other items of clothing as well?"

"Yes." A bare whisper now.

"That was generous of her. It just occurred to me that she might have taken you with her when she went out, you know, to play a joke on people by appearing together, like twins."

"Twins?" she faltered.

"Just a fancy. After all, the Countess was high spirited; you said so yourself, and I wouldn't be surprised if she enjoyed playing games. You did say that you occasionally went out together, dressed alike?"

"Who told you that?"

"A lucky guess on my part. You know that's half the pleasure of being a detective. You get the chance to guess about people and with practice you often guess right. I'll tell you why this is important to me, and then you will be able to help me. You were very close to your mistress, adored her, didn't you? And you wanted to be like her, learn from her, and imitate her voice and manners. Perfectly natural on your part. And she responded, gave you pointers, how to walk and, you must forgive me, perhaps even flirt like a gentlewoman. It is an art, after all, that has to be learned from an expert. And you were an apt pupil, quick and eager and she liked that. You became more friends than mistress and maid. Certainly a sign of the Countess' democratic inclinations. Now why am I telling you this, since you know it already? It's simple, really. This closeness, say intimacy, must have led her to confide in you and perhaps she told you something that would lead us to solve the crime, to find her murderer and you want that don't you?"

The girl had grown very still.

"Well, let's begin with your little expeditions together, nocturnal weren't they, because in broad daylight it wouldn't have been so effective, this *charade à deux*. Now the question is where did you go and whom did you meet?"

The girl took a deep breath, folded her hands in her lap and suddenly threw back her head, breaking into a harsh laugh.

"How you frightened me with your story. Oh, for a moment I thought I was at the Grand Guignol again. The mistress used to take me there. Oh yes, that was as far as it went, to the Grand Guignol! And the drives in the park and long walks in the summer on the estate. But there were no nocturnal expeditions. Is that what you called them? What a fanciful idea. You are right of course about dressing up, but that was just in the beginning. She hasn't done that in years. After all, I'm really just her maid, you know."

"So I didn't guess right after all." Vasiliev stood and glanced at his watch. "You see how you have charmed me. I scarcely noticed the time. Here we are chatting idly while I have serious business elsewhere. You have been very patient, mademoiselle."

He bent over her hand and felt the softness of her palm. She rose too, giggling, and curtsied extravagantly, as if to mock him. Vasiliev strode out of the room annoyed with himself. He should have pressed harder, or perhaps he had been too clumsy in dealing with her. He wondered whether he had just lost a chance to break open the case.

Chapter Thirteen

At headquarters Vasiliev packed the metal fragments in cotton wading and sent the parcel with a messenger boy to Professor Slepov at the Mathematical-Physical Institute of Moscow University. A telegram from Borka reported Tarashkin was headed west possibly for Moscow. Another from Ivan's men in Nizhnyi Novgorod identified the dead body of a one armed man fished out of the Volga as Kolya Ilin, blacksmith's assistant from the village of Osholovo, Semenov district, Nizhegorod Province. "A local boy," muttered Vasiliev.

From the bookshelf behind him he pulled down the register of the nobility for Nizhegorod Province, his fingers quickly locating Bagration where he read a list of the family's landed holdings. They included a large estate in Semenov district. Then he paged to Ushakov and, no longer surprised, found a listing for a neighboring estate and among its villages, Osholovo. "Quite a place," Vasiliev spoke out loud. "Let's see, also Tarashkin's place of birth and wasn't there something else?"

He turned to his cardboard files and pulled over one marked OL-OSH, leafed through the clippings until he came across an item from the newspaper *Golos* date June 2, 1878 bearing the caption, "Khlysty Horrors in Nizhegorod Province. Savage Rites Claim Two Lives." He got up from his chair and rummaged in his bookshelves, taking down one volume after another, skimming through them until he found what he wanted He placed a marker in each one and set the book on his desk until he had assembled a precariously balanced pile. Then he settled down to try to make sense of it all. There was Dobrotsvorsky's articles on the radical sects in *The Orthodox Companion* for 1858 and 1860, the first systematic account he could find, Next he read the ramblings of a certain father Sergeev from Kaluga Province from 1809 under the imprint of the Holy Synod followed by Archimandrite Dosifei's sketch of the schism, the sects and heresy. Vasiliev remembered Prince Meshchersky's claim that whole towns in Kostroma Province were secretly sectarian. He found the article that reported on a ring of Orthodox priests in the same province who ran a profitable business peddling fake baptismal certificates. Much of the information seemed vague to him, some of it was downright wrong. He knew the newspapers feared printing material on the sects; police reports avoided the subject whenever possible. Yet there was evidence of sectarian activity everywhere. Vasiliev had his own store of memories about the sectarians, and this made him all the more doubtful that the killings in Nizhegorod Province were the work of Khlysty. It sounded more like *Pryguny*, the Jumpers, a more aberrant sect with a propensity to violence as he had cause to remember only too well.

The images were still sharply etched in his mind. Foma, always the guide to the twilight worlds of Russia, had taken him deep into the forest, making him promise no matter what he saw never to reveal it to anyone. He could still remember as they moved stealthily into the thicker underbrush how the low branches caught at his shirt as if to hold him back. Then Foma gently pushed him down to the humid earth. They began to crawl until Foma signaled a stop. Lying side by side in the heavy brush on the edge of a glade they watched the local peasants lash themselves into a religious frenzy. It had begun quietly, he recalled. An old man reciting by memory long passages from the Book of Revelations accompanied by moans and gnashing of teeth. As the old man's voice reached a crescendo the peasants gathered around him howled and writhed, ripping their blouses and exposing their nakedness. They tore their hair and beards, screaming as they lacerated one another with switches of birch branches. The flogging drove them to a pitch of sexual excitement. They began to jump into the air as if the fires of Hell had scorched the ground beneath them, and when they landed they fell upon one another, men and women indiscriminately, rolling over in the grass and copulating like farm animals he had seen in the village.

Had he ever felt real fear before then? He recalled how he had trembled all over until Foma's gentle hands closed over his eyes. Vasiliev felt strong arms lift him to his feet. Foma led him back through the woods. But he still heard behind them the bleating of the Jumpers, "Oh my soul. Oh God! God the tsar, my soul, the tsar!" And for many months afterwards he had awakened at night, shivering and crying out "My soul!" until his nanny secretly brought him to the local wizard who cast a spell. Perhaps it was hypnosis. Whatever the case the nightmares ceased. Vasiliev caught himself staring at the pages in front of him without seeing a word.

His tea had become lukewarm. He gulped it down and opened another file labeled Sacher-Masoch. He reread the Austrian's story *The Prophetess*, which he knew to be second hand stuff and full of errors, but it had titillated Russian high society with its lurid descriptions of the rituals of the Khlysty or Flagellants as Sacher-Masoch had called them. Vasiliev was reminded him of how bored Russian aristocrats sought erotic stimulation to satisfy their jaded palettes. He was still scribbling notes when Serov made his appearance, wearing a silk blouse; his hair cut in a military style and dyed the color of straw.

"Very dashing, Sergeant. I hope you're not settling into your new life too comfortably." Serov cocked one eye at Vasiliev, groaned and kicking off his leather boots, padded over to the samovar. He filled his glass and leaned against a file cabinet assuming the pose of a city dandy.

"Well, tell us my friend, what secrets you've uncovered."

"Bits and pieces, Vasili Vasilievich, only bits and pieces."

Serov took a lump of sugar between his teeth and sipped his scalding tea.

"The servants are a tight-lipped bunch, all from the same village. Downstairs they have the look of a happy family. They liked the coachman, 'a good sort' they called him, and it pleased them to have a hero in the household, won a St.George's Cross stormin' Shipka Pass. They like the Count but the Countess is a different story. They were respectful, I guess, but, well, seemed uneasy like when talkin' about her. That is all except one. She didn't fit the mold, the upstairs maid, that is. Or, as she told me huffy like, she was the Countess' personal maid, a real beauty with that sort of hair that reminds you of fine spun flax, and eyes a sort of violet color. Never saw the like of those eyes. She puts on airs; when she's out for a stroll, dresses up like a real lady That's why I had to upgrade myself, you see. That's the reason for all this." Serov passed his hand rapidly over his hair. It was then Vasiliev noticed then that Serov had made the supreme sacrifice by getting himself a manicure, but he said nothing.

"She stuck her nose in the air and I could see trouble in tryin' to strike up an acquaintance. So I took a short cut, beggin' your pardon, but you wouldn't mind, I thought, tellin' me time was short. Anyway, I arranged a little theft, you know. My sister's son, Serezha, you remember him, a bright lad,well I got him to snatch her purse. Now I told him this was a serious matter and he could only do this once in his life and, well I used your name Vasili Vasilievich. I told him the Inspector needed him to do this. Then I ran after him and caught him though the little devil led me a merry chase. I pretended to box his ears and let him slip away and that was that. It's an old trick, but as you've said they're the ones that work best. She fell for it, and we became real chummy, and I could see her again if you like." Serov rolled his eyes, poured some tea into a saucer and went on.

"Between what she told me and a bit of gossip from the tradesmen here and there, I'm gettin' a picture of the place. The Count and Countess led different lives. His was workin', hers was playin'. Her playmates, if you'll pardon the expression, are a lumpy sack of potatoes. To begin with there are gypsies, nothing special there, but also sectarians. They show up at the country estate. It was them all right, no mistake. They wore those long white calico blouses with the wide sleeves all the way down to the tips of their fingers, and the women had the white sarafans and covered their heads with kerchiefs with red spots. Oh, they're Khlysty all right. The Countess was crazy enough to invite them to Moscow sometimes, though she kept them mostly out of sight on the estate, the one in Nizhegorod Province...."

"In the Semenov district, near a village called Osholovo?"

Serov sucked on his sugar cube and sipped his tea from the saucer. "Ah, there's no movin' very far ahead of you, Vasili Vasilievich. Now what's the sense of my gettin' all spiffed up and courtin' a pretty woman when you sit here nice and comfortable puzzlin' it all out?"

"A lucky guess, my friend, but I think you're right about Khlysty. Take a look at this." Vasiliev handed Serov the clipping from *Golos*.

Serov shook his head. "But killing isn't Khlysty work unless..."

"Unless what?"

"...unless gentry get mixed up in it, beggin' your pardon. They're lookin' for somethin' different in it, and I've know of some terrible doin's when gentry get mixed in."

"So you think the Countess was playing with fire?"

"I don't know, Vasili Vasilievich, but there's signs burnin' along that way."

"Signs of burning? Rather poetic of you, Serov."

"Well, you were tellin' me the Count's a deputy minister and if his wife is invitin' Khlysty to the manor house, that's a risky business seein' that the government calls them one of the pernicious sects and all. I mean it's illegal to have commerce with 'em."

"Did the maid say anything about sectarians?"

"She just told me how they looked; she didn't call them what they are."

"Do you know much about the Khlysty beliefs, Sergeant?"

"Can't say that I do, except those crazy dances and the floggin' they do."

"Let me tell you about them. They believe that they can be inhabited by God, or Christ or by the Mother of God. And every commune of the Khlysty, which they call a ship or vessel, is led by a nurturer. If it's a woman then she is inhabited by the Mother of God. She has an assistant, a young girl whom she raises and trains to prophesize and who will succeed her at her death. Your pretty little maid, Sergeant, is a dead ringer for the Countess. It's my guess that the Countess was so fascinated by the resemblance that she tried to make the girl over into a version of herself. If they were involved with Khlysty, then the chances are good that the Countess would have played the role of the nurturer and the girl would have served as her assistant and, well, now as her successor."

Serov's eyes widened as Vasiliev closed the file.

"So that's what she meant."

"Another bit or piece you forgot to tell me?"

"She said she had to get back to the countryside. Said she was wanted there and if she didn't go they might even come for her. And I thought it was her family."

"You're right in a way. The commune is the family, whether Khlysty or something more sinister like the Jumpers. That's what surprises me, why she waited so long to leave. Perhaps she doesn't feel ready to take on the burden of the nurturer. She may be frightened by what's in store for her. She's bold and saucy and sly but there is a lot of the child in her."

Vasiliev stood up abruptly. "Listen, Serov, we have to split up again. I need you here as my eyes and ears. Borka may get in touch. He'll be on Tarashkin's trail. If he comes back to Moscow I want you to take over from Borka who operates better in the countryside. Stay close to him. I have to know how deeply the Countess was involved with the sectarians. That means I'll have to go to Osholovo. We can't forget that Tarashkin was born there and may head back that way. Be careful in tracking Petya. He is beginning to be a nuisance. He tried to kill me again."

Serov gasped, but Vasiliev waved his hand in a dismissive gesture. "Yes, yes. I'll take precautions, but I don't need a body guard. You've better things to do."

A knock on the door announced a messenger from Moscow University bearing a note from Slepov. Vasiliev recognized the hasty scrawl.

Dear Vasili,

So you haven't forgotten an old professor. Good! Even better that you give me a practical task. Science has solved tougher mysteries than yours. Here is my preliminary analysis, always subject to revision after another set of tests. The fragments appear to have come from a shell casing or grenade of foreign manufacture, probably French, dating from the early years of this century. Now, if you will permit a little speculative leap, I would guess that this fragment comes from a hand-thrown projectile used by Grenadiers of the Grande Armée in the campaign of 1812. Where on earth did you dig it up?

Vasiliev remembered Slepov warning his students about guesses, yet impressing them with his intuitive powers. And here he was once again making one of those guesses—what did he used to say in his pedantic way?—'that forced the eye to adjust to an unexpectedly sharp angle of refraction.' How they loved to quote him. But Slepov had not known that the fragment came from the pillar of the Ushakov mansion or that Prince Bagration had a collection of memorabilia from the War of 1812.

Chapter Fourteen

The girl had coarse hands but she unwound the bandage with a tenderness that surprised him. Her arms moved up and down in an easy rhythm. The edges of her calico blouse with its wide sleeves reaching to the ends of her fingers caressed his face.

"Be still, now, I have to cut off the rest. I don't want to soak it with water or it will start to bleed again."

Magician caught her hands and kissed them, bringing color to her cheeks, but she did not pull away. He heard himself saying to Marko how useful servants could be if you treated them right. Now the memory of it made him feel ashamed.

"You are inhabited by the Mother of God." He tried to mimic their way of speaking, to strike the right note of humility. There were worse things than hypocrisy to worry about. Besides, he thought, she did have a serenity about her that was actually touching. She wasn't pretty, but he had enough of pretty women for the time being. He felt her fingers pass over his thick blond hair as though she were anointing him.

"You have given me shelter, little sister, and I am eternally grateful. You do believe in me don't you?"

She nodded.

"I swear to you that we shall find the killer who robbed you of your nurturer."

She nodded again, a tear rolling down her cheek. Magician resisted the temptation to brush it away. He kept telling himself he was not in a lady's drawing room. And how would she interpret his gesture? Better to avoid giving her the impression he was one of those city boys who took advantage of peasant girls.

"Your master doesn't understand, does he, that we are working for the same ends? Why are you crying?"

"Life has changed and it has changed the master too."

She was cutting off the bandage, and he winced. "It's all right, you didn't hurt me. What do you mean he has changed?"

"We are not in good hands."

Magician had a great affection for the peasantry but sometimes he found it damned hard to understand them. They did not seem to think logically. There was all this mysticism. The sectarians lived in a different universe, a kind of parallel Russia. Hadn't he read somewhere about such things? The trouble was that as soon as you thought you were getting close to them they went off in an unpredictable direction. And how did all this fit into a future for socialism? That was something he really didn't want to think about.

"But your master is good to you, isn't that so?"

"Yes, but she is a harlot," the girl exclaimed and covered her mouth, "May God forgive me."

"She?" Magician felt at a loss. His eyes wandered over the smoothly planed floorboards and white washed walls. Hoarfrost on the window dimmed the sun, a blur behind a scrim of clouds. He wondered whether the roads were open and when someone would come to relieve him of this terrible boredom.

"The dark side of the Countess," she whispered.

"The dark side of the Countess," he repeated mechanically. "Ah, you mean her maid, the one in Moscow who resembles her?"

"Yes, she is to be our nurturer," a sob caught in the girl's throat.

"But what has that to do with the Count?" Why did he have to ask these endless questions, and how long would he have to remain buried in this provincial hole with only a few servants for company. He had grown up here, he reminded himself, but he had forgotten how insufferably dull the countryside could be.

"She has bewitched the Count."

"Cast a spell on him?" Where was all this nonsense going? he wondered.

"She has betrayed her calling. She has not come to us. Instead she crawls into the Count's bed for earthly pleasures. She plays at being the Countess, but she was to be our nurturer and now she has gone over to the Jumpers. She has told the Count that your friend is evil."

"What! You mean the police Inspector?"

"Yes, your friend is a good man. My sister and her husband said he was kind to them when he came to the house in Moscow, but now the Count will not see him. He has fled to Piter and she is to follow. She has gone over to the Jumpers and poisoned his mind."

Magician seized his head in both hands. Who would have imagined that happening? My God, how stupid it all is. The world has lost one bitch and another takes her place. Silently he cursed them all. He sat for a long time, not moving, pondering how to get the maid out of the Count's bed. Really, it was too much. These ridiculous Russian nobles with their ideas of reforming the world and seducing parlor maids. Or had it been the other way around? Yes, she had seduced him. Even worse.

The girl lovingly rewound the bandage over his head, her eyes lingering on the line of his jaw. 'If only he would be truly possessed by the spirit,' she prayed. She stooped to pick up the basin of water, discolored by his blood, when she heard distant sounds that sent a pang through her heart. They were coming for him. She could not bear to have them take him away, not yet, perhaps never. She gathered the soiled bandage, scissors and basin and glancing at his bent head once more she left the room.

Magician was vaguely aware she had gone. He heard another sound in the corridor, footsteps, heavy boots. He stood up, expectant, then hope giving way to fear, fear of arrest, of being thrown in a dark hole, of being beaten again. He faced the door, half expecting a hob-nailed boot to kick it open. Instead, a series of knocks—three loud, two soft—and a flood of relief. He wrenched open the door and fell into the arms of three figures muffled in furs, the wet snow on their collars soaking his blouse and sending a pleasant chill through him.

"Comrades, welcome! God, how good to see you." Marko pounded him on the back and bombarded him with questions without waiting for answers until Norka took command. She demanded a full account from him.

"Of course, yes, everything in good time. But first, tea. You must be starving. They are good to me here. He rushed into the passage and called for the samovar, bread, sausages and pickled mushrooms.

"Yes, everything, you will hear everything that happened. Marko, you missed out on the excitement."

The girl in the calico blouse brought in the samovar and then cutlery and baskets of black bread, plates of cheese and mushrooms, all the while casting glances at Swan who sat quietly by the window. Magician had gone over his story many times at night, lying in the darkness, his head throbbing. After a time, he began to forget some of what had happened and began to believe in what he had invented as a plausible substitute. Of course, he had to leave out this and that. But, he told himself, these details were not essential to the story. There was no reason, for example to drag in Petya. An unknown assailant would do just as well. And as for his conversation with Vasiliev, here it was necessary also to do a little editing. Let them think that his courage had been sorely tested.

He carefully observed their reactions, noting with satisfaction how Marko was soaking it all up, grinning and nodding his head like a tipsy peasant and Norka pretending to give away nothing while being taken in completely. It was only Swan who worried him. She was staring out the window. Suddenly her eyes flashed at him as if to say, no, that's too much. Her mouth was set in a firm line; her hands were folded primly in her lap. These were all signs he had come to interpret as skeptical even disapproving.

"Do you think that Vasiliev is leaning in our direction?" Norka asked. "That would confirm what Swan has reported."

"You have seen Vasiliev?" Disappointment was written all over Magician's face. Hadn't it been agreed that he would make the contact? And what had Vasiliev told her about the Volga encounter, the truth?

"Not only that, but Swan has information from the other side as well."

"What do you mean?"

"From General Shuev."

Magician fiddled with his bandage. Swan kept staring out the window as if absorbed in the snow squall outside. Marko began to say something but Norka nudged him to be silent.

"The Gendarmes are having fits about Vasiliev's investigation.

Van der Fleet seems more upset than Shuev. The headmaster is always more self-confident, the arrogant pig. We must have been right from the beginning; they staged the whole thing themselves in order to discredit the reform", said Norka. Irina caught herself thinking that Norka sounded pretty self-confident herself.

"What about our friends in the People's Will; do they agree, or will they accept this?"

"They are fools. And they are paying for their obstinacy. Mikhailov was taken last week. God knows what that will do to their organization. He knew everything."

"You'd almost think that the Gendarmes were working for us," Marko grinned.

The others fell silent.

"Will there be a constitution, then?" Magician asked.

"Not in so many words." Swan, speaking for the first time, had taken off her hood, scattering ice crystals all over her hair where they sparkled briefly before melting away. She was conscious that they were all staring at her. She felt her color rise but she plunged ahead. "The political changes will be extensive; representatives of the public will be taken into the State Council to help draft legislation. The optimists see this as only a first stage. Much then will depend on the reformers keeping their nerve."

"That's where we may be in trouble." Magician felt compelled to reclaim their attention. As he expected, they turned to look at him. "Apparently, Ushakov is backing off."

In the chorus of exclamations he heard only Swan. "I can't believe it," she blurted out. Still, she had already feared something like that would happen. Why else would the Count have decamped to St. Petersburg? There was no other possible explanation.

Magician folded his arms and stared directly at her. "It seems as though a stronger influence than yours has intervened." And he related what the servant had told him.

"We've got to get her out of Moscow and prevent her from going to Piter. It's the only way to loosen her control over the Count. Listen, she's tied to the sectarians, right. You know them, Magician. Think, there must be a way to get her out here."

Magician looked out the window as the rim of the sinking sun touched the horizon.

"You're right, Norka, but we don't have much time."

"How long?"

"A fortnight, until the solstice."

"We'll leave tomorrow."

"They speak of a blizzard."

"Then now!"

"The horses are exhausted."

"Let me go. My wound has healed, I can travel faster alone."

Norka thought for a moment. "You're sure you can get her to come? Well, then all right. What do you think?"

Marko nodded, Swan hesitated but Norka had already made up her mind. "There seems to be no opposition. Can we stay here safely for a few days? Just until the horses are rested and the weather clears."

"Yes, the Khlysty are reliable people. They don't trust the government any more than we do. But I have to warn you. Don't try to win them over to our way of thinking. They are fanatics in their own way."

"We're too exhausted to do anything like that. Let's give our wounded herald some time to pack." Her rough joking always fell flat. But Marko obediently followed her into the corridor. Swan paused on the threshold, turning to face Magician.

"We must talk, Iuri." He was startled that she used his real name, another bad sign. "You have a lot to explain. I haven't told the others about what really happened at Bagration's. But I can't stay quiet much longer. I'm already…"she hesitated before blurting out "…breaking discipline." She immediately felt awkward. Conspiratorial language still sounded a false note in her ears.

"For God's sake, not now. What did Vasiliev tell you?" He did not wait for an answer but plunged ahead. "He's exaggerating. Anyway there's no time. I have to get ready. There are only a few hours of daylight left. You must trust me, Irina. I swear to you that what happened to me at Bagrations has nothing to do with the murder. Please believe me."

"Come Swan," Norka's voice grated on their ears. It was a reminder that she took seriously her duty to guard against sentimental attachments from developing within the organization.

Chapter Fifteen

Vasiliev was seated at his desk pondering his next step. He felt blocked at every turn. The Bagration family had gone off to the Crimea. Despite two written requests, he still had not received a list of the guests invited to the ball. Shuev refused to divulge the names without the permission of the Prince;"a matter of common courtesy," was his excuse to Vasiliev. Count Ushakov was also avoiding him. Why had everyone lost interest in the case? The countryside seemed to have swallowed up Magician and Borka as well. Serov had not reported any success in tracing Petya.

He turned things over in his mind. There was nothing straight forward about the case. The highest officials in the government had called him in to investigate the possibility that the Gendarmes had covered up the murder of the Countess for their own reasons. But why would the boys in blue go to such lengths? They had already demonstrated their skill in hunting down revolutionaries. What more did they have to prove? Or, what was necessary for them to conceal?

He involuntarily shook his head. Were they so concerned about the reforms? Why take the chance of ruining their reputation in order to sow panic among the nobility? It seemed far-fetched.

One thing was certain: from the beginning someone was desperate to get rid of him. Who would hire a thug like Petya to do the job? Certainly not the Gendarmes. They had their own professional methods. It seemed obvious that it had to be the murderer. He wondered how he, whoever he was, had found out about his assignment. It might have a highly placed official who had leaked the information. Or else an agent who had penetrated the Ministry That would point to the terrorists. But they had even less reason to assassinate the Countess. Unless they were aiming to kill the Count, and there had been a mix-up in the operation. But why target the Count? And why not use the dynamite bomb? That was their weapon of choice. Professional criminals or terrorists deviated from their normal patterns only in only two situations. Either they panicked, or else they were forced to act quickly. But neither explanation seemed the right one in this case. It seemed like the work of an amateur. Then what was the motive?

Another loose thread was Irina and her friends. What stake did they have in all this? They claimed to favor reform not terror, but they were illegals, socialists. And what had turned Irina into one of them? He had searched his memory for the slightest sign of her previous interest in politics. He had found none. It seemed that no one in Moscow knew what happened to her over the past two years. People closest to the family thought she had gone to Como with her parents. He had not tried to get in touch with them. Perhaps that had been a mistake. Tarashkin, Magician was another puzzle. He seemed like a very confused young man. Yet he was a friend of Irina's and she was not a stupid girl. Not stupid or flighty. But why think of her virtues only in negative terms? His feelings for her had never changed. And now he was concealing his contact with a group of revolutionaries. They might be of help. Or was he just deceiving himself? Down deep he knew the real reason he was working with them.

He spent the rest of the day leafing through his files again. He did not know exactly what he was looking for. There had to be some connection between the Ushakovs and the Bagrations. What was it? When he returned home an invitation was waiting for him. The Golitsyns were giving a big party. He tossed the engraved card aside. Later he picked it up again. An idea suddenly came to him. The cream of Moscow society would be there. If he could not interview the principals in the case, he could pick up the latest gossip about them. The information might be just as valuable. Besides the Golitsyns were famous for their buffet suppers. His cook had the day off. He prepared his own modest supper: salted fish, cucumber salad and a small vodka. He worked for several hours on his Pushkin article. Then he took out his old flute and played some mournful melodies. He ought to practice more, he thought. At midnight he went to bed feeling pleased with himself.

The Golitsyn mansion on the Petersburg Road stood near the Petrovsky Palace. Vasiliev's history books had taught him that in the old days the tsars took up residence there before entering the city for the coronation. The place still looked the part, its massive brick corpus flanked by two semi-detached wings, a broad circular drive leading to a covered portico supported by marble columns in the Doric style. In the entrance hall he ran into a group of general staff officers. Most of them had served with him at Plevna during the war with Turkey. There was no way to avoid their boisterous greeting. They recalled how he had solved the battlefield murder of Colonel Grekov at Plevna. It always ended the same way; "you restored morale to the army and we went on to storm the Pass, eh Vasili?" Then, the teasing began about his bachelorhood in a world of beautiful women. By the time he entered the grand salon he felt as though his own coronation was about to begin.

A ripple of excitement passed through a coterie of young women when he bowed to them. They fluttered their fans in unison. He knew the rumors about him, that he had a secret love or a hopeless love or a dead love. They had turned him into a Byronic hero. And then there was the matter of money. Someday, they said, he would be a very rich man, the only male heir of old Count Vorontsov. It was times like these he understood the dilemma of Tolstoy's Pierre Bezhukov, but he was not going to be trapped like poor Pierre by some latter day Hélène with a bewitching bosom. Princess Golitsyn was doing her best to steer him in that direction, presenting him to the most suitable heiresses. Wealth has no fear of marrying wealth, he thought, wondering whether the idea was original or not. Vasiliev decided to turn the tables on his old friend, the Princess. He insisted on escorting her to supper. She was flattered, and none of the young women could take offense.

A chef from Paris had been imported to prepare the banquet. Were the Golitsyns trying to outdo Bagration? It looked that way to him. He tasted the *poche à l'aumônière*, the beggar's purse, French crepes stuffed with sturgeon caviar. Princess Golitsyn explained it had been first prepared at Le Grand Verfour in Paris. "Just pop them into your mouth. They melt immediately," she exclaimed as they moved along the table passing by the *vol-au-vents* with mushrooms and sweetbreads, the sterlets poached in champagne, and the braised quail with walnut and pomegranate sauce, a mound of buckwheat kasha for the local patriots, a salad he did not recognize and at the end a *sharlotka* created originally by the great Antoine Carème for Alexander I and known to the rest of the world as *charlotte russe*. Arranged like sentinels on their own table stood a group of wines ranging from Vosne-Romanée for partisans of the reds and Puligny Montrachets for the whites. Dish after dish reminded him of his childhood when the old Count, his father would entertain on the same lavish scale. Vasiliev would stuff himself with sweets and be sick afterwards. The temptation was still there, he knew. But now he only sampled to taste. Others, he noticed, were not so fastidious. He wondered how it had been at Bagration's.

He imagined that the Golitsyns would draw the better crowd, more titled aristocrats, more beautiful and unattached young women. He was aware that most people stared at him. Aside from the officers very few of the guests approached him. It was always the same. They thought about his inheritance but were queasy about his mixed blood. He was surprised then when the French ambassador, René Lafebre de Laboulaye, demanded an introduction. It turned out that he admired Vasiliev for having crossed swords with his diplomatic rival, Strafford de Redcliff, the British ambassador to Istanbul. Vasiliev had no desire to rake over those dead coals. He launched into a discussion of Prince Bismarck's latest moves. He would have been even more surprised had he known that later that night the ambassador sent a long cable to Paris summarizing Vasiliev's views as reflecting the opinion of the Foreign Ministry.

Vasiliev pushed himself forward into small groups of officers, using the skills he had learned from his father in his best Polonius style. He remembered all the stock phrases: "be witty but not coarse, flatter but not slavishly" and the rest of the silly repertoire. He was always amazed that it worked, or that he could do it so well, dropping a *bon mot*, relating an anecdote and moving on. He kept an eye peeled for Princess Golitsyn whose matrimonial intrigues he was determined to foil and the dancing master who apparently had orders to recruit him for a quadrille or a mazurka. He was looking for a certain retired general, the best-informed gossip in Moscow, who invariably showed up at most of these parties in search of a fresh audience for his stories. In the hall, he ran head long into his hussar friends from the Volga. They too grabbed hold of him.

"We're glad to find you here, Vasili, surrounded by the most beautiful women in the world." Had Princess Golitsyn conspired with them as well?

"Listen, I need reinforcements. I haven't felt so outnumbered since Plevna."

"We know how well you did in the Balkans. And here the women here are a lot more attractive. We hear that you've been tracking hussar officers from our regiment. What deviltry are we accused of now?"

"No deviltry I can think of, at least none I can arrest you for. To tell the truth I'm not here for the women or the food, though they're both tempting. I've been assigned to look into the murder of Countess Ushakova. I'm looking for some eyewitnesses, you know, people who were at the Bagration ball and might have seen something that might help me."

"Why we were there!"

"What! Both of you? Impossible, but why didn't you mention it on the steamer?"

"It didn't come up. We were too busy hacking off arms and such things to have a polite conversation. Besides, you disappeared after we chased those two thugs over the side. We wondered where you had gone. We even thought we had somehow offended you."

"Good God, no. You saved my life."

"That did occur to us. We were afraid we might have been too familiar with you, joked too much. A man's honor is a personal thing. But we should have known better in your case. Tell us, did you ever track down the animal called Petya. What did you do with the detached limb?" They laughed. "See how outrageous we can be."

"I gave the arm as a present to an old friend. Petya has been giving me fits since then. But let's get back to the events at Bagration's ball." Vasiliev shook his head. "I can't believe you were right in my hands. The beautiful women will have to wait." Vasiliev guided them into a room occupied by a grand piano and a harp facing rows of empty chairs.

"I've never believed in coincidences, no detective ever does, but I am going to have to make exceptions. Either that or fit you into the conspiracy."

"On the Volga? No! We were only conspiring to seduce the merchant's wife. Remember her, with the slim waist and the terrible hat? Just a moment, we'll save the story for later. You want to know what we saw the night of the murder. I'm not sure we can help very much."

Vasiliev let them talk. He had long ago reached the conclusion that questioning people directly was not always the best method. It could just as well narrow the inquiry as opening it up. It turned out that they had known Prince Bagration slightly before the war, but that he had virtually adopted the regiment ever since it had been assigned to guard the railroads. He had taken a personal interest in the campaign against terror.

"Always invites us to his grand affairs, balls, dinners. Almost all the officers in our regiment have been there one time or another. He packs us in, as many as he can accommodate. Without him, I tell you, life for us would be fairly dull in Moscow. We are Petersburgers tried and true, you know."

"I'll forgive you for your sins. And the Moscow balls attracted interesting people like the Ushakovs."

They exchange glances. "Oh yes, the Countess was a favorite among us, from a distance of course. Terrible that she was cut down in her prime, a spirited woman, quite literally the belle of every ball. Too popular, in fact. We couldn't even squeeze onto her dance program, Bagration's name was all over it."

"So you watched from the sidelines, kept an eye on her did you?"

"Hard not to."

"Anyone else besides the Prince get a chance to partner her?"

"Hussars of course," they laughed again. "And then there was the poet."

"Poet? At Bagrations?"

"Our nickname for him. What was his name, Mitya? I don't recall. No, nor do I, perhaps he never told us. Anyway we ran into him in the library where he was scribbling some verse and we hit it off right away. A clever chap with words, like you Vasili. At some point, I can't recall exactly when, early on I think, he broke into the quadrille opposite the Countess. She didn't seem to like it one bit. He was an odd character. He looked like a poet, oh not like Pushkin or Lermontov, but more like our modern poets, not exactly shabby but a little rumpled. She cut him dead. Then the Prince materialized out of nowhere. He stopped the orchestra and carried off the Countess in a waltz. God, what a stunning pair they made."

"And your poet, what happened to him?"

"We lost sight of him. I don't think we ever saw him again what with the Terek sword dance and all."

"What did he look like?"

"Mid to late twenties, a real Great Russian type, blond, thick almost glossy hair, full beard and moustache, good figure, though a bit stooped, too much scribbling I guess. He moved nicely on the dance floor. In fact, the more I think of it..."

"...the more he resembled the young man who was talking to me on the steamer deck, except for the beard and moustache. His name is Tarashkin."

"I told you, Mitya, that they looked alike, but we got only a brief look at him on board and then the beard and moustache were gone. What's wrong Vasili?"

"Gentlemen, you have the honor of being in the presence of the most short-sighted detective in the empire. At the very beginning of this case, on board the steamer, I had within reach three witnesses of the Countess' last hours and I failed to discover any one of them."

"Back luck, Vasili."

"The bad luck of a man who drowns in a teacup." Vasiliev prayed that Borka was sticking close to Magician. But then why pray? Borka had never failed him.

"Let's go back to the moment when you met, in the library. I need to know about the doors; where did they lead?"

"Let me think. One led to the ballroom and the three of us sailed out that way, arm in arm. There was another door on the opposite side of the room, I seem to recall, but I don't know where it led. Why is that so important?"

"I'm trying to figure out how Tarashkin got into the house. He wasn't an invited guest, I'm sure of that. There's no reason you should know, but he belongs to an illegal group, the Repartition of the Land. The boys in blue want him for questioning. Sorry to say he was a gate crasher, and you two provided him with the perfect escort."

"So much for picking up strange poets in other people's houses."

"You couldn't have known. As you say he is clever. That's why his revolutionary pseudonym is Magician. But tell me what he did once he joined the party? How did he act toward the Countess?"

"He came out to her like young Lensky. We even joked about that. The orchestra had been playing Tchaikovsky's new waltz from Eugene Onegin, so the whole thing struck us as something right out of Pushkin. Plenty of drama on the dance floor too, because the Countess was not happy to see our poet. I believe she actually hissed at him, and he looked as though his face had been slapped. It was then that Bagration stopped the music, quite literally."

"You must have watched the Prince and Countess, then. How were they with one another?"

"Vasili, you are really straining our memories. I had the impression, didn't you Mitya, that she didn't look like a woman rescued from a cruel fate. No, there was something cool and even aloof about her, at least when they swept past us. You'd have to have known her, Vasili. She was like a young girl when she danced, gay, laughing and, well I hesitate to say it now, but very much alive. And here she was looking very much put out with her poet and not too happy about her savior. Still, the two of them, she and Bagration, danced beautifully together. It was almost as if..."

"...they were old acquaintances," Vasiliev finished. "How long did you watch them?"

"Just a few minutes, then the Prince gave a signal. He tossed his head, and the Cossacks came stamping in. After that things got confused and the two of them disappeared. Come to think of it, at the same time we lost sight of...what did you call him, Magician?"

"And the Count, did you see him at all?"

"Only briefly, he seemed to be attached to that pretty girl, remember, Mitya, the one General Shuev took a fancy to."

"Shuev pursuing a girl?"

"Well, in a manner of speaking. God, Vasili you must think we had nothing better to do than spy on people like a pair of old women."

"No better witnesses than spying old women. Go on, you are giving me more than I could have hoped for."

"The headmaster is not known to be much of a ladies' man, but he danced every mazurka with the little charmer. I said a pretty girl, but that's not quite right. She had a strong face. Does that seem a strange thing to say? Well, if you were comparing her to the Countess you would say she was a typical Russian beauty while the Countess was more European, French or Spanish. Mitya was quite taken with her, and tried to strike up an acquaintance but she wasn't interested. His first failure in years."

"You know, Vasili, since you are dragging the bottom of our memories, I'll confess that this young girl was positively brusque with me. I never ran into that before at a ball. I'm no Adonis, but to prefer Shuev. It was a hard thing to take. And when I saw her tonight..."

"She's here?" Vasiliev felt the coincidences were multiplying on him like rabbits.

"Yes, and it was the same thing, she snubbed us."

"My friends, I'm sorry to cut this short, but as they say on the Volga, when the current is strong it's a sin not to catch it. Shakespeare said it better, but you get my meaning. I've got to find this charmer of yours. She has a big part in this little drama."

"Lucky for you, Vasili. I wish I had the force of law behind me on this one." Vasiliev left them laughing, he thought, ruefully.

Swan had arrived before Vasiliev with the same purpose in mind. But she was quicker to find her prey. She cornered the famous gossip in the card room where he looked bored watching several officers play Boston. She remembered him from childhood when her father had referred to him as "the dullest dinner companion in Moscow." Her mother took great delight in his scandalous gossip. He did not recognize her after all those years but perked up at the prospect of entertaining a pretty young woman. It occurred to Irina, without much satisfaction, that she was perfecting her technique of cultivating older men. She steeled herself to endure a lengthy monologue dealing with people she no longer cared about. But she finally steered him to the subject of the Ushakovs.

"So, my dear, you must understand there are very few who know the story behind the bad blood between Count Ushakov and Prince Bagration. It all goes back to the days before the Turkish War, in Tiflis. It was hushed up at the time. When the war came we all had more pressing things to think about. I was surprised the story took so long to get to Moscow. After all this is where all the juicy scandal comes home to roost."

The general paused, took out a cigar from his breast pocket but after glancing at Irina, he replaced it with a sigh.

"I had it first hand from the Prince's personal adjutant in the winter of seventy-two. Ushakov was in charge of the Viceroy's finances. A damn stickler—forgive my rough talk, I am not accustomed to chatting with young ladies any more—let's see where was I? Yes, a damn stickler for detail was our Count. He demanded an accounting for every kopeck. Enter Bagration. He used his connections with the heir, Alexander Alexandrovich, to get himself appointed vice-governor. From the beginning he had his eye on the main prize. Dreamed of being governor, even married into Georgian nobility, a Dadian. You know her I'm sure. He kept her hidden away like some oriental despot. Got involved in a quarrel with Ushakov down there. Oh, they had known one another for years, owned neighboring estates in Nizhegorod Province. But the families had never gotten on well, one of those interminable legal squabbles about estate boundaries. But in Tiflis it was something else. They became rivals for the reigning beauty at the viceroy's court, a dashing woman, great rider, fashionable European clothes and so forth. They put on quite a show for the rest of us. Imagine a dry as dust fellow like Ushakov competing with a tiger like Bagration."

The general cast a wistful look at a thin layer of smoke drifting in from an adjoining room. He reflected how much more pleasant it would have been to have this conversation with a man who might have shared his taste for tobacco and a few choice oaths.

"Am I being too coarse? No? Good. The two of them...well, the Count can be quite charming, I admit, if he sets his mind to it, and in those days he did so. He was a lively suitor, surprised us all, maybe it was the mountain air. What did Lermontov say?"

Swan smiled sweetly.

"Yes, well the old goat cooked up a little plot to discredit his rival. Details a bit fuzzy here, and I don't want to make up anything, have to keep my reputation." He chuckled. "Where was I? Oh yes, Ushakov, the financial wizard, got the Prince to draft a plan to tax the native chiefs. Encouraged him in a vague sort of way, even loaned him an expert from his own department, promised to support him at the council, they say. Of course, Bagration should have known better. But he wanted a big success to become governor or maybe just to impress his lady. It all came apart at a full dress meeting of the Viceroy's council. The Count just pulled the rug out from under our tiger." The general slapped his knee and waved down a servant.

"Over here, my good fellow, yes a brandy please, Armenian if you have it, of course you do." He turned back to Swan. "Have to show our loyalty these days to our dictator of the heart. Never mind, I got used to it in Tiflis. Mostly Armenians there you know, and to tell the truth their cognac is just as good as Courvoisier. Surprised are you?"

"We Russians always assume foreign things are better."

"Capital! But you aren't one of those slavophils, are you? Terribly preachy people."

"You were telling me about the duel between Ushakov and Bagration," Swan prompted.

"Was I? Yes, quite right and it almost came to that, I mean a duel, a real one. Bagration didn't realize that he had been building a house of cards until it collapsed on his head. He had to resign, lost the lady too. Well, what did he expect after that, and he was married even if he kept his wife in a *terem*."

"Quite a sordid little affair," Irina said.

"Ah well, for your innocent ears, yes. But I must say for us grizzled veterans—I'm afraid I will shock you—it was amusing. Bagration got everything he deserved. Sad part about it was that his son's life was wrecked. Bagration had been married before, wife died of consumption, I think, and the boy was frail too. Bagration had set him up in a sinecure, but he couldn't even manage that. He was a bit queer if you ask me, too much religion, or rather of the wrong kind. He got interested in sectarians, a parcel of them down there in the Caucasus, you know. Then the funniest thing was that the boy took his father's disgrace to heart, insulted the Count at a dinner party. Some people expected a duel, but I don't think the boy or Ushakov for that matter would have known which end of the pistol to point. It had all the makings of a French farce. Still, I felt sorry for the boy. Can't hold a candle to papa, but he is the sole heir. They say he has become something of a recluse these past years, shows up at the oddest places."

"Sad to think that the last descendent of the General is a weakling," Irina hated to play the role of a mindless female. She had hoped to drop all pretence when she joined Land and Liberty. Instead she was drowning in it.

"Right. The worst thing for the Prince was being ostracized from court. Our Viceroy down there, Grand Duke Mikhail Nikolaevich, took a dislike to him after the tax scandal. Bagration tried to go over his head, petition the tsar directly. I guess he was counting on the heir to back him up. But the tsar couldn't very well decide against the Viceroy, his own brother after all. Bagration never forgave the tsar. But that seemed to bring him closer to the heir. You know of course that Alexander Nikolaevich and his son are not getting on too well these days. The marriage to Princess Yurevskaya didn't help. Did you know her when she was still Ekaterina Dolgorukaya?"

Irina shook her head. "If the Prince is still bitter it seems strange that he would have anything to do with the Count, let alone invite him to his balls."

"Why that's the Countess' doing."

"Why is that?"

"My dear, she was the delicious prize in that sordid little affair as you so delicately put it."

"Of course, how silly of me not to have seen that."

The general sipped his brandy and began to reminisce about the war. Irina hardly listened. After what she considered a suitable interval she slipped away feeling she could no longer breathe in an atmosphere so redolent of her past. In this state she almost collided with Vasiliev in the corridor. Suddenly he was holding both her hands in his. They both spoke at the same time. "I must speak with you," he said. "We must talk", was the way she put it. Vasiliev was struck by the subtle difference. For her they were allies, even friends, or at least former friends while he was still conscious of being the

Inspector. Yet they had both reverted to the familiar "thou" form of address. Was he over interpreting what they said to one another, or the way they said it, finding more than there was or perhaps looking for something that no longer existed? Good God, he was even interpreting his interpretations. What had gotten into him?

Swan was conscious only of the pressure of his fingers and a feeling of relief and comfort at seeing him.

Vasiliev was the first to recall where they were and releasing her hands he bowed, offered his arm and led her into the ballroom.

"So much in this case seems to hinge on what happens on a dance floor," he bent over to whisper.

A hundred pair of eyes followed them while the fans ceased to flutter.

"You must smile, Irina, at least at my jokes, or else the guests will think that something unusual has just happened."

"I can think of nothing more unusual than what has just happened."

"Sometimes the best disguise is to appear natural. And I see that you have not forgotten your waltz steps in the underground."

"Nor you on the battlefield. Not surprising since we had the same instructor."

"Ah, yes, old Professor de Schweinitz. I often wondered whether he deserved the title. Still, you must admit that attending balls does seem a curious occupation for an enemy of society. I hope you have no plans to generate the same excitement as last time."

"I am not an enemy of society, just of this society. And my intention is always to avoid excitement not cause it."

Neither of them was aware any longer of the couples swirling around them.

"You did not tell me that Tarashkin, or should we call him Magician, had shown up at Bagration's ball where he created a near scandal. If we are to be allies in this, even if only allies of convenience, then it would be best not to conceal facts that might have a bearing on the case."

"Magician did not kill the Countess."

"Unless you can tell me who did, I shall have to leave the question open."

"Perhaps I can give you a more logical alternative. I came here tonight to help solve the crime. I had a conversation that might interest you. Prince Bagration was a rival of the Count for the favors of the Countess, I guess that is the most polite way to put it, before her marriage. The Count not only won the contest but also engineered a plot to humiliate the Prince. It worked. Bagration was disgraced and forced to retire from public life. It seems that the Countess did not lose interest in the Prince, or vice versa. You may know that there was some kind of —what shall I call it—galvanic attraction between the Prince and the Countess at the ball. I saw it with my own eyes, but I cannot explain it any more clearly than that. They left the ballroom together and she was never again seen alive."

Swan did not add that Magician had followed them, but it was not up to her to offer explanations for Magician's behavior. She did not understand it herself. And she had agreed to give him more time but for what she was not certain either. Vasiliev was right, of course. She was concealing evidence, but she felt torn between her desire to help him solve the case and her belief in Magician's innocence. She promised herself that unless he told her the truth— and she felt her mind trip over the word—she would have to tell Vasiliev what she knew.

"There is something else you should know. The reason you have had trouble seeing the Count is, how shall I put it?"

"...that he has been under the influence of the maid, Nasya, and the influence has, I take it, been strong." It encouraged him to see that she could still blush. "I think you would make a good detective, Irina."

"And you would certainly have made a good revolutionary, Vasya. But there is more. We saw to it that she was out of the way for long enough for you to see the Count."

"You don't plan..."

Swan laughed. "No, no, don't worry, Vasya, no kidnapping, no mayhem, no murder. We are just arranging it so that she will play out her role as nurturer during the winter solstice when her presence in the countryside will be expected."

"You mean by the Jumpers of Osholov district."

"Very good, Inspector. You live up to your reputation. Just remember that it is we who arranged the diversion. I told you we could be useful."

"All right, I accept that, but perhaps it would be wise in the future not to rely on chance meetings at the houses of the aristocracy. How can I get a message to you?"

"I.N. Lebedeva (Swan), Poste restante, Moscow will reach me. You see, pseudonyms are good for something besides confusing the police."

The waltz had come to an end, and they broke apart. She had been hardly aware that he was holding her in his arms, his touch was so light. Suddenly, she felt something missing. Vasiliev was bowing and asking her to join him at the buffet.

"It would be better if you found another partner to stop tongues wagging."

"That sounds like the suggestion of a co-conspirator. All right if we have to be discreet then we should leave now. Let's go separately. You first." As they crossed the room he noticed no further movement from the fans. After making a formal bow, he wasted a half an hour in the card room before making his excuses. Princess Golitsyn was disappointed. She was still trying to find out who the girl was when he bade her good night.

The night was frigid. The crystalline air stung his nostrils. Perhaps there was more to learn from Osholovo than from Ushakov at this point. It was tempting to imagine all the lines meeting there, the adjoining estates of the two families, Bagrations and Ushakovs, Tarashkin's birthplace and now the site of the coming Jumpers' celebration of the solstice with the maid Nasya presiding as nurturer. Despite the cold Vasiliev remained for a while in the shadows of the east portico. He was thinking of Irina, of how she had grown up and grown away, of how waltzing with her had brought back so vividly the hours of practice under the stern beat of Professor de Schweinitz, of how he kept wondering what had turned her from a carefree girl into a radical, a believer in socialism and an illegal. He decided that he was thinking of her too much.

Out of the corner of his eye he had been studying the traffic pattern in front of the Golitsyn palace. He noticed how one cab kept pulling out of line as its turn came to move into the first rank and returning to the end of the line only to repeat the maneuver a second time. More surveillance? Yes, but at a distance. Vasiliev who was unarmed decided to switch tactics. He ordered his driver to turn down a side street and slow the cab to a walk. He handed up some bills, jumped out and walked rapidly through a courtyard before emerging on a parallel street where he knew there would be another cab rank. He climbed into the first one and turned to peer out the rear window. Another cab had picked up his trail.

Having cabs running down parallel streets was a very clever procedure, a new technique, he recognized, developed by the secret police in tracking revolutionaries. So someone had given up on amateurs and had acquired some professional operatives. Or was that the wrong conclusion? There might be two groups in this game. Were they acting together or separately, for the same or different ends, to protect or obstruct him?

Chapter Sixteen

Vasiliev was rehearsing paradoxes. For a time nothing was possible now everything was. He was in the midst of his preparations to leave for Osholovo when a message arrived that the Bagrations had returned from the Crimea and would now receive him. On top of that a telegram landed on his desk, 'Your presence urgently required. (s) Ivan.' Vasiliev packed two different valises and set out for the Bagrations. By the time he arrived the sky was filled with snowflakes blowing in all directions. He was reminded of what a chaotic place the world had become.

In summer the Bagration mansion would be screened from prying eyes by beech trees, but now he could see the portico clearly from the street. It was supported by eight fluted columns surmounted by a frieze portraying the Argonauts, an example of Girardie's best work. A footman in black and white livery led him through a succession of rooms jammed with furniture of half a dozen different styles. What had happened to the taste of the aristocracy? His father kept to the old style of Catherine the Great, and people snickered behind his back. Well, let them snicker. For once he was on his father's side.

At the end of a long corridor they passed into a salon that radiated light and warmth. He had the impression that he had been transported into a Caucasian villa. At the end of the room windows extending from floor to ceiling faced south onto a terrace and miniature garden surrounded by a low brick wall. The shrubbery and flowerbeds had been covered with burlap that was sagging under a blanket of snow. The ancient beech trunks standing at regular intervals outside the wall had been topped so that the sun, even at its lowest point on the meridian in mid-winter, flooded the room. On the south side, flanking the windows, stood two ceiling-high stoves ornamented with yellow and green Yaroslavl tiles, the only Russian touch in the entire room. Rugs from Daghestan covered the walls and were draped over the low divan on which Princess Bagration reclined. Her feet encased in jeweled Persian slippers rested on an ocelot skin. A great beauty in her youth, Vasiliev had heard, she was not aging well. He was reminded of Medea.

The figure of the Prince, looking more like Hercules than Jason, stood by a marble fireplace. He was dressed in a pale yellow linen suit with a raw silk cravat held in place at his throat by an emerald stickpin. Vasiliev met a pair of dark eyes that never left the Inspector's face. A sardonic smile played over the Prince's full mouth. The total effect was meant to impress, indeed, thought Vasiliev, to over-awe.

"You are most kind to receive me," Vasiliev bowed, "and in this magnificent setting."

"It is a pleasure, Inspector," the Prince replied, "that we have too long postponed. I believe you passed through Tiflis on your way to the front while we were on a tour of the mountain tribes. Since then we have neglected to make up for our loss."

"Please sit here, Inspector," the Princess had kept more than a trace of her Georgian accent. Vasiliev found the lilt of her soft voice to be charming in an exotic sort of way. She turned to gaze at her husband with a wistful expression. "This room is called Bagration's folly built to comfort a princess in exile from her sunny Georgian homeland." Vasiliev glanced out the windows where the wind stirred eddies of snow in the garden. It reminded him more of winter on the Georgian Military Highway. The Prince's face was impassive.

"You must forgive me from intruding into your private world, and so soon after your return from the Crimea. I'm sorry to revive unpleasant memories. As you know I am here because my duty obliges me to pursue an investigation into the tragic death of Countess Ushakova."

"We have already been visited by an officer of the Gendarmes," the Prince said, "a certain Van der Fleet. He assured us we would not be disturbed again. He told us the outrage was the result of an attack by terrorists. It seems they were aiming to assassinate Count Ushakov but the attempt miscarried. Poor Countess Ushakova was the unintended victim. I assumed that this was the official position. Am I wrong? Or has it changed?"

"No, Your Excellency, the official position remains the same. But the assassins are still at large despite the best efforts of the Gendarmes. The Minister of Interior has authorized me to expand the preliminary inquiry. There are some loose ends. Not everything we have fits into the official explanation. It seems strange, for instance, that the attack came when and where it did given what we know about the methods of the terrorists. Then there is the question of the explosive device. That too does not fit any known model previously used by the terrorists. There are one or two other trifles I need not bother you about. One lead I am following comes from a suggestion that there might have been a relay system of communications between Prechistenka and Povarskaya."

"Surely you are not implying that one of our guests was in contact with the terrorists?" The Prince sounded more amused than outraged.

"Perhaps Inspector Vasiliev means that someone was posted outside our gate to keep watch and alert his confederates when the Count's carriage departed."

It was the lisp that gave the Princess' accent such charm, thought Vasiliev, but her Russian was stilted as if she had learned it late in life.

The Prince did not deign to glance at his wife.

"My dear, you show remarkable deductive abilities."

The Princess fluttered her long eyelashes and her cheeks turned the color of dull rose.

"The Princess' observation is an interesting one, Your Excellency. It seems likely to me that sometime during the evening the Count and Countess were being watched rather closely. But one thing still puzzles me. Why did the killers wait until the Countess was alone before launching their attack? After all, they could have killed the Count quite easily earlier but did not even try. Was she their real target?"

"There are several possible explanations. They might have tried once before and failed. Their bombs might not have gone off. It has happened before."

"Quite right, and all the more reason why they might have relied on inside information to time their second attack. That is why I cannot rule out the possibility that the terrorists had a confederate among your guests or your servants." Vasiliev knew he had to speed up this part to forestall an interruption. "Remember that the terrorists are very skilled at this sort of thing. They penetrated the Winter Palace itself. One of their top people named Khalturin, disguised as a worker, smuggled himself into the basement and dynamited the imperial dining room."

"We know all this, Inspector, what is the point?"

"The point is that if they could penetrate the tsar's residence then they can penetrate anywhere."

"So you want a list of our guests and servants. How charming." The Prince flicked away an imaginary speck on his tunic.

"More than that, Your Excellency, I would like your help in clearing up several obscure points about the events during that tragic evening. I would like to know, if you will indulge me, whether you saw anyone being particularly attentive to the Countess."

"I don't understand your obsession with the Countess. The question is irrelevant. It was the Count they were trying to kill." Vasiliev caught the change in Bagration's tone, a rising note of impatience.

"That is the official position, and as I have said there are problems with it. I have to consider other possibilities. Nothing is really irrelevant in the early stages of investigating a murder."

"A murder?" The Princess faltered."Surely you mean…"

"Astounding!" the Prince interrupted. "This is too much. Perhaps you would like to search the house?" The Prince moved for the first time since Vasiliev had entered the room, spreading his arms wide as if to embrace everything he possessed.

"I did not mean to offend you," Vasiliev said. "Only the express wishes of His Majesty in this case forces me…."

"Ah, the Emperor, our tsar liberator," cried the Prince, ignoring his wife's movement on the divan. "Hunted like a wild animal in his own country. God spare him, but you know, Inspector, he really has brought this on himself. The sixties were bad enough. Now it's even worse. Most of us warned him against the emancipation, taking away half the nobles' land and turning it over to the peasants. Short of a revolution it's never been done before in history. Do you realize that? Even the Americans with their crazy egalitarian ideals did not give the slaves land when they freed them, and that was four years after we had freed our serfs with land! After, I repeat, Inspector, after! Then our emperor had to set up the local government boards where we have to rub shoulders with the rabble. Oh, I don't mean the peasants. No, at least they still know their place. But the merchants and riff raff from the towns, puffed out with their own importance. God, you should see they way they arrive for the sessions, overdressed, overfed, letting their mouths run on with so much drivel. And the school teachers, they are the worst, every one of them a nihilist, preaching their watered down socialist rubbish, priests' sons, most of them, who don't know how to wipe their noses properly."

Vasiliev stood with his hands clasped behind his back, giving his best imitation of the respectful listener while the Princess lay motionless, her eyes shut and her features composed like a death mask.

"Now he's shoving Loris-Melikov down our throats. Man can't even talk a proper Russian, spits and froths like a Yid. Planning a constitution, they say. Imagine a constitution for Holy Russia. Next thing you'll see a revolution with ink stained clerks and teachers running around chopping off heads.

"And to top it off, yes, the final insult of our anointed of God is to drag that damn Dolgorukaya woman into the palace. Scandalous, ruinous! The Empress was still alive when he installed her there. Did you know that? Then he married her while poor Maria Alexandrovna was hardly cold in her grave. What kind of a man is this? I can tell you that even his son despises this so-called Princess Yurovskaya. What an absurd name. It means nothing in Russian history. At least Dolgorukaya has or had some distinction before she dragged that illustrious name in the mud. Did you know she dabbles in railroads? Yes, she's nothing but a common speculator. Her friends are unsavory as well. They are selling Russia, piece by piece."

The Prince had seized the mantle piece with both hands as if he were about to tear it from the wall. A moan escaped his wife's tightly compressed lips. The Prince jerked his head to look at her, and suddenly fell silent. Had she brought him back to his senses? He stared at his hands, slowly relaxing his grip. Vasiliev was gazing out the windows at the thickening snowfall.

"So the Emperor commands you. All right, you shall have the lists. I suppose you will want to know that one of our servants has taken a leave to return to his home in Georgia, our beloved major domo. As for those dancing attendance on Countess Ushakova, it would be hard to say who was most attentive. Men swarmed around her like bees hunting sweet nectar."

The Princess opened her eyes and threw her husband one of her imploring looks. Vasiliev was getting to know the repertoire.

"Yes, she had a fascinating way about her," he added. "One of Dolgorukaya's little gang. Does that surprise you? She liked to sparkle at court, and also to dabble in railroad securities. But I've already told you that. Poor Ushakov, it embarrassed him. After all, a deputy minister."

"Was she always that way, I mean an intriguer?" Vasiliev decided he would swim with the current rather than be swept aside. But he was ready for the storm to break.

"How should I know?" Bagration growled, taking a step toward Vasiliev.

"But you were acquainted in Tiflis," said Vasiliev surprised to see the effect of his remark on the Princess where he had least expected it. She struggled to her feet, and for an instant Vasiliev thought she might collapse. He had not noticed before how tiny she was. Her upper lips trembled and the color drained from her face as she gripped the edge of a carved mahogany table for support. Vasiliev had to check himself from hurrying to her side.

"Inspector, we cannot keep you from your duties with our idle gossip." Her Georgian accent was now more pronounced. "Every minute must be precious. Please excuse me while I arrange for the list. It will take me only a few minutes to find the information you want."

Without extending her hand she glided past him, her jeweled slippers brushing the carpet like a caress, the only sound in the room.

The Prince waited until they could no longer hear her retreating steps and then whirled on Vasiliev.

"What prompted that remark?" The storm had indeed broken in his dark eyes.

"Nothing in particular, Your Excellency. Everything about Countess Ushakova interests me, her railroad speculations, her old ties, her present friends."

"I did not know the Countess when I served in the Caucasus."

"Ah, then you must excuse me again. But," Vasiliev added as he moved to leave, "you did know her husband then, I believe."

"Yes, a small man in every way. We served in the same chancellery under Grand Duke Mikhail Nikolaevich. Ushakov is another misguided reformer. He loves the peasants, at a distance. He will do anything to become minister and almost anything for a new decoration."

"It was generous of you to invite a political enemy as a guest."

"My wife takes pleasure in mixing breeds. Is that all Vasiliev, or do you wish to interrogate me further?"

"Did I seem to be interrogating you? How clumsy of me. You must forgive my impertinence."

A lackey crossed the threshold of the Georgian room holding a sheet of paper and murmuring a few words in Georgian to the Prince.

"My wife regrets that she is indisposed and cannot bid you adieu. You will understand how delicate the health of a southerner is in this frigid weather. This is a list of our guests that I myself prepared. You will see my wife made a few corrections. I fear this rather domestic product will have to serve."

Vasiliev folded the sheet without glancing at it, and slipped it into his tunic. Neither man said a word as they passed through the cluttered rooms. When they reached the central hall, Vasiliev wheeled to face the Prince.

"Just one more thing, Your Excellency. My army friends tell me you have a fine collection of trophies from your grandfather, General, Prince Peter Ivanovich. I'm something of a student of the campaign of 1812. I would very much like to see it, if I might, at your convenience, of course."

The Prince stood very still, the penetrating gaze back in place.

"You are very well informed about my life. Yes, there is a small 1812 room, but it contains only family mementos, nothing of interest for a connoisseur, Inspector."

Chapter
Seventeen

Vasiliev was unhappy about the summons from St. Petersburg. Knowing Ivan as he did, he interpreted the laconic message – "Your presence urgently required" — as a warning signal. Urgently required by whom? He distrusted the passive tense. He put Serov in charge of Bagration's list to distribute names to the detectives the chief had put at his disposal for routine tasks. He pulled out some files, dumped them in his English portmanteau that he had already packed with a few travel necessities. He ordered a first class compartment on the night express to the capital.

A fresh storm was raging over Moscow as if exacting revenge for the Indian summer when Vasiliev settled in his compartment. He was looking forward to a solitary ride over the six hundred kilometer track laid down straight as an arrow between Moscow and St. Petersburg. According to legend it had been built to specifications dictated by Tsar Nicholas I who had resolved a dispute among his engineers over the best right of way by applying a ruler to the map. There was little enough for which to thank Nicholas Pavlovich, Vasiliev reflected. But the slow passage of the train over the gentle gradient always produced in him the same feeling of detachment from the world. The snow muffled the sound of the wheels. Frost glazed the windows with abstract designs. Outside the drifts half buried the log cabins. Snow layered the long pine branches, reminding him of the long cotton sleeves of the sectarians.

He idly turned the pages of his files but found nothing of interest. As he expected Tarashkin's name did not appear on the guest list, but neither did Irina's. It bothered him that the major domo had left Moscow. On leave, a major domo? Unlikely. He would know all the secrets of the house. He'd been a servant in the Dadian household before the Princess was born. Vasiliev wondered if his old friends in the Tiflis force would be able to track him down. The evidence seemed to be scattered all over the Russian empire.

And why he asked himself, had the Prince really invited the Ushakovs? Why had they accepted? It seemed strange that the Count had left his wife in the house of an old rival and driven home by himself after he had been a witness to their flight upstairs. And what had Tarashkin-Magician been up to other than embarrassing the Countess? He too had disappeared after the Sword Dance. It came down to the three men, didn't it, Tarashkin, the Prince and, yes, even the Count. The Prince, mercurial, a former suitor, still involved in some way with her and the last person to be seen with her. The Count was politically embarrassed by her death and had brought him into the case. But now he was playing a cautious hand and inviting Nasya into his bed. Tarashkin, unstable, a raw youth Dostoevsky would call him, clearly obsessed by the Countess, but how close had they been? There were no clear motives but plenty of opportunities. Each man had access to the grenade, though he was pretty certain the Countess had been killed before the explosion. Where and how? He hadn't quite literally a clue. Of all the suspects in the world his were a couple of aristocrats and a revolutionary, not the easiest people in the world to deal with much less to investigate. He threw down the files and pulled out a volume of Pushkin's verse, always the best antidote to confusion, he kept reminding himself. Just before he fell asleep the thought came to him that what awaited him in Piter would just complicate matters further.

Early the next morning the snow covered engine pulled into the Nikolaev Station in St. Petersburg. The wind had all but died. Only a few lonely flakes were circling the city. The Neva was frozen solid except for a narrow passage kept open by cutters breaking through from the Gulf of Finland to the foot of the Admiralty Wharf. In another week, Vasiliev reflected, they too would be immobilized by the ice. An army of peasant shovelers, struggling to keep the main thoroughfares clear, had erected pyramids of snow along the Embankment.

The police sleigh glided over the icy Nevsky Prospekt and passed under the arch of Palace Square. Vasiliev had been absent from the capital for six months and the changes astonished him.

The place looks like an armed camp, he said to himself. Guards were stationed everywhere, it seemed, even under the small canal bridges. Mounted detachments of Cossacks patrolled the front of government buildings; groups of soldiers huddled around bonfires in the vast squares. The Winter Palace itself was under heavy guard, Cossacks circling the perimeter at irregular intervals. Sentries from the Semenovsky Guards, shouldering standard army rifles loaded he later learned with live ammunition, were posted at the side and main gates. Before they reached their destination the sleigh was stopped three times and officers scrutinized Vasiliev's documents. The last checkpoint was a temporary guardhouse warmed by a pot-bellied iron stove. "Documents, please!" A few questions, a cursory wave of the hand. A sentry escorted him into the Palace. They encountered more armed guards.

A Guarded Small Canal Bridge, St. Petersburg

Ivan's secretary, grown old in service, admitted him. The office had been furnished for a middle rank bureaucrat: a desk covered with papers, a deal table and a few chairs. A full-length portrait of Alexander II in his coronation robes hung between curtained windows. Had Ivan been demoted? If so, Vasiliev concluded, then his case had suffered a comparable fate.

Ivan embraced him, poured two brandies — Vasiliev did not dare ask its venue — and raised his glass. "You see how we live now! To your success, *mon vieux*. And how is it going, your investigation?"

Vasiliev, sensing that Ivan was ill at ease again, wondered why he had this effect on people. "I thought we were through fencing, Ivan. What's happened? What's got you worried, why the urgency and the telegram in a passive voice? You know how that raises my hackles. Have I tread on anyone's toes?"

"Sorry, Vasili, I didn't mean to be coy. It's just that this damned case is so sensitive. All right, I'll be frank. We've had one complaint, nothing from our side, mind you, at least not...well...."

"You expected loud noises from the boys in blue, didn't you, and from trouble makers among the ministers? You were the one who warned me. Perhaps you didn't take your own warning to heart."

"Of course I expected trouble, but not from this source." Ivan seemed to have lost his touch again, or was his touch suitable only for courtiers? "There have been developments. I'm embarrassed to say that Ushakov seems to be annoyed. I don't know what's got into him, but we'll come to that in a moment."

"So what of it? Do my orders still stand, and the guarantee as well, no interference?"

"Now Vasili don't get your back up. The situation keeps changing in unexpected ways; that's all. We have to talk it out. There are things going on at many levels, you must understand that."

Vasiliev leaned back in his chair, sought salvation in the bottom of his brandy glass and waited. He would not make it easy for his old friend.

"The Gendarmes have achieved a major breakthrough. Now listen to what I am saying. They nabbed Mikhailov, you must have heard of him. He was a member of the Exec-Com of the People's Will, known as *dvornik*, the yardman, you know their jargon, because he controlled the entrances and exits, so to speak. A key person in the organization. The Gendarmes had a bit of luck, but that doesn't diminish their achievement. It was a big catch. Van der Fleet got the credit and Shuev struts like a cock of the walk, boasting that it was his men who brought it off."

"Did Mikhailov confess to the Ushakova killing?"

"No, but he didn't deny it either. I was at the interrogation. What he said was 'Such trash doesn't concern us.'"

"He's probably telling the truth."

"For God's sake, Vasili, suppose he is. That doesn't help us."

"You don't expect help from the terrorists do you, Ivan? If they know what's going on inside the government, and I think they do, then they'll play the same game with us as Van der Fleet wants to play with them, set one faction against the other, get us tearing at one another's throats."

"All right, I won't argue the point. But let me tell you what the Gendarmes are up to. They are using Mikhailov's testimony to revise their theories. They are very shrewd over there. What they are claiming now is that the terrorists' indifference to killing has corrupted the younger hot heads in the organization, those still in their teens, turned them into moral monsters. They say that the organization is beginning to split into small extremist groups which have lost all political sense. This is a new phenomenon. These kids are sworn enemies of the nobility and committed to indiscriminant killing. The Countess was the first victim of these mad dog attacks. It's an explanation that suits everybody. It even covers one of your objections, that this was the work of amateurs. Meanwhile the Gendarmes keep showing brilliant results..."

"...while I show none."

"I'm not blaming you, Vasili, it's just that it is going to be harder now to push ahead. There are strong pressures and some backtracking."

"By whom?"

"Aside from the Gendarmes who keep complaining about your playing a lone hand...."

"And who may have me under surveillance."

"What! Do you have proof, Vasili?"

"Right now, no, but that's because I haven't made a fuss. You see how well I am behaving myself? I've not dragged their agents out of the cabs trailing me. What a scandal that would create! And the Gendarmes would claim they were taking precautions to protect me after what has happened. No, to force proofs would play into their hands. The only possibility...tell me, Ivan, are you having me followed?"

"Good God, no. Really, Vasili, sometimes you are exasperating."

"If you were, I'm sure you would have your own good reasons. Strange times, these, and old loyalties get stretched to the breaking point. Self-protection is a powerful instinct," Vasiliev spoke so softly Ivan could hardly hear him.

Ivan bit his lip and said nothing. There was a long pause.

"Who else is complaining?"

"Besides the Gendarmes, there is Bagration."

"Already! Understandable enough, but I thought he was in bad odor here."

"You forget he is on intimate terms with the heir, Alexander Alexandrovich. They knew one another as boys, had the same tutor and all that. Bagration even stays with him at the Anichkov Palace when he is in the capital."

"That explains a lot. But it's your problem to deal with the political complications and mine to follow the leads wherever they go."

"You may have been a little rough with the Prince."

"I was almost servile."

Ivan could not imagine that, but let it pass. "Worst of all," he went on, "Ushakov is having second thoughts."

"Again? That was a quick change of heart."

"The mad dog explanation appeals to him. It means the terrorists did not single him out, so he saves his political reputation. It was not *une crime de passion* so he saves his personal reputation. I told you the Gendarmes were shrewd."

"Is that all he is worried about?"

"Well, he mentioned that his servants were shaken up a bit."

"Only one of them?"

"Listen, Vasili...."

"That's all I've been doing."

"Please, you have to put the case in a larger perspective. Loris-Melikov needs Ushakov's expertise, his financial skills, his willingness to supervise the Gendarmes. The Count is also preparing a labor reform to go with the other changes. The reactionaries, Katkov and Company, are fighting him inside and outside the government. They gain strength every day. So you see how other issues assume equal or even greater importance right now."

"So everyone has lost interest in the case."

"What are you saying, Vasili?"

"It's a fair observation. You remember, Ivan, how I saw this coming. First the fate of the empire is dumped in my hands, then poof! It's out of my hands. That's why I was so stubborn, so reluctant to take the case when we talked in Nizhnyi. Now, to be fair, are you pulling me off the case?"

Ivan had given a great deal of thought as to how he would answer this question. He knew that it might not be possible to order Vasiliev off the case without weakening his own position. He could not drop him now without looking foolish. Besides, the wheel might turn again, and it might be useful to know, if not to make public, who had killed Ushakova. There was also the chance that Vasiliev had invested too much of himself in the case to give it up no matter what he was told to do. Ivan knew him well enough to realize that. So there was the danger of cutting him loose from all restraints.

"Absolutely not, Vasili. You may think I've become an opportunist, but I'm not going to sell you out. No, it's a matter of being more discreet. You really don't suspect Ushakov of murdering his wife do you? So why offend his servants? Must you pursue Bagration so openly? We chose you for your discretion."

"Tell me about Ushakov. Did you speak to him personally? What exactly did he say?"

"He was very polite, asked whether you could go easier on his staff. They were upset by your questions about the Countess."

Vasiliev swallowed the rest of his brandy and smiled across the deal table, calculating how deceitfully discreet he could be, if that was the price he had to pay. He would begin with Ivan.

"I see your point, Ivan. Perhaps I was pressing too hard in the interests of time. Actually to answer the first question you asked me today; the investigation is going better than I had hoped at this stage. I have three good suspects and will be closing in on one of them very soon." Vasiliev smiled his crooked smile and watched the frown fade from Ivan's brow. "Of course, this means I will have to follow some irregular procedures."

"Fine, fine, just don't confide them to me. You realize that you are in an exposed position?"

"That was clear from the beginning. But I need to see Ushakov again. I thought he promised not to interfere.Or did you misunderstand him? No matter. Now I have to deal with the mad dog hypothesis. What next? Ivan, do I get to see Ushakov as a reward for my good behavior?"

"I'm certain I can arrange it in a day or two."

Vasiliev could tell that Ivan had already made the arrangements on the assumption that the interview would turn out as he planned. But there was no sense scoring points at this stage, after all, discretion was the watchword.

Chapter
Eighteen

There were fewer guards outside the Ministry of Interior than at the Winter Palace, but they spent more time scrutinizing his documents as if they had been trained to uncover counterfeiters rather than terrorists. Ushakov's office was nestled within the deeper recesses of the building. There were the now familiar check-points to be passed. Vasiliev entered a narrow anteroom. The Count's private secretary was standing in front of a padded leather door. He clicked his heels and ushered Vasiliev into the inner sanctum. Vasiliev concluded that he was back in favor from the fact that he had not been required to cool his heels in the anteroom. At least his probation was over.

Ushakov's office was in the form of a large cube of what looked like mathematically precise proportions. On three sides the walls were lined with bookshelves, always a good sign in Vasiliev's eyes. They were crammed with leather bound statistical handbooks, commercial codes and official reports uniformly bound in red morocco, each volume stamped in gold with the armorial crest of the family. The fourth side was draped in velvet. In the center of the folds hung an antique Tibetan banner portraying a tantric god with many arms clutching flaming swords, scepters and maces; his three faces colored red, blue and green looked left, right and straight ahead; he wore a necklace of skulls that reached down to his ample paunch. Vasiliev thought he looked angry. He drew close enough to read the inscription engraved in Russian and Chinese on a brass plate. The banner was a gift from the Chinese Emperor. Hadn't Ushakov helped negotiate the Treaty of Aigun that delimited the borders between the Russian and Celestial Empires? A man of many parts.

Vasiliev detected a peculiar odor in the room, of Russian mahogany mingled with dried out leather bindings and incense. The Count peered at Vasiliev from behind a mountain of papers stacked like barbicans on top of a long desk.

"*Entrez. entrez, monsieur l'inspecteur! Avez-vous fait un bon voyage?*" The Count rose from his seat. "*Vous me pardonnerez...*,"he gestured at the papers and waved Vasiliev into a seat some distance from the desk. Always the obligatory opening in French, Vasiliev mused. What a quaint custom; no one else practices it except for the Ottoman court and, of course, in Paris.

"Was my invitation unexpected?" the Count switched into Russian. "Let me tell you why I waited until now to meet you. I wanted you to conduct your preliminary investigation free of pressure or bias on my part. Now that you have done this, I can take pleasure in making my position clear. Intermediaries, even ambassadors, do not always convey nuances. Don't you agree? I began to realize that you must find yourself in an unusual, one might say unique situation. Isn't that so? I am partially to blame. Cigarette Inspector? Turkish tobacco blended in England..."

"No thank you, Your Excellency." Vasiliev wondered why the Count was so expansive.

"Never acquired the habit, not even on the Grand Duke's Staff? I thought an after dinner smoke was *de rigueur* in his company. Well, no matter. I am speaking to you man to man, not as a minister and intimate of His Imperial Majesty, you understand. I referred just now to your awkward position. What I meant is that you cannot interrogate all the principals as though we were suspects, eh? It's not like the murder of an old seamstress, is it? Discretion, you are the soul of discretion, they say, and this requires you to take what I believe you military men call the indirect approach. Clausewitz, isn't it? You see, Inspector, I am not just an animated statistical table." The Count smiled and lit another cigarette, blowing smoke toward the tantric god who looked back angrily. "Of course," the count went on, "the phrase is only a metaphor, and we are not at war are we?"

"When it is a question of the enemies of His Majesty, it amounts to the same thing. Besides, Clausewitz also said 'war is the continuation of politics by other means', so he ended up blurring the differences." Vasiliev wondered what the Countess had found attractive in this man. Then again with Bagration as the alternative, perhaps she had little choice. There was his high rank, the promise of an even higher one.

Ushakov had reached the conclusion that perhaps Vasiliev was not quite so discreet as his reputation. Undoubtedly intelligent but a bit prickly. He would have to draw him out and set him straight.

"Perhaps, but we men of peace are bound to lose everything if we declare war. Yes, you quote Clausewitz rightly, but I interpret him differently, more in a moderate spirit. I am a diplomat, and I do not like these different means, they can get out of control so easily. To fight is to acknowledge the failure of the civilized response. I hate the expression to fight fire with fire. We cannot become like our enemies in order to defeat them. Let the Gendarmes pursue their tactics. They have their uses but they are not builders like we are. Are you a builder, Inspector?"

Vasiliev gave a non-committal shrug. He did not think he was supposed to give an answer, just sit and listen. Perhaps he would hear something worth the visit. Perhaps not.

"Builders are obliged to make compromises, to take into account the nature of the terrain and the materials at hand. They are not like architects who dream of perfect order in abstract space, people like revolutionaries and policemen—yourself excepted of course. You understand the difference; we builders find allies among artisans who place brick upon brick. In the end we have completed a structure, not perfect in every detail, but one in which people can live decent lives."

The Count stubbed out his cigarette and reached for another.

"Let me be frank with you, Inspector. There was a time in this... case," he pronounced the word as if it were distasteful, "when I was prepared to sacrifice my reputation, accept scandal, all for the good of the state, so that the structure would remain sound. But that is no longer necessary. I am happy to give up my heroic role; it never suited me in the first place."

Vasiliev was tempted to remind the Count that smoke was bad for morocco bindings, but he repressed the impulse.

"The Gendarmes may be relied on to carry out certain tasks, though they are not builders. Did you know that they arrested Mikhailov, an enterprising young man. He would have made an excellent investigator like you, intelligent, even imaginative. But he wanted to be an architect. That is almost always fatal unless you are in authority and even then it can lead to tragedy. Look at Napoleon. The little corporal was a contemporary of Clausewitz, wasn't he, but I'm not sure he ever read him. A pity. But back to Mikhailov. It turns out he is a master of the well-rounded phrase. Referring to my wife he said, 'such trash doesn't concern us.' A real swine, you see, but an honest swine, yes, honest. He is telling us that the terrorists had no rational plan to assassinate my wife or me—I believe we can safely conclude that Mikhailov would place me in the category of trash—yet he does not deny that his organization had something to do with her death. You were absolutely right. Up to a point, that is. He accepts moral responsibility for the act. Perhaps he is even a high-minded swine, if you can accept the paradox. But he did not agree to confess to the crime. What are we to conclude? That undisciplined elements within the People's Will launched an attack without authorization. The executive committee—the Ex Com as they like to call themselves—of which Mikhailov is a prominent member does not disown these random acts, but it refuses to justify them. A nice distinction, don't you think? Under these circumstances it was irrelevant whether I was in the carriage or not. A mad dog does not discriminate among his victims."

Vasiliev understood why the Count had been entrusted with the Aigun negotiations. He was very good, much better than Ivan in laying out the revised official policy. But perhaps the Chinese had not grasped the implications of chain-smoking. The Count was ill at ease, Vasiliev concluded, even nervous. Except for the incessant smoking he concealed it well enough.

"Now we come to you, Inspector, or rather to the question of whether you are a builder or an architect, a practical man who wishes to leave behind a lasting monument or a dreamer who spins castles in the air."

"Do I assume, Your Excellency, by castles in the air you mean the pursuit of Truth and Justice with capital letters, just in case my inflexion is weak."

"That was unworthy of you, Vasiliev. You see now why I prefer metaphors, they reduce the chance of arousing primitive emotions."

"Let me be frank in turn, Count. You have found a logical explanation that enables you to put this tragedy behind you and move on to your main order of business which is to reform Russia. Logic may be a convenient substitute for truth, and frequently is in criminal cases, in trials and sentencing. But I am faced with a different problem. I have evidence that has to be explained, or explained away. Like you I need a logical explanation, but one that fits the evidence. It may not be a truthful or a just explanation, but by training and instinct I need it, you understand."

The Count began to wonder whether he had not underestimated Vasiliev. Then he remembered that the Inspector had also negotiated with Orientals. The Turks were less subtle than the Chinese but they too looked to save face. And Vasiliev had outwitted Strafford de Redcliff, no mean opponent. Ushakov placed the tips of his fingers together. He might have enjoyed this duel, he reflected, if there wasn't so much at stake.

"How can I help you build a logical but realistic explanation?"

"I would like to take you back to that terrible night, painful as it must be. As luck would have it, I have been able to interview a number of those present, not all of them guests. Their testimony when pieced together adds up to a complicated set of personal dramas. There were several illegals attending the ball...;" had the master diplomat blinked?

"...and some kind of intrigue involving the Prince and, I suspect your wife, but I still have too little evidence to unravel it."

Vasiliev had to admire the Count's self-control, but he saw signs of growing agitation. The chain smoking increased in tempo.

"However, I believe, Your Excellency, that you witnessed an incident that might shed light on this intrigue. Someone saw you at the time and noticed that you appeared to be very upset."

"Inspector, you are treading on dangerous ground that has nothing to do with this case but involves my personal affairs."

"Rest easy, Your Excellency, nothing I have said eliminates the possibility that the killing was done by one of the illegals for reasons I do not yet know. But here is where I need your help. If you could give me a full account of what you saw and heard that night, I could fill in some of the blank spaces. I have enough other witnesses to verify some of what you can tell me. Of course, you cannot know what part of your story I can confirm."

"You are blackmailing me, Inspector."

"Your Excellency! Nothing is further from my mind, but I cannot make the case without your testimony. In the event of a trial it must conform to the other facts that I will present to the court."

Ushakov glanced down at the gray ash at his fingertips, felt for another cigarette in his breast pocket, and then let his hand drop to his side.

"I have the testimony of General Shuev, the Bagrations, several hussar officers...." Vasiliev let his voice trail off apparently absorbed in drawing imaginary arabesques with his fingers on the arm of his chair.

"So, this version of yours is composed of guesses, nothing more than a few disconnected facts tied together with speculative flights."

"Guesses, Your Excellency? Why, I suppose you are right. But there are guesses and guesses. Have you ever heard of a young American called Charles Peirce? No? Of course, he is not famous, yet, but I guarantee that he will be some day."

"Is this one of your mystery witnesses, Inspector, I can tell you that no one by that name.,"

Vasiliev smiled his crooked smile. "Oh no, Peirce is a philosopher who has never been in Russia. I met him in London last year. Quite an interesting mind. He has a theory about guessing. He told me a fascinating story of how he had tested it in a little affair that came his way in his own country. I shall not bore you with the details. It was a matter of Peirce using his methods to expose the criminal in a petty theft. The lesson he drew from it confirmed what I have believed for a long time. You see, he and I were discussing proofs in philosophy, history and detection, and we agreed that the mere accumulation of facts about an occurrence will certainly not lead to an understanding of how and why it happened. Too many facts, irrelevant in a sequence of important, we may say causal events, confuses rather than enlightens the investigator. Peirce spoke of inspired guessing, or musing, as he called it, as a means of linking the unusual or surprising fact into a hypothesis and then testing it. But the key to his theory is the notion that while there are a great many possible explanations of a random accumulation of facts, the mind, or the trained mind, seeks to organize them according to nature's pattern. The mind is predisposed to guess correctly about the way things really are. So guessing for Peirce—and for me—is not blind. He made another point I never thought of. Upon reflection I believe it to be equally true. When we trained observers guess, we are often drawing conclusions from something we have seen or heard but cannot specify. In this respect our mind is acting just below the level of consciousness, you follow me? We react like a bird in flight, wheeling, diving with great precision and snaring its prey. The bird does not reason but acts on an imitation of the real. This is something different from instinct. Well, perhaps this is getting too philosophical."

Vasiliev had pressed the tips of his fingers together in imitation of the Count. He wondered when the Count would realize that he was being toyed with.

"Peirce and I had a delightful time comparing the methods of fictional detectives, Poe's Dupin and Gaboriau's Lecoq. Have you read Gaboriau? Well, not in your field. Both of them firmly believed in what Poe called ratiocination, or some might say the science of deduction. But the point is that it really is not a science—no laws, no experiments that can be repeated, in many cases no objective reality, just opinion or impressions. No one is denying the role of precise observation and measurement, even chemical analysis. Without these I could not have reconstructed the nature of the bomb and the effects of the blast that killed your wife and your coachman. But once that has been done, then the real mental work begins."

The Count was staring at him, his lips parted. Vasiliev intercepted his glance at a carafe of water on the desk, a brief struggle with temptation, then submission to caution. At all costs, Vasiliev thought, the diplomat must not show any signs of uneasiness; dryness in the throat is a dead give-away.

"Now you must realize that my guesses are something more than wild speculation as you put it. They have taken me to a precise point. The evening of the murder you were overcome by what you saw on the staircase of Bagration's mansion. I guess it had something to do with the Prince and your wife. We must remember that she was last seen with him. It seems that they left the ballroom during the Terek sword dance, and you may have caught a glimpse of them. Were you surprised? Shocked? Did you see it as a betrayal of some sort? You see I am guided by what I already know of the relations among the three of you going back to your days in Tiflis."

Vasiliev had observed many people under the strain of interrogation. It seemed to him that Ushakov he had almost reached the point of crisis. Either he would burst out in anger, or cave in. Vasiliev decided to play his trump.

"Let's return to our illegals. They may hold the key to all this. Did you recognize Tarashkin at the ball?" Ushakov appeared to relax at the change of subject. Good, thought Vasiliev, my little verbal bomb is going to demolish him.

"Good heavens! Was he there?"

"Yes, please tell me, what were your relations?"

"He was the local priest's son, on my estates in the countryside, a bright young man. Elena and I took an interest in him. We treated him like one of the family, taught him manners. But like so many young people today he thought he could change the world."

"In short he aspired to be an architect."

Ushakov smiled wanly. "You could say that."

"How far did he go in that direction? Nihilism? Terrorism?"

"I don't think…." Ushakov paused as if he had sensed an opening. "I don't know, one can't be sure of what goes on in the heads of these young people."

"Would he have been capable of taking revenge against you for some insult, real or imagined?"

"Perhaps," the Count mused. "Yes, it's quite possible. Once I tried to straighten him out, you know one of those classic fathers and sons conversations. He reacted quite strongly, actually denounced me as a relic of the 1840's. Of course, I took it as a compliment. But he was very angry, said I was patronizing him."

Ushakov reminded himself that it was Vasiliev who was sitting across the desk from him. I mustn't jump too quickly, he thought. Let it come out naturally as though the meaning of it all has just dawned on me.

"There were more scenes, and the upshot was that I forbade

him to come to the house, cut him off. I imagine he was bitter about it. He was an impulsive young man."

"And your wife snubbed him at the ball when he tried to embarrass her into acknowledging him."

"Really, I hadn't noticed. That would be just like Elena. You may be on to something, Inspector. It hadn't occurred to me before. I'm not a psychologist after all, but now that you take me back over the years I can see a pattern of violence developing."

"I wonder how he wormed his way into the Bagration's," Vasiliev murmured as if to himself.

"Wait a minute, Inspector. This is really quite extraordinary! I think your lesson in method has inspired me. My coachman, Arkady, told me a curious story when he drove me home. Of course, that must be it. Arkady had run into a figure in black scurrying along in the back corridor of the Prince's place. He thought it was a house demon. You know how superstitious the peasants can be, even the most intelligent like Arkady. But suppose it was Tarashkin in a dress suit."

"He managed to slip through a rear entrance or an open window."

"Yes, more like a window, for the rear entrance leads directly to the kitchen where the coachmen were warming themselves. But that means he must have had an accomplice in the household."

Vasiliev had not seen Ushakov so animated since he entered the office. Vasiliev decided to strike. Now that they were working together and not at cross-purposes the Count was vulnerable.

"And the girl with Shuev?"

"Eh?"

"Who was the girl with Shuev?"

"Oh, the Davidova girl, Irish...Irina Borisovna, she...;" Ushakov hesitated an instant. Surely there was no harm in telling Vasiliev the rest. "A charming young lady."

"Irina Borisovna Davidova, her father Colonel Davidov the highly decorated officer?"

"Yes, do you know him?"

"My dear Count!"

"What is it, Inspector?"

"How well do you know her?"

"Since childhood, but...."

"Have you been in touch with the family lately?"

"No, they've been living in Como, it seems."

"Como, yes. I knew them well. Her brother was my boyhood friend. He was killed in the war. But Irina, my dear Count! Did Shuev really pursue her? More important were you seen with her?"

"There was no question of pursuit, Inspector."

"Did she question you about politics?"

"Why yes, as a matter of fact, she seemed well informed. But I don't understand."

"She is a nihilist, Count, an illegal, member of the Repartition of the Land Party."

"Impossible! Why she...she was the one who recommended you. She called you 'the best detective in the empire.' She doesn't sound like a nihilist to me."

"That fits. She was Tarashkin's comrade. They belonged to the same organization. I wonder if she was also his accomplice?"

"I must ask you to explain."

"Count, this changes everything, a serious matter. I had no idea. It would not do to have it known that you and the headmaster were consorting with an illegal on the night your wife's death was organized. Let me think. Few people have heard about her break with the family. Her father has hushed it up. Besides she moves in the underground with an alias. Still if word got out...very damaging."

Ushakov pushed himself out of his chair, leaning on the desk, only to fall back as if his legs had given way. Vasiliev arranged his features into an expression of grave concern.

"Do you wish me to ring for your secretary?"

The Count shook his head. Vasiliev fixed his eyes on the head of the Tibetan god. Did he seem less angry? Perhaps just annoyed. It would be easy now to get the rest of the story out of Ushakov, he thought. And he would have no further trouble from him. But he did not feel like gloating. His triumph had been won at the heavy cost of betraying Irina.

Chapter Nineteen

Deep snow had slowed his pace, but Vasiliev figured he could still reach Osholovo before the solstice. He knew the inner clock of the countryside. You could not simply show up in a small village in provincial Russia and expect the peasants to accept you for what you claimed to be. Rumors would have to precede you. He hoped they had reached this village: an itinerant peddler headed in your direction, might show up in a few days. Let them get accustomed to his presence before he appeared. If he rushed in no one would trust him. Even so, to travel in this weather could raise eyebrows. More worrisome, the villagers might think he was crazy. It would have been better to have waited until spring. But he knew he couldn't delay any longer. He felt sure the solstice would provide a key to the puzzle. The blizzard had passed to the north. An early thaw was setting in, but no telling how long it would last.

He came into the village at dusk as he had planned. It had been hard going all day and he was exhausted. The cabins were scattered at random on both sides of a wide track of cleared land churned into a sea of mud by peasant carts and melting snow. On the outskirts several cabins had been burned down by *krasnyi petykh*, the red cock, the worst calamity that could befall a peasant household, a flash fire ignited by a toppled candle, a half-extinguished match or outright arson. He noticed there were no chimneys to be seen, a sure sign that these were all so-called black cabins where the smoke from stoves could only escape through the door and the atmosphere inside was suffocating. He saw too that many cabins were tipped to one side, as if the earth were intent on swallowing them up. The shutters and door-frames were plain, no wood carvers in this village. A layer of wheat sheaves and dung was tightly packed around the outer walls right up to the lower edge of the window sash. Wattle fences were mostly in disrepair or had completely collapsed. Mud spattered hens picked at the puddles of melting snow in what seemed like a hopeless search for a few grains of oats. He saw no signs of horses, and he knew that whatever goats and pigs the peasants owned were inside the cabins sharing quarters with the family. He compared it to his mother's village, with its gaily painted wood carvings decorating the facades. Her *izba* was a white cabin with a chimney and red windows with panes of green glass and an annex with a Dutch stove, the lap of luxury compared with this miserable place. When he thought of the Bagration house, with its formal French rooms and the Georgian folly, he felt the familiar anger of a peasant's son, a sense of helplessness and even a spark of sympathy with the Repartition of the Land.

He walked past the first group of cabins. There was no one in sight. The sun had touched the horizon, casting a few shadows from isolated trees onto the central track. He kept moving until he came abreast of a cabin that looked more solidly built. It was standing upright. The roof and fence were in good repair. He shifted the pack of iron pots to his right shoulder, pushed back his fur cap and lifted an earflap to scratch his head. A peddler in winter was a rare sight, but he hadn't been able to come up with a better idea. He had played the part before. He looked around and waited. It must have been five or ten minutes before the door to the cabin opened a crack, then swung wider revealing a tall peasant wearing a black woolen cap. Vasiliev chose not to notice him for a time, then glanced over and raised his hand in greeting. The other made no sign. Vasiliev hitched the pack higher on his back and the pots rattled. The peasant coughed and spat, his mouth opening like a dark hole.

"Good day, brother," he said at last.

Vasiliev saluted him again. "Good day to you, brother. I seek the elder. Can you show me the way?"

"He is here, brother. God has led you to him."

As soon as Vasiliev crossed the threshold an acrid smell of animals, cabbage and human waste assailed his nostrils. He had forgotten how pungent the odors could be. Geese cackled in the

The Elder's Hut, Osholovo District

corner. In the gloom he could make out the irregular shape of the stove, and long wooden benches around the walls. A tallow candle burned in the icon corner. Vasiliev bowed in that direction, crossing himself before he let the pack slip to the ground. Three women huddled together around another candle; their heads bent low over their sewing.

"There's little to be gained by selling in this village," said the elder as they crouched by the samovar. The tea smelled of fish and the sugar had been nibbled by mice.

"Aye, it's a harsh life", Vasiliev replied.

There was a long pause punctuated by the sound of the old man lapping up tea from the saucer. Vasiliev asked whether it was far to the next village.

"Too far to get there before sundown. It's not good to stray in these parts at night."

"Wolves, hungry are they this year?"

One of the women looked up for her needlework, but no one replied. Vasiliev could not tell how long they all sat together breathing the fetid air. His head was beginning to throb, his eyes closing.

Suddenly the door was flung open with great force and two figures staggered into the cabin, one supporting the other who groaned in pain before collapsing on the earthen floor. The older woman shuffled over and muttered something Vasiliev could not hear, then louder, "Marya, hot water."

The women bustled around the fallen figure, while the other man slumped down on the bench, breathing heavily. The woman called Marya was carrying a steaming earthenware jug into which she dipped a rag and at moment later Vasiliev was shaken by an agonized scream.

"Hold his arms, for the love of the Mother of God."

Without a thought, Vasiliev seized one of the flailing arms.

"What happened?" the elder spoke from his place near the stove.

"A fight," answered the man from the bench, slowly getting to his feet. He stumbled out the door and a minute later Vasiliev heard him working the pump.

The elder stoked the fire and the smell of cabbage grew stronger. Vasiliev picked up his *tulup*. He had bought the bulky sheepskin coat, the front faced with dirty yellow leather, at a bazaar in Moscow. He tossed it over the injured man. He sat down on the bench and folded his arms. A wooden bowl was set in front of him and he heard the elder mumble a blessing. He dipped a crust of dried black bread into the thin soup before gulping it down.

The elder signaled Vasiliev to take a place on the stove. Vasiliev shook his head and nodded to the man on the ground. He dragged his pack to the bench, heaved it up beside him and stretched out using it to pillow his head. The elder grunted something unintelligible which Vasiliev interpreted as thanks, while the older woman bowed to the icon and muttered her prayers.

Vasiliev fell into a troubled sleep with the moaning of the injured man in his ears. During the night he was awakened by a light touch on his shoulder. He could barely make out the figure of the younger woman, Marya wasn't it, kneeling beside him. He heard her breath rattle in her throat.

"May I touch them?"

Vasiliev raised his head and quietly untied his pack. She was only a slip of a girl, trembling in her coarse linen gray shift. She slid her hand inside and rummaged around for a minute. Vasiliev could not see the expression on her face, but he felt the warm tears fall on his hand.

In the morning there was only strong tea and moldy bread dipped in water to soften it. The man on the stove was still groaning.

"Does it hurt badly?" Vasiliev placed his hand on the man's forehead. He was feverish and his eyes were fluttering. "I've some training in these things. I can help." Vasiliev had turned to the elder, but it was the young girl who nodded vigorously and stroked her mother-in-law's arm. The old woman squinted at Vasiliev.

"He's in a bad way," Vasiliev insisted. She nodded.

Vasiliev asked for the candle. He examined the cuts across the man's forearms, defensive wounds, and on the abdomen, gashes on the side of his head and cheek. "Boiling water, auntie, and boil some cloths in another pot. Here use this," Vasiliev began ripping up his only clean shirt. He worked rapidly cauterizing and dressing the wounds. With his back to them, he was able to apply tincture of iodine from his pack. He should have done it right away. But he had sensed the need to wait. With the help of the elder and the other son he was able to stitch up the gashes by the light of a wood splinter. He wiped his brow and said to the elder. "I'd be taking his place for a day or two, if you'll let me stay and rest. I've had no luck selling and need some nourishment."

"You're not a sorcerer are you?" the old woman croaked.

"Nay, this they taught me in the war."

"The war, aye, my oldest never came back," she answered crossing herself.

"God's will," said the elder.

The elder took Vasiliev's internal passport off to the bailiff who pronounced himself satisfied with the new *batrak*, a hired hand, now employed to help cut timber in a remote corner of Count Ushakov's estate in the Semenov district of Nizhegorod Province.

Every day at dawn Vasiliev accompanied the older brother and a gang of peasants from the village to the cutting area. It was three versts distance. Vasiliev thought he was in good condition, but this was back breaking work. At the end of the day his hands were bloody. He fell asleep right after consuming the soup and bread that passed for supper. Without his hidden supply of sugar rations, he could not have kept up. How the peasants fed on thin soup and dried bread could stand the pace was a mystery to him, even though he came from the same stock.

The thaw ended and the ground froze. Snow fell and they had to build sledges to pull logs to the edge of an ice-covered tributary of the Volga. There the timber would lie there for four months until the stream thawed and it could be floated down to the mill. Whenever Vasiliev wandered away from the teams of cutters, the older brother warned him of danger from the sorcerers. When pressed he would say no more about them. The clipping from *Golos* in Vasiliev's file was never far from his mind.

Near dusk at the end of a brilliant cloudless day Vasiliev was alone, trimming a majestic pine his team had just felled. He heard the low whistle of a quail from the heavy undergrowth in a ravine short distance away. He continued to chop rhythmically for a few minutes, looked around, stretched and drove his ax into the fallen tree. He moved down the slope into the brambles without being seen. In the shadow of a blasted oak he spotted the familiar figure of Borka squatting next to his bitch hound.

Vasiliev's question followed a quick handshake. "The student?"

"At the Ushakov estate. They are hiding him in the servant's quarters."

"The servants?"

"Khlysty."

"Any visitors?"

"No one, but he waits."

"What do you know of the sorcerers?"

"Jumpers, they will soon be active."

"I may need help."

Borka moved to the stump and showed Vasiliev where to conceal a message. Vasiliev nodded. They agreed that in an emergency he would fire three shots from his service revolver. He patted the hound. Borka melted into the woods.

Sunday morning Vasiliev attended the village church. After the service he asked to accompany the priest home. The cabin had been well-built with wood carvings on the eaves and window frames. But signs of neglect were obvious to Vasiliev. The priest too had seen better days. The worn cassock covered a large but sagging frame, much like the village *izbas*. There were traces of spirituality in his face, but the eyes had dimmed. The spark had been extinguished.

"Humbly beggin' your pardon, little Father, I'll be needin' a letter to my kin. My mother, now she'll be frettin'. She's not had a word for a great age. Here, I've managed to scratch out a few lines as best I could."

"You have been taught your letters well." The priest coughed as he corrected the grammar and orthography.

"Yea, Father, a good man like yourself gave me a little learnin', but he hadn't as many books as you." Vasiliev ran his fingers over the worn bindings on a shelf over the priests cot.

"K-a-r-a-m-z-i-n," he spelled out. "Aye that was his favorite too, after the holy books."

The priest looked wearily at Vasiliev but did not ask him to go. "Would you like some tea, my son?"

"Aye, Father that would be good, for I've been fastin' since yesterday."

"Have you read Karamzin?" asked the priest as he stirred boiling water into the *zavarka*. Vasiliev thank him, turned to the icon and crossed himself.

"Ah, no Father. It's beyond me, but I enjoying having parts read to me, about the Troubles and how Russia was saved. But they did teach me to cipher in the army, during the war."

The priest gave a start and coughed into his handkerchief. Vasiliev saw spots of blood. "Did you fight the Turks, my son?"

"Aye, Father, and strange it is you should ask. A lad from these parts was with us, a real gentleman he was, a reader like yourself, a student he said, but he was writin' all the time."

"A clerk, then?"

"Aye, that's what they called him. He was with us rough fellows in the rank and file. Must have been a political. But he said nothing of that."

Vasiliev avoided the priest's gaze and waited. The old man seemed to withdraw into himself as if pondering whether to let the subject die or not. The house was silent except for the scratching of mice under the floor boards.

"There were not many like the one you speak of from the nearby villages," he said finally.

"We called him Iuri, a stout lad with that thick yellow hair the girls are fond of, beggin' your pardon, Father."

The priest turned away, running his hands through his own thick hair which was almost white, and then said in a voice Vasiliev would not easily forget. "He was my son, but is no longer."

"Lord be praised! Vasiliev exclaimed. "But Father he survived the war. I know it. Your son is alive."

"He is no longer my son," the priest repeated. "He turned his face from God."

"Lord as my witness, I knew him to be a good man, a loyal comrade."

The priest went on as though he had not heard Vasiliev. "He was raised in this house and taught to love the Lord, to read and cipher. His mother died giving birth, and I loved him though he took her from me. I thought I did the right thing. But the learning made him proud and the landowners corrupted him. Yes, they too were attracted by his thick blond hair, his fine figure, his easy manner. I taught him to be humble but not to bend his knees to any earthly power save *tsar batushka*. But they taught him to ride and shoot, to kill God's creatures for sport. They turned him into their play toy, a pet to amuse themselves."

He whirled to face Vasiliev, fire back in his eyes. "Yes, the landlords hereabouts are voltairians, worse, pagans who have immersed themselves in the filth of the black arts and schism of the pernicious sects, Khlysty, Jumpers."

Vasiliev crossed himself. "It's a wonder to hear, Father, that the Prince would dabble in the black arts and Jumpers, Lord preserve us."

"Not the Prince, the Countess! But the Count is also to blame. A liberal and a freethinker, he has let the churches on his property fall into disrepair. But his wife is a fiend, feeding like a leech on the bodies of the young and innocent. God be merciful." He crossed himself. "Even now I cannot forgive her evil work."

Vasiliev felt a knot in his stomach. He disliked having to open the old man's wounds.

"Aye, he spoke of her beauty."

"So her image pursued him even onto the battlefield. Well, she had a devilish way about her that no man could resist. He was not her only victim. She led others astray as well, first to the Khlysty. That was not enough for her insatiable lust. No, then she fell in with the Jumpers who have fallen so low that their worship has lost all semblances to Christian rites. They steep themselves in filthy practices, celebrate the black mass."

"The Lord save and protect us, Father. But the authorities, surely they don't permit this."

"They are in her hands. My complaints to the bishop were buried in the files of the Holy Synod. The police are indifferent or fearful. Who else is there? The Marshal of the nobility is Prince Bagration and she has some influence over him, perhaps through his son, I do not know. She was a wicked woman, wicked. But now without her protection perhaps they will leave our district, these sorcerers as the peasants call them."

"They linger on, Father. They attacked my friends, not these many nights ago."

"God be merciful! Have they returned? Of course, I forget, the winter solstice is coming nigh. They will celebrate it in their horrible fashion."

"May the plague take them, forgive me, Father. My friends and I, we could take them by surprise, give them a sound hidin' and drive them away, out of the district. Do you know, Father, where they practice their dark rites?"

"In the abandoned mill on the northwest edge of the Ushakov property, near the boundary of the Bagration estate, four or five versts from here. But beware, my son. They are many and they are fierce. Three years ago, but you've a soldier's training, haven't you? Our peasant lads led by a man of your courage can stand up to anyone. Perhaps you will prevail. May the Lord protect you." The priest made the sign of the cross over Vasiliev's bowed head and kissed him farewell.

It was snowing lightly when Vasiliev reached the blackened stump of the oak. He wrapped a message around a stone and placed it inside where the snow could not drift in. As he looked up the leaden clouds parted for a moment disclosing the sun then closing in again. The orb seemed veiled and sullen as it moved toward the point of the winter solstice.

Chapter Twenty

On the morning of the winter solstice Vasiliev awoke after a night of troubled dreams. No one was stirring in the cabin. Vasiliev slipped the revolver from his pack and emptied the cartridges into a pouch which he tied around his neck. Using his foot cloths he bound the gun to the inside of his right leg. Then he slung his *tulup* over his shoulder, picked up his boots and padded across the earthen floor to where the elder lay asleep. Vasiliev touched him on the shoulder.

"Listen Uncle, tonight I may not return from the cuttin'. Wait three days for me. Then take the pots and hand them out as you see fit. Let auntie and Marya choose first what they will." The old man nodded, but Vasiliev saw the fear in his eyes. The elder followed him out of the cabin and stood, hatless watching Vasiliev until he passed out of sight.

The clouds had broken up, the last of them disappearing behind the line of firs, but there was no trace of a ground breeze. The cold, crisp air stood motionless. To a superstitious mind it would have been a portent of great events. On the way to the logging camp the older brother kept glancing around uneasily. When Vasiliev asked him to take him to the mill at sundown, he stared at the ground and shook his head. Vasiliev showed him the revolver and promised that the sorcerers would never harm them again. At the cutting site he avoided heavy work and rested frequently. The men had never been talkative. Today they seemed to him like dumb animals communicating with each other in a secret sign language.

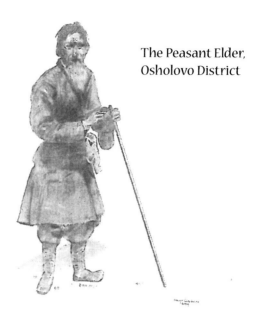

The Peasant Elder,
Osholovo District

The moon had just cleared the edge of the pine forest when Vasiliev and the older brother reached the top of a low rise over looking the mill. The cold had become more intense. Vasiliev turned to say a word of farewell, but the peasant had fled, running into the growing darkness. Vasiliev pulled up the collar of his *tulup*, fastened his ear flaps, and posted himself behind a screen of young firs several hundred meters from the ruined mill. He kept moving his arms about and stamping his feet. From time to time he pulled off his mittens and rubbed the exposed parts of his face. As the hours passed he consumed the last of his sugar. Fatigue began to set in. He knew the warning signals, drowsiness and a creeping numbness in his limbs. It was now a matter of minutes before he would have to end his vigil and find a place to build a fire. Otherwise, frostbite would cripple him. His hands were too numb to remove his mittens. Had he waited too long?

At first he thought the lights might be a hallucination. He blinked rapidly to keep his eyelashes, already coated with frost, from freezing shut. The flickering grew brighter as more lights appeared. A line of torches undulated through the woods toward the old mill.

He crept painfully to the edge of the clearing, keeping behind the cover of the small pines. He cursed himself for having failed to prepare a torch of twigs and pitch. He reached the point where he had first seen the lights emerge from the forest. Most of the procession had already entered the mill. None of the stragglers took any notice of him when he fell into step behind them.

As he stumbled across the threshold a blast of hot air struck him full force. Tongues of flame from a dozen bonfires shot high into the air toward the gaps in the roof where the boards had long ago rotted and caved in. The crackling of the pine logs sounded like volleys of rifle fire. The walls of the mill took on a reddish hue darkened by moving shadows. Snow that had fallen through the opening in the roof was rapidly melting into puddles and rivulets. A nice setting for a Faustian drama, thought Vasiliev, but one mounted in a Russian hell where frostbite was part of the torture. He felt his flesh thaw with frightening speed. It began with sharp pains in his ear lobes and the tip of his nose. He felt as though his face was being scraped with a dull knife. His fingertips stung as if immersed in boiling water and every step was agony.

Forty or fifty men and women had gathered in an irregular semi-circle around the fires. A stone altar had been erected in an open space at one end of the mill. Over the roar of the fire Vasiliev heard a murmur coming from the congregation. Most of them had already thrown off their sheepskins and flung them in heaps against the walls. He pulled off his *tulup* with difficulty. His frozen fingers seemed reluctant to obey him. He slumped down in the semi-circle, lowered his head and vigorously massaged his face.

The worst of the pain was subsiding when the man to his left handed him a wooden mug containing a thick liquid. Vasiliev raised it to his lips and threw back his head but did not drink. The stench repelled him. Fighting down his nausea he thrust the mug into the hand clutching at his sleeve. Dim figures passed behind him shouldering earthenware casks. They refilled the mugs as quickly as they were emptied. Vasiliev feigned drinking again. He felt an almost irresistible urge to relieve his parched throat. Part of him felt encased in ice while the rest of his body was heating up like a furnace.

The huddled figures began to sway rhythmically from side to side. The murmuring grew louder. It sounded more like a chant.

Vasiliev could not make out the words but there was something familiar about the gibberish that made his flesh crawl. He started to sway with them. He watched with horror how the men clawed at their throats and uttered guttural cries while the women pulled their hair. The fires were burning lower. Suddenly a man jumped into the shrinking circle of light. He crouched like an animal, then leaped into the air, soaring to an astonishing height. Vasiliev's neighbor sprang to his feet and vaulted over him landing with a jarring thud. Others followed in quick succession. All around him men were leaping and emitting terrible cries. Some fell heavily and did not rise. The most athletic hurled themselves into the air again and again, each time bounding higher and higher. They extended their arms as if to embrace an invisible world. In the center of the circle the lead jumper collapsed after spectacular leap. As he lay there writhing and moaning, men and women tore at his blouse and stuffed the tatters into their mouths.

Vasiliev began to make sense of the guttural cries. "I rise to God and God hurls me down, Oh my soul!" The words brought back with terrifying intensity the nightmare of his childhood. It was as if he were lying next to Foma again, deep in the village forest watching the Jumpers for the first time. He felt the hair rise at the nape of his neck. These Jumpers seemed even more savage.

A few feet in front of him the fallen man struggled to rise. Vasiliev could not believe his eyes. The female Jumpers were scraping the man's naked flesh with their nails, emitting howls of delight. He drove them back with his cry, "Let me rise!" He staggered to his feet. Shreds of clothing hung down from his body like strips of birch bark torn from a tree. He launched himself into the air, his body twisting and turning. He crashed to the ground. Vasiliev heard his ankle crack like a pistol shot. The man rolled into the fire. The Jumpers threw their bodies on him and smothered the flames, but the stench of burned flesh hung in the air.

Outside the semi-circle the Jumpers stripped a woman and poured the foul smelling beverage over her naked body. Half a dozen pairs of arms snatched her up, carried her into the shadows and spread her out on the altar stone. Vasiliev lost sight of her. The man next to him was tearing his own hair and babbling incoherently. His eyes rolled wildly showing only the white orbs flecked with red veins. Vasiliev recoiled as he bared his teeth, foamed at the mouth and snapped the air like a mad dog. Men and women fell on him and stripped him.

Vasiliev sensed his turn would be next. He broke out of the circle and ran for the deep shadows along the wall. He was jerked from his feet by a powerful pair of arms wrapped round his neck. As he fell he jabbed the man with his elbow. He lashed out with his boot. A scream of pain merged with the cries of ecstasy. He scrambled to his feet. Jumpers hurled themselves on the fallen man, tearing and stripping his clothing. Vasiliev felt a sudden surge of excitement. It was a part of himself he did not fully understand. Something had been stirred up from deep inside. The point is, he thought with grim humor, not to end up horizontal. He pushed past a group of kneeling Jumpers. It was no easy matter to keep from stumbling over bodies strewn all around him. He kept clear of the walls, looking for space to maneuver. He realized with a pleasurable shock that at this point a sensible man might be looking for a way out. But he sensed that the main attraction had yet to come and that was the reason he was in this madhouse.

He scrambled on top of a pile of sheepskins, pulled his revolver out of the leg wrapping and loaded it with five cartridges. Then he stuffed it into the pocket of his *tulup* and hid the coat behind a grinding stone standing on end that was visible from all corners of the mill. He leaped back into the circle, matching athletic jumps with the best of them, surrendering to a sensation that frightened as much as it thrilled him. All around him half-naked bodies jumped, stomped and shrieked. Vasiliev heard himself screaming too, as if he had been transformed into a wild being he no longer recognized.

Suddenly, a bell tolled behind the altar. The whirling bodies flung themselves on the ground. He lay among them, straining to make out the shadowy figure that stepped to the front of the altar. Torches were inserted into iron fixtures mounted on either side of the empty slab. They revealed a large bearded man wearing only boots and a necklace of bear claws. He was fully aroused sexually. The prostrate figures twisted around to face the altar. They began to chant. Several men raised a naked young woman from the ground and bore her toward the altar. Her body twitched as if charged by a galvanic current. They lifted her like an offering over the giant, who sprawled on the slab, and lowered her until he impaled her. Accompanied by the monotonous chanting, they celebrated the black mass time and again as woman after woman was dedicated to the insatiable giant. Intermittently, a female voice cried out above the rest, "Petya, you are the rock on which we shall build our church." The blasphemous incantation was taken up by the men. "Aye, aye, Peter, Peter the true tsar, give us truth and give us true freedom, our souls cry out for freedom."

Petya raised his head and gestured toward the threshold. Vasiliev turned with the others to watch. A young woman had entered the mill on the arm of a slender youth. She slipped off her hood and her sable cloak fell open displaying a white gown deeply cut over her dazzling bosom, a collar of jewels and matching earrings that sparkled like ice crystals. A shawl of Orenburg goat's fleece covered the coils of yellow hair piled high on her head. The young man, a boy really, dressed in the fashionable foreign clothes, snatched off his Karakul hat and bowed deeply to Petya.

"Hail, ye golden people of Ophir!" Petya roared.

They advanced toward the altar with mincing steps. An absurd thought struck Vasiliev. They looked like lovers on a stroll along the Nevsky Prospekt. The effect was spoiled by the tangle of bodies that broke up and scattered in their wake. The young man hesitated as though he had just noticed them. Vasiliev saw clearly the grimace of horror that suddenly came over his face.

Petya jumped down from the altar stone. He swept the young man up in his arms he retreated into the shadows. The woman turned away disdainfully. She flung her cloak over one shoulder and surveyed the figures gathering around her. They seemed to be kneeling and murmuring something. Vasiliev could not make out the words. Arms were raised toward her as if in supplication. Her eyes swept over them and came to rest on him as he crouched in front of a dying fire. His face was in shadow. She picked her way towards him, slipping off the sable and trailing it across the bodies that groveled at her feet. Vasiliev kept his eyes fixed on the cloak, wondering how it would feel sliding over his bare skin. She walked toward him as if hypnotized by the sight of his torso gleaming like burnished copper in the firelight. As she came closer she exaggerated the movement of her hips. She was almost upon him when he recognized her, the pouting mouth, a ringlet of blond hair falling over her forehead. He started to rise, but she uttered a sharp cry and sprang at him. She clung to him fiercely as they rolled over on the earthen floor. A desire to inflict pain swept over him.

He came to his senses breathing in her French scent. The sable cloak lay across his body. Her face was buried in his chest. Her hair had loosened and fell over her bare shoulders. He heard the snapping of the dying embers. Cold air was beginning to seep into the mill. So this was what the Countess had been like, he thought. She had taught her successor well. He tried slowly to disengage himself, but she stirred and wrapped her legs tightly around his. He murmured an endearment and caressed her. "Not yet," she whispered.

"What about your Petersburg dandy? Won't he be jealous?"

She giggled, nuzzled him and sighed. "Not that weakling. He isn't interested in women anyway, not any more."

Vasiliev felt drugged. He tried to remember whether he had swallowed some of that evil smelling liquid. No, it had been the heat, the jumping, the rending of garments and speaking in voices. The Biblical invocations had affected him strangely. These were filthy practices. What was it then that had taken possession of him? He was terrified by the idea that somehow the Jumpers had touched an unknown part of his inner self, a throwback to his peasant ancestors. Or had he just been caught up in playing his role as one of them? That must be it, he thought. It was all part of the disguise. Foma's training had taken over. He had forgotten the difference between acting and being. And then he had succumbed to pure lust. Nothing more to it than that. He struggled to reassure himself and forced his mind in another direction. What had all this to do with the Ushakova case? he asked himself. Here was another link between Petya and the Countess. But it led him nowhere. And who was the young man? Another thread torn from a pattern he could not make out. He needed Nasya to tell him. She hadn't recognized him yet. She had only seen him once in full uniform. His beard had grown; his hair was dyed and tangled. He counted on deceiving her with his peasant accent perfected long ago by Foma.

Nasya was stirring again. "He's a silly boy. Now his true nurturer is gone. Just when he had learned to drink at her bosom. But he's not important any longer. Not to me."

"But he's real noble stock ain't he," Vasiliev muttered.

"Better than that," she chuckled, rubbing against him. "He's a princeling, a famous one. I'll bet even you've heard of him"

Vasiliev stiffened.

"Don't worry, my darling. He's a Bagration but nothing like his papa."

"Good God!" Vasiliev exclaimed. Something in his voice finally betrayed him. Her head snapped up. The muscles in her face that had grown slack with passion, tightened as she tried to focus on him. He bent to kiss her and force her back but she elbowed free.

"Who the devil are you?" she rasped at him. She rose to her knees, her bare breasts swinging out of his reach, her features twisted in fury.

Vasiliev raised his arm to cover himself in what he knew was a futile gesture

"You are...Holy Mother of God!" She screamed and lashed out at him with her bright red nails. He grabbed her wrist, twisted it and sent her sprawling with a blow of his open hand. In an instant he wished he had snapped her neck. She lay stunned, blood trickling from her cut lip, whimpering. Then she rolled away from him. He jumped to his feet as she began to scream again. The fires had all but died out; there were only faint points of light scattered around the mill. He was disoriented. In the darkness he could not locate the grinding stone. He began to run, stumbling over bodies. He stopped short when he realized he had been heading toward the altar. He raced back past her, shaken by her screams. "Petya, Petya, a spy among us. God Almighty, Petya save us, he'll betray us. Petya!" She was pounding the earth with her fists, her blond hair lashing her shoulders and breasts like tiny whips.

Vasiliev felt along the wall until he reached the grinding stone. He groped for his *tulup* and found his revolver. He kept telling himself to move deliberately. The Jumpers were exhausted. It was just her damned screaming. He had to find trousers and boots for protection against the cold. Clothing was scattered all over the ground. Down on all fours he pulled a pair of trousers out of a pile and struggled into them. Bent double, he ran along the wall in his bare feet. He seized hold of a body stretched out in front of him and tugged at the boots.

Nasya's screams seemed to grow louder. They resounded throughout the mill. "Help, help, Petya, a copper, he'll give us away."

The boots were too small and forced him to hobble. He only had five cartridges and there were scores of men in the mill. How many between him and the doorway? But they were drugged, stupefied by that hideous drink. It was only the girl, Nasya, who hadn't poured the stuff down her throat. They might not even hear her.

He was sweating now in his heavy *tulup*. He spotted Petya who had reared up behind the altar, swaying from side to side. The girl was hoarse from shrieking, "Kill him, kill him!" Her body was outlined against one of the smoldering fires. Vasiliev took aim with his revolver but hesitated to shoot. The report might rouse them all. He saw another figure appear behind the girl. Damn it, the Jumpers were beginning to stir. He took two running steps and tripped over a man who was crawling toward him. He reached out to catch himself but crashed against the wall jarring loose his revolver. It went flying into the darkness. He went down on all fours again, fumbling along the ground, snatching at emptiness.

What the hell was he doing? Run for it and leave the revolver, he told himself. He saw more figures looming up in front of him. They were blocking the door. He would have to shoot his way out. There were too many of them. His fingers ran along the edge of the wall. The sharp stones tore his nails.

Petya shambled toward the girl. He was shaking his head and bellowing like a wounded stag. "Get up, you fools. There's an enemy among us, a traitor. Seize him before he gets out, You'll be slaughtered in your sleep. Block the exit. He's over there."

Vasiliev's hand closed over the revolver just as a Jumper grabbed hold of his leg shouting, "Here's the swine, Petya." Vasiliev struck out; the butt of his revolver slammed into the man's head. He pushed his way past another Jumper who was staggering to his feet. He could see more bodies rising from the ground, like the resurrected on Judgment Day. The girls' voice had sunk to a moan punctuated by sobs.

A torch flared, casting his silhouette against the wall. A second and then a third torch illuminated the front end of the mill. They could see him clearly now, but he could see them as well. Some of the Jumpers were closing in on the doorway. Petya was heading toward him, lashing out with his boots at the bodies within reach and shouting, "Cut him down, we'll all die if he escapes."

Vasiliev waved his revolver and shouted at the Jumpers clustered at the entrance. They swore back at him and brandished their torches. Vasiliev fired three quick rounds. Two men dropped without a word, a third cried out and went down on his knees. His torch tumbled into a pile of sawdust, igniting it. Vasiliev charged the open doorway. Petya hurled his torch. Vasiliev saw it coming too late. He threw up his arm to protect his face. A searing pain shot down his arm from elbow to wrist. The revolver spun out of his hand as he stumbled into the frigid night. He shuddered, plunged his burnt arm into a snow bank, and began to run. The tight boots cramped his feet. He kept slipping on the icy patches where the snow had been trampled down.

Petya's voice rang out close by, "He's lost his gun. No need to fear him. Seize him, tear him to pieces."

Vasiliev felt his ankle buckle and he fell heavily into the snow. He got to his feet and limped forward. He hoped the naked men would be stunned by the intense cold. It had been idiotic to have come alone, to have lost his head and taken the girl. The cries were close behind him now. The cold had not stopped them. They had been aroused, their sexual passion yielding to blood lust. He knew he offered an easy target silhouetted against the snow by the light of the full moon. He lost his balance again and toppled into a snowdrift. He struggled to rise, sensing he had lost his last chance. Perhaps they had already found his gun, two cartridges remaining. It would be better to die that way, quicker.

He heard the first shot and a second, but felt nothing. Could they have missed at that range or was he already dying, dead? More shots, four, five, six. Was he imagining them? He twisted his head and looked behind him toward the mill. A clump of bodies lay in the path; torches burning out in the snow; dark shapes looming in the doorway; the sound of more firing. Suddenly, through the pain it came to him. The shots were not coming from a revolver. He was hearing the rapid fire of his Martini-Henry carbine.

He heard muffled hoof beats on the path from the forest. A shaggy steppe pony was cantering toward him, Borka crouched low in the saddle. Vasiliev raised both hands over his head, a greeting and a celebration of life.

"Can you mount?"

Vasiliev clambered up, Borka grabbing hold to haul him up by his good arm.

"How in God's name...?"

"We agreed on three shots as a signal, Vasili Vasilievich."

Vasiliev couldn't help breaking into a hoarse laugh despite the pain. Borka wheeled the mount and rode back toward the village. They came to a halt at the top of the small rise where Vasiliev had caught his first glimpse of the torchlight procession. From the gaping hole in the roof the flames shot up into the sky illuminating the path choked with bodies. The air was motionless, as it had been all night. Vasiliev whispered a prayer of thanks that the sorcerers' funeral pyre was not his as well.

Chapter
Twenty-One

Vasiliev was awakened by the smell of burning wood. For a moment he was back in the abandoned mill, running and tense with fear. His arm and ankle throbbed. He was lying under furs in a felt tent. Borka was brewing tea over a low fire, his hound pressed by his side. Vasiliev threw off the fur and tried to rise but the ankle buckled and he fell back with a groan.

"Petya, the woman and the boy all survived and left by sled." Borka spoke into the flames. "The trail is easy to follow. Best to rest the ankle, Vasili Vasilievich." Borka knew that what he said on this matter would not count for much. "The student has gone to Moscow. The stable boy, a Komi, told me. Serov will pick him up in Nizhnyi." Vasiliev swallowed the hot tea. Borka handed him a crust of bread and some salted fish.

"What no banquet, Borka?" Vasiliev smiled his crooked smile. "The bitch gets even less." Borka smiled back and produced a long, heavy stick whittled to a point that would serve Vasiliev as a cane. Borka pushed open the tent flap and saddled the pony. Vasiliev hobbled out behind him and mounted up. Borka collapsed the tent and packed it up while Vasiliev looked on helplessly. Borka took the reins and led the pony along a trail in the snowfield that only he could make out. His hound trotted beside them. At the next village they bargained to hire a horse and cart. They found out that the trio had split up. Petya and Nasya had continued on the sled. The princeling had hired the best horses from the stationmaster and was headed for the nearest railroad on the Nizhnyi Novgorod line. Presumably he would change there for the express to Moscow.

Vasiliev sent Borka after Petya and the girl. He had to face the problem that they were only two to follow the three of them.

"If Petya and the girl split up, follow Petya."

Vasiliev's cart made slow progress along the snow packed road. When he arrived at the Nizhnyi station, the young Prince had long since departed, having bought a ticket all the way to Petersburg. Vasiliev sat in the telegraph office for a long time staring at the blank message form. Then he picked up a quill and shook his head in wonder at what he was about to do.

Vasiliev caught the next train to St. Petersburg. When he arrived he registered at the European Hotel where an envelope was waiting for him. It contained a ticket to a reading by Fedor Dostoevsky at the Needy Student Benefit. Those who attended long remembered it as the last great social occasion in the reign of Alexander II when the two extremes of Petersburg society sat down together peacefully. Vasiliev's uniform stood out in the mass of top hats and formal dress mingling with leather belted blouses and colorful *shotlandsky*, the plaid Scottish scarves that he recognized as the hallmark of the radical students.

He barely had time to scan the audience before Irina slipped in seat next to him. She greeted him like an old friend. Well, wasn't he? She looked even younger in her blouse and Scottish shawl.

"It's taken a long time for the Russian public to catch up with Fedor Mikhailovich," she began. "Hard to imagine that he published *Poor Folk* thirty years ago. Remember what Belinsky said at the time? 'Do you yourself know what you have written?' What do you think, did he know? I mean know how important it was back then to write about the 'insulted and the injured'?

"I think he did, but that's when he was a socialist, after all. Now, it's different isn't it?"

"You mean the religious conversion? Yes, but he can still reach almost everyone."

"The Pushkin monument speech did it. Reminds me. Right after you picked me up for the first time at the Nizhnyi station in Moscow and I raced back to headquarters. I took a good look at the new Pushkin statue and thought of Dostoevsky's speech. It didn't have much to do with Pushkin, did it?

"I suppose not, but he got us and the reactionaries equally excited about Mother Russia."

"Pushkin and Dostoevsky, it's like moving from light to dark. It takes time to get accustomed to the Russian darkness."

"That sounds quite profound, Vasya. I used to think that you were one of the few who could bridge both worlds. Most of the intelligentsia could only imagine what life was like in the village. You knew it first-hand."

"That was a long time ago. But it's still true that the village people don't have the slightest idea what the intelligentsia are talking about. That is your main problem, Irina."

"Well, this isn't the time for a discussion of the burning questions of the day. But since you gave me an assignment, I'll try to carry it out. So pay close attention. A few minutes before the reading begins, Anna Grigoryevna, Dostoevsky's second wife, will dash in to her seat. She stays with him backstage as long as possible to calm his dreadful nerves. You see, over there, they reserve that seat for her on the aisle, right behind young Prince Bagration."

Vasiliev gave her his crooked smile. "You always had a wonderful flair for the dramatic. How did you know he would be here?"

"Magician knows his habits. Young Bagration has been coming to the readings on and off for the past few months."

"Ah, Magician, and where is he now?"

"Confidential information, Inspector. But don't underestimate him as an ally. He is well informed about a lot of things."

"I must have caught him in one of his off moments," Vasiliev replied, keeping a straight face.

Swan thought it unnecessary to reply. "They say the young Prince has sent a large contribution to the Literary Fund.He will probably will make a large donation tonight as well. It seems he takes the readings quite personally. I heard he actually broke down sobbing at Fedor Mikhailovich's reading of Nekrasov's *When from the Murk of Sin.*"

"The young Prince seems to be in a repentant mood these days." He intercepted Irina's quizzical look and was about to explain when a ripple of excitement passed over the audience as Anna Grigoryevna took her seat. A moment later a diminutive, slightly bent figure dressed in a dark suit shuffled across the stage, greeted by a burst of applause. Dostoevsky bowed, his thin lips trembling. Vasiliev was shocked by the writer's frail, sickly appearance. But there was something else there too. Vasiliev had never before felt himself in the same room with such a palpably spiritual presence. It crossed his mind how great a moral distance he had traveled in the last few days, or had he? Perhaps Dostoevsky understood better than any other writer of his time the dark side of Russian religiosity.

Young Bagration had leaped to his feet when Dostoevsky appeared and was clapping wildly. Vasiliev thought of him on the altar in the old mill. The young Prince seemed hyper-excited as if he were about to what? Levitate? Dostoevsky waited patiently for the applause to subside, his eyes riveted on his young wife. Did Bagration think the writer was staring at him? It seemed so to Vasiliev, for the boy suddenly dropped his arms to his side and stood as if transfixed until his neighbor tapped him on the shoulder. He shuddered before sinking into his seat.

Dostoevsky began to read the epilogue to *Brothers Karamazov*, "Illusha's Funeral." He spoke quietly and without gestures. Vasiliev felt deeply stirred by some indefinable quality of the voice, but he kept his eye on young Bagration who had bowed his head as if in prayer. When Dostoevsky came to the passages describing the appearance of the boy's dead body, Bagration's head snapped up. From where he sat Vasiliev could not see the expression on his face. Vasiliev listened to the muffled sobs around him. People were beginning to weep openly and not just the women. Bagration buried his face in his hands. Dostoevsky's voice had died down to a whisper as he reached the climax, forcing people to strain to hear him though, apparently from the way they moved their lips, many knew the passage by heart. Vasiliev made an effort to focus his attention on young Bagration, whose shoulders were now shaking uncontrollably. Vasiliev did not know what to expect, but it was clear that Bagration was going through an inner torment.

Dostoevsky raised his head from the text and his words came out strongly but in a strangely cracked tone; "'Where have you taken him away?'"He recited. "'Where have you taken him?' the lunatic cried in a heart rending voice." He stopped. The reading was over. A storm of applause broke out, apparently breaking the spell over young Bagration who threw back his head, uttered a cry and bolted from his seat. He rushed down the aisle his face wet with tears. Vasiliev jumped to his feet and brushed past Irina, having almost forgotten she was there. All around him people were standing, shouting "Bravo", crying and embracing one another. Dostoevsky stood with bowed head as if he had spent his last ounce of energy and was waiting for the applause to revive him. Vasiliev was blocked by people who had stepped into the aisle to get a better view of the stage. He almost collided with a general, seized the man by the shoulders and spun him around, muttering apologies and pushing his way through a crowd of young people. He limped across the parquet floor. The heavy doors swung shut behind him, cutting off the sounds of the demonstration. Bagration's boots clattered on the marble steps leading down to the cloakroom. Vasiliev slid and skidded down the stairs, his ankle threatening to give way at every step. When he reached the ground floor he saw Bagration ahead of him, scampering toward the double glass doors. The doorman, an astonished look on his face, rose to his feet. An old woman leaned across the counter of the cloakroom and cried out, "Prince, Prince, your coat, my God, it's frigid outside. Wait for mercy's sake!"

The young prince stopped abruptly, his arms swinging backwards and forwards. He slowly turned his head. Vasiliev registered the frantic look on his face. He raised his arm to signal the doorman who moved in front of the prince and bowed. "Prince, you must have your coat."

The young man fumbled in his jacket and tore the wooden coat check out of his pocket. It slipped from his fingers, and fell to the floor. It landed on edge and rolled toward Vasiliev who had also stopped in his tracks. They all watched as if hypnotized, the doorman, the old woman, the prince and Vasiliev, as the wooden disc teetered and fell at Vasiliev's feet. Above them the loud noise of applause burst forth as someone opened the doors to the hall.

Vasiliev bent over and fixing his eyes on Bagration he picked up the disc. He smiled his crooked smile and held it out at arm's length as he walked slowly towards the Prince. The young man shrank back.

"What a pleasure to be of assistance to you, Prince." Vasiliev was suddenly struck by the close facial resemblance between himself and the Prince. It was as if he were looking at a younger version of himself. Or was it more like a reflection in a dark mirror?

"It must be some time since we last met. You remember me of course?"

"Who are you?" he gasped. "My God, how can you be?" He raised his arm before his face as if to defend himself. Footsteps resounded on the main staircase but no one else had yet descended to the entrance hall. The young Prince lowered his arm and pointed at Vasiliev.

"My God, my God, you are my double! You are the devil and the devil is my double." Bagration whirled and with an agility that caught Vasiliev off guard, he scampered to the entrance waving his arms. When it appeared that he would not stop before crashing through the glass, the doorman pushed open both doors in rapid succession. The Prince plunged into the frosty night.

Vasiliev realized at once what had happened. The Prince had been deeply immersed in the nether world of Dostoevsky. He saw the physical resemblance as a sign that Vasiliev was his *doppelgänger*, his spiritual double. The idea had obsessed the writer. Now it was invading Vasiliev's case. The Countess had her double in Nasya, and now he had acquired one.

"This is all I need", Vasiliev lamented. "My criminal investigation has become some kind of crazy spiritual quest." He spoke out loud to the astonishment of the old woman and the doorman. Another inner voice reassured him; this will serve you well. He would have good reason to remember those words.

"Wait, your coat," he shouted to the Prince's back. He hobbled over to the old woman. He pressed the wooden disc and a silver ruble into her hand. "Quick, the boy is ill."

Grabbing hold of the Prince's furs he hurriedly limped to the door just as the first members of the audience began to appear behind him. The shock of the cold air surprised him until he realized that he had forgotten his own coat. Suddenly he was surrounded by a group of students carrying a large wreath for Dostoevsky. Had he come as a personal emissary from Fedor Mikhailovich? They wanted to know. They gathered around him eagerly, a babble of voices, friendly faces. He looked over their heads for the Prince. Suddenly Irina was at his side. She seized his hand.

"Let him through, you must understand, there's a demented man, he's run away." She plunged into the crowd, pulling Vasiliev behind her.

"He went that way, I saw him." The students opened up a path for them. "You'll freeze like that," someone said. When they reached the street Vasiliev caught a glimpse of Bagration in an open sleigh pulling away from the curb, his chalk like face illuminated by a street lamp as he twisted his head from side to side. Swan ran into the thoroughfare with some of the students and signaled to another sleigh. Vasiliev squeezed her arm as he jumped in, a dozen hands helping him, waving as sleigh shot forward.

Vasiliev stuffed a silver ruble into the driver's mitten. "Another ruble to match it if you catch up with that charcoal black runner." Shivering, he burrowed under the fur blankets.

The full moon threw an ethereal glow over the pyramids of freshly shoveled snow and the pastel facades of the buildings along the Embankment. The sleigh sped past the Gostinnyi Dvor, its thick arcades casting grotesque shadows. Why did everything look different to him? Sharp lines seem to blur and solid objects to melt into one another. It must be the light, he thought, or was it his mind playing tricks on him. It was as if the Petersburg he loved, Pushkin's city with its classic elegance was disintegrating before his eyes, and out of the shapelessness was emerging the Petersburg of Dostoevsky with its conspiracies and demented young men seeking salvation from real or imagined horrors.

They were catching up but not fast enough, for he had guessed at the Prince's destination. He leaned forward and prodded the driver. A whip cracked like a pistol shot in the transparent night air. They continued to gain, but the charcoal black runner was fast approaching the ochre mass of the Anichkov Palace, the extravagant, rococo residence of the heir to the throne, Alexander Alexandrovich, the friend and patron of Prince Bagration. Only four sleigh lengths separated them when a troika materialized out of nowhere, overtook Vasiliev's sleigh and cut sharply in front of it. His driver had to swerve in order to avoid a collision. The right runner of the sleigh struck a pile of snow jolting Vasiliev and forcing the driver to rein in. Vasiliev watched helplessly as Bagration's sleigh passed under the arch of the Anichkov Palace, the guards snapping to attention. The troika continued at full speed to the Fontanka Canal, shot off to the right and disappeared from sight.

Vasiliev's driver was cursing as he brought the sleigh to a halt under the ochre walls. "God be praised, your honor, we'd have had him if the troika hadn't cut us off."

"Yes, yes. You did your best, you'll get your silver ruble. Drive back to the theater," growled Vasiliev. He repressed a foolish impulse to storm the Palace. The whole case was absurd. How could he press an investigation against people who enjoyed the protection of the highest powers in the land? The driver turned the sleigh and crossed the Anichkov Bridge. Vasiliev stared ahead, hardly noticing the swarms of skaters gliding over the frozen Fontanka Canal under a canopy of gaily colored Chinese lanterns.

Chapter
Twenty-Two

They entered the Moscow safe room, one by one. Vasiliev waited until they were all accounted for. Irina had again proven true to her word. Even Magician had shown up along with Norka, Marko, Letchik, the healer.

They had arranged the meeting in St. Petersburg after Vasiliev had returned from his pursuit of the young Prince. Irina had been waiting in the deserted hall following the benefit. He had taken precautions so that they would not be followed on their midnight stroll along the Embankment. She had silently linked her arm with his, helping to take the pressure off his game ankle. He had related the incident of the troika.

"No accident, of course. Instead of trying to kill me, they must have thought it was more important to protect the young Prince. I should be pleased, but it puzzles me." He had suddenly found himself pouring out all his feelings about the case. "Too many leads going nowhere, Irina, too many plots and sub-plots. Attempts to get me off the case from the beginning. I don't know, yet, but I can guess, by whom and why. Ushkov and Bagration were old rivals in the Caucasus for the favors of the Countess. The old Count wins out, but the Countess keeps in touch with the Prince. What is her game? Ushakov gets me on the case but then draws back. Why? Because his wife's maid seduces him and warns him against me. Who put her up to that? She is involved with Petya and the Jumpers, who drag in the young Bagration. What is their aim? And then there is your Magician."

"You cannot put him in the same *kasha.*" Irina sounded indignant. She had defended Magician once before, but he could not figure out why she continued to do so.

"Perhaps, but he's not a neutral bystander." He decided to test her. "Your Magician was involved with the Countess before. Did you know that?" She looked at him uneasily. "No, I expect not. A long story. I met his father in Osholovo. Claimed the Countess had seduced his son and turned him into her poodle. No doubt that was before your time. In any event, Magician is in this up to his neck. He sneaked into the ball, acted like a damn fool, or was he being terribly clever? Later, on the steamer he is assaulted by Petya, another relic of his checkered past. And he was hanging around the Ushakov estate right until the winter solstice. Why was that?"

"He was recovering from his injuries. Remember he was the one who arranged for Nasya to play out her role as nurturer. We had to break the connection between her and Ushakov long enough for you to get to see him. It worked didn't it?"

"Yes, but it almost cost me my life." She had been visibly shaken when he told her his story of the black mass. "And my visit to the Count may have had its effect, but I'm not even sure about his role in all this."

"Surely you cannot suspect him"

"I can think of three good reasons why he might have arranged to dispose of his wife. And how do we explain his strange behavior that night, the fainting fit."

"It's absurd to make so much of that. He fainted because…" she hesitated uncertain how much she had already told him.

Vasiliev had whirled on her. "Again, you know something. For God's sake you could spare us all by telling me the whole story of that evening rather than parceling it out." Swan had chewed her lip, just as she had done as a child when she was caught fibbing.

"I would have told you, but you would have drawn the wrong conclusions."

"And you have drawn the right ones? Good. Tell me what they are."

"The Countess and the Prince left the ballroom together. It was during the excitement over the sword dance. The Count saw them as they rushed up the staircase. He collapsed and was carried into the Georgian Room by the major domo. I did not see him again."

"And what about Tarashkin, when did you last see him?"

"Magician followed them up the stairs..." She hesitated again, should she tell him everything? "He disappeared. I lost sight of them all."

"Irishka, Irishka, what else have you concealed? All right, nothing. I believe you for the moment. So where does that leave us? Three men went missing after she did; all of them may have had a motive to kill her. Where did they go? And now there is young Bagration who was supposed to give letters to your Magician. He too was wandering around upstairs. It's beginning to look more like a French farce than a murder mystery."

"Do not call him my Magician," her tone had been icy.

"Well then, whose Magician is he?"

"Vasya, I suggest we stop quarreling."

"All right. But let me clear up a few things first, with your help. I need to see *Magician* and ask some pointed questions. He is not under any powerful protector." He had been tempted to add "except for you". But he restrained himself. "And there is something else, too, but that can wait until we have a meeting. Can you set it up?"

"Yes, but it will have to be with the entire group."

"So he is in need of protection."

"You are always free to arrest him, of course."

"Nicely parried. All right, I agree to your terms."

And so they were now gathered all together in t he safe room under the watchful eyes of Nikolai Chernyshevsky. This time Vasiliev had spent half the day making sure he was not followed. He hoped others had been as cautious. It would not do for the Gendarmes to find him consorting with nihilists. He arrived in civilian clothes and unarmed. Norka had already commandeered the desk, assuming her right to chair the proceedings. Instead of a gavel, Vasiliev noted, she has her Browning revolver within easy reach. A tallow candle flickered on the desk beside it. Swan glided in next followed by Letchik, then Marko and finally Magician, looking furtive and tired.

Norka led off. "We have agreed to have this extraordinary meeting in order to clear up all allegations about our comrade and to hear Inspector Vasiliev's proposal to bring his investigation to a just conclusion." Vasiliev considered what she had said for a moment, not exactly the way he would have put it, but never mind.

Vasiliev had hardly opened his mouth when there was a knock on the door, the secret code unmistakably rapped out. Norka seized her revolver and waved it in the air, rather recklessly Vasiliev thought. "No one else knows the signal," she whispered.

"Oh yes, one person," said Vasiliev as he went to the door, trusting that Norka would not lose her head and accidently shoot him in the back.

"Come in Sergeant," said Vasiliev. "You are acquainted with some of these people." Serov bowed to Swan. "Most recently with that young man, Vasili Vasilievich, over there. Some's in the habit of callin' him Magician, I suppose."

"I'm sorry I haven't had the honor," Magician gave a low bow.

"What the hell is he doing here?" Norka snarled.

"Yes, Sergeant what in hell, in a manner of speaking, are you doing here? Did you just amble by?"

"Amble by!" Norka repeated. "Nonsense, he came with you. But what's the reason for this charade?"

"Wrong, Norka, I haven't seen Sergeant Serov in several weeks. Tell us, Sergeant, how you just ambled by."

Serov had been studying each face carefully before answering. "Just carryin' out orders, beggin' your pardon, your Honor."

Norka winced at what she considered a display of slavish mentality. "You see."

"And what were those orders, Sergeant?"

Serov seemed pleased that Vasiliev was giving him the best lines.

"Why as you said, Vasili Vasilievich, just keep my eye on this young man, Magician. I took over from Borka who went to meet you at Osholovo. And then just a few days ago the strangest thing happens. Someone else is on his tail as well. And then it turned out that someone was tailing the tail. Well, that does get a bit confusin', doesn't it? But I don't mean to confuse you."

Vasiliev seemed to be the only one amused by Serov's story.

"Here, I'll have to confess somethin' to you. The tail of the tail picked me up before I saw him. But these Komi tribesmen," Serov shook his head as if in wondrous admiration. "You know how they are. Move like a spirit ghost."

"If I can interrupt for a moment, Sergeant". Vasiliev was smiling broadly now. "The man following Magician, that is the tail in Serov's account, had to be our old friend Petya, for the simple reason that the Komi tribesman by the name of Borka, had been ordered to follow Petya, and hence emerges here as the tail of the tail."

"Exactly as it was, Vasili Vasilievich. So Borka and I split up, no sense our followin' one another. He was to go back and pick up the trail of the girl. Ol' Petya had left her in the Kolomenskoe suburb, it seems. That's where Borka is now. I came on followin' Petya, who was still trailin' Magician here."

Serov paused to scrape his heel on the floor.

In the silence of the room someone, was it Marko? whispered, "Jesus."

"And what kind of a merry chase did Petya lead you"

"Well, your Honor, if truth be told, I tracked him right here."

Norka rose to her feet as if in a trance. "Idiot", she spat out at Magician. Then she realized with a pang that she had made a terrible mistake. She had failed to post one of them on the street to watch.

"Did Magician ever come to the safe room with Petya on his tail?"

"Twice."

Everyone seemed to be standing at once. Norka rushed to the window and flattening herself against the wall drew the curtain aside. To Vasiliev she looked almost comically conspiratorial.

"You've given us away," Norka cried letting the curtain drop."We must leave quickly."

Magician had buried his face in his hands. Vasiliev moved closer to the table. He suddenly realized his own mistake in coming unarmed. "By twos," Norka went on, "and at close intervals. Swan and Letchik will...." But she never finished the sentence.

Vasiliev was the first to react to the sound of pounding boots in the corridor. But his shouted warning was drowned out by the crash of gunfire and the splintering of wood. He dove for the revolver, knocking over the candle, and came up firing through the shattered door. The report of his small caliber weapon was barely audible above the volley of rifle fire. It was over in a few seconds.

A current of cold air poured in from the shattered window. Serov lying flat on the floor felt a trickle of warm, sticky liquid under his fingers and experienced the soldier's fear of having been hit. But the blood was not his.He rolled toward the overturned table where Vasiliev was crouched, and they grasped hands as they stood up. The light from the corridor filtered through a haze of gunpowder. There were bodies lying in the room and across the threshold. Serov wiped his hands on his trouser leg. Someone was whimpering. Vasiliev picked up the candle and lit it.

"Letchik?" Vasiliev called out.

Like a god damned battlefield, thought Serov; the gunfire, the moans, the silence and the call for medics.

Letchik stumbled to his feet and almost at once went down on his knees bending over the body of Norka, his fingers moving from her wrist to her neck. He was up again and crossing the room. Marko lay sprawled in a corner, his chest perforated in three places. On the couch Swan was cradling Magician in her arms. The whimpers came from his blond head buried between her breasts.

"We have lost two comrades," Letchik announced. Serov saw his hands were also covered with blood.

"They have paid an equal price," said Vasiliev. "This one is Petya." He turned the heavy body over with the tip of his boot. "I don't recognize the other. Give me a hand with them, Sergeant. Any identification?"

"No papers."

"But the rifles, Serov. Look at the rifles!"

Serov picked up a warm barrel, ran his fingers over the stock and whistled. "Berdan army rifle, model IV, the latest."

Vasiliev rummaged in his pockets, produced a pencil stub and a sheet of foolscap.

"Serial numbers," he ordered.

Serov picked up the second rifle, Petya staring him in the face, a hole through his right eye.

"We have to leave the dead where they lie," said Vasiliev.

"We can't leave our comrades to rot here," said Letchik.

"What do you propose?" asked Vasiliev.

"I don't know…but…"

"I take it that as a revolutionary you have no religious convictions. It's just a matter of sentiment. Imagine what will happen if we try to cart the bodies around with us. We can't be sure if these two were alone. Probably they were or we would have more company right now. Still, the racket was enough to bring the police. They might show up at any moment. We have no choice. The authorities will take some time to figure this one out. We'll leave the revolver next to Norka. What do you think, Iri...Swan?" She nodded but he thought her eyes were reproaching him. The hell with it, he thought. What does she expect? He was angry at them all; at Magician for his carelessness, at Norka for her arrogance, at Marko for his childishness. What kind of revolutionaries are these? Amateurs.The hard cases were all with Khalturin and Zheliabov. This lot didn't stand a chance. But he bottled up his rage. He had to work with them, and needed them now more than ever. Damn it! And there was Irina to think about, to protect. God, what a mess I've gotten into to. He'd do what he could to cushion their loss.

"Let's follow Norka's advice, Swan and Letchik out first, waste an hour on the streets, then go back to your rooms. We'll meet in another twenty-four hours. Do you have another safe place?"

"My room will have to do," answered Swan. She gave them an address in the Taganka district. "I'll make certain the yard man is occupied when you arrive."

Letchik was removing all evidence that might identify the bodies of his comrades. There wasn't much to take away. In Marko's pocket he found an unopened letter addressed post restante, the return address indicating it was from his father. Letchik shook his head in disapproval. Vasiliev admired his cool demeanor, his efficient movements. Perhaps, he thought I might have been too harsh in judging them all the same way.

A noise from the hall startled them, but it was only Magician retching.

Chapter
Twenty-Three

"The Apple jelly is all gone, Vasili Vasilievich."

"There is no justice in this world, Serov, none at all."

They were sitting in Vasiliev's office, the samovar bubbling happily, though, as Vasiliev himself had remarked many times, its repertoire was limited.

"I think the war was easier on me than this case." Vasiliev examined his ankle which was resting on a footstool that Serov had appropriated.

"In the war they'd have you in a field hospital, beggin' your pardon."

Vasiliev grunted. "So, Tarashkin and Petya led you a merry chase."

"Merry, I'd not be saying, but the late deceased Petya did keep strange company. All sorts of mysterious goin's on in that feller's life. I wonder that he could make a livin'."

Serov was back in his taleteller's mood, Vasiliev could tell by his singsong. He let Serov ramble on. Tarashkin had taken the cheapest conveyances, it seemed, boats, wagons and only at the last stage, the train, Petya at his heels but taking care not to be spotted, no mean feat in Serov's eyes, given his bulk. Magician was squeezing every kopeck, subsisting on bread and kvass, so far as Serov could tell. Back in Moscow he took up lodgings in Big Tatar Street, while Petya found a room in a boarding house in the Kitai Gorod. Serov had decided to keep tabs on Petya since he seemed to know where to find Tarashkin. Once Petya had located the safe room, he posted a man across the street probably the same one Vasiliev had shot to death. Then Petya seemed to lose interest in Tarashkin. He hardly stirred from his room which he shared with several other men, peasants working as carters, down on their luck by the look of them. Serov had found out that they were *zemlyachiki*, peasants from the same village commune on the Bagration property, living together as an *artel*, an informal workers' cooperative, sharing the same lodgings and helping one another find jobs.

"Comes Thursday, and everythin' changes. It was a good day for ol' Petya. Toward eventide he slips out of his lair and creeps along the streets, wary now, like a bear in strange country. All of a sudden he grabs a cab when there was none other in sight, and off they go, me keepin' up just by luck as another cab comes out of a side street. And wasn't I surprised when the rogue stops outside the Pompei. Well, isn't it one of the gilded halls of our White City? But he doesn't get out, our Petya, but sits there in his cab, so I pays and strolls into a nearby courtyard. But I'm wonderin' who's going to pick up the tab for this little ride. Still he sits there pilin' up the fare. It's gittin' on to midnight when I find out. A man, all muffled up, comes stampin' out of the Pompei like a high spirited stallion leavin' the startin' gate. He goes straight for the cab, swings open the door and pops in, just so. Now I'm cursin' myself for lettin' my cab go, but no. They just sit there. There's no way for me to find out what's goin' on. How long it was I don't know. I'm feelin' a bit chilled when Petya's out of the cab, bowin' and scrapin' right there in the street, and off goes the cab, mysterious stranger and all. Petya's standin' there watchin', but he's a different man. I tell you, Vasili Vasilievich, a different man. No more creepin' around for him. He marches down Tverskaia and grabs the first likhach he sees, a likhach mind you! This gives me a fright. I'm not ready for this. Again I'm lucky to find a cab, but not one of them that can fly like that, and I'm prayin' that he's not off on some trip. I'm also squeezin' the last coppers in my own pocket. There's the silver ruble sewn in my jacket, but that's to go only to save my life, beggin' your pardon. And then the likhach pulls up at a very respectable address, if I may say so. From then on, Petya treats himself right, a new pair of boots, a trim for his beard, he strolls about in the parks, drinks tea in the high class traktirs, and spends a couple o' nights in a good brothel, if you're askin' my opinion. But he don't say a word to no one, save the girls of course and they hadn't anythin' to tell me. That is no one until the next Thursday, which I'm thinkin' a lucky day for him, if you get my meanin'. Back he goes to the Pompei and the same adventure befalls him, as they say. And I'm beginnin' to wonder if it'll happen thrice, as in the folk tales."

"And tomorrow night is Thursday by some nice coincidence." Vasiliev broke in.

"That's correct, Your Honor."

"And Petya will not be there, but we will."

"Somethin' of the sort occurs to me as well, beggin' your pardon."

Vasiliev had hoped for a clear, cold night and got more than he bargained for. Twenty degrees of frost gave him a good excuse to pull the fur blanket up to the tip of his false nose. Under the fur hat with the flaps down, only his fake bushy white eyebrows could be seen. Serov was out of sight at his post in the courtyard where, with the help of a bottle, he had struck up an acquaintance with the yard man and got to share his fire. Vasiliev wished they had been able to take Petya alive, but with any luck he would find out very shortly who the professional was behind the amateur.

Shortly before midnight, the door of the Pompei restaurant opened and a figure wrapped in a long cloak made for the cab in long strides, just as Serov had described him. Vasiliev drew himself into the far corner of the cab. The door was flung open and the coach tilted under a man's weight. Vasiliev gave a visible start and exclaimed in a cracked, high-pitched voice.

"Eh, eh! What's this? Is that you Afanasy?" He pulled down the fur blanket and thrust his Dundreary whiskers close to the man's face half concealed by a muffler. The man let out a curse and reached inside his cloak, going to the belt. Vasiliev was wrapped tightly in furs and there was no question of giving resistance, nor, he hoped, was there any need.

"Who the devil are you?" The figure stepped back to the pavement leaving the door open. Vasiliev pulled back into his dark corner.

"Why you're not Afanasy!" he exclaimed. "My, what a start you gave me. Where is Afanasy?" Vasiliev whined. "You ask, sir, who I am. Well, I might well ask the same of you, giving me such a fright as I sit here peacefully waiting for my brother Afanasy." Vasiliev dropped his eyes and began to fuss with his furs, calling out to the cabby, "Not yet my man, not yet, Afanasy has not come yet."

The figure stood motionless on the pavement, his long cloak pulled to the side, his hand resting on the belt of his tunic.

"You ask who I am, sir. Ah, I repeat myself. Allow me to introduce myself," Vasiliev coughed. "The cold air, please sir, either join me here inside or close the door." After a moment, the door swung shut and Vasiliev rolled down the window a few inches. "I am, sir, Collegial Councilor Arkady Konstantinovich Shaposhnikov, at your service and in a state of some impatience, I can tell you, waiting for my brother, Afanasy Konstantinovich, a Privy Councilor, no less. Have you had the pleasure of meeting him? Did you see him by any chance at his table in the Pompei, always the same table sir, an honored patron, like yourself, perhaps. I would be obliged if you would tell me sir, whether you did in fact see him."

The hand moved away from the belt to pull down the muffler.

"My apologies Arkady Konstantinovich, I thought, mistakenly as I now see, that this cab was free. As a matter of fact I did see your brother, in very lovely company and in no mood I would guess to leave. It is rather thoughtless of him to keep you waiting."

Another cab rolled up behind them, Serov having timed it perfectly.

"Perhaps I shall have better luck with this cab," the figure saluted smartly and backed away.

Vasiliev leaned forward. "Thoughtless, yes, you are right sir, my brother is thoughtless, and I shall wait no longer, but whom have I the pleasure...?" But the figure had turned on his heel and was striding toward the second cab. Vasiliev pounded on the roof with his cane and his cab shot away from the curb. Through the rear window Vasiliev watched the figure in the long cloak open the door to the second cab and stand irresolutely on the pavement. Vasiliev knew he was peering into empty space. Serov had paid the cabby, given the address and then slipped out of the cab by the door to the street. An old trick, Vasiliev mused, but never used to quite this effect. The figure turned, watched Vasiliev's cab until it disappeared from sight before climbing into the second cab. After waiting for some time he ordered the cabby to drive off.

Vasiliev threw off the heavy furs and rummaged in the folds of his coat for a small kit. He doused his handkerchief with a strong smelling solution and soaked his Dundreary whiskers and the white eyebrows before removing them and pulling the putty off the end of his nose. He felt pleased he had solved one problem by establishing the link between the professional operation and the amateurs, but the question of what this had to do with the murder of the Countess still puzzled him.

When they met again Vasiliev told them his plan, and took careful note of their reactions. Taraskhin twitched nervously, running his hands through his hair, his eyes fixed on the floor. Swan was pale and drawn as if from a sleepless night, but her eyes never wavered from Vasiliev. Her hands were folded demurely in her lap. Letchik balanced his chin on his thin fingers laced tightly together, studying Vasiliev like a student in a lecture hall. He was the first to break the silence.

"I shall need a few medical supplies."

"Good. Give Sergeant Serov a list." After a short pause Vasiliev added more as a statement than a question, "So you think it's feasible."

Letchik shrugged. "I can't really say. It depends on many factors. But it's not impossible."

Vasiliev turned to Swan. "I'll leave you in charge of things on your side. We will meet at Kaluzhskaya Square, at the intersection of Donskoi Lane. You know the place? Good. Try to look as much like trading peasants as you can. It's time to put your affection for the people to some practical use. Space out your arrivals at irregular intervals between four thirty and five o'clock. I''ll be there waiting."

Swan stood up, annoyed by Vasiliev's sardonic tone, but refusing to be drawn into another quarrel. "It's good we're joining forces this way. If perhaps from the beginning...." But she realized that everyone bore some of the blame for what had happened. "I shall leave first, then you, Letchik, and you last," she signaled Magician with a toss of her head as if it had become too painful for her to speak his name. Vasiliev felt reassured that she was taking over from Norka. She had the talent for quiet leadership. She made a graceful exit, too, leaving Magician to hold his head and Letchik to scribble down his list of medical supplies. A few minutes later, without warning, Tarashkin jumped to his feet and headed for the door.

"Breaking discipline again," Vasiliev rapped out. Tarashkin stopped, turned and stared at the man he now considered his tormentor. Vasiliev stared back not hiding his contempt for the man he considered a revolutionary without honor, a foolish man who had led the killers to the safe room and caused the death of his comrades. Letchik put down his pencil and brushed past Magician, tapping him lightly on the shoulder as if to give him encouragement. He closed the door noiselessly behind him.

Vasiliev ran down the list Letchik had handed him. Serov peered at Magician, drawing his own conclusions; restless as a flea, he mused, a bad sign,.

"Iuri, I have some questions that you will have to answer. I didn't want to embarrass you any further in front of your comrades, though I hardly imagine that anything you say would be worse than what you did. But perhaps I am wrong. So let's begin with the night of the ball. Then we can fill in the many other blank spots in your life. You crashed the ball. Why? Was it just to confront your, what was she, former patroness, former mistress?"

"Elena was a bitch."

"I had reached that conclusion without your help. What interests me is how you made the discovery."

Magician, thought Vasiliev, has run out of tricks. Perhaps he never had many to begin with, just the thick blond hair, the boyish charm, the smattering of learning.

"I'll make it easy for you. I know you had an affair with Ushakova, your father told me that story."

"You had no right…"

Vasiliev slammed his hand down on the table.

"Damn it, I'm sick of hearing people tell me I have no right. I damn well do have the right; it is you who have none, no rights, you are an illegal, but worse you have betrayed the trust of your comrades. The only reason you are still free is that you may still be of use to us. So let's start with the night of the ball. You had a scheme in mind when you broke into the Bagration house, a scheme you did not share with Swan or Norka. As for Marko, we'll never know, will we, whether he was in on it or not. We have only your word to go on. And you will forgive me if I don't put much faith in that. But I haven't much choice but to hear you out. Just remember I have other witnesses whose testimony could probably send you to Siberia."

"No need to threaten, Inspector," Tarashkin sat down hard and rubbed his face with both hands. "All right, I made a mess of it, but you'll see that I'm not guilty of murder or any other criminal act. As for believing in socialism, that's not a crime in civilized countries."

"Please, Iuri, spare us your secular sermons. If you do not know where to begin, then let me prompt you. How did you meet her, the Countess Ushakova?"

"In the village. I'd been sentence to administrative exile, but you know all that. I met her when she drove over to visit my father, claiming she wanted to borrow books. She heard he was a learned man, but later I found out that was only a pretext. She knew exactly what she was doing. She had keen antennae. Someone must have told her, possibly her servants, that I had come back from Moscow. A very exciting event in the countryside, don't you see? A certified nihilist, expelled from the university, someone to spice up the dull fare of provincial life. You must know how boring it is on those country estates, miles from your nearest neighbor, surrounding by peasants, the dark people. All right," he lifted his hands, "no propaganda! Winter was her salvation, Moscow, Petersburg, balls, dinners, theater; as the wife of a minister she was received at court. But she hated the summer months, languishing in that backwater, nothing but mosquitoes, heat, rain, endless boredom. She couldn't stand Turgenev, did you know that? Of course not; doesn't make much difference. 'He and his damned thunderstorms,' she used to say. Poor Turgenev, he did paint pretty pictures of Russia's provincial muck."

Magician scrapped his shoe on the rung of his chair and began to hum a tune. For a moment Vasiliev thought he had lost him.

Magician stared into space frowning. He looked back at Vasiliev as if he had forgotten where he was.

"Well, once she saw me…, I don't flatter myself, Inspector, but I am fair, well built, in a word not without physical attractions especially for a youngish woman married to a dried up stick..."

How wrong you are, thought Vasiliev.

"...and I had read a few books and been arrested after all. Do you know how many respectable people sympathize with us? Well, let it go. Anyway, I became her newest diversion. Oh, she carried it off well, She was something of an actress herself. I mean she had real talent. She even fooled my father, no mean judge of character I can tell you. She snared him right away, bold slut, got him into a discussion on Lavrov. Imagine! How she knew my father had read the atheists, I don't know. Perhaps something he had said in a sermon, some denunciation of their godless ways. But she too had read a little or picked someone's mind who had. She knew just enough to deceive the unwary. And who else could my father discuss Lavrov with? Certainly not me, who worshipped Lavrov. Poor father, the truly enlightened cleric, one in a hundred thousand parish priests, or is it a million? And he was ripe for her plucking. Then she let it slip out that she subscribed to a few of the thick journals. But she waited to drop that bomb until I could hear her. Oh! That was a master stroke. She knew I would be desperate to read them."

"Clever", said Vasiliev. "She saw you were cut off from your friends, sunk in the dark life of the village, irritated by the misguided efforts of your father to save you from eternal damnation. She offered salvation of a different sort. But still, Iuri, you must admit you were naive, a Countess flaunting socialist theories?"

"You're right, but you didn't know her. She was superb and I was lonely. That first day, I remember every detail as vividly as a Turgenev sketch," he grinned for the first time. "She gave me a few books and promised to return with some journals. When she was gone traces of her scent lingered in the air. My father muttered something about a fresh spirit in the countryside. She was that magnetic. In one short conversation she had enchanted a bitter old priest and a fiery young nihilist."

"And soon it became too much trouble to send over those weighty volumes. She enticed you to the estate."

Magician nodded. "Yes, I know it seems so obvious now. But I was starved for conversation, tired of arguing with papa who sank back into his gloomy moods. So I went. It was all quite innocent, really, the first time. Elena had a flair for surrounding herself with people who showed off her talents, the usual assortment of provincial gentry, a few pompous asses. But each time I came she managed to round up somebody of interest; once it was a privy councilor who had read at least one book, another time an argumentative lawyer or a landowner who had recently come back from seeing a play in Moscow. Hardly sparkling conversationalists. But they were live bait and I went for it."

"And she was beautiful."

Magician gave a hollow laugh." Yes, Inspector, she was beautiful."

"And then what, more meetings, I suppose, greater intimacy."

"Not so fast, Inspector, if you want the whole dreadful story then you have to follow my descent into Hades, circle by circle. No, first there were the visits to the local orphanage, another masterful stroke, don't you think? The staff fell all over themselves. She had been cultivating them for some time for her own purposes. I was taken in too; I eager to see only the best in her. She may have despised Turgenev, but she took his heroines as her model, the noble heroines of our sad Russian countryside. Beneath it all, I see now of course, she was as cunning as the old witch, Baba Iaga. She was probing for my weaknesses; not a tough job, you say. But still I didn't flaunt them, not then. She plied me with questions about my studies, my aspirations, the lofty ideals every young Russian is supposed to cherish. I poured out my soul, all my romantic yearnings concealed under my armor of the realism. Yes, I wanted to be like our dear Nikolai Gavrilovich Chernyshevsky. Of course, it was I who tacked up his print. But I couldn't quite bring it off. It was life imitating art again. She listened, my God how beautifully she listened. We read to one another, wept together, took long drives in the summer heat. In the evening she sang for me, a rich mezzo voice. It was a glorious time, just one summer, even the weather conspired to entrap me, dry and warm with delicious breezes from the south."

"And the Count, was he oblivious to all this?"

"He was rarely in evidence. When he made an appearance he seemed preoccupied. He said little, saw less and retired early to his study. He scarcely noticed I was there. Elena was bored with him. 'He crinkles like chancellery paper,' she used to say and give that throaty laugh of hers. She confided in me, or pretended to. God knows how much was invented. She said she only married him because he saved her from someone worse."

"You ended up falling in love."

"It wasn't difficult, Inspector, not difficult at all."

"Then she seduced you. You weren't shocked by her advances? After all you were engaged in a pure communion of souls."

"So, I was a fool. I don't deny it. Don't think I haven't cursed myself a hundred times. I've gone back over every scene in my mind. How many men fell into the same honey trap? She knew how to make it all seem so natural. Who was it who said, 'To be natural is the result of great efforts'? No one? Perhaps I made it up." He pushed his fingers through his hair.

"How did you get involved with the Jumpers?"

"So you know about that too."

"That was how you got to know Petya, wasn't it. You were never beaten up on Hunter's Row, were you? It was all made up, the story you told me on the Volga."

"Yes, what corruption, what filth. She had befriended some Khlysty. They were servants in her household. They were flagellants all right, but the mild kind. I don't know whether they ever really whipped themselves. They seemed so meek. I think the Synod makes up half the horror stories about them, may be more than half. But their scourges fascinated her. She confessed she dreamed of being whipped and begged me to whip her. I couldn't do it. One of the few violent sectarians introduced her to Petya. He worked on the Bagration estate. I don't know what he did, part time coachman, whatever. He was the one who led her to the Jumpers. He lured her to a black mass, promised to protect her and then he raped her and forced her to take part. She became utterly debased. They made her their nurturer. She begged me to join them."

"And you couldn't resist her; she dragged you down with her."

"Wrong for once, Inspector. No, I never joined them. I was revolted by what I saw. We had a terrible quarrel that night, coming back. I called her the devil's whore, and then I struck her. She groveled at my feet, implored me not to desert her. I can still see her face, streaked with tears. My head was pounding. I wanted to reach out to her, but the sight of those people disgusted me."

"You left her?"

"Yes."

"Yet you couldn't keep away; you were obsessed with her."

"Yes, yes,! My God do I have to wade through this filth again. What are you Inspector, part of this police conspiracy to force us to confess and repent, and then let us hang ourselves in some airless cell."

"Don't play the fool, Iuri, I'm trying to find out who killed her and why the police are covering up. I haven't the slightest interest in your spiritual salvation."

Magician threw back his head. Vasiliev wondered again whether he was going simply to fall apart. Magician pounded his knees with his fists, almost shouting,

"Yes, I loved her, desired her madly, dreamed of her. It was a disease." He was sobbing now. Vasiliev glanced at Serov who was examining his nails.

After a few minutes Magician recovered his voice.

"I came to hate her too. At night I used to steal into her garden. I kept thinking about the times we had wandered there. A charming place, overgrown paths buried in wild pear and crabapple. I stood outside the window and listened to her sing melancholy Russian romances. I hoped she would not see me but I desperately wanted her to know I was there. The perfect nihilist, eh, Inspector?"

"What did she tell you about her relations with Bagration?"

"Ah yes, the villainous father and the weakling son. Shakespearean stuff."

"Let's cut to the chase, Iuri, and drop the literary allusions. Did she tell you that Bagration, the father, had been her lover."

"Ever the good prompter, Inspector. Yes, Bagration had been one of her conquests, only she reversed the order, claimed he had seduced her when she was much younger."

"But that was in Tiflis, before her marriage, ancient history."

"True, but she had made a new conquest in Moscow, also in the Bagration family."

"What, the son too?"

"And the wife."

"Good lord."

"Ah, even the great Inspector Vasiliev can be shocked. Yes, but I know little about the two women, just what the boy told me. What attracted him was her passion for the religious life. That was fakery too. While she took me to orphanages, she took him to the local monastery, some mystic father so and so. And that led to visits to hermits in caves along the Volga and on and on through the Khlysty to the Jumpers. He didn't tell me everything, but it was clear enough that she had found the ideal sexual playmate. You know Sacher-Masoch's *Venus in Furs*? That was her. Apparently she could only be aroused in that way. There's where Petya came back into it, and also Nasya, her maid. They were all part of it."

Magician rubbed his cheek with the back of his hand.

"But then Elena passed beyond villainy to crime. She tried to blackmail the Prince. She threatened to expose the dark side of his son and heir. She soon tired of the boy, but he was confused. Let me give you another literary reference, Inspector. He was wandering in the twilight zone of sexuality. Who said it? I forget. It's not important, but it is a nice turn of phrase."

Magician rubbed his hands together as if, Vasiliev reflected, he was washing them of sin.

"I may have ended up with socialism to console me, but young Bagration became bi-sexual and despairing of his soul, though not doing very much to save it, I dare say. Well, you saw him at the Dostoevsky reading. There were other such occasions. He was a seeker but filled with self-hatred, so corrupt in his own eyes that he couldn't find a way out. Funny, isn't it how we had something in common, though he couldn't guess what it was. We met at literary evenings; papa let him out on occasion, seemed to think they provided a safe outlet. The princeling began to confide in me. He told me how the Countess was using him to blackmail his father. I don't know, maybe she was extorting money from the Princess as well. She was capable of anything at that point."

"But surely money was not the issue."

"Of course not. Elena had to exercise power over people. It was her ultimate form of sexual domination."

"So you decided to turn her weapon against her and the Prince. Was that why you broke into the Bagration house, to get the letters?"

"Yes, well it was for the sake of the movement, damn it. We had to have cash. The People's Will rob banks and dribble a few kopecks down to us when we beg for it. Just for old time's sake, you know. What do you think we live on?"

"Certainly not on student stipends. Did you also intend to take revenge on her?"

"What do you mean?"

"As you say, she was committing a crime. If you were going to use the letters to get money from Bagration, then you could also get it from her. Or perhaps when the well ran dry you could denounce her anonymously to the police."

Magician groaned and covered his face with his hands.

"Steady, Iuri. Tell me the rest. What possessed you that evening? You ruined your own plan. Let me warn you that there is already enough evidence against you in this case to hang you."

"I didn't kill her for God's sake."

"Then you will have to explain what you did do. I know most of it anyway. You and Marko approached the house early in the evening. You got in through a window on the ground floor left unlocked by a confederate, presumably a servant. You were wearing a dress suit under your street clothes. You changed in an unused room and made your way along a passageway in the rear of the mansion. The Count's coachman saw you and thought you were a house demon. Did he frighten you too? You made your way to the library where you ran into two hussar officers. They thought there was something poetic about you. They got you into the ball without knowing who you were. You cut into the quadrille, confronted the Countess. She hissed and cursed you. Bagration intervened, stopped the orchestra and whisked her away in a waltz. Then the two of them used the Sword Dance as a cover to escape together. You followed them up the staircase to the first landing. And there is where I lose sight of you. What happened next?"

"My God, how could you know all that?'

"You wanted a detective, and you got one. Let me backtrack for a moment. Why did you jeopardize your meeting with the young Prince by bursting into the quadrille like that?"

"Why?" Magician seemed confused by the question."Why?" He repeated as though the question had never occurred to him."I don't know. Perhaps it was the same ridiculous impulse...."

"Hardly an impulse; you dressed for the part, ergo, premeditation."

"I knew she'd be there. I needed to see her once more, even to touch her, nothing more."

"All right, we'll grant you a pass given your romantic nature. But romantic natures can turn violent. What happened when you got to the 1812 room?"

"That crazy place, full of guns, banners, all the crap of Russia's glorious past. I went through it as fast as I could and headed for the young Prince's room. It was then I heard the scream. I panicked and escaped down the rear staircase. I was smart enough to have memorized the house plan. I got it from the princeling. Lucky that I did.That scream."

"Didn't you recognize it as the voice of the Countess?"

"I don't know; it was unearthly; it could have been."

"You didn't see the boy and you never got to read the letters."

"No."

"Do you know anything about them, how many, what they said, where he might have hidden them?"

"Nothing, except that they compromised Bagration."

"Did you try again to make contact with the boy?"

"No. After she was killed, I was afraid. But I knew he would be going to the Dostoevsky reading. I told Swan when she asked for my help."

"Do you know the worst of it, Iuri? I'll tell you if you've forgotten. The worst was that your escapade in the ballroom—forget about the blackmail scheme—threatened to compromise your organization. And you put at least one of your comrades in terrible danger. If I had been in your group I would have kicked you out immediately."

"What the hell do you know about our group? You're a cop, for Christ's sake, and what is your group but police stoolies."

Vasiliev lashed out with his open hand, striking Magician across the face, snapping his head back.

"Get out Tarashkin!" Vasiliev felt the urge to thrash him but he was ashamed too that he had let his anger get the best of him. And over what? Over Magician's betrayal of Irina? But who was he to pass judgment on that score?

"Get out," he repeated, quietly.

Magician brushed past Serov who had come back into the room from surveying the street. "Always lookin' like a lost child," he said.

"Think of him as the next Minister of Justice," Vasiliev sneered, rubbing his hand as if to erase a stain. "Strange people these revolutionaries," he said, "and yet sometimes I think that there but for the grace of God go I."

"That could never be!" Serov protested. Vasiliev bit his lip. He had almost forgotten the limits of their friendship. Ever since they were children, Serov had refused to countenance any weakness in Vasiliev. To have done so would have shattered his world. Vasiliev knew he could never share his doubts with Serov, his youthful hunger for social justice in Russia even at the cost of violence, the terrible Russian rebellion as Pushkin called it. If it hadn't been for his father, cynic though he was, and the Davidovs, who knows what paths he might have followed.

"Perhaps not," he smiled laying a hand on Serov's shoulders. "You remind me Sergeant that soul-searching is for adolescent intellectuals. We have too much to do, beginning with tracing the serial numbers on the rifles, then collecting the medical supplies, shovels, kerosene lanterns and a crowbar. We'll work out the delivery later on."

Serov came smartly to attention, relieved that Vasiliev had snapped out of his mood. "Vasili Vasilievich, there's one thing still puzzles me. Who was meetin' Petya at the Pompei?"

"Ah, the guiding hand, the professional behind the amateur. None other than our elegant Gendarme, Colonel Kostya Van der Fleet."

"Mother of God!"

"I can't be certain that Van der Fleet hired Petya to kill me. That seems rather extreme. And I don't know whether he is playing a lone hand or acting on behalf of someone else, possibly Shuev. I guessed pretty early on that there is more to the Ushakova murder than meets the eye, or most people's eyes. The political side was always there, but Van der Fleet is risking his neck in this, and he's too smart not to know it. Just to prove a point? What does he gain by it? Are the Gendarmes trying to get the nobility to rally round the tsar by scaring them? Too tricky, it could boomerang and drive them farther away. Or are they worried about the reform? Why should they care about a consultative assembly? Or why care about it enough to compromise their organization? Look at this way, Sergeant. They have penetrated the People's Will, arrested some of its top people, Goldenburg, Mikhailov, probably others we don't even know about. They're riding high. Yet Van der Fleet gets mixed up with a petty thug like Petya. Is he really out to get rid of me? If so, why not use his own agents? Oh, they trail me, but why don't they strike? I'm missing something, something I fear that's very important."

Serov knew Vasiliev would figure it out. He always did. His only worry was where to pick up the medical supplies, shovels, lamps and, what else was there, a crow bar?

Chapter
Twenty-Four

Vasiliev felt Irina pressing against him as they sat on the curb of Kaluzhskaya Square watching the bulky peasant carts rumble past. He shifted his weight until his shoulder touched Tarashkin on his left. He needed to concentrate and having Irina so close wasn't making it easy. A light coating of snow covered the roofs of the houses surrounding the square but there was no sign of it in the muddy ruts that crisscrossed the road. Another mid-winter thaw reminded Vasiliev with no great enthusiasm of Osholovo. He glanced at Irina but her eyes were fixed on something beyond the wet roofs. On her other side Letchik sat with his chin in his hands. Vasiliev admired his long, tapered fingers, the fingers of a surgeon.

The four of them attracted no attention, wrapped in sheepskin coats, with burlap bags slung over their shoulders. They looked like a hundred other trading peasants from the villages come to Moscow to sell their wares at the big open markets. Magician pulled a crust of black bread out of his pack and tore off a chunk with his teeth. Swan began to hum softly. Vasiliev had to smile to himself. They were playing their parts well.

A lamp lighter was making his round along the perimeter of the square. He walked toward them along the Neskuchny Garden where Donskoi Lane separated from the main thoroughfare and meandered toward the monastery. They waited until he came near and then slowly got to their feet and made their way down the Lane past the massive green walls of the debtor's prison, the notorious Tity, as it was known to Muscovites. As they shuffled past a row of tall beech trees, a wagon drawn by four powerful dray horses, steam pouring from their nostrils, turned into the Lane. When it came abreast of them, the driver slowed the horses to a walk, leaned back and tipped a long flat box off the side of the wagon. It splashed into the mud.

"Hey, brother, you've lost part of your load!" Vasiliev cried out in the harsh accents of a peasant from the north. The driver gave no sign of having heard and cracking his whip, urged the horses forward. The wagon rumbled out of sight.

Vasiliev stepped into the road and gingerly poked the box with the tip of his boot. He turned to his companions, shrugging his shoulders while his eyes darted up and down the street, missing nothing. He bent over and spelled out loud the letters that were barely visible in the growing dusk. "G.G. Z-A-V-O-D-O-V-S-K-Y A-N-D S-O-N-S. Swan stared after the wagon, Letchik surveyed the Square. After a few minutes they gave the all clear signal.

"Altogether now, lift," muttered Vasiliev, "and quickly into the gardens."

They pushed their way through the wet bushes until they came to a windowless shed. The padlock was new but the fittings had been loosened. Serov had done his work well. It took them only a minute to pull out the rusty screws and drag the box inside. They pried it open. Vasiliev picked up each item, examined it and passed it along. It was all there, the four spades, three shuttered kerosene lanterns, a coil of rope, a crow bar and a small box containing medical instruments wrapped in cotton wadding. Letchik turned these over in his hands. In the darkness no one could see the grin of childish pleasure on his face.

At one end of the shed wooden boards had been arranged on the bare ground; an odor of resin filled the air. Serov had made their beds as well. They lay down on the boards and waited. No one slept. Vasiliev was conscious of Irina's body next to him, but this time he did not move away. They only stirred when the great copper bells of the Donskoi Monastery began to toll. They all counted the twelve strokes. They got to their feet and left the shed, walking in single file. Vasiliev led them down narrow paths until they could reach out and touch the walls of the monastery. Overhead banks of low clouds masked the stars. It was a night of the new moon. Vasiliev uncoiled the rope and attached it around their waists leaving a length of three feet between each of them. They made their way to a small iron gate set into the recesses of the southern wall, a private entrance for high-ranking visitors who might wish to enter the cemetery unobtrusively. Vasiliev flicked the rope and they came to a halt. He fumbled for the wire that should have been attached to the lower end of the grate. He breathed a sigh of relief. Serov had not failed him. The bolt slid noiselessly in its socket. The hinges had been oiled recently and the grate swung open at his touch.

Vasiliev glanced up at a point of light above them. A taper burned low in the window of a single cell built to house the monk who served as watchman. Vasiliev could barely make out the shape of an alarm bell suspended outside the door and connected by a length of cord to a pull above the monk's cot. He had agreed with Serov that it was too risky to cut it. Once they had passed the grate, Vasiliev began counting to himself. He had been over the ground in daylight and measured the distance: a hundred and three paces straight ahead, a right turn, then thirty-five paces. Looming over them they could see a dark mass, the Church of Our Lady of the Don. Swan remembered how vivid its blue cupola had shone in the autumn sun. It seemed half a lifetime ago.

"...thirty three, thirty four, thirty five." Vasiliev tugged the rope twice and the line of four halted in their tracks. They should be standing directly in front of the grave of Petr Chaadayev, who fifty years before had been judged officially insane by Nicholas I for having questioned official truth. The chiseled letters of his name stood out boldly against the gray granite. Vasiliev wondered whether his friend Ivan would have seen this midnight escapade as the work of another madman.

He raised his lantern and opened the shutter a crack, letting a narrow beam of light fall on the headstones crowded together as if to provide one another everlasting comfort. Vasiliev moved the lantern until he saw a mound of earth strewn with wet and withered flowers half buried in the melting snow. There was no stone to mark the grave. He closed the shutter and opened it again. No need to speak, they knew this was the place.

As they moved into position a sharp clanging noise rang out only to be smothered. One of them had nicked the edge of a headstone with a shovel. "Tarashkin," muttered Vasiliev. He and Swan held their lanterns high on opposite sides of the grave, while Letchik and Tarashkin removed the dead flowers and began to dig. The men spelled one another at fifteen minute intervals. The earth was soft but heavy with moisture from the melting snow. They made slower progress than Vasiliev had planned. He began to regret not having brought along Serov. They were spattered with mud, and their muscles ached. They were breathing heavily now. Vasiliev signaled a short rest. Swan lowered her lantern to the ground. They stared into the deep pit.

Vasiliev picked up a shovel and climbed down alone, working steadily until his spade struck a hard surface. Magician and Letchik joined him. They cleared the top of the embossed oaken casket until their hands were caked with mud. Swan stood over them. She remembered a nightmare from childhood after a sermon she had heard on the resurrection of the flesh; the three men now looked like corpses rising from their graves.

Confined in the narrow space they took turns trying to pry open the casket with the crowbar but they kept slipping in the muddy soil. The seal resisted as if some supernatural force were holding down the lid. Magician imagined the Countess fiercely clinging on from the inside, desperate to protect her secrets. He gave a shudder and exerted his full strength. The last clasp gave way with a crack like a gunshot. The three men leaned back exhausted against the muddy walls of the grave.

Letchik signaled to Swan and she handed down a small box. He unfolded the wrappings, removed four squares of double gauze bandage and soaked them in alcohol. Using a clean cloth he wiped the mud off their faces and tied on the masks. He passed another up to Swan. She thought they looked even more ghastly now. For the first time the word ghoul sprang to her lips and she felt a wave of nausea. A momentary giddiness overcame Magician. He reached back against the wall of the pit to steady himself. They listened to one another's ragged breathing, waiting for Vasiliev to give the signal. He nodded and seized one end of the casket. Together they raised the lid. Swan opened the shutter of the lantern and light flooded over the decomposing face of the Countess. Her lantern wavered for an instant then steadied. Vasiliev glanced up to meet Irina's wide-open eyes. So, he thought, she would spare herself nothing.

Vasiliev lit the second lantern and held it directly over the corpse. Letchik began his examination, head bent, his hands moving deftly, choosing instruments from his medicine case. Magician looked away as Letchik exposed her breasts. Plucking Vasiliev's sleeve Letchek drew the lantern closer and pointed to dark marks on the dead woman's throat and breasts. Suddenly, he squeezed Vasiliev's hand. A triumphant expression lit up his face. He guided Vasiliev's fingers over the stiff flesh under the Countess' right breast. He pressed his mouth against Vasiliev's ear and whispered. "Could be the fatal wound, a stab wound."

Vasiliev stared at the Countess' golden tresses set in an elaborate coiffure and then at the withered features, the face of a hundred year old woman. He glanced around. Magician was slumped against the earthen wall of the grave, his head averted, his chest heaving. Vasiliev guessed it was no longer from exertion. Letchik was cleaning his instruments before putting them back in the medical case. Swan stood rigidly at the head of the grave, holding her lantern high. Vasiliev set down his lantern and drew a deep breath. He had been right. The Countess had been murdered, half strangled and stabbed before she was dumped into the carriage. The grenade had been rigged in haste to cover up the crime. The Gendarmes had not bothered to examine the body or draw any conclusions from the unusual kind of explosive device. He still was not certain who had killed her, but all the evidence now pointed to one man. More puzzling was the connection was between Petya and Van der Fleet. It did not make sense that a decorated officer who was hunting down terrorists with great success would conspire with a common thug to get rid of him. Yet it was a fact.

He was about to raise his arm as a signal to replace the lid of the coffin when a terrifying scream split the air. He whirled and pulled out his service revolver, accidentally kicking over his lantern. He could see nothing beyond the circle of Swan's light. The shutter on her lantern slammed shut with a metallic ring and they were plunged into darkness. "Don't move, anyone," Vasiliev said, and then realized how foolish that must have sounded. He heard Tarashkin's hoarse whisper, "Swan, are you all right?"

"Quick, give us a light Irisha!"

The scream had given way to a wailing sound that seemed to

come from farther away. The shutter swung open, the beam catching Swan's frightened features as she held high the lantern. Letchik had raised his shovel as if to strike out, but Tarashkin had dropped his in the mud and was now staring at the face of the Countess who seemed to be winking at him, a lump of mud from Letchik's shovel having fallen on her right eye. An image from Pushkin's *Queen of Spades* flashed through his mind. He shuddered.

Vasiliev was crouched over the casket aiming his revolver at a figure that squatted on the mound of earth above them. It was flailing the air with its arms, a mass of white hair framing its head like a nimbus. Its body was draped in rags so shredded in places that they trailed off in wispy threads. The wailing was dying down, giving way to groans. Then the figure rose to its feet and began stamping the earth in what looked to them all like a grotesque dance. Vasiliev lowered his revolver, straining to understand the jumble of words tumbling out of the toothless mouth.

"Oh, ye wicked, wicked children of Beelzebub..." that much was clear, but then he could make out only disconnected phrases like "agents of Hell" and "violators of sacred soil." Vasiliev made out the figure to be an old man or perhaps only an emaciated one. Whatever he was, he was angry. He fell to his knees, snatched a handful of soft earth and hurled it down on the face of the Countess where it landed with a dull thud. The impact sent another tremor through Magician. The words came out more clearly, "What is your evil purpose, ye demons of darkness? A curse upon ye for all eternity." He reared back and extended his arms so that his body took the shape of a cross.

"Christ, who is this madman," growled Letchik between clenched teeth, his shovel still poised over his head.

"Wait!" Swan exclaimed, "Don't touch him, he's harmless, a *yurodovy*, a holy fool." They looked at her as if she too had gone mad, but Letchik's shovel wavered. Vasiliev lowered his revolver.

"Ilarion," Swan was saying, "Ilarion, brother, do ye not know your sister and brethren?"

The man's head jerked sideways and he went down on all fours, peering across the open grave at the girl who was also kneeling, her arms extended, holding out the lantern, as if in supplication.

"Drop the shovel," Vasiliev said quietly, but Letchik had already let it slide to the ground.

"We have come as agents of good will, not Beelzebub. Do you not see the signs? We are simple Russian people, not demons. We seek the truth here." Listening to her voice Vasiliev felt a strange sensation. It was pitched in a lower register than he had ever heard, and it sounded as if she were crooning a lullaby. It seemed to have touched a chord in the *yurodovy's* mind.

"Nay, child," he answered her. The note of hysteria was gone. "The truth is not found in graves of the violated."

"But the dead have been wronged, but not by us. A lamb has been slaughtered and the great and powerful conceal their sins behind fine phrases and empty gestures. Hear me, o wise Ilarion, who has spoken of the three famines and the five plagues."

The man raised his hand as if to shield his eyes, and Swan lifted the lantern so that the light fell on her face. Vasiliev was shocked to see her ecstatic expression. For an instant she looked to him like the Angel of the Lord in a fourteenth century icon of the Annunciation. He felt a thrilling sensation go right through him. What was happening to him? Dostoevsky seemed to be writing the script again. Was he beginning to succumb to the crazy Russian mysticism he had always disdained? Letchik brought him back to earth. "For God's sake!" he rasped. "This heavenly dialogue is going to land us all in Siberia."

"Can you think of an alternative?" Vasiliev replied, dropping a hand on Letchik's shoulder.

"Holy Russia is always with us," Magician sneered.

Vasiliev felt suddenly annoyed. "It's a hell of a lot better than Jumpers," he muttered.

Ilarion folded his arms. "Speak, child, but do not let thy tongue be led astray by false prophets."

"Dear, wise, Ilarion, before thee lies the mortal remains of Elena Borisovna Ushakova, unjustly slain by the enemies of truth. We disturb her temporal body to grant her eternal rest. Look for thyself, see the marks of violence upon her" Irina intoned, pointing into the grave.

The *yurodovy* crossed himself and leaned over the edge of the pit where Letchik, feeling himself thrust in the middle of a medieval mystery play, pointed silently to the wounds. The *yurodovy* crossed himself again and began to sway from side to side his hands clasped in prayer, his eyes fixed on the mud spattered face of the Countess. Then his head sank slowly on his chest and he remained motionless.

"Close the lid," Irina said. Vasiliev nodded. Was any casket ever closed with greater reverence, he wondered. Poor *yurodovy*, if he had only known...

"Now gentle Ilarion, cast the first handful of earth to cleanse the defilement."

The *yurodovy* showed no sign of comprehension but continued to sit as if dazed or transported onto another plane. Vasiliev had been listening to the faint night sounds beyond the ring of light. He started as the great copper bells of the Great Cathedral boomed the hour. The night air was frosty but he felt the sweat trickling down his back.

Letchik had picked up his shovel and was leaning on it, softly cursing to himself. Tarashkin, slumped against the earthen side of the grave by the head of the Countess, looked as though he might be sick again or else collapse. Swan stood over them, her hands clasped in front of her. Still, they waited. The quarter hour sounded, followed by the dull thud of a clump of earth falling on the lid of the coffin. Ilarion was now pushing the dirt into the grave. They clambered out and stood around him. Swan moved to his side, took his hands, lifted him to his feet and led him away.

"Fill in," Vasiliev ordered, and they thrust their spades into the earth with savage energy. Swan knelt with the *yurodovy* at the edge of the circle of light, speaking to him too softly for Vasiliev to hear. When they finished replacing the earth, they shoveled the withered flowers back in place. The *yurodovy* crawled over to the mound, picked out a sodden, discolored blossom and, gazing at it for a moment, stuck it in Irina's hair. She rose and motioned the others to follow. They reformed their rope chain, shut the lanterns and retraced their steps past Chaadayev and the poets, Vasiliev leading them out again. When they reached the monk's cell they noticed that the taper had burned out. On the eastern horizon a faint glow was visible. Vasiliev slid back the well-oiled bolt and then paused to listen. He thought he could hear a faint hum hovering over the cemetery, but perhaps it was just his imagination playing more tricks on him.

Chapter
Twenty-Five

They came back the way they had gone, threading their way through the paths of the garden to the shed. Magician could not rid himself of the image of the Countess. His father's incantations range in his ears, "the flesh corrupts and then is corrupted." Letchik's thoughts turned to the dissecting table at the Institute. Had he performed his last autopsy? Or was it too early to give up his dream of becoming a doctor in a free society. After all, some day, they would topple this government or it would shrivel from internal weakness like a diseased organism. But how long, how long? Swan let her mind drift back to the days when Ilarion had been a novice at the monastery. Vasiliev had already enrolled in the Page Corps. Had the two men known one another then? Probably not, she thought. Now, years later their three paths had crossed, the holy man, the detective and the revolutionary—of sorts. All from the same class of Russian society. How was it possible to grow so far apart? Her musings were cut short by a tug on the rope. They had returned to the shed and she heard Vasiliev whisper, "no light" as they crossed the threshold, and then, "hand me your tools."

In the darkness Vasiliev could tell from the fleeting touch of her fingers that it was Swan who handed him the coil of rope. Two ideas kept chasing one another inside his head. He knew he would have to confront Prince Bagration in his lair but he was not certain how best to do it. He had long resisted his second and more disquieting thought. He was falling in love with Swan or else he had always been in love with her, but it had been different those many years ago when she was only a child.

"We have a few hours to rest." He found himself issuing unnecessary instructions just to distract himself, but it wasn't working. All he could think of was her amazing self-possession. At every critical moment her intuition had guided her to do the right thing. It was probably the first time she had ever seen a decomposed body. There were men who fainted over less, as he knew from having walked enough battlefields. Her quick reaction to the appearance of the *yurodovy*; it was as if she understood his world and then was able to entered into it. That extraordinary dialogue and her ecstatic look. What had it meant? He doubted she was dissembling. Who was it had compared the Book of Revelations and the catechism of revolution? Perhaps the two worlds were not so far apart.

Shortly after dawn Serov drove his wagon down Donskoi Lane past files of men trudging back from their work as trash collectors, wood carriers and night cabmen. He scanned their faces, gray as the leaden sky above them. In the distance he spotted the four figures seated on a box outside the gate to the Neskuchny Garden. He reined in the horses and looked around him. A porter emerged from a corner house and, sniffing the air, began to sweep the wooden boards that lay across the muddy path to the Lane. Two women carrying large wicker baskets came out of the courtyard. Farther down the street a dog had been let out and was barking at imaginary enemies. Serov had watched the morning routine for several days and concluded that nothing was out of the ordinary.

He drove the wagon up to Vasiliev and his crew, as he liked to think of them. He jumped down and helped them load the box. He noticed how closely their faces matched those of the tired men passing them on foot. They climbed into the wagon, lay down and pulled burlap sacking over their legs.

Serov guided the horses past the monastery walls, blood red in the morning light, beyond the city limits, into the suburbs where clusters of wooden cabins gave way to open fields. He reined in on a deserted patch of ground.

"So she was stabbed," Vasiliev began, deciding that he could get more out of Letchik by not questioning him directly.

"Yes, it looks that way. The cause of death too, as I told you. But you know everything I say is more like an informed guess, since I was not able to make an internal examination. My conclusions have to be tentative."

"I understand. It is often the same with my work."

"Deep wound under the heart made by a sharp instrument, most likely a dagger, curious wound."

"A dagger and not a knife, interesting that you make a distinction."

"Hard to say, still, it looked to me like the wound was made by a broad, thin and possibly two edged dagger of Eastern origin."

"And the bruise marks? Was she man-handled before being stabbed?"

"Correct. The bruises around her neck and throat indicated an attempt to strangle her, but the skin was not broken, the thorax was intact and there was no indication that she was suffocated. None of her vertebrae were broken; in other words her neck had not been snapped. Another curious thing. She had some superficial injuries on her legs that seem to have been made by flying pellets or metal fragments."

"Let's go back to the dagger wound for a moment. Would there have been a great loss of blood?"

"Absolutely, a pool of it, I would imagine."

"That's very important." Vasiliev glanced at Letchik's swollen, blistered hands caked with dried mud. How much of a chance that he could ever become a doctor in Russia? All of them were counting on a revolution and then offering their service to the people. But why not begin now? Perhaps Letchik could get a degree abroad. Zurich was a good place. He knew lots of émigrés went there. If he could get out of the country with a little money, would he go? Vasiliev caught himself wondering how he might be smuggled across the frontier. Healthy thoughts for an Inspector of police. You see these people as human beings and then what happens?

"It hardly looks premeditated," he murmured as if to himself. "Someone knocked her around and then the same person or someone else decided she had to be killed and then what? Had the killer seized the first weapon at hand? I wonder why the attempt to strangle her failed; lack of strength or second thoughts?"

Serov had climbed down to feed the horses. Letchik and Magician were dozing. Swan was staring at him. Huddled in her sheepskin, a stray strand of hair caught in the corner of her mouth, she still looked less of a peasant to him than the rest of them. He turned to her, "You saved us in there. It was quite a performance."

She cocked her head as if listening to the bells now far in the distance summoning the monks to matins. Her eyes followed a flock of gray crows just dots in the sky, circling the walls of the Donskoi.

"You didn't recognize him, Vasya? Well, even a wise man stumbles, to quote Serov, our fount of popular wisdom. You might have known him as Kharitonov. No? Well, he renounced the easy life, like you. He entered a seminary, took his vows but then he quit his sanctuary for the wilderness like a hermit. In the old tradition he went north across the Volga, disappeared from sight. It created quite a stir at the time, but you had gone off to Petersburg by then. You knew the family though, old nobles, tracing their line back to Grand Duke Gedimin of Lithuania. They had high hopes that with his learning and talents he would rise in the hierarchy and become an abbot, perhaps even metropolitan, rich, comfortable and powerful, a credit to his illustrious lineage," she added with a rare touch of sarcasm. "You know these ambitions; so do I."

Vasiliev nodded watching the wind play with her hair, now whipping the strand across her cheek like an arabesque.

"In the early years your old friend, my brother, and I tried to trace him. One summer we discovered his cave but he refused to see me, a woman, for fear of temptation. Soon after, we heard that he had moved off into a more remote area. He had become something of a legend. It was fashionable to drive out and look at his cave, catch a glimpse of the holy man. I like to think my brother and I had different reasons than vulgar curiosity. What a strange country. We venerate the holy men but treat them like prime specimens in a zoo. It was said he went mad from loneliness and became a wanderer." A far-away look came over her.

"There are lots of stories about him, but they can't all be true. Some say he got as far as Mount Athos; others claim to have seen him in the Church of the Holy Sepulcher in Jerusalem. There are the usual tales of miraculous deeds. So he did become celebrated, but not as the family wished. I wonder if the same will be true of me. What do you think?"

Vasiliev shrugged and said nothing.

"You don't want to predict martyrdom for me?" she smiled sadly. He felt a lump in his throat.

"It's been many years since I saw him, but last night I thought I recognized him though I knew he wouldn't know me any more. What stirred him were the verses from the Apocalypse. Strange how that book was always my favorite. It seemed to me to read like a fairy tale. That's all there is to it."

Vasiliev was pursuing a different set of images, of a tall, slim girl just entering her teens with a single long braid falling down her back, wearing a dress of white muslin and standing on the veranda of a big country house. She was waving as he and her brother rode off to hunt. Of this same girl pursuing him in a game of blind man's bluff and he allowing her to catch him because he knew from her brother that she was subject to dizzy spells if she was blindfolded too long. Of crackling fires and the aroma of pine resin burning. Of Antonovka apples under wet leaves. Of a small terrier yapping at them as they picked wild strawberries.

"It seems so long ago," he said out loud and immediately thought how inane that sounded, how foreign from what was really in his mind. But he realized too this was an impossible love. A greater gulf separated them than between Romeo and Juliette, or Heloise and Abelard.

The crows had spotted them and had come on fast, circling over head, then landing nearby in hopes of picking up grains of oats that fell from Serov's feeding of the horses. Suddenly, they shot upwards again wheeling over the muddy fields still covered with patches of snow and disappeared over the crenellated battlements of the monastery.

"Something has frightened the crows," said Swan. "Perhaps it's time we left here." She closed her eyes and lay back on the floor of the wagon.

"Let's be off, Sergeant, take the road along the embankment."

It was getting colder again, the muddy ruts were beginning to freeze up and the ride back subjected them to a hard pounding. But Vasiliev did not notice, preoccupied with his own thoughts.

What an odd generation we are, coming of age in the sixties and seventies, he thought. If we call the roll we find a detective whose idea of justice has as little appeal for the government as for its opponents, a holy fool who may be simply mad, but is venerated because of that, a woman revolutionary, or at least an illegal who does not believe in violence, her brother, a patriot who died in war to defend Slavdom and Russia, a feckless romantic who falls in love with the depraved Countess. We were raised in the same places, played the same games, shared the same books and dreams. Yet how far apart we have been cast. And when we are gone how will they look back on us, in fifty or a hundred years? Who among us will have better served the people? And what is Irisha thinking? Perhaps the same thoughts?

With a sharp jolt the wagon bounced back onto the Valovaya, the road marking the old boundaries of the city walls. The ride became smoother but they were hemmed in by a crush of carts and wagons, the air ringing with the curses of drivers and the neighing of horses. Opposite the Old Tatar Quarter, Tarashkin slipped off the back of the wagon and disappeared in the jumble of old houses and shops of Small Tatar Street. Soon after they passed over the boards of the wooden Krashnokhomsky Bridge, Letchik scrambled over the side. Vasiliev was left alone with Irina. He thought of many things to say to her, but the words died on his lips. And then, suddenly, she too was gone. He watched her figure until she was lost from sight. Even at a distance no one could have mistaken her for a peasant. She held her head too high, she moved her arms too freely, her bearing was too proud.

Chapter
Twenty-Six

Borka was keeping watch on the cabin where Petya had left the girl. He had concealed himself in the shell of a burnt out cabin diagonally across the way. It was a quiet lane in the southern suburb of Kolomenskoe. In the distance he could make out the tent shape of the Church of the Dormition. The cold was penetrating but he had wrapped himself in his sheepskin and the bitch hound was pressed closely against him for warmth. Hours passed without a sign of movement inside Petya's cabin. But a tell tale wisp of smoke drifted out of the chimney.

Borka dozed off. The sound of retching woke him up. He sprang to his feet. The bitch hound was missing. He found her in convulsions in the yard, at her feet a half-gnawed bone stinking of rotten meat. He cursed himself for not having fed her when they first settled in. He had been thinking only of keeping watch. He carried her to the roofless annex of the cabin where the walls were still standing, sheltering her from the wind. He forced her to throw up again and again until he was sure that the poison was out of her belly. Then he covered her with his sheepskin and stroke her flank until she slept. He started a fire to keep himself warm. No need to worry, he thought, about the smoke giving him away. It seemed clear to him, judging by the charred remains of other fires, that the place had been used before as a shelter, probably by beggars or wanderers. But all this had taken him away from his observation post. He had not seen the troika sleigh pull up in front of Petya's cabin and drop off several men in sky blue uniforms before disappearing around the corner.

When the hound began to breathe normally he went back to the front of the cabin. He squatted down again by the boarded up window with the broken slat. It gave him a clear view of the lane. He sensed immediately that something was wrong. Across the way smoke was no longer coming out of the chimney, and the gate to the yard looked as though he was slightly ajar. He felt uneasy. Vasiliev had told him to follow and to watch. Now he felt at a loss. He feared he had failed the only white man he had ever trusted. What had happened while he was attending the hound? The girl might have left; or someone might have entered the cabin and carried her off, or done something worse to her. He could not tell enough by the signs. Vasiliev would talk about guessing. He had understood what he meant; he did the same thing when he was tracking or hunting in the forest. But he wasn't in the forest now. In the shadow of the great city of Moscow the signs were different, and there were too few. He would have to move in closer. It was risky, he knew. But he couldn't sit there wondering if he was watching an empty dwelling. If she had left or somebody had come there would be signs in the snow. Or perhaps he would have to go into the cabin. He felt for the hunting knife at his belt. As for the carbine, he had left it in a safe place; a tribesman in the streets of a village here could not be seen carrying such a weapon. But now it was out of reach.

He waited until the cabin was hardly visible in the dusk, and the wisdom of waiting longer had worn thin. What decided him was the absence of candlelight in the window. He went back to the annex to check that the hound was resting. Then he slipped across the lane and made his way to the rear of Petya's cabin.He peered through the thick green glass of the window, fearing that he had waited too long. All he could see were the dark shadows of the furniture, tables and chairs. He edged his way along the timbered wall until he came to the front of the cabin. Bending low he examined the border of the path and was alarmed to see the snow had been trampled down. Small clumps of snow were melting on the top step of the porch. They could not have fallen from the eaves which jutted out beyond the porch.

Borka vaulted over the steps, holding on to the wooden pillar that supported the eaves, and landed noiselessly on the porch. He touched the heavy door and it swung open. Once inside he closed the door and listened. The inside of the cabin was pitch black. A slight creaking sound brought him to a complete halt. In the forest you could tell whether the snapping of a branch was made by an animal, a man or the weight of new fallen snow. But inside a cabin who was to know. It might be a rat, the settling of the foundations, the contraction of a window frame in the cold. He had to make sure; so he waited. But there was no further sound. He made his way along the wall until he reached an opening. He knew it led into the single large room that occupied the entire left side of the cabin. Every peasant cabin was built along the same plan. There would be two smaller rooms to the right of the hallway and a storage room behind them. He eased himself around the fore post and entered the large room. Here the odor of fish soup was strong, but the room was getting cold from the lack of a fire. He felt his way past the oven, an iron-bound chest, chairs and table. His foot struck something soft lying under the table. He went down on one knee and moved his hand over the body of a woman. It was warm, but rigid. She was obviously dead, her long hair slippery with blood. He pulled back and knocked against the side of a chair.

Another sound came from the hallway, someone approaching, crossing the threshold. Borka decided to charge him before he got too close. He drew his knife, leapt up from his crouched position and bounded across the room. He collided with a man, seized him by the throat and cut off his breath. The knife went in just below the man's ribs. He gurgled as he crumpled to the floor, dragging the knife with him as he fell. Borka heard shouts and the crunch of boots. He turned to run but was knocked to his knees by a terrible blow on his neck. He tried to cover up his head, but he was stunned by a blow to the side of his face. He collapsed.They continued to beat him, breaking his arms and smashing his skull long after he was senseless.

Vasiliev and Serov were still some distance from the village of Kolomenskoe when they heard the howling of the bitch hound, then a shot and silence. Vasiliev dug his heels into the side of his mount, but the ground was too soft and the snow too deep to give a firm footing and the horse struggled to break into a canter. Between the cabins they caught a glimpse of half a dozen sleds scattered in the lane around Petya's place. Torches illuminated a cluster of sky blue uniforms. Several peasants were standing at the side of a sled, folding up a rough stretcher. A Gendarme shoved some papers into their hands and waved them off.

For an instant Vasiliev felt an impulse to ride into their midst, cursing and scattering them in all directions. Intuitively he knew Borka was lying senseless at the bottom of the sled. He knew too what Borka would have wanted, to have his body returned to the ancestral burial grounds. Instead he reined in. There was nothing he could do, dressed like a peasant without documents. They would not hesitate to shoot him down if he tried to intervene. That did not make it any easier to sit in the saddle with a sick, empty feeling in the pit of his stomach.

Serov had already dismounted and stood quietly beside Vasiliev, finally reaching up and touching him on the knee. Vasiliev nodded, swung out of the saddle and together they walked the horses behind the annex and waited until the last of the sleighs had driven off. The villagers began to come into the street, forming a knot around the entrance to Petya's cabin. Vasiliev and Serov pushed their way through. They asked for torches, handed out a few roubles and entered the cabin. Vasiliev found plenty of signs to read, two pools of blood at different places in the big room, the edges of one already drying, the other fresh. Outside they followed Borka's foot prints back to the burned out cabin where the remnants of Borka's fire had burned itself out. In the annex they found the bitch hound covered with a sheepskin, a bullet through her head.

The peasants said they knew nothing except that the Gendarmes had come and carried away three bodies, two men and a woman. Serov listened as Vasiliev tried to reconstruct what had happened. "Borka's hound got sick and he tended her. That's the only reason he would have left his watch. Then something aroused his suspicion, you can see how his footprints go around to the rear. He decided to enter and found the girl, presumably already dead and her murderer still there. They struggled. Did they kill one another? Not likely. Borka had the advantage of surprise and was a formidable fighter. But why had the Gendarmes shown up and not the regular police? How did they get here so quickly?" Serov understood there was nothing for him to say.

Vasiliev returned to Petya's cabin and found the answer to one question in the storage room to the right. The floorboards were still wet in places. "It looks like several men were standing here in wet boots for some time. Borka had walked into a trap. They were waiting for him or someone, possibly us." Serov had never seen such a look of despair on Vasiliev's face, but he also saw madness in his eyes.

Magician climbed four flights of stairs clinging to a wobbly banister that threatened to collapse under the pressure of his weight. A different, nauseating mixture of odors greeted him on every floor, human sweat and urine, cabbage soup and putrid meat. He was sweating and pulled at his collar, though it was already open at the neck. At the third floor landing he began to doubt whether he could make it up the last flight, but pushed ahead. His legs seemed to move mechanically. He grabbed hold of the door jamb for support and fumbled for his key, but the door swung open revealing a wizened old man smelling of candle wax. Magician cursed him under his breath; he hated the old man for his constant spying and the cackling laugh with which he greeted his tenants. But he pitied him too. Years ago he had been a doorman at a fancy restaurant until he let the door slip out of his hand and strike the back of a general. After he was thrown out of work he lived by renting his rooms and sleeping in the corridor. Magician edged past the old man, wondering how much longer he could stand living there. He stumbled into his room. Two men were waiting for him. He recognized them immediately.

The shorter one was powerfully built as if his body had been hewn from a granite block by a strong but unskilled sculptor who forgot to provide him with a waist. The second man, taller but well proportioned had always reminded Magician of an icon of Elijah, his beard and hair forming a reddish halo around his head. Magician reached back for the door, but an unseen hand had closed it and locked him in.

"No need to be frightened, Magician, we are just taking elementary precautions. Surely, you can understand that."

Magician nodded, fearing he might collapse from the trembling of his legs.

"We need your services, just briefly. It's a simple and straight-forward mission, isn't that so, Stonemason?" The man addressed as Stonemason folded his arms on his chest, giving the impression that he had suddenly doubled in size.

"Your relations with Vasiliev are still amicable, I trust?" The red beard moved up and down. It seemed to Magician that the entire halo was in motion.

"Yes," he heard his voice crack.

"Excellent! One has to choose one's messengers carefully these days. You are not ill, are you?"

Your solicitous tone doesn't fool me, Magician thought, but he did not dare to trust his voice again and shook his head.

"So this is the message. We possess half the correspondence between Ushakova and Bagration. Let us agree it is the best half. You shouldn't look surprised, Magician. We work more slowly than you, but more methodically too. Had you remained with us you might have enlarged your bag of tricks. Perhaps you will return to the fold someday. But as for now, you can tell the good Inspector that we are willing to share this treasure with him under certain conditions. We do not intend to negotiate. He will do what we say. He will need to be convinced that we have the letters, and that this is not one of your little games. So, you will tell him that the murder weapon is a Caucasian dagger that hangs on the south wall of the second floor library of the house on Prechistenka Street. You will commit to memory that simple sentence. He may wish to confirm it. Perhaps he will realize that he has more to learn from us. If he wishes to obtain the letters he must meet with us in Piter, not here, and according to our instructions. You remember the book store routine? Good. The author is Karamzin, second edition, volume four. He will be told that they never break up sets. He will reply that a friend took his copy to Berlin. The clerk will then offer to sell him an odd volume, and he will buy it. The message will be inside. Is that clear? Hmm, not very talkative today are you? Perhaps that is all to the good. Tell him the offer is open for seventy-two hours. You will please go now, and, of course, you still remember the penalty for defaulting."

Magician raised his fingers to his lips.

"My dear fellow, how thoughtless of me. You wish a glass of

water. Nothing is easier." He poured from a pitcher standing on the bedside table. Magician always wondered how the man's simplest gesture could convey such a terrifying impression of immense strength and will power. He would always be grateful to Irina. She had given him the courage to break free of this man's domination. He gulped his water and turned to leave. Stonemason clapped his hands and the door flew open. Magician kept his eyes fixed straight ahead as he walked across the landing and down the stairs.

He made his way through the narrow streets of the Old Tatar Quarter as if in a trance, his mind leaping from one image to another: Elena's mud spattered face, the holy fool wailing his doomsday prophesies, the man in the reddish beard pouring water like a statue in a Roman fountain. He felt feverish. It was only after he crossed the river that he became aware of his surroundings and began to take precautions. He ducked into a traktir, ordered tea and looked over the street traffic from his window table. He could not afford to make another mistake like the last time. He moved in and out of courtyards, doubling back, taking some comfort from his thorough knowledge of the Quarter. One thought dominated all the rest; only Swan could help him now.

A street urchin delivered the message to headquarters. He ran back into the street and was lost in the crowd before the dispatcher could catch hold of him. Vasiliev read it out to Serov, "Urgent, meet at Swan's."

"All messages in this case are marked urgent, Sergeant. I wonder if there are any normal occasions to be reckoned with anymore." Serov decided it was all right to joke again. "And, beggin' your pardon, I'm close to forgetting who I'm suppose to be anymore." They went out the rear door in their peasant disguises and within twenty minutes had taken up residence in Swan's safe room. Magician had observed their arrival but waited another ten minutes before he followed them in. He rapped out the signal and entered the room in a rush, slamming the door behind him, already prepared to meet Vasiliev's anger.

"Please Inspector, no lectures today. I took every precaution. This is not one of my tricks as you call them. This is serious and real. I have something for you that you very much want. So give me a chance to speak."

Vasiliev was determined to keep calm. He motioned Tarashkin to be silent and moved to the door and flung it open. He peered into the corridor, holding his service revolver in his pocket. He pointed to the stairs and Serov went down to the ground floor while Vasiliev mounted to the next landing. When they returned Magician was standing by the window, a disconsolate look on his face.

"If you follow my advice, Iuri, you'll give up this revolutionary business. You're not cut out for it. Become a scholar, a monk, abandon the world or go abroad, study law and enter a nice bourgeois profession. I don't care what you do, but leave overthrowing the government to others."

Magician seemed not to have heard what Vasiliev was saying. "I have just come from a meeting with members of the Exec-Com of the People's Will. They told me they have Ushakova's letters to Bagration. They are willing to share them with you under certain conditions."

"How thoughtful of them. I am simply bursting with curiosity. How do you know they aren't bluffing? Did you see the letters? I'd be satisfied with one of them. No? I thought not. Why didn't you ask for proof? And how will this sharing take place? A clandestine rendezvous or delivery of an unmarked parcel? Then there is the question of why they chose you as the messenger. Have you considered the implications of how they went about this? No, again. So, you want me to believe that the Exec-Com has taken time off from their daily routine of plotting to assassinate the tsar in order to give us a helping hand. Perhaps out of the goodness of their hearts? Wonderful! How I've misjudged them. They are really an organization of good Samaritans in disguise."

"They told me something else."

"Another fairy tale, go on."

"The Countess was stabbed by a Caucasian dagger that is presently hanging on the south wall of the second floor library on Prechistenka Street."

"Not bad, Iuri. Of course, you could have told them as much. Letchik guessed a dagger of eastern origin, and you have been on the second floor of that house, though we have only your word as to what you were doing."

"I swear to you, Inspector, I told them nothing, nothing. They didn't give me a chance and...."

"So you were summoned to hear their orders, eh?"

Magician felt his excitement melt away. He reminded Serov of a peacock stripped of its tail.

"Did you recognized any of them or were they hooded?"

"One of them, I knew one of them"

"And would you be so kind as to give me the name or does your revolutionary code of ethics preclude that?"

"It was Zheliabov."

"Zheliabov? Are you sure?"

"It's hard to mistake him, the reddish hair and beard, the voice like a drum beat. Besides, he towers over everyone else."

"If it was really Zheliabov...Damn it, Iuri, if I could only believe you. Zheliabov eh, the top man himself, taking quite a risk. I wonder what their game is." Vasiliev rubbed his chin and walked to the window gazing out at the traffic.

"What's to be the contact?"

Tarashkin told him. "And they want you to meet them within seventy two hours; that's their absolute deadline."

"Are you to report back?"

"No."

Vasiliev turned to Serov. "We'll have to check up on the dagger first. It will be a close thing."

Vasiliev extended his hand. "Thank you Iuri. For once I owe you an apology. This could be a breakthrough. But I'll have to think about it. You had better go now. We should not meet again. I think it would be best if you stayed under cover for the next week. Above all, do not take any independent steps, no surprises. You've done your part. Think about retirement".

Chapter
Twenty-Seven

The light was already beginning to fade, casting shadows on the portico, when two men walked briskly from the rear entrance of the Bagration mansion across the open ground to the stables. Within minutes a coachman wearing a long black coat with red trim brought out the prince's landau drawn by a team of four prancing chestnuts and led them up to the main entrance. Not a minute passed before the prince hurried out of the mansion and flung himself into the coach. An equerry leaped to his place, still buttoning his tunic just as the coachman cracked his whip. The landau shot forward, made a sharp turn onto Prechistenka. It thundered down the street toward the center of Moscow, sweeping from its path a film of snow that had accumulated the previous night. The only observer of the prince's departure was a peddler dressed in an assortment of multicolored castoffs, wearing a top hat with a broken rim. The long pole he balanced on his shoulder held a number of purses, handbags and umbrellas, all imperfectly finished or slightly soiled. As the landau sped past he took several strides into the street so that one end of the pole almost grazed the side of the coach, prompting the equerry to flinch and utter a mother curse. He glanced back to see the peddler pirouette into the middle of the street and open a bright orange parasol; he cursed him again. Turning to face forward the equerry did not catch sight of a horseman galloping out of the gathering gloom at the opposite end of the boulevard. Without slackening his pace, the rider turned into the cobblestone drive of the mansion. His full cape billowed behind him, revealing an officer's uniform

He swung out of the saddle and tossed the reins to the stable boy standing at the foot of the steps whose attention had been distracted by the peddler's antics. The yardman, sweeping the rear court, caught a glimpse of the uniform and scuttled off to his shed where he lay down on the stove and covered himself with his sheepskin.

"Inspector, Major Vasiliev to see Princess Bagration on official and urgent business," he announced to the liveried butler who opened to his insistent pounding. Vasiliev had to smile to himself; if everyone else could toss around "urgent" so could he. He brushed past the stammering servant into the reception hall and then whirled around.

"Well, are you going to stand there with your mouth wide open or will you announce me to your mistress?"

Instead of waiting in the hall, Vasiliev followed the butler through the now familiar period rooms, Through a partially open door he caught a glimpse of leather valises and boxes tied with heavy cord. Vasiliev strode into the Georgian Room, assuming a proprietary air quite different from his first visit.

"A thousand pardons, Princess, for bursting in on you on the eve of your departure, but I have my instructions. My superiors have summoned me to a high level meeting in St. Petersburg. No doubt General Loris-Melikov himself will preside. I have completed my report except for one small but vital detail. It is a matter of filling in the picture as completely as possible, you understand." Vasiliev smile his crooked smile as he slapped his gauntlets against his thigh.

"With your permission I wish to take a quick look at the second floor. A witness has testified to seeing something strange going on there on the night Countess Ushakova was killed. This may have an important bearing on the case. I'm a bit skeptical, but I have to follow up every lead. It's a matter of being absolutely sure; I need to convince myself, and now others as well, that I've examined every scrap of evidence."

There was no mistaking the growing confusion in the Countess' features as she stared at him. Her hand reached out for support, but finding none it remained suspended in air.

"Inspector, I am at a loss. What can I say to you? What witness is this? A woman? I do not understand. My husband is not here,

He will return shortly. A brief visit to the center. We are about to depart for Piter. Everything is in turmoil. What could you possibly expect to find?" The Princess cast an alarmed look toward the door as if appealing for help, but all around them the house was silent. Vasiliev swung the cape from his shoulders and dropped it on the divan. The Princess looked shocked at this breach of manners.

"My dear Princess, I am sorry this comes at such an awkward moment for you, but in these terrible times we cannot always observe the niceties of life as in calmer days. You see, I too must leave at once. I haven't a moment to spare. Even now I shall have to ride hard all the way to the rail station. It is just a formality, a matter of a few moments, a glance at the rooms will be enough." Vasiliev pulled out his watch, his smile faded.

The Princess let her hand drop to her side. "My husband would be angry if I denied him the pleasure," she stammered.

"My apologies, madame." He cut her short and snatching up his cape he backed out of the room with a bow, closing the door behind him. He hurried back through the empty rooms, coming face to face with the butler at the foot of the grand staircase.

"Where have you been, my good man. Your mistress rang several times. Didn't you hear? She is quite agitated and requires your services immediately." Vasiliev adjusted his cape, pulled on his gauntlets and made for the entrance. The butler hesitated a moment and then hastened in the direction of the Georgian Room. Vasiliev listened to his retreating footsteps, then turned and vaulted up the staircase. He paused when he heard a faint cry from below. He pushed open the oaken doors and entered the 1812 room.

A current of air coming from a small opening in the rafters stirred the regimental standards, producing an eerie effect. He felt the uneasiness that all shrines aroused in him. Yet there was no denying the strong impression made by the etchings and prints of the battles of Borodino and Maloyaroslavets, the French crashing through the ice at crossing of the Berezina, the Cossack outriders and peasant partisans. He studied the portrait of General, Prince Bagration. He was struck by the contrast with the present Prince who resembled a bad copy of the original, showing signs of decay in a once illustrious house. Below the painting hung a pair of crossed sabers.

He began examining the glass cases housing medals, buckles, epaulets, helmets with faded plumes and a variety of weapons. The last case contained an assortment of small arms and cannon shot, dark round balls and canister. He noticed that some objects had been rearranged leaving indentations in the black velvet underneath. He tried to lift the glass cover but it appeared to be locked. He pulled open the narrow drawer beneath, groping for the key but felt only parchment, prints and maps. He went down on his knees and worked at the keyhole with his pocketknife until the lock snapped. He raised the cover and rearranged the arms and cannon balls so that they fit into their former places leaving a spherical indentation about six inches long, identical in shape to a Napoleonic grenade.

There was just one more point to check. He hurried down the hallway opening doors until he found the library. Behind him, coming from the staircase the Princess could be heard scolding the butler. Vasiliev shut the door and examined his surroundings. A small candle burned under an icon of the Mother of God in the corner. The main illumination came from two standing candelabra in the shape of acanthus trees. An Anatolian rug covered the floor. The rest of the room was overcrowded with furniture: a sofa, several over-stuffed chairs, an ornately carved desk, a chest with brass fittings, a malachite table, an Oriental screen, book cases lining the walls. A door at the far end led presumably to an inner room. Suspended on the south wall over the mantelpiece a Caucasian dagger of rippled steel glistened in the candlelight. Vasiliev came closer, running his fingers over the surface. He had seen similar weapons in the Caucasus. It was the work of a Chechen armorer, keen to the touch along both edges and honed to a fine point. It was attached to the wall by a metal bracket one end of which had been bent as if the dagger had been wrenched from its socket with great force. Suddenly the room was filled with bright light.

The butler stood in the doorway holding high a candelabrum with twelve tapers. The Princess swept in, panting and gesturing with both hands.

"Inspector, your behavior is shameless. You have no right to invade our privacy. I shall make a formal complaint to your superiors. The heir shall hear of this." Vasiliev was struck by the dramatic change in her appearance. Her face was flushed and her hair in disarray. She glanced at the dagger and he was reminded of Lady Macbeth, but rejected the idea at once. He was after the real killer. He felt more concern over the butler, another loyal Georgian no doubt, who had assumed a menacing stance. Vasiliev now regretted that he had come unarmed. But he had wanted to avoid any suggestion of intimidating the Princess. There were already too many weapons in the house.

"My husband has a famous temper. You must go at once or else there may be terrible consequences."

Vasiliev bowed and murmured an apology, but as he started to leave he was struck by something peculiar about the room. He stopped in mid stride and slowly turned around, as if he had never seen the place before. He had completely forgotten about the existence of the Princess and her butler.

"What is wrong, Inspector. My God, what's come over you," the Princess followed his gaze, slowly raising her hand to cover her mouth.

Vasiliev ignored her. Suddenly it came to him. The arrangement of the furniture was all wrong. The divan had been squeezed into a narrow space to the right of the door through which he had entered. The antique chest with brass fittings stood too close to the mantle, covering one end of the fireplace. Nothing balanced it on the other side. A high back walnut desk, eighteenth century by the looks of it, partially blocked one of the tall windows that over looked Prechistenka. There was no chair where it should have been, in front of the desk and he found it half hidden behind the Oriental screen.

Vasiliev dropped to his knees and ran his hands over the thick pile of the rug, searching for indentations that the furniture must have left after having been moved. "So now it's become a case of indentations," he muttered shaking his head. Behind him he heard the low moaning of the Princess. He looked back to see her collapsed on the divan while the butler stood transfixed in the doorway.

"Close the door and bring the light over here," he ordered. As he reached out to touch the desk leg, the door to the inner room slowly opened allowing a thin shaft of light to fall directly on his face. All he could see was a silhouette and beyond it a large canopied bed and two tapers burning in the icon corner. The figure stood motionless as if undecided whether to enter the room. Vasiliev immediately recognized young Prince Bagration. At first he took no notice of Vasiliev crouched by the desk but riveted his gaze on the Princess sprawled across the divan. Then he lowered his eyes, saw Vasiliev and sprang back, his hands raised in front of him as if to ward off an impending blow, uttering a guttural cry like a small animal trapped in its lair.

"You...you again."

Vasiliev pushed himself upright, bracing himself on the desk.

"Don't touch it!" The boy's arm shot out. Vasiliev stepped out of reach and faced the young Prince.

"Iuri, go back to your room," the Princess whimpered, raising herself on her elbow. "I beg of you for the love of Christ. You are still ill, go back and close the door." She gave another cry when she saw the two identical profiles etched by the candlelight, inches apart from one another.

"There's no way to prevent the truth from being uncovered, Prince. It lies hidden under this desk," Vasiliev said.

Holding Bagration's gaze, Vasiliev leaned his shoulder against the desk, braced his legs and pushed with all his strength. The desk groaned and yielded, slowly pushing the door back in the face of the young prince who was rooted to the spot, his mouth open in a silent scream. It was as if he had fallen into a trance. Then, suddenly, he leaped forward. Vasiliev brushed him aside, knocking him off balance. As he fell he clung to Vasiliev's cape. Sprawled on the carpet he dug his fingers into the thick pile. "Please, for the love of all that's holy. Don't force me to look again at the mark of the beast."

Vasiliev knelt beside him, grasping his shoulders. "I promise to spare you, but you must bare your soul. If you tell me the truth, then your nightmares will cease. You will be left in peace. Tell me the truth. It is the only way to exorcise your devils."

"Iuri, be silent," the Princess gasped and then called to the butler, "Fedya, quick fetch the master. Oh my God, save us."

The butler rushed from the room plunging it into semi-darkness. Young Bagration shrank back from Vasiliev.

"Why are you doing this to me? You've made it all come back just as it was; the candle, the same shadows again, just three of us."

A shiver passed through him and he reached out to wrap himself in Vasiliev's cape.

"When was it like this?"

"Are you really my second self?"

"No, Prince, I am like you, though, a seeker for Truth."

"But you appear in my hours of torment. Are you right then to ask me for the Truth? If you are the devil the Truth will exorcise you. If not then of what use is the Truth? I thought the Truth was noble and radiant in its searing light, but the Truth has become monstrous and the telling of it awful. How can I believe that the Truth shall make me free?"

"Tell it and you shall see, but you must have faith."

The young Prince looked back into his room where the tapers flanking the icon seemed to burn more brightly. Then he turned to Vasiliev, his face untroubled, his voice steady. "She was standing by the bed, gowned, bejeweled and radiant. But I get confused. How can beauty and wickedness be joined together? Is that how they tempted Christ in the wilderness? No, it must have been different. She taunted me, mocked my manhood with cruel words that fell heavily on my heart. She said I was a puppet stuffed with straw, whereas my father was an animal who had forced himself upon her and that my step-mother...."

"Iuri, I forbid you to go on. For the love of God be silent. You are raving. Inspector, he has been sick spiritually and physically. The doctors...he needs rest...heaven help us." The Princess was sobbing as she slid from the divan to the floor and began to crawl towards them.

"She was a bitch goddess, that's what she was, God forgive me. I was weak and tempted by her. I remember her laughing and how it tormented me. Imagine, laughter! But laughter means joy and happiness not humiliation. You see how everything was twisted. I waited for a sign. I turned away from her and felt a breeze behind me. It was like the breath of an angel. Then the candles by my icon fluttered and went out. Another light from somewhere threw her shadow on the wall. Suddenly, it was clear to me what I must do. I seized hold of her, but she broke away. Was I not manly enough? I pursued her, caught her there and the instrument of my liberation fell into my hands."

The voice of the young prince had sunk to a whisper. Was he imitating his idol, Dostoevsky, reading the climax of the Ilusha reading? Vasiliev felt mesmerized and was not prepared for what happened. The young prince moved with surprising agility. He dashed to the mantel piece and wrenched the dagger from its bracket. He whirled to face the Princess and then flung himself on the divan, plunging the blade repeatedly into the silken cushions where she had been lying minutes before. Vasiliev was sickened by the sounds coming from his throat; they were scarcely human.

The Princess lay curled up on the carpet, her body heaving with dry sobs. Vasiliev stepped quickly to her side, but saw there was no need to protect her. The young prince had fallen face down on the divan. The dagger had slipped out of his hand onto the floor.

Vasiliev stood over them. His thoughts moved in all directions. How much was real and how much was fantasy? Could he ever sort it out? Young Bagration's ravings seemed to come from a bad novel, but his torment was real enough. Still, was hard to believe that the young prince had really murdered the Countess. If so then who had arranged the fake bombing? Was the entire household involved? And why was Van der Fleet willing to risk his career to cover up the crime? One mystery solved opened the door to others.

A sharp whistle from the street interrupted Vasiliev's thoughts. The peddler was signaling that the landau was on its way, bringing the Prince back from his errand.

Chapter
Twenty-Eight

Young Bagration's hands felt stiff and clammy as Vasiliev raised him to his feet. "There is no reason to be afraid any more. Your nightmares are over. We've exorcised your personal demon. You can forgive yourself."

The boy had the glazed look Vasiliev knew so well of the criminal who had confessed and was emotionally spent, no longer capable of anger or remorse. He stood uncertainly, then turned and with lowered head shuffled back to his room closing the door softly behind him.

Another shrill whistle from the street announced the arrival of the landau. As it rolled up to the entrance Vasiliev stepped to the window and parted the curtain. The snow had let up but the sky had grown darker, the eastern horizon showing a thin streak of bright orange. It reminded him of a Ural sunset and his sorrow; the hunt would never be the same without Borka.

Vasiliev watched the Prince climb out of the carriage. The butler hurried down the steps to meet him, gesticulating toward the upper floor, his mouth working furiously. Vasiliev made no attempt to conceal himself when the Prince lifted his eyes to the window. As soon as the Prince disappeared under the portico, Vasiliev lit a candle from the mantelpiece, placed it on the carpet at his feet and tried again to move the desk from its place. It required all his strength to ease it inch by inch toward the young Prince's room until he had blocked the doorway completely. He knelt down to examine the large, irregular stain that was now exposed. An effort had been made to wash it out, but he had no doubt that it marked the spot where the Countess' life had ebbed away. He straightened up and drew aside the drapes, folding them inside out to reveal a jagged tear in the inner lining that ran from top to bottom. A clumsy attempt had been made to repair it. He released the drapes, letting them fall back into place just as Prince Bagration stormed into the room.

"What is the meaning of this, Major Vasiliev? Have you gone mad? Tamara my dear, what has happened?" He towered over his wife without looking at her, his eyes glued to Vasiliev. The Princess had managed to drag herself back onto the divan. She could only manage a helpless gesture that went unobserved by either man.

"Prince, it is my duty to inform you that Countess Ushakova was murdered in this room. The proofs are unmistakably clear. Here is the murder weapon." He held out the Chechen dagger. "And there is the mark of her life's blood on the carpet. Before she was killed she had been beaten about the face. An attempt had been made to strangle her. She must have fought for her life. She broke away from her assailant, tried to flee, but was caught and stabbed. As he fell she clutched at the drapery. The weight of her body ripped the inner lining from top to bottom. You can see the crude efforts made to conceal the evidence by washing the stain from the carpet and sewing up the rent in the lining." Vasiliev pointed to the floor and pulled the drapes aside. Bagration's eyes did not waver but became narrow slits.

"I do not believe the murder was planned, but I may be wrong. In any case, the killer or killers tried to conceal their crime. They hit upon an ingenious solution to dispose of the body. They wrapped the Countess in her furs and carried her down into the courtyard probably by the rear staircase. There they dumped her in the back of her coach. The killer or an accomplice must have removed an old French grenade from the 1812 room. The objects in the case were rearranged so that the casual observer would not notice that anything was missing. I have just been down there. I saw the mark on the velvet where it had been. Someone rigged up a crude triggering device, is my guess, a wire attaching the grenade pin to the door of the coach. When the door was opened the grenade would explode. The device was primed by someone who understood the particular preferences of the Countess. She always insisted on leaving the coach from the left side. When she stepped out she wanted to face the entrance so that she could mount the staircase directly. The coachman had strict instructions to be sure he made his approach so that her side would always be turned away from the street.

"How do I know this? The Ushakov coachman told his wife he had been annoyed earlier in the evening. Someone brought the coach from the courtyard to the entrance of your house. He did not like a stranger handling the horses. That was the time when he drove the Count home. I think it was a dress rehearsal for the killer. Later the maneuver would be repeated in order to fool the coachman and conceal the fact that the dead body of the Countess had been placed in the coach while it was in the courtyard. Considering the awe, even fear with which the coachman regarded the Countess, he was unlikely to investigate further. The coachman was a loyal servant. But he had been cleverly distracted and tricked into thinking that the Countess was alive when he drove her home.

"The explosion that killed him concealed the fact that the crime was committed elsewhere. It eliminated him as a witness. Alive, he could have provided information that would have broadened the investigation. But the investigation was perfunctory. The Gendarmes have the habit of attributing violence to terrorists. From the beginning I was suspicious of their report. There were no bloodstains inside the remains of the coach. I found metal pellets in the cushions and in the front pillars of the Ushakov house. That convinced me that this was not a terrorist attack. The People's Will use only dynamite or nitroglycerine. A final point. The mad dog theory did not match a number of facts, too many—the place of the attack, the nature of the weapon, even the identity of the victim. I dismissed it out of hand.

"The conclusion is obvious, Prince. Someone in your household is deeply implicated, someone with access to your private rooms, someone with a professional knowledge of weapons, someone who was involved emotionally with the Countess and was driven to kill her in a moment of rage. Only a few moments ago your son, in the presence of your wife, confessed to killing the Countess. I think the Princess is right. Your son is obviously mentally disturbed. He may be living in a fantasy world. I have already seen other evidence of that. For the moment we can leave open the question of his guilt.

Who else could have committed the crime? You are in the best position to answer. You were the last person to be seen in her company by an independent witness. As the chief investigator in this case, I must ask you respectfully for an explanation."

While Vasiliev was speaking the Prince had seemed to be going through an inner transformation. His blustering manner had vanished. He knitted his brows as his eyes darted around the room coming to rest on the desk jammed against the door to his son's room. For an instant he seemed bemused by the sight; a faint smile passing over his features. Then he threw off his beaver coat and began to pace up and down in front of the divan as if to screen his wife, throwing warning glances in her direction.

"Inspector, you quite amaze me. I have heard about your speculative power or should I call it your poetic imagination. But you have really outdone yourself. You should have been a playwright. But this is poor theater. Of course, you have had some help from my son who also suffers from an overheated imagination. No doubt you know all about him through your snooping. It is none of your business, but he has been under the care of physicians for a long time. They have told me that his nightmares can turn into fantasies in his waking hours under the pressure of external stimuli. So, you see, I agree with you. The boy lives a fantasy life. You cannot take him seriously. Or perhaps it is my wife who has inspired your flights? She comes from an ancient and rich culture steeped in epic poetry. At times the poetry and the prose of life become mixed together. You have seen the Georgian Room. Right out of a fairy tale isn't it? My dear, you should not have encouraged the Inspector's wild imaginings when he last visited us."

"I meant no harm," the Princess whimpered.

"Of course, and none has been done unless the Inspector insists upon pursuing his absurd theory."

"My theory, as you call it, is not absurd, Your Excellency. I have examined the Countess' body in the presence of a physician. The knife wound was mortal. Your son is involved with the Countess in an extremist sectarian community. He has taken part in their violent rites. I have a witness to that too. Your son's confession of what happened the night of the murder matches all the physical evidence. If he did not kill her he saw who did and made the crime his own. It is a familiar phenomenon. The psychologists now call it called transference. The net is drawn too tightly, Prince. You cannot slip out so easily.

"All right, Vasiliev, you shall have your explanation," the Prince snarled. "But first you will have the decency to allow my poor wife to retire to her room. Fedor, come here."

The butler entered and set down his candelabra on the malachite table. It seemed to Vasiliev as if the stage had been lit for the denouement. The Princess took the butler's arm and swaying unsteadily left the room. Vasiliev folded his arms and leaned against the mantelpiece still holding the Chechen dagger. The Prince rubbed the palms of his hands together and resumed pacing.

"Now Vasiliev, you have gone beyond the limits of an invited guest. But then again no one invited you here. You forced your way in. So much the worse for you. You have become quite tiresome with your petty spying. I am going to have to teach you to take your dirty police work elsewhere. Are you ready for some vigorous exercise? You enjoy the reputation of being a gentleman even though you are a bastard."

Vasiliev lowered his arms and stiffened.

"Good! I have touched your honor. I expect you were taught how to defend it. Sabers were always my favorite."

The Prince stalked from the room returning a moment later with two cavalry sabers, the same ones Vasiliev had seen crossed under the portrait of the General.

"Since your fancies attract you to Napoleonic moments in history, we shall play out the rest of this comedy in period style. Don't worry about the blades. I keep them well honed." The Prince slashed the air with his saber, flung the other to the floor and kicked it across to Vasiliev.

"Don't play the fool, Prince. We are not living in the age of Pushkin. These are hardly conditions for a duel. I am obliged to arrest you."

The Prince acted with astonishing quickness. Wielding his saber he knocked the dagger out of Vasiliev's hand. It went spinning across the room. The sword point ended up resting on Vasiliev chest.

"Excuse me, Inspector, but we should be armed equally! Pick

up the saber and fight." The Prince sprang back into position.

A noise behind them coming from the young Prince's room checked Bagration. The door was banging against the desk. They heard a plaintive voice, at first incoherent and then more plainly crying out. "Papa, papa, let me out. I have confessed my sin, but I am free, I am free from all guilt. God has forgiven me."

A grimace passed over the Prince face." Stay in your room; this is no place for you. Go back to your prayers."

"Your son seems to have more sense than you do, Prince." Vasiliev said, picking up the saber. He had not fenced in years and sabers were not his favorite weapon.

"Yes, Vasiliev, you have discovered the murderer, that poor creature bleating inside there. Having satisfied your miserable little curiosity bump, I'll now dispatch you into the next world. Elena, the clever bitch, thought she could enslave and destroy us, but she lost her risky game, just as you are about to lose yours. Poetic justice, isn't that the cliché?"

"You are insane, Prince. The game is up. My men have the house surrounded. You will be taken immediately, and tried for murder."

"Your men? Marvelous, Vasiliev," the Prince forced a laugh. "The lone wolf has suddenly acquired a pack. No, no, Inspector. Your foolish ploy only reveals your desperation. There are no other men, Inspector, just you and I. *En garde!*"

"Prince! For God's sake stop, you will ruin everything!" A figure blocked the doorway of the library and the firm voice of command was unmistakable. The Prince kept his arm extended in the French position.

"No, Colonel, you must not interfere now." Bagration shouted.

The three men held their positions like a tableau vivant. The odor of gutted candles hung in the air. The door was banging again and a small voice cried out, "Papa, papa." Van der Fleet moved first. Entering the room, he tossed his cloak over one shoulder and unbuttoned the leather flap of his holster.

"Prince you have no right to jeopardize our sacred mission for a personal vendetta. You must put up your blade or I will be forced to disarm you."

Bagration's sword arm held steady. "No," he said.

Van der Fleet drew his revolver and pointed it at Vasiliev. "Drop your saber, Inspector." Vasiliev threw it down; his hand was trembling.

"Prince, you cannot slaughter an unarmed man once you have challenged him. No need to worry. We will take care of Vasiliev in our own way. He will do no more harm. But if you kill him you will lose your usefulness. You will have wasted years of planning and destroy our entire operation."

The saber point wavered.

"Damn you, Van der Fleet, damn you."

"When the time has come, Prince you will thank me. Ask yourself what is more important; duty to the empire or self-indulgence?"

The Prince flung his saber across the room and collapsed into a chair. "All right, I had him as good as cleaved. Well, what now? You're not going to let him walk out of here?" He threw his head back against the cushion.

"No, at least not until we have finished what we have to do. Then he can walk all he wants, anywhere he wants. Right now, Inspector Vasiliev deserves a rest from his Herculean labors." Van der Fleet had assumed his familiar bantering tone. "Call Fedor and have him bring a coil of stout rope."

Vasiliev's only thought was to coax Van der Fleet into revealing the conspiracy that bound the two men together. He would have to act the fool.

"Colonel Van der Fleet, I am grateful, you saved my life. But perhaps you do not understand the situation. I have placed the Prince under arrest. He is guilty either of murder of being an accessory in the Ushakova case. The evidence is clear. If you persist in ignoring it then you will become an accessory yourself."

The two men ignored him. While Bagration gave orders to Fedor, Van der Fleet lolled on the divan, peeling off his white gloves and cradling the revolver in his lap.

"Inspector, your lonely mission is at an end. I see that despite your zeal you are still in the dark. I regret that I cannot enlighten you just yet. I shall have to reserve the pleasure, but not for long I hope. Your trouble, my dear fellow, is a common one in our ranks. Your pride, that insufferable arrogance of yours, and your narrowly professional view of things have blinded you to the importance of this moment in our history. Things have been moving too fast in our patriarchal Russia. Ever since the serfs were freed in sixty-one, our leaders have made a number of rotten compromises. Our intelligentsia expected our peasants to become little socialists overnight. They thought we could apply Robert Owen or Fourier to our dirty, ignorant masses. Ah, you are surprised that I know something about the socialists. What did Karl Marx call them—utopian socialists? Well, that's one thing he got right. I've read their works. Dreamers, Vasiliev, dreamers. Even in Western Europe where you have a literate, thrifty and hard-working peasantry, they are utopian dreamers. And what do they sound like in Russia? Our brilliant subversive, the father of them all, the *flaneur* Herzen once said that 'a Russian peasant scratches himself when he pronounces the word God.' I have no doubt that he is right. But do you think he will cease to scratch himself when he pronounces the word socialism?"

"A waste of breath, Colonel, talking to him. He is just a cog in the wheel. Too bad Petya didn't dispose of him long ago," said Bagration.

"I fear my dear Prince that you made a mistake in hiring Petya to do the dirty work. We could have handled this without him. I suspect that he may have led Vasiliev to you."

"Rather to you, Colonel," said Vasiliev. "Or don't you remember your encounter with Collegial Councilor Arkady Konstantinovich Shaposhnikov outside the Pompei?"

"Ah! So that was you. *Touché,* Vasiliev. Yes, that did puzzle me. So it was Petya who led you to me, and I was just trying to pay him to do nothing, whereas the Prince..."

"How was I to know Petya was mixed up with Elena's gang of sectarians. What a depraved woman she was," said Bagration.

"Since you have me at your mercy, gentlemen, perhaps you will tell me what happened at the Kolomenskoe cabin."

"Vasiliev, it is better for your health, and your health is in danger these days, if you restrain your curiosity about everything under the sun. I think we were talking about more important matters like Russia's future. So, do you think that these swinish bastards running around with dynamite charges are capable of running a government? Not even you believe that. And they are the first to admit it. We won't need a state, they say, following that madman Bakunin. No, the whole structure, the police, army, courts, will vanish overnight. What a ridiculous idea. Let me tell you, if they succeed it would be best for Russia if all our institutions did vanish because the Goldenbergs, Khalturins and Mikhailovs would not know how to run them. The revolutionaries are incompetent, hopelessly incompetent.

"You don't need to be convinced of that. But then why this attachment to your idea of abstract justice? The Countess is dead, no great loss to humanity, as I'm sure you have discovered. But you move heaven and earth to discover the real murderers. Meanwhile the terrorists run amok. What a fool you are. You still miss the main point. It is them or us. There is no middle ground in Russia. This is not England or France. Perhaps some day there will be something like it here, but not in our lifetime, my unfortunate friend."

Van der Fleet sighed, tucked his folded gloves into his belt and replaced his revolver in its holster.

"I am not concerned with abstract justice, Colonel. This is a case of murder pure and simple. The evidence is here to prove it, the murder weapon, the blood stains, signs of a struggle, the confessions of both father and son. I can't say which part of their stories is correct. I suspect both were involved in one way or another. The boy may lack the will or strength to kill, but I'm not even sure of that. You did not see how viciously he assaulted the divan. You can see the slash marks where the Princess had been lying. It was as if he were performing the ritual murder of his stepmother. I think the Prince knows the reason why."

"You bastard, Vasiliev," the Prince sprang from his chair."God damn it. I'll skewer you yet."

"Please Prince, the man is just trying to provoke you. Vasiliev, you too should behave yourself. You are a guest in this house."

"You forget too, Colonel, that the Countess was not the only victim."

"Not the only victim? Oh, you mean the coachman. Vasiliev, Vasiliev! Your concern with insignificant individuals is really touching. First the Countess who was no better than a whore if you prefer that to blackmailer, and then a coachman. My God, Vasiliev, a coachman!"

Bagration wrenched himself out of his chair, "I've had enough of this." He picked up his sabers and marched out of the room. Fedor passed him in the hall. "Make damn sure he can't get loose, Fedor."

As Fedor closed the door behind him, they heard scratching behind the desk.

"For God's sake," exclaimed Van der Fleet, "is the poor fool still in there? If he hadn't become involved with that devilish woman none of us would be here. Thank heavens for one thing. He is too mad to give us any further trouble. No one will believe anything he says. Up to now he has been nothing but an embarrassment to us all. The Prince may have his temperamental weaknesses, but he is a man of vision. Unfortunately, in his son the weakness has become a thoroughly debilitating trait. He ranks high among your insignificant creatures."

"There are no insignificant people in the eyes of the law, Van der Fleet. You, unfortunately, share that misconception with the revolutionaries. But you do not have any more right than they do to justify murder on the grounds of some higher cause. If the government violates the law — as it has consistently done in our unhappy land — then what moral force can restrain the people from doing the same? And for all the efficiency of your police and the army, you cannot force Russians to obey the law. You cannot manufacture law-abiding citizens. You can only execute the criminals you do catch. Some day, not yet, I agree with you there, but some day there will be too many for you to catch. The roles will be reversed. They will arrest and execute you with the same brutal disregard for the law."

"Vasiliev, I would very much like to continue this philosophical discussion, but I have the feeling that neither one of us is going to convince the other. I would have welcomed you into our ranks. We need honest men, and no one has ever denied that you were that. But you are also insignificant in the larger scheme of things. Perhaps you will recognize this while you will sit here and we will decide the fate of the empire."

Chapter
Twenty-Nine

Van der Fleet came onto the porch. He leaned on the balustrade and surveyed the boulevard with the trained eye of a professional. A few coaches drove past. The lamplighter had completed his round. Opposite the mansion a porter was clearing snow from a circular drive. Farther down Prechistenka a peddler was dickering with an upstairs maid over the price of a used silk purse. Apparently satisfied that everything looked normal, Van der Fleet went back inside only to emerge several minutes later and drive off in his own carriage. He was followed almost immediately by Prince Bagration and his son, supported by a lackey. Before they left, the Prince gave some orders to the stable boy who led Vasiliev's mount around to the rear courtyard.

Serov who had been cutting his asking price kopeck by kopeck promptly accepted the girl's offer. He watched her strut down the boulevard delighted with her shrewd bargaining. He hesitated. His training dictated that he follow the landau; his instinct told him Vasiliev was in trouble. He did not hesitate for long. He was thinking of Borka at Kolomenskoe. He ambled down the street, heading for the Bagration stables in the rear courtyard of the mansion.

"Hey, lad, any of the womenfolk 'round here want to pick up a bargain?" He did not like the looks of the stable boy, a thick set peasant type with lowering brow whose gnarled hands were unsaddling Vasiliev's horse. Serov stepped across the threshold of the stable.

"Go on, beat it, uncle, before I lay a horsewhip on your mangy hide," he snarled.

"Easy does it, young whipper-snapper, why so jumpy? Hey, that's not one of your horses." Serov spat and dropped the pole, purses and umbrellas on the stable floor.

"Why you son of a bitch, I'll hide the skin off your ass." The stable boy pulled down a whip from a peg on the wall and ran at Serov who dashed out the door and flattened himself against the side of the building. The stable boy, surprised at the peddler's nimble moves, rushed headlong across the threshold. Serov tripped him and knocked him unconscious with a powerful blow to the base of his skull. He dragged the limp body back into the stable, pulled down a pair of reins hanging on the wall and trussed him up. He stuffed his mouth with a rag torn from his own collection. Then he saddled Vasiliev's horse and a mare he selected from the Prince's stud. Leaving both horses hitched inside the stable he walked to the servants' entrance and knocked loudly.

"Well, what do you want?" bawled the cook. Another prize specimen, thought Serov. She was loose-limbed with stringy hair, wearing a dirty smock. Where are all the neat and tidy Georgians? he wondered. Behind her stood a lackey, his black jacket slung casually over his shoulder.

"Listen, auntie, give us a crust in Christ's name. There's been no sellin' today."

"What a nerve beggin' on this street," she began but the lackey interrupted her, "Go ahead give him a couple of kopecks and get rid of him. The master wants no fuss."

The cook stepped away from the door and reached up on the stove. Serov hurled himself at the lackey butting him on the jaw and driving him against the wall. He slid down senseless to the floor, blood streaming from his broken mouth. Serov stifled the cook's scream with one hand and twisted her arm, pinning her against the stove.

"Where is the Inspector?" he growled in her ear.

"I don't know any Inspector. Oh God! Fedor told us the master gave orders not to let anyone in. Have mercy! Take the money on the stove."

"Who else is in the house now?"

"Fedor, the butler, her Excellency and the maid, that's all, I swear. The others left for Piter to get the house ready."

"Put on your shawl and fetch a policeman. If you try to run away we'll clap you irons. Which way to the upstairs library?"

Serov released her and she fled without answering. He lifted the lackey on his shoulder, dropped him in the pantry and bolted the door. Picking up a butcher knife from the kitchen table, he went into the passageway leading to the front of the house. He experienced a twinge of fear. If he had made a mistake it would be the end of him. Assaulting the servants of a Prince without good cause, —he could hear the magistrate already. His work as a policeman would be finished. They would bundle him off for life in Siberian exile. The thought did not stop him.

He paused at every doorway, peering into darkened rooms where the furniture was covered with sheets, his ear cocked for the slightest sound. Nothing. It was as though the house were a mausoleum. The only light he could see was burning at the end of the passageway, probably in the central hall. It would have been better to have found the rear staircase, but at least he could make out the main entrance and the tall candle stands flanking the double doors. He crept along the side of the grand staircase edging his way past a marble column and then stopping again to listen. From now on he would be in the open, climbing in full view of anyone standing on the landing above. Vasiliev had told him about the 1812 room directly overhead. He would head for that and take his bearings. He slipped round the column and froze in his tracks. A shadow had moved on the staircase, he was sure of it. Had he been seen as well? He couldn't be sure. He was partially hidden by the balustrade. He strained his ears but no sound reached him. Had the shadow gone back for help, or was it waiting for him to make the next move? He decided to stay where he was. He extended his arm aiming the butcher knife at the spot where anyone coming down the stairs would come into sight. His eyes were smarting from the strain of staring into the gloom. Yes, it was best to wait. As a child he had excelled in the game of waiting. His friends called him *stolb* the post. In their endless play at hide and seek, he would sit immobile in a dark hole until everyone else had been caught and the seeker would tire and lose interest in finding him. Then he would dart out and with a shriek dash into the circle drawn in the dust, freeing his companions who chanted *stolb, stolb, stolb*. True, Borka had also waited, but not long enough. Serov kept his breathing shallow and willed his muscles to relax to avoid them cramping up.

Without warning the figure of a man hurtled across the balustrade and landed a few feet away. But having misjudged the distance or having slipped on the polished floor he lost his footing and sprawled full length. The saber he was brandishing was jarred from his grip and skittered out of reach. Serov timed his own leap so that he would have struck the man full force in the chest. But instead he missed him entirely and slammed into the opposite wall, The impact knocked the knife out of his hand as he too tumbled to the floor. For an instant the two men faced one another and then simultaneously burst out laughing.

"What a pair," gasped Vasiliev, "damn near killed one another."

Serov had propped himself against the wall and was holding his sides, still incapable of uttering a word.

"Sergeant, what do you think do we qualify as Jumpers?" This set off Serov again and he collapsed with laughter.

"Order, order," Vasiliev cried out, tears streaming down his cheeks. "Give me a hand, Serov, I'm an invalid. I hope to God I didn't twist my ankle again in that last *grand jete.*"

Serov had no idea what a *grand jete* might be, but it did not stop him from breaking out into another paroxysm of laughter. It was good to feel the nervous tension drain away.

"What about the butler, Fedor is it?" asked Serov

"Fedor will give us no more trouble. He's resting upstairs. How about the others?"

"Stretched out in the stable and the pantry in much the same condition."

They burst into laughter again.

"We're mad, Serov, completely mad. Come on, give me a hand. I'm a bit shaky but it'll pass. We can't lie around here any longer. They've got a good head start. God! I've bungled this one from the start."

"No, Vasili Vasilievich, I let 'em slip by me."

"All in a good cause, Sergeant. I'd be the last one to blame you for coming to rescue me. Besides, neither you nor I were in shape to take on the whole gang. In that outfit you couldn't have gotten very far. No, you did right. Peddlers can run Princes to ground, but only after a change of clothes. We also need some luck right now. We have about forty-eight hours to meet Zheliabov's deadline and get those letters. And we have to intercept Van der Fleet along the way."

"I've two horses saddled in back. Cook has run off, huntin' a constable if she has any sense."

"Well done. See if you can find some brandy for me. They didn't offer me a thing to drink. Damned impolite."

They found the lackey in the pantry where Serov had laid him out and Vasiliev soon had his brandy. They had just mounted when two constables came through the archway with the cook urging them on from the rear.

"There he is, the wretch!" She screamed as she saw Serov.

The two men barely glanced at the peddler, snapping to attention when they recognized Vasiliev.

"Perfect timing. lads, who is it, Kharlampov, right?"

"Yes, Your Honor."

"Good, couldn't have picked a better man myself. Now listen carefully. Sergeant Serov and I are on the track of the killers, the Ushakova case. There isn't time to explain. Your orders are to place all the servants under arrest including your cook friend who looks as though she is about to slip away. The rest of them are harmless for the moment though you might want to give the lackey in the pantry some first aid. Check the stable for another miscreant. A third one is stretched out in the upstairs library. Oh yes, and give my compliments to Princess Bagration. You'll find her in the Georgian Room at the end of the corridor, probably with her maid, possibly in a hysterical state. Tell her to stay where she is, for her own protection. That should keep her quiet. I'll get some higher ups from headquarters to handle her arrest. Yes, sorry to say she is an accessory. No one is to be allowed to leave or enter the house. Don't worry I'm taking full responsibility. Here give me your note pad and I'll write you an order. I'll make sure you get reinforcements quickly. Now get to it, lads."

Having seized the cook by both her arms, the two constables saluted. They exchanged grins as the peddler and the major rode out together, the most unlikely pair of horseman they ever saw. "Another Vasiliev and Serov story," said Kharlampov.

Vasiliev held the reins with one hand as they cantered down Prechistenka Street.

"Get yourself back in uniform, Sergeant, and meet me at the St. Petersburg Station in two hours. Book us two berths on the midnight express. We still have a chance to catch up with them before it's too late. The question is too late for what? Damned if I know. But Piter is the only place to settle the fate of the empire. Don't look surprised, Sergeant. I'm not being melodramatic again. There's enough of that in this case. No, those were Van der Fleet's words. They were off to settle 'the fate of the empire.' He is not a man to use words lightly. It seems that the murder of the Countess was not the main attraction, only a sideshow and a spontaneous one at that. From what Van der Fleet said it was something of an embarrassment, threatened to upset a larger plan."

"What about your leg, Vasili Vasilievich?"

"Ah, Sergeant, I never was able to teach you the right sense of values, putting a friend's welfare above the fate of the empire. Where did I fail? Never mind. I'll tell you this. I promise to use my two hours as wisely as you will. I'll let Dr. Zubov take a look at it before I report to headquarters. The chief will be a very unhappy man at the turn of events. He'll not relish keeping a Princess and wife of an intimate of the heir to the throne under house arrest. Not something that might boost his career. To hell with him. Here's where we part, Sergeant. God's speed."

Serov saluted, wheeled his mount and galloped off, his ragged cloak flapping behind him, looking for all the world like a horseman of the Apocalypse.

Vasiliev kept his mount at a slow trot as he rode toward the sounds of the early evening traffic on the ring. He crossed Prechistenka Boulevard and turned left past the Alexander Military School. As the light faded the snow fell more heavily and the wind whipped it into strange shapes. Vasiliev felt light headed, fighting drowsiness, his head nodding, his mind wandering. Was it a campfire he was looking for, Borka's fire beyond the next clump of firs? A mongrel ran into the street and barked. He thought he recognized the bitch hound. A curse from a yard porter broke his reverie. But he was soon imagining figures moving through the screen of falling snow, Bagration swaggering across the street waving his saber, Van der Fleet tossing his cloak over his shoulder, hand at his holster. The next time he saw him he would have to kill him. The idea came too easily. Could he really do it? There seemed no other way to avenge Borka's death. No court would ever convict him, a Gendarme Colonel, for killing a tribesman. Even if it did, he would be pardoned. But what about his own beliefs? Hadn't Van der Fleet mocked his rigid adherence to the law? Would he now mock it as well?

The snow was driving hard. It felt refreshing on his parched lips and face, or were those tears running down his cheeks?

Through the fog of his mind one phrase kept repeating itself, "the fate of empire", and he struggled to grasp something at the edge of his consciousness, but he could not hold on to it.

His horse shook the snow from its mane and Vasiliev started in the saddle. Had he really fallen asleep? He had been dreaming of being thrown into a river bound by heavy chains. As he was sinking below the surface he heard Foma's voice, "exhale, then inhale." The chains fell away.

Fedor's rope had yielded to Foma's secrets. The old man had taught him the escape trick years ago. It was just a matter of expanding your chest and flexing your muscles at the moment they were tying you up, Foma would say. Then by contracting them you got enough slack to wriggle out of the most complex knots. How had the old man learned to be an escape artist, from a circus performer or a darker source? Vasiliev had never found out. But he suspected that Foma had mastered the art for practical reasons. The old man had a pathological fear of being confined. He couldn't bear to wear tight clothing and went around in a loose blouse and trousers that threatened to fall off at any moment. Vasiliev guessed that Foma had been in chains at some time in his life. All he had ever said to Vasiliev was that no living creature, not even a goat, should ever have a rope put round its neck.

Vasiliev reined in. He had almost missed Zubov's house. He dismounted and limped up the steps in a haze. Zubov fussed over him just like Serov, scolding Vasiliev as he applied a tight bandage to his ankle and recommended two weeks rest. Reluctantly, he gave Vasiliev a vial of laudanum accompanied by as stream of cautionary advice. Vasiliev extricated himself as politely as possible, agreeing to abandon his horse and take a likhach to headquarters.

He hobbled into the chief's office and gave his report. He couldn't have said later on whether he had been shouting or whispering. The chief had assumed his morose look, nervously picking at a scab on his chin until it began to bleed. He pressed a handkerchief against his face and glowered at the small red spot it absorbed.

"So you've placed the Princess under house arrest, and beat up the Prince's servants. They may flay you alive for this Vasili and your great friend Ivan, the iron colonel, will send his condolences, nothing more. Oh, it will be all right in the end for you. Retire to your father's estates, become a gentleman farmer. But what about me, out on the street without a pension, eh?"

"One more thing," Vasiliev said. "I've asked Professor Zubov of the Medical-Surgical Institute to apply his new blood test to the stain in the Prince's library."

"Blood test? Never heard of it. What next?" The chief wagged his head slowly as if it were too heavy to hold upright, reminding Vasiliev of a hippopotamus he had once seen in the Jardin des Plantes. "And all this business about sectarians and psychological crimes. You know what Vasili? You are beginning to sound like that fictional detective, what was his name, Porfiry wasn't it? But my dear fellow we are not characters in *Crime and Punishment*."

"No, but you realize, don't you that Dostoevsky took his crimes out of real life. He probably has a clipping file as thick as mine."

"In my day we did without files and blood tests. We just used our fists. Results were the same, or better."

"I've only got half an hour to get to the station, chief, and I need to send a coded message, police priority to Ivan. I've got his cipher so..."

"Of course you have a secret cipher! And I don't know any more what you tell him anyway. What kind of a bureau am I running?" The chief was worrying his chin so ferociously that his handkerchief was stained a deep crimson.

"...so I just need your permission."

"You have it, Vasili, the whole thing is out of my hands now."

"And the household staff at Bagration's?"

"Yes, yes, of course, we'll haul them in for assaulting a police officer, the butler, lackey cook, whatever you've got down there, dressed in the Prince's livery and all."

Vasiliev bowed and left the room having taken a final glance at Alexander II suspended over the chief's desk. The tsar was still looking melancholy. He went through the office, ignoring the whispering of his colleagues, and sat down next to the telegrapher where he composed a coded message to Ivan.

Irrefutable proof Bagration's son killed
Ushakova/stop/ father accessory or material
witness/stop/Van der Fleet involved in
covering up major conspiracy/stop/ request
both be placed under surveillance your office
/stop/ arriving a.m./dated/ 27/II /signed/

He handed it to the dispatcher then pointed to the chief's office where the telegrapher could see through a half open door a dim figure daubing his chin. "It's been approved." The telegrapher's fingers rapidly picked out the unfamiliar sequence of letters. He had known Vasiliev for many years, but the Inspector was wearing a grim expression he had never seen before. Later he spread around the story that it reminded him of the look on the face of his commanding officer leading the charge at Shipka Pass moments before a Turkish bullet went through his brain.

Chapter Thirty

Ivan met Vasiliev in his new suite of offices dominated by an enormous map commemorating Humboldt's second voyage across Siberia. The furnishings struck Vasiliev as stylish if a shade too lavish. The faint odor of eau de cologne hung in the air. Ivan in full dress uniform with all his decorations was standing by a baize table, the tips of his fingers resting on the green cloth.

"Vereshchagin!" exclaimed Vasiliev.

"What?"

"You look as though you are posing for an official portrait by Vereshchagin. Very impressive, Ivan."

Ivan sighed and waved Vasiliev into a chair. "I will never get used to your humor."

"In the past you had less trouble with it."

"Your telegram made quite a stir, Vasili."

"Well put. I should have thought the more appropriate cliché would have been—ruffled some feathers."

"We've followed your instructions, I want you to know. We were waiting for Van der Fleet at the Nikolaev Station. All very discreet of course, a picked group of our most trusted men. It won't surprise you that the Gendarmes were there in force as well. They closed around him and the two Bagrations like a regimental square. I must admit there was something chilling about the maneuver. No question of our intervening. After all we did not have your full report and we have no authority to detain let alone arrest...and I didn't read any such intention in your message, right?"

"Right, or rather, not yet. Where are they now?"

"Our men followed them to Van der Fleet's residence on the Moika Canal. All three of them are still in there. The house is surrounded by a cordon of Gendarmes. A few sharp shooters posted on the roof. We have the place under surveillance, but we can't match their numbers without giving ourselves away. It's a damned irregular procedure, you know. I had the devil of a time convincing Loris-Melikov to spy on someone under his command."

"Did you ask him whether he had authorized a Gendarme detachment to serve as Van der Fleet's personal bodyguard?"

"Not in so many words. Remember Van der Fleet has a good deal of autonomy in the Corps. After all he has a remarkable record."

"So you have told me. But the regimental bodyguard must have struck General Loris-Melikov as odd."

"That's what helped me convince him. Still, we're in a tight spot now. We have to come up with something more than your word against theirs. I believe your story, extraordinary as it is. But I trust you as a friend, while Loris-Melikov only knows you by your reputation. As you know, a reputation here is a fragile thing. And the Gendarmes have been spreading rumors about you. We have to have the strongest proofs that Van der Fleet is criminally culpable. Otherwise it could be damned embarrassing. Van der Fleet could simply deny everything that happened in Moscow. Bagration would back him up, and he has the ear of the heir. The son is hardly a reliable witness. Van der Fleet could turn the tables on you. He could accuse you of being a double agent. After all you have been in touch with the nihilists. You admitted as much to me. And they probably know about it. You said you were being followed by professionals. His men no doubt. What they didn't see they could make up. He holds most of the cards."

Vasiliev had rehearsed the conversation with Ivan, and so far it was proceeding exactly as he anticipated. No one close to the center of power could take on the Gendarmes at this point. But he had decided to press Ivan hard in the hope of squeezing more information out of him about the current state of things. Perhaps he could pick up a clue as to what Van der Fleet meant by "the fate of the empire."

"It seems to me, Ivan, that the campaign against subversion

is getting out of control. When a superior officer cannot demand explanations from his subordinates, when a subordinate commandeers police units for his own and his friends' protection, all in the name of fighting revolutionaries, one wonders if the terrorists haven't already accomplished half their mission. It looks to me, as I have told you before, that the state power is divided against itself. We keep undermining our own authority and what is worse, our moral integrity."

"These are extraordinary times, Vasili. Yes, I know you are tired of that old refrain. But, listen, there is something that has recently come up and you should know about it."

They were interrupted by Ivan's secretary who served tea and left a plate of macaroons on the table. Vasiliev had resolved to play the civilized man, no severed arms or stories of black masses and wild sectarians. He needed Ivan in a good mood.

"English bone china," he remarked holding his cup to the light. "Don't see much of this outside the Home Islands. Too fragile to export." He knew Ivan had the mentality of a collector, and porcelain was his weakness.

"Yes, Vasili, an extravagance. My son-in-law was on a diplomatic mission to London and I persuaded him to supervise the packing and shipping. I thought you might appreciate it. Your father was always such an anglophile."

How pleasant it would be, thought Vasiliev, to spend a few hours sitting in Ivan's comfortable office discussing the manufacture of porcelain, comparing designs and styles. He knew he was fully capable of enjoying it, but not today, perhaps not for a long time to come. He bit into a macaroon.

Ivan put down his cup and took out a cigarette but remembered not to offer one to Vasiliev.

"Let's see, right, the newest developments. About a month ago—no need to tell you that this is still secret—Van der Fleet and Shuev exposed a double agent named Kletochnikov. It now looks as though he was the last member of the People's Will to penetrate our security services. Somehow he got a job as a confidential clerk in the Department of State Police and wormed his way into the confidence of the section chief. Brazen, these chaps, eh? He ended up transcribing reports from the Gendarme secret operatives in the field. Thank God he was not entrusted with all the correspondence. But he got his hands on enough information to help his people sniff out most of the big raids that were being planned. As soon as he found out that Goldenberg had been turned and was our source for planning the raids, he could anticipate our moves before we thought of them ourselves. You know how these fanatics are—living in poverty, denying themselves every comfort, even those they can afford, pouring the whole of their miserable salary back into the party coffers. No one suspected this miserable gray blur. But because of him we failed again and again to spring our traps. The Exec-Com— I keep slipping into their jargon—well, the executive committee got away just as the nets were closing on them. Then Kletochnikov made a mistake. He possessed an extraordinary mind and was able to commit to memory the most intricate details. You can imagine that he dared not write down a thing despite the flow of information passing through his hands every day. The pressure began to wear on him. He couldn't sleep. He lost weight and finally fell ill with bronchitis. Still, he refused to miss even a day's work; too much was at stake. His comrades depended on him for survival. He began to fall asleep at his desk. One day, recently, he came across a crucial report outlining a big Gendarme operation aimed at rolling up the entire executive committee. But he could not absorb all the details. So he scribbled a few notes on a scrap of paper and concealed it in the sweatband of his hat. That was the day a security check was scheduled. They found the paper. He was arrested. With Kletochnikov gone there will be no more leaks, no more near misses. The Gendarmes are closing in on the last surviving members of the executive committee, Zheliabov, Perovskaya, the lot. Van der Fleet promises that he'll soon haul in the biggest catch of all."

Vasiliev gave every sign of listening intently, but his mind was trying out fresh combinations and getting nowhere.

"You say nothing, Vasili."

"To be honest, Ivan, I can't figure out why Van der Fleet's every move seems to strengthen the hand of the reformers. He and Bagration have not made any effort to conceal their contempt for a constitution or consultative assembly or whatever Loris-Melikov has up his sleeve. Bagration is even openly critical of the emancipation, the zemstvo reforms, the whole package of reforms. And he despises our tsar, Alexander Nikolaevich. If Van der Fleet wanted to discredit the reformers he would be a shade less efficient. No one would have noticed if he had been."

"Be fair, Vasili. Van der Fleet made a mistake trying to protect his friend's son. But we have no idea why. I've been thinking about it a great deal. Suppose, for a moment, just suppose without wishing to excuse the man, you understand, that he thought the affair involving the young Bagration would destroy the career of the Prince and even cast a shadow on him as a close friend. Remember that the young Prince was involved with the Jumpers, a pernicious sect under the Code of Laws, and that he also was in touch with a nihilist. You see how the whole thing could have exploded into a major scandal. Of course, if Van der Fleet has done something criminal he will have to pay for it. But stand back and look at it dispassionately. He is an officer, much decorated who does not agree with your politics but who..."

"...who is shielding a murderer and has tried to kidnap a detective investigating the case, not to speak of abetting a hired thug..."

"But no proof, Vasili, again, no proof except your word against his. You know as well as I do that in the dirty business of hunting revolutionaries the police have to deal with some unsavory characters. We cannot control their every move or even always know what they are up. Just consider the possibility that this hired thug was acting on his own, or on Bagration's initiative without Van der Fleet being involved. You may be looking for too much complexity, Vasili."

"Look for a simpler answer, you say. Curious, Ivan, you are the second person to brandish Occam's razor over my head. The first one was a nihilist. It bothers me to think that people on both sides of this war think the same way. Van der Fleet is not a phrase maker. He says only what is absolutely necessary unless he is chatting about the ballet. Yet, when he ordered me bound and confined like a prisoner, he was quite ecstatic, you get my meaning, ecstatic when he said he was off to settle 'the fate of empire.' It would be a mistake to ignore his boast."

"You attack so hard, that you force me to defend the man. Surely the phrase has several possible meanings. He could have meant the destruction of the executive committee of the People's Will. If he did he might have feared that your accusations would have led to an official investigation and prevented him from following up on the capture of Kletochnikov and wiping out the last nest of terrorists."

"Sorry, Ivan, but there is no direct connection between the murder of Ushakova and the activities of the People's Will. One conclusion is simple—that's what you want isn't it—simplicity. Van der Fleet is determined to protect Bagration's reputation at all costs. Here I agree with you. But not because he is a friend, or because he would be embarrassed by scandal. No, he needs him, and needs him so desperately he violated the law and jeopardized his whole career. What is the reason? I'm missing something obvious. It must be staring me right in the face."

Ivan rose and leaned over Vasiliev, laying his hand gently on his sleeve. It was always like this, he thought; the man's intensity is irresistible, even though it sometimes irritates the hell out of me.

"My dear fellow, in two days the emperor will sign the draft project reorganizing the government. Loris-Melikov has been working on it like a fiend. I can tell you that it gives the educated public a real voice in advising His Majesty. The liberals will be won over, perhaps even some of the moderate revolutionaries; the terrorist will be isolated, cut off from any sympathy and then we'll hunt..."

Vasiliev jumped to his feet, overturning his chair, knocking his tea cup to the floor where it shattered and driving Ivan back on his heels. For an instant Ivan was sure Vasiliev's mind had snapped under the strain. Vasiliev reached out to him but Ivan retreated to the desk, frightened by the wild look in Vasiliev's eyes.

"Christ, I've been blind!"

"My God, Vasili, what's come over you? Are you ill? Shall I call a doctor?" Ivan was moving toward the door, but Vasiliev waved him back. He stared at the fragments of bone china at his feet and muttered something. Then he seemed to pull himself together and made a great effort to speak in a normal tone of voice.

"Ivan, the tsar is in imminent danger."

Ivan stared at him incredulously. "Vasili, what the devil is wrong with you? Of course, the tsar's life is in danger. What do you think we have been trying to do for the last two years but save that precious life. Seven assassination attempts. We have spared no effort to track down the madmen. Have you been living in a dream world? When you speak like that, I begin to wonder."

"You miss my meaning, Ivan. Hear me out if our friendship means anything to you. I am not raving, I am not sick, I am not a fool. The emperor is the target of a plot so cunning, so monstrous that there is no way he can defend himself against it."

"Sorry, Vasili, you are raving, if not mad. What do you mean? We have all the means to defend him. The entire security apparatus has been mobilized. We are in a state of siege. Petersburg is an armed camp. The tsar is surrounded by bodyguards whenever he ventures out of the Palace. Loris-Melikov has the power to forbid him to move without his approval. Do you understand what that means? No tsar has ever granted that kind of power over his person to anyone else. And the terrorists have lost their best people, their eyes and ears inside our operations. Their organization has been decimated, their double agents turned, their most ingenious attempts have failed. They are reduced to a few frightened, hunted survivors. No defense you say."

Ivan whirled and strode to the window and fixed his gaze on the Alexander Column, struggling to master his anger. "You go too far," he murmured, no longer sure that he could reason with his old friend. "You've had a terrible time of it, you are exhausted, your nerves are shot," Ivan spoke without turning around.

"Could you tell me, Ivan, who is in personal command of the tsar's bodyguards?"

"Vasili, you are out of your depth. You are a criminal investigator and a damn good one. Your work on this case was first rate. You've done your job, but now I see you veering off in another direction like a runaway carriage. Why the sudden interest in the security arrangements of the tsar? It makes no sense. You say you see no connection between the terrorists and the Ushakova killing. You've convinced me, but apparently you are not sure about it yourself. Since you are so agitated, let me reassure you, our Emperor is in good hands."

"Who is responsible? I must know."

"Easy, *mon vieux*. There is no secret about it. You have a right to know." He was still worried Vasiliev might break down in front of him.

Ivan's secretary entered with papers to sign averting his gaze from the fragments of china littering the floor. Since the Colonel gave no order and both men seemed oblivious to the accident, he silently gathered up the documents and left the office. Outside he caught the eye of the chief clerk, shrugged his shoulders and rolled his eyes, meaning another stormy interview with the legendary Vasiliev.

"Let me fill you in. General Loris-Melikov has assumed full personal responsibility for the safety of the tsar. And I need hardly tell you that his attention to detail is obsessive. Nothing gets past him, not the slightest change in the tsar's travel plans or daily routine. I admit things were lax before he took over. Now it's quite different. The Winter Palace is sealed tighter than the frozen Neva, triple sentries at all entrances, check points inside. Special security details patrol the corridors at irregular times. There are no fixed schedules even for changing the sentries. The tsar's personal aides de camp guard the imperial apartments. When His Majesty leaves this fortress he is accompanied by a Cossack bodyguard, all Companions of St. George. They are splendid riders, superb marksmen, every one of them hand-picked by the Minister of Interior himself. In addition, the tsar is attended wherever he goes by the St. Petersburg Police Chief, Adrian Dvorzhitsky. You know him well, I think. A first class man. He has a large body of plain clothes detectives under his command. They are stationed throughout the city, but concentrated on the streets and squares where the tsar will pass when he travels by coach. They are experienced and highly trusted. Are you satisfied? You can't fault the arrangements can you?"

Ivan felt as though he had just delivered a most respectful report to the tsar himself. He was pleased with his performance and felt a great sense of relief.

"One more favor, Ivan, and please don't refuse me. It's a small thing, really. For the next twenty-four hours, no more, I need direct access to General Loris-Melikov. Can you arrange it?"

Ivan felt a surge of impatience. "But Vasili I report to the General every morning. I enjoy his full confidence. Whatever you bring me, I'll show to him immediately if you insist. Just be sure it's hard evidence. I'd never screen you out, you know that, even if I have doubts about your theories. You asked me to put Van der Fleet under surveillance. I went ahead and did it, even though it could cause me some embarrassment to put it mildly. Do you need more proof than that?"

"Don't be annoyed with me. I know I try your patience. I appreciate your tolerance. Let me explain why the next two days are critical. In a few hours I will get hold of the hard evidence you require. There are letters providing proof that Bagration was involved in the murder of Ushakova. Once I have them even you will have to admit that Van der Fleet is an accessory. Then we will have to move fast to prevent a greater tragedy. Chalk it up to intuition if you like, but it is more than that. There is a chain of logic here that I have tested carefully. It has no weak links. I don't have to indulge in guesses this time. But we have so little time. That is why I want direct access. I could ask for an even greater favor, a personal audience with His Majesty. It would not be out of place. But then you would surely think me mad. So I'm willing to compromise."

Ivan smiled in spite of himself. "The ultimate negotiator! You offer me a compromise. You really are delightfully infuriating. You always manage to surprise me, though I've known you for twenty years. How do you manage to persuade me every time? Well it doesn't matter, except that you should have been in a courtroom or on the stage."

"People are always telling me that I belong somewhere else or should be someone else than the person I am."

Ivan burst into laughter. "You shall have your access, Vasili. I will speak to the General's private secretary this afternoon. But I'll take you at your word. Your privilege expires in forty-eight hours."

"Many thanks, Ivan. I hope to God I do not have to use it. If I do it will only be to warn the Emperor of the most ingenious and devilish plot yet devised to assassinate him."

Chapter
Thirty-One

"What do you think, Serov, a monocle or a pince-nez?" Vasiliev bent closer to a highly polished mirror framed in metal garlands and laurels. The rays of the weak afternoon sun barely penetrated into the corner of the hotel room where Serov sat hunched over, casting disconsolate glances in Vasiliev's direction.

"The pince-nez, Vasili Vasilievich. Why play the Prussian when there's no need."

Vasiliev settled the pince-nez in place and leaned back to examine the result.

"Right you are, the monocle would have been out of character." He daubed a bit of mascara on his left eyebrow and rubbed it in.

Serov had wandered over to the window and was starring out into the courtyard of the European Hotel. Several porters wearing leather aprons were unloading barrels of flower from a wagon parked under an overhanging corrugated roof.

"Beggin' your pardon, Vasili Vasilievich, but suppose I was to follow at a distance, just keepin' you in sight, as it were. No harm in that."

Vasiliev turned his head from side to side. The face of a middle-aged barrister of a vaguely central European mien stared back at him.

"Not a chance. No risks this time and no mistakes. They're a skittish lot and for good reason. The smallest hint of a police trap will blow the operation sky high. There will be a dozen pairs of eyes on me all the time, you can be sure of it. Even the best disguise wouldn't conceal you for long. You're good, of course, and they might not pick you up right away. But after a while they couldn't help but spot you tagging along behind me."

"I could walk a broken pattern."

"Sergeant, stop clucking over me like a brood mother. There is no reason for us to be afraid of the People's Will. If they wanted to get rid of me, they could easily do so without going through this rigmarole. Now tell me, have they finished unloading down there?"

"Yes."

"Then off you go. You've got your story right?"

"My story is your story, Vasili Vasilievich. You're a famous lawyer from Dresden. You've come to Russia to take on a case. But the client is a high personage, don't want any public fuss. Whole thing is hush-hush. We're puttin' together a quiet little exit for you, back entrance, curtained cab. Only the concierge knows what's up. He'll get a couple of silver rubles to keep his mouth shut. Cab is under the roof, now. No one will spot you leavin'. Cabby knows what to do, another silver ruble. It's up to me to jostle the organ grinder over there by the Mikhailovsky Gardens just in case he is what we think he is. I'll make sure he doesn't see you."

"Good. After you've distracted the organ grinder, you'll do a full sweep of the emperor's route — Winter Palace, Riding Academy, Grand Duchess Catherine's Palace and back. I want to know where the bottlenecks are. You'll check the shops for double exits and schedules of daily deliveries. Get inside as many as you can. Watch out for any clerks who are indifferent or hostile to customers. Keep your eye peeled for any fresh construction work. Check the roofs of the buildings. You know the drill."

"I'll just be trampin' over ground churned up by the plain clothes men," Serov grumbled, slouching against the windowsill.

"They won't have been looking through your eyes. The detectives may be good but they don't know the difference between a beggar and a student posing as one. They're trained to check papers, and that's about all. They lack imagination. Look how quickly you spotted the organ grinder."

"He was playin' out of tune."

"My point, exactly. Now listen. I should be back by midnight."

"And if not?"

The Winter Canal, St. Petersburg

"Send out the bloodhounds."

It was shortly after six o'clock when Vasiliev's cab drew up to an address in the center of Nevsky Prospekt only a few blocks from the hotel. He had ordered it to drive first in the opposite direction and then double back along the Embankment. They returned by the Catherine Canal. The sight of the Winter Canal brought back romantic memories of a time before Irina, a better time than this, he thought. And things could get much worse. That was what drove him on, the urge to prevent a disaster.

The cab was back on Nevsky. It stopped under the familiar oversized replica of a book suspended over the entrance to Plavilchikov's Book Emporium. Pushing open the glass door, he made straight for the antiquarian section and began to browse through the history books. The sales clerk, a young man in a greasy, threadbare jacket, was occupied wrapping a package for an old woman who was lecturing him on Tolstoy's conversion. Vasiliev waited until she had left and waved over the clerk.

"Do you have, by any chance, volume four of Karamzin's *History of the Russian State*? I want the second edition."

"I'm sorry, sir, we never breakup sets, especially not the second edition."

"What a pity. I loaned the volume to a friend who took it away with him to Berlin."

"We might have an odd volume from a later edition. Would that do?"

The clerk never took his eyes off Vasiliev as he rummaged behind the books on an upper shelf and extracted a much used copy that had been wedged in against the wall. It was free of dust.

"It will have to do, won't it."

Vasiliev paid and left at once, mixing with the dense evening crowd that surged across the pavement into the small restaurants, bars and concert halls that lined the street. He went down a flight of steps into a high-class traktir that was still half empty. He ordered *thé citron*, speaking with a heavy German accent, and opened the book at random. He concentrated on reading until the waiter glided up to his table as smoothly as if he were on skates. Vasiliev sipped his tea, occasionally glancing round the room. He watched people come and go until there was a complete turnover of customers. His fingers quickly found what he was looking for in the pages of his Karamzin – a theater ticket and a wooden cloakroom disc. He slid them up the stiff cuff of his shirt, glanced at the wall clock and threw down some coins. He left the book on the table where it was immediately picked up by his skating waiter.

He examined the ticket in the washroom. It was for a performance to be held that evening at a concert hall known since Pushkin's day as Engelhardt's House and situated on Nevsky Prospekt a short walk toward the Neva. Vasiliev remembered it as the most beautiful small hall in the capital. He walked across the bridge over the Catherine Canal. The façade of Engelhardt's House was brightly lit. by kerosene lamps.

The lobby was crowded. The air was filled with a subdued hum of polite conversation and the scent of French perfume. Every audience creates its own atmosphere, he mused. A few military uniforms were like points of light among the dress suits and dark gowns. No Scottish shawls here. Vasiliev was out of place in his street clothes, but they must have planned that as well. Since no one else was dressed as he was, they could pick him out from a distance and watch his every move.

A concert poster announced in bold blue letters the final appearance of the season by Anton Rubinshtein. The program—Beethoven, Schumann and Liszt. So his invisible friends knew his tastes as well. Or was it only a coincidence that they had chosen this event among all others in the capital that night? No, they were out to impress him.

The cloakroom attendant who looked no different than others of his tribe handed him a wooden disc identical to the one in his pocket and a slip of paper. His seat was a good one too, center left in the parterre and on the aisle. More evidence of careful attention to detail. The hall was rapidly filling up. He consciously restrained himself from scanning the audience. This was not his operation. Instead he let his eyes wander over the rococo ceiling where Greek deities larger than life rose out of clusters of acanthus leaves surmounting cream colored pilasters.

There was something godlike about Rubinshtein himself as he emerged from the wings, his massive head, his mane of hair brushed back from a high forehead, craggy, knitted brows and firmly set, thin lips. His hands descended in a rush of octaves and Vasiliev felt himself swept up in the sonority of the playing. The pianist stormed through the allegro assai of Beethoven's opus 57. Vasiliev lost all sense of time and place. The applause was a harsh reminder of why he was there. He remained in his seat during the intermission, going back over the music in his head until most of the audience had left the hall for the lobbies. He took out the piece of paper, read the short message and put it back in his pocket. There was nothing to do but wait for the audience to file back to their places. When a fresh burst of applause greeted Rubinshtein, Vasiliev got to his feet and walked to a side exit. As he let the door close behind him he caught a last glimpse of the pianist his body erect, his large hands poised above the keyboard, waiting for the rustling in the hall to die down. Vasiliev had no sooner taken a few steps than he heard the opening of Schumann's *Faschingschwank aus Wien*. What else, he muttered to himself, but the fate of the empire could have dragged him away from this music.

He paused at the end of the corridor, the staircase of another theater coming to mind, but this time there were no deranged young men, no echoes of Dostoevsky, only the faint strains of Schumann. He was in the hands of men and women who had thought out every step of the way. The cloakroom attendant was not the same man. Vasiliev dropped the two discs on the counter. Without a word the man shuffled out of sight and was gone for several minutes. He reappeared with Vasiliev's coat under his arm, and before helping him to put it on, he patted one of the pockets. Vasiliev handed him a coin but he ignored it and disappeared behind a rack of coats. In the back a door slammed.

He stood under the announcement of the spring subscription concerts. By the light of the gas jet he took out the second message from his pocket, read it and tore it into small pieces. Leaving the building by the side entrance, he was greeted by a blast of air that almost tore the door out of his hand. He let the wind carry away the bits of paper. The night sky was star-studded. The street was deserted except for a cab standing fifty meters away. Beyond it he could see along the embankment the monumental granite figures of two griffins flanking the Bank Bridge. As he approached the cab he made sure that the cabby was hatless, turning over his fur cap in his hands. Vasiliev resisted the temptation to look behind him. As he pressed down on the metal cab handle he wondered whether this too would ever become a normal action. But there was no one waiting for him, no explosive flash. He settled back against the cushions as the cab started up. The horse maintained a steady trotting pace.

Vasiliev went over the arrangements. They seemed to have been designed to prove to him that they still had a network in place despite the arrests that had presumably crippled the organization. Their people were disciplined and well trained, apparently drawn from all classes. No superfluous instructions, every move controlled and monitored.

They traveled along the Catherine Canal, across the Moika past the brilliantly illuminated rococo facades fronting the Neva, splashes of pastels traversed by white columns. This was the Petersburg he loved. But the spell lasted only a few moments until they reached the Alexander Bridge and then crossed to the Vyborg Side. The cab swerved to the right and plunged into the rabbit warren of narrow lanes beyond the Finland Station.

The whole area was unknown to Vasiliev. The cabby negotiated a succession of turns that confused his sense of direction and must have discouraged any pursuit. The last of the gas lamps had long since passed. The cab was now bumping over unpaved and rutted lanes. He could discern an occasional candle flickering behind a thick glass window. The buildings here were one-story houses with plaster walls, gradually giving way to wooden huts. The roadway narrowed.

The horse slowed to a walk and came to a stop. Vasiliev heard the driver climb down from the box and then the sound of harness jingling. He stepped out into the crisp snow. The driver had moved round to the opposite side. The precaution seemed unnecessary. In the darkness it was impossible to make out the man's features. The cabby clambered back on his box and drove off, cracking his whip for the first time. A natural sound was always the best signal.

Vasiliev began to walk in the direction of the disappearing cab. The only sound was the crunch of snow under his boots. He had covered a few hundred meters when he hesitated at a fork in the road. A low whistle came from behind him. He waited, rocking on the balls of his feet. Hearing footsteps behind him Vasiliev felt his body stiffen. The arrangements had been good, perhaps too good if the organization had really been crippled by arrests. And what about the possibility of double agents? He drove these ideas out of his mind. There was nothing he could do now but hope that his instincts had been right in the first place. The steps halted right behind him. Then a whisper.

"Easy. We are going to blindfold you."

"Unnecessary. I have no idea where I am."

"Good. We'll keep it that way."

A cloth fluttered over his eyes and gentle fingers tied it behind his head. The guide took his arm and led him through a sequence of turns that he made an effort to memorize. This kept his mind from wandering through its own maze. A door opened and they trudged down a flight of rickety steps and along a narrow passageway where Vasiliev's shoulders kept brushing against the walls. Up another flight of steps, through another door and more steps, the odors becoming stronger, always the same in these hideaways, rancid cabbage soup, human waste. His guide rapped on the door, an intricate rhythm, but Vasiliev was sure he would be able reproduce it if he could ever find this place again. He was brought into a room. Two men wedged him in and pressed down on his shoulders. A chair was shoved roughly against the back of his legs. He sat down hard letting his arms hang by his sides. Strong hands gripped his shoulders while the blindfold was removed. He blinked into the flame of a single candle placed directly in front of him. It was the only light in the room.He breathed in the fetid air of wet sheepskins and human sweat.

"Very good. Please remain seated just as you are. Do not move your head until you are instructed to do so." The male voice behind him had a distinctive resonant quality.

"We shall be brief. On the table to your right there is a packet of letters. They were written by Prince Bagration to Countess Ushakova over a period of two years from June of seventy-eight to September of last year. We do not have in our possession the other half of the correspondence. Quite possibly she did not write him at all, for her own protection. That is irrelevant for our purpose and yours. The letters make clear the Bagration was being blackmailed. The proof is there, if you want it, that he had good reason to murder her."

Vasiliev heard whispering. Could it have been a woman's voice? His eyes were beginning to water but he kept them level with the flame that fluttered from the breath of the man behind him.

"We believe", the voice continued, "that the letters will help you solve your case. Is this correct?"

"To answer that, I would have to read the letters."

"All in good time, and under certain conditions."

Tears began to roll down Vasiliev's cheeks. He felt ridiculous; it might look as though he were mourning the dead Countess.

"We will give you the letters if you agree to have them published in one of the major Petersburg or Moscow dailies."

"Sounds simple," said Vasiliev finally forced to shut his eyes. "But think about it for a moment. No editor in his right mind would dare print them if they say what you imply. The censor would issue a warning, possibly even impose a fine. Perhaps suspend publication. Don't forget we are dealing with a man who is a favorite of the heir. Too risky."

"You underestimate our press lords. For a sensation like this they'll risk a warning, even a fine. We doubt it will come to suspension. These letters do not contain state secrets. Bagration might howl, the heir might stir his mighty buttocks, but our Loris-Melikov has to tread lightly in dealing with the liberals these days. He won't risk upsetting his precious public opinion in order to punish an editor who is just exposing a filthy private affair, a fait accompli. Besides won't a *crime de passion* satisfy their needs? The political motive goes out the window. Loris will be sitting pretty. And Ushakov, well too bad, he married a whore."

"Why don't you print them yourself? You have your own presses."

"Come, come Vasiliev, you are playing games, bargaining like a fishmonger. Do you want the evidence or not? Or have we misjudged your devotion to Truth and Justice.?"

"No more than I have misjudged yours."

"Son of a bitch," another voice snarled.

"Silence! We have no intention of negotiating with you. You know our aims. We have never concealed them. Terror is a refined method. Surgical if you like, intended to cut out a diseased organ. Our quarrel is with those who hold power, not with parasitic nobles, helpless without the state behind them. We have no need to blow up degenerate women or men. They are destroying the morale fiber of their class. Let them wallow in their debauchery. Who would ever elect them as leaders if given a choice? No, we have the autocrat to deal with. We are revolutionaries, not common criminals."

"Suppose I agree but fail to find a publisher?"

"Anything can be published. It depends on how hard you try."

A chair scraped and more whispering broke out behind him.

"We have great confidence in you, Vasiliev. We're not worried. With your connections you will succeed. If you fail in Moscow and Petersburg, there is Berlin or even Paris. The correspondent for *Le Temps* is staying at the European Hotel in a room down the corridor from yours. Once Paris publishes, the Russian papers will snap it up. But this must be done quickly. No one likes stale news."

"I can't promise anything without reading the letters. I have to verify the handwriting, they might be forgeries."

"You are tempted; that's encouraging. You may examine the

letters right here. Take one with you when you leave. That way you can verify the handwriting as you say. By itself the one we give you will prove nothing. If you are satisfied that the letter is genuine, then you will have to come back for the rest. But you only have until tomorrow at this time to make up your mind."

"May I read the letters now?"

"First, we must have your word of honor that you agree to our terms. Let's be precise so as to avoid any chance of misunderstanding. Verification in twenty-four hours, publication in forty-eight."

"All right, I agree if the letters prove genuine. But I would like to know how you got hold of them. That might help to convince me they are genuine."

"Ah, Vasiliev, always rooting around like a good detective. But we cannot reveal our sources. You will have to rely on your investigative skills. Are you ready to read them under our conditions."

"Yes."

Vasiliev watched a hand with stubby fingers and dirty broken nails reach over his shoulder and push a packet tied with a white silk ribbon into his hands. He raised the letters to his nostrils and inhaled. Above the stench of men sweating in their sheepskins he could still detect the faint scent of her perfume. The white ribbon slid through his fingers. Could they have duplicated these things? A sulphur match blazed, lighting another candle that was placed on the table.

He counted the letters. There were twelve of them. The envelopes bore no stamp. Hand delivered. The address was scrawled in large bold letters. Just her name, Countess Elena Borisovna Ushakova. The envelopes had been slit open by a thin knife. He took out the first letter. It was not dated.

My dear Elena,

You can imagine my surprise at receiving your curious invitation. It has been several years, and the scars have not healed. Do I detect a threatening note in your summons? You have always fascinated me, but now, I fear, like a rabbit to your cobra. I know how dangerous you are—but I cannot resist. Friday afternoon, then, at three o'clock, the Selenki wood, by the pond on the second Luchevoi Prospekt.

Your Aleksei.

"The first letter can be your handwriting sample. Take it with you. It is the only one not dated. Our scheming Countess made certain, thereafter, that her evidence was better documented."

Vasiliev slipped the note inside his jacket and unfolded the second one which showed, judging by the change in the handwriting, that Bagration was in a highly agitated state. It bore the date, June 2, 1879.

Elena!
You are as vicious as I thought, but even more clever, diabolically so. You demand that I contribute to my own enslavement. I have no choice. I'll play your game for his sake. But I will never write anything you can use against him, only against me.

That's part of the bargain isn't it? You know just how far you can push me.

If you push too far you will unleash my devil. I accept your terms, but I cannot help but be amused that I am subsidizing the wife of a deputy minister of interior. Does he keep you on such a short leash?
Aleksei.

Vasiliev found the remaining letters to be written in the same tone though Bagration's hand had become steady again. He was protecting his son from scandal over his relations with the Jumpers. The Countess extorted over 200,000 rubles. But she was not satisfied with blackmail. She insisted on humiliating him, summoning him to secret rendezvous, demanding invitations to his home. Vasiliev detected a plaintive note in his later letters. The last one was dated a week before her murder.

Elena!
You frighten me, yes, me your former tiger. Are there no limits to your brazenness? What is 'this urgent question'? You know how dangerous these meetings are in my own house, and on the night of the ball. Damn you! But you leave me no choice. Just don't make a spectacle of yourself.

You can do that much to protect us.
A.

He memorized as much as he could, though none of it surprised him. The letters changed nothing in the case, and they did not answer the questions that still bothered him. What was the urgent question she raised to force him to invite her to her last ball? Was she taking revenge for Bagration's having raped her as a girl? Or was that story a fantasy of the young Prince? What did it matter any more, he thought. The letters provided enough evidence to head off the insane conspiracy of Van der Fleet. He had planned to settle the fate of empire, all right, but in a way that could only be disastrous for the country. He placed the letters down on the table. Someone blew out the candle. This time rougher fingers blindfolded him. The meeting with the Exec Com of the People's Will was over.

Chapter
Thirty-Two

Swan had been staring for some time out a window overlooking
the Fontanka Canal. Her fingers were tightly holding a knotted
silk cord that fastened the velvet drapes as if she feared falling into
the icy water. All day she had watched clouds swollen with moisture hovering motionless over the city, threatening to deposit a fresh
blanket of snow. The lamps had been illuminated hours ago. In the
distance she heard the mournful tolling of the bells of St. Isaac's
Cathedral. She was turning over in her mind the inner struggle that
had brought her to this point. None of the comrades had encouraged her. Magician and Letchik fell silent when she explained her
plan. It had to be her choice. She respected them for their silence.
The one thing she refused to do was to accompany Shuev in public.
He was just as happy to have her all to himself. He seemed to want
to keep her in secret. That was just as well. It would be disastrous if
Ushakov found out. She no longer dared to visit him.

Her fingers released the cord when she heard the tell tale click
of Shuev's boots resounding in the hallway. She had long ago ceased
to be a believer but now she muttered a prayer in spite of herself.
Tonight he was late and he might be weary from official meetings.
They seemed to consume most of his day. His hearty greeting dis-
pelled her hopes. She had prepared distractions, a platter of his favorite *zakuski* and a carafe of iced vodka. When his arms encircled
her, she buried her face in his tunic. The hardest thing, she realized,
was to look him straight in the eye.

"I always worry when you are late," she murmured. He stroked
her bare arms under the fur-trimmed sleeves of the silk gown he

had given her. "You risk so much in your war against the terrorists." She reached behind her and tugged the silken cord releasing
the drapes and cutting off the light from the gas lamps along the
embankment. The room darkened. The candle by the icon in the
corner flickered briefly and then resumed its steady flame. She no
longer felt disgust. So long as she could shut down her feelings
and slip into a trance like state she knew she could bear the few
minutes he embraced her. At first she had been surprised when he
seemed not to notice how deeply she withdrew into herself at those
moments. Later she realized he was too much absorbed in his own
pleasure. Reading novels didn't prepare one for this and no one
talked about it. Afterward it was easier for her to resume the role of
the kept woman. At least he was never brutal, although she had no
basis for comparison.

Like most men who wore a uniform Shuev seemed greatly di-
minished in his shirtsleeves. Or was she being spiteful? No, she
concluded, it was the same with her father. Shuev faced her across
the small table with the platter of *zakuski* between them. It pleased
him that she did not drink, not even a glass of wine. She said little
but that suited him too. She hardly had to ask him any questions.
He relished telling her about his work, the web of conspiracies, the
arrests, the work of the double agents. Most of all he enjoyed repeating the conventional praises of his superiors, acknowledging
his services.

"...and I quote his very words..." a refrain that grated on her
nerves. But this time she detected something new in his voice. He
was spooning beluga caviar from a silver dish onto a diagonal of
toast that was not quite as crisp as he liked. He left untouched the
finely diced hard-boiled egg on the side. "No need to dilute a good
thing,," he was fond of saying, leering at her.

"It really is a pity about Vasiliev," he began, neatly snapping
off a bite. "He has many fine qualities. But he seems to have gotten
himself into a real jam this time. Mixed up with one of the terrorist
splinter groups..." Swan felt her eyes drawn again to the icon.

"Hmm, well, maybe just a drop," he held out the slice of toast.
She could almost feel the pleasure he took from squeezing the lemon
wrapped in cheesecloth. She had taken a dislike to his constant look
of self-satisfaction. In her mind the sound of his jaws crunching
toast assumed a sinister meaning.

"Who is this Vasiliev?" Irina prompted.

"Vasiliev?! My dear you are an innocent. He is the bastard son of Count Vorontsov who threw over the chance to be one of us. Why did he do this? You may well ask. A personal flaw inherited from his peasant mother. The old Count should have left him in the village, or else packed him off to some relative in the provinces. But no, he became infatuated with the boy. Oh, yes, infatuated. Well, Vasiliev was, they say, a charming little fellow."

Irina turned away to hide her smile. "Yes", she thought, "and just how charming you will never know." A sequence of images flashed through her mind, like a lantern show each slide tinted sepia: her first dance with Vasiliev under the baton of Professor Schweinitz; Vasiliev and her brother setting off with Foma on their first hunt, waving back at her. Why was she always standing on the porch waving to them? Good bye, off to the hunt, goodbye, off to the war...and then only Vasiliev coming back.

"...besides which he seems to be completely off the track on the Ushakova case."

Irina simulated a yawn, another one of her practiced poses. The yawning woman, a good way to encourage him to babble on.

Shuev prepared another caviar and toast taking time to study the small grey eggs. What was so interesting about them? She wondered. It was another habit of his that irritated her. He sipped the vodka. Knocking it back was plebian, he once confided to her.

"He is either a dupe or a fool but I cannot agree with Kolya Van der Fleet that he is disloyal. Still, we will see very soon. Thursday it will all be clear. So don't expect me that evening, my dear. You know how much I sacrifice for duty." He reached across the table and she was forced to extend her hand. He squeezed it like the lemon in cheesecloth. His fingers were sticky.

"I must tell you, Irisha, that we have achieved an extraordinary success. If I were an artist I would call it the sublime moment."

Irina lifted the carafe from its bed of melting ice. "Is the vodka chilled enough for you, Grisha?" Anything to keep her hands busy.

"Ah, my dear, here I am about to tell you that we have penetrated the Exec-Com of the People's Will and you are concerned about the temperature of my vodka." He laughed harshly. "But that is why I adore you."

She poured with a steady hand.

"So, we will test our good friend Vasili Vasilievich. Yes, it will be a nice touch to put Vasiliev on Vasilievsky Island though it was not our intention. Perhaps Zheliabov and his gang have a sense of humor."

Shuev stretched out his legs, admiring the sheen of his highly polished boots.

"Shall I order supper? Solyanka soup and cutlets."

"How determined you are to attend to my well-being in all ways." She felt a rush of revulsion at his lascivious smile.

Shuev enjoyed displaying his exquisite table manners while Irina barely managed to swallow a few spoonfuls of soup. She arranged small bits of cutlet on the edge of her plate where they might be less noticed. She repressed the urge to find out the identity of the police spy in the Exec-Com. But that would be too obvious a departure from her feigned indifference. She wracked her brains but could think of no way of teasing the name out of him. One thought dominated all the rest; she would not give him Vasiliev.

"I have always had fond memories of Vasilievsky Island," she murmured.

Shuev grinned at her. "Well, so will I after we spring our little trap. It really is quite simple. We will make sure that Vasiliev has an opportunity to get in touch with the Exec-Com. If he acts alone – that's his style you know—without informing his dear friend Ivan or any of the rest of us, then we will take him and them as well. We are so close, Irisha, to destroying the terrorist center. And when we do it will give an unmistakable sign to the liberals that they cannot continue to flirt with terror in order to pressure the tsar into making concessions. Whatever his faults our tsar, Alexander Nikolaevich, will never grant a constitution."

Shuev pushed back his chair and began to pace, hands clasped behind his back, a sure sign to Irina that she was in for a long lecture. But it was better than the alternative, she thought.

Chapter
Thirty-Three

In his hotel room Vasiliev sat down with Serov to compare the handwriting of the letter with the guest list Bagration had written out.

"See how distinctive the 'e' with its pointed top like a pennant, and the flourishes in the final 'y'. The paper is an expensive rag bond watermarked with the Prince's crest. It looks genuine to me. I never thought my paleography class at the Page Corps would turn out to have been so practical. You know for all my faith in inspired guessing, I believe in science as well."

"Well, somethin's to be learned from you every day, Vasili Vasilievich. But I'll be settlin' for the guessin' part."

"Did you pick up anything on your tour?"

"Lots of ground to cover. Slow work, it is. Tomorrow I'll finish up."

"We'll both get an early start. I'm off to *The Russian Courier.* Lanin has a reputation for bearding the nobility. Made a fortune selling champagne. He's wealthy enough to pay a fine if he has to without turning a hair."

Vasiliev considered himself lucky that Lanin was still in the capital visiting his warehouses. But then again, he reflected, in this case luck has been in short supply. Lanin greeted him effusively. When he heard Vasiliev's proposal he rubbed his hands in glee, his bushy eyebrows dancing up and down, reminding Vasiliev of a classic stage villain.

"I'll publish the lot, the day after you hand them over. The censor be damned. That's the business end. Now listen, Inspector, I've just had a shipment of Möet, brut 1879. They say it is easily the best in years. Let's test it right now."

Lanin led him past large barrels lining the walls of his warehouse. He kept up a running commentary on the latest vintages. "Ah, but you know, your father is the true connoisseur. Oh, my dear, his orders. No one knows the champagne country like does. Must have spent a long time there. All the winegrowers remember him from the late sixties. My own daddy, bless his departed soul, would have given an arm, perhaps both, for your father's *goût* and even his gout," Lanin giggled at his *bon mot*.

Lanin insisted on sending a case of the Möet over to Vasiliev's hotel. "A tribute to your daddy," he said and promised an article on the first page.

Prompt to the minute Vasiliev showed up at Plavilchikov's. There was no one at the counter, but he heard a man and a woman quarreling from behind a curtain in the back of the shop. He went back out, waited a moment and entered again slamming the door behind him. The voices ceased and after a minute or two the young man appeared, still wearing his greasy coat.

"I need volume seven of Karamzin to complete my work."

"I'll see what I can do. But don't you read the volumes consecutively?"

"I don't like to read about the Time of Troubles."

The clerk left him again and returned with the book already wrapped. Vasiliev sensed that this time the clerk was nervous. He appeared relieved when an officer and his wife entered the shop, and he hurried off to serve them.

Vasiliev had only taken a few steps along Nevsky when he felt a light touch on his sleeve and an arm slip through his.

"You should be ashamed of yourself for ignoring me for so long. I really should be very angry with you." He was stunned by her appearance. The tight fitting gray coat with black frogging and a beaver collar matching the fur hat perched on her elaborate coiffure, a single auburn ringlet falling on her neck. Tan colored French kid gloves matched her soft leather boots. There was a trace of rouge on her lips. He breathed in a delicate scent as she turned her head and spoke to someone behind her.

"Thank you Igor, Monsieur will see me home." Vasiliev caught sight of a man wearing livery who was quickly swallowed up by the crowd.

Vasiliev saluted her but muttered so only she could hear, "You are mad." She pressed his arm more tightly so that he could feel the pressure of her breast. His first impulse was to jerk free. Whatever she was up to now, she had chosen the worst possible moment.

"What a naughty man you are. So wrapped up in your books that you never come to see us any more. Now that I have you, you'll have to pay a price for your thoughtless ways. You shall have to take me to Dominique's for an ice."

"My dear Irina, normally nothing would give me more pleasure. But tonight I have one of those appointments in life that is truly impossible to miss. You understand?"

"Don't be too sure about that," her voice dropped. "There isn't a chance you will succeed tonight."

It would have been a simple matter to walk away and leave her standing there. Why did he hesitate? Something in her voice, the pressure of her arm. He found himself under the sign of Dominique's restaurant. It was where he promised to recommend Borka and his recipe of grouse. "Karamzin, volume seven, page 101, a ticket on the omnibus to Vasilievsky Island. You'll walk into a trap. Please go in with me."

The doorman in an ankle length, bright blue coat bowed deeply. Inside white damask tablecloths, cut glass and silver, oil paintings and mirrors.

Vasiliev ordered raspberry ices and *petits fours*.

"Do behave yourself, Vasya. I tried to avoid this kind of scene. The clerk in Plavilchikov wasn't cooperative. He used to be a reasonable boy, but the People's Will has ruined him. At least you won't run away now. Take a look at your book if you still doubt me."

Vasiliev unwrapped the parcel and flipped through the pages. The ticket was wedged between pages 101 and 102. In the margin a pencilled message. "Last trip, last stop, head north toward Smolensk Field." He shrugged and unfolded his napkin.

"The last omnibus doesn't leave for an hour. You have time to hear me out. Don't worry they'll be waiting for you."

She had reached out, seized his wrist, and then released it.

She was lovely in her light blue dress. It was no hand me down, but the height of fashion with a touch of lace at the throat and the broach he knew so well, the cameo of Antigone. But he saw sadness in her eyes.

"I'm listening, my dear."

"Magician put you in touch with the People's Will. Good. Zheliabov is an honest man whatever else you may think of him. What he does not know is that a police informer has penetrated the Exec-Com. The informer has betrayed your meeting with them tonight. The Gendarmes have planned a raid to take them and you as well. You'll be branded as a double agent. You'll be finished for good."

"Have you warned Zheliabov and the others?"

"They won't believe us. The trouble is that we cannot positively identify the double agent. Zheliabov is suspicious of our motives. He thinks we want to delay them from carrying out their plan until it's too late to put it into operation. Besides, he argues, the circumstantial evidence is against us."

"What does he mean by too late?"

"You must know about the proclamation of the reforms? They intend to kill the tsar before the public announcement."

"And the circumstantial evidence?"

"Zheliabov sees no reason why the Gendarmes should have waited this long to roll up the rest of the Exec-Com if they really have a double agent in place."

"How do you answer that one?"

"You are the answer."

The raspberry ice was melting in her dish. Vasiliev lifted his spoon to his lips, his eyes now fixed on the entrance to the restaurant.

"Eat your ice, Irisha. We are supposed to be enjoying ourselves. Don't furrow your brow. You look as though you are quarreling with me."

She broke into a smile and applied herself to the raspberry ice.

"How strange it tastes. It's been years since…" she didn't finish.

"Sounds too elaborate to me. Too risky for them to wait until I show up."

"If the Gendarmes make mistakes it is on the side of arrogance. They think their plan is fool proof."

"Why didn't you tell Zheliabov your source. That might have convinced him. By the way, what was your source."

Irina selected a miniature éclair and nibbled at it.

"You can't expect me to answer that, Inspector."

"Then you can't expect me to believe you any more than Zheliabov does."

"But I do, because you are logical and they are dogmatic. You can see the logic of the plan. You understand how important it is for them to discredit you. If you prove your case Bagration will be disgraced and Van der Fleet will lose his access to the heir. Their political plans will be ruined."

"Irina, let me say something. I mean this, sincerely. You are a brave woman. I appreciate the risk you are taking in meeting me. That should be enough to convince me. But I'm a difficult type, as you know. If you do not tell me your source, I shall walk out of here in a few minutes and rendezvous on Vasilievsky Island with...whoever turns up."

She shook her head, her eyes glistening now.

"Please don't force me."

"Look if you were just here to save my skin, I'd be inclined to believe you. But you have your own political motives, and so in a way do I. I have to know."

How could she tell him that political motives were no longer involved. She had never ceased to love him ever since she was a child. The love had changed, the war, her own spiritual crisis, the long separation, the underground. The gulf had widened, become unbridgeable. But she did not want him to know how much she had sacrificed. He would not understand. But she knew she would tell him. It was the only way to save him.

"Shuev," she whispered in a half-throttled voice.

It occurred to him then that he knew so little about what had happened to turn her into a revolutionary, to bring her to the point where she was prepared to sacrifice the last shred of her upper class respectability for a cause he considered quixotic and doomed to end in exile or on the scaffold. Life in the underground was shorter than that of a lieutenant on the battlefield. But was her rage against the arrogance of her own class—whatever may have fueled it—any different from his? He had never felt one of them, the nobility, despite his education. They were selfish men, but incapable of running their own affairs, a ruling class that was incompetent to rule. He shared her hatred of the privileged and of the secret police, Van der Fleet and his kind who had tried to have him killed, had trapped Borka and was pursuing a murderous plot against the tsar. But he had taken another path from hers. He felt pity and a pang of remorse. What could he have done to spare her? All this passed through his mind in the time it took to lower his spoon to his plate of melted ice and touch her wrist as she had touched his. It was strange, he reflected, how even our gestures toward one another are poorly timed and fail to coincide. Then he looked up at her. Her eyes were fixed on his. The voice may have broken but the gaze remained steady. It was as close as they would come, he and she, to a joint declaration of love.

"A heavy sacrifice," was all he managed to say.

"Others have made heavier ones. There was no other way."

"How long has Shuev been confiding in you?"

"About a month."

"Did he give you any details about the operation tonight?"

"Not exactly. He said that there was a good chance his men would arrest the remnants of the Exec-Com along with a detective. He mentioned your name and made some unflattering comments about your character. Called you either a dupe or a fool. He said there were others who considered you a traitor, but he couldn't believe that, knowing your father. He made a bad pun out of your name and the Vasilievsky Island."

"What about the contact in the bookstore."

"They know all about Plavilchikov now. The informer, of course. I tried to warn the clerk, but none of them believe anyone outside the organization. At least I got him to tell me about the arrangements they made with you. We were classmates and comrades before the Land and Liberty split. Sometimes the old ties still bind."

"And the timing of the raid?"

"Presumably the Gendarmes will have their people on the street and hold off until you are in the house."

"I might be able to get to Zheliabov before they do." He folded his napkin and looked for the waiter.

"Wait. You are making a mistake. It's too late and you cannot risk being taken. Listen to me, for God's sake."

"Quickly then."

"One member of the Exec-Com will not be at the safe house tonight. Shuev doesn't know that, but I found out, no need for you to know how. It is Sophia Perovskaya. Zheliabov is her lover. They have planned a last ditch attempt on the tsar's life. I didn't learn the details, place and timing of the attack. I have one more chance to find out later tonight."

"I need the letters."

"Not at the cost of the tsar's assassination. Don't you see? We can work together to head off the assassination, but only if you avoid the trap. No one in authority except for you will believe my story. The first thing they would ask me is what's your source? Isn't that what you wanted to know? I would have to admit I had made contact with the revolutionaries. I can hear Shuev now: 'And how my dear Irina did you do that?' If I admit being in the underground, that would end it right there. But with the information I can get you tonight you will have the best chance to forestall the attack. The letters won't do the job. They will only compromise Bagration and Van der Fleet, but it will be Perovskaya or one of her people who will throw the bomb."

"Your logic has one flaw. Van der Fleet is part of the plot, and the People's Will don't know that. We have to expose him and the only way is to get the letters."

"So it's a stalemate. You think without Van der Fleet, the terrorists will fail; I think Perovskaya is the key. Unless we neutralize her, they will succeed."

"Not a stalemate. We are not adversaries in chess. We have to work together to prevent *shakhmat*, the death of the king."

"And how do we do this?"

"We go our separate ways. You meet your contact, I'll meet mine. We rendezvous tomorrow early and plan the next move. Leave me a message at the European Hotel, just name a place and time."

"But the trap?"

"I'll take a likhach right now and arrive at the safe house well ahead of the last omnibus. I'll get the letters and then leave. What happens after that is an affair between the Gendarmes and Zheliabov."

"You are taking the greater risk."

"Up until now that has been true of you; this may make us even."

The waiter appeared and Vasiliev paid. They left Dominique's and walked to a cab stand. He bent over and brushed her gloved hand with his lips.

"Be careful."

"Good luck."

Vasiliev watched her cab move into the heavy traffic and then hailed a likhach. He thought back on their conversation. He always seemed to be saying one thing to her and thinking another. He wondered whether it was the same with her. He glanced at his watch. He tried to convince himself there was still time to get the letters and beat a retreat before the trap was sprung.

The cab crossed over to Vasilievsky Island and turned down 23 Line Street when a boy ran out into the roadway in front of them. The likhach swerved and bounced up on the sidewalk. The right wheel struck a lamppost and cracked in two. Vasiliev jumped out. The boy was lying in the street and the traffic was beginning to back up behind the likhach. A policeman ran up and seized hold of the cabby by the collar.

"It wasn't his fault," Vasiliev began, adjusting his pince-nez." We'll see about that, sir," said the policeman. "Get back all of you," he shouted at the gathering crowd. The boy seemed more dazed than hurt. He was sitting up and crying. Vasiliev went over and examined him. "He's all right, just shaken up."

"And are you a doctor, sir?" asked the policeman taking out his note pad.

"No, but he isn't bleeding or bruised."

"Well now, we'll see about that, sir."

Vasiliev shrugged and backed off.

"Just a moment, sir. You are a witness. I need your statement and your papers please." They were hemmed in now by a circle of onlookers. Vasiliev didn't like the look of them, a rough crowd.

"It's a crying shame, if you ask me," said an old woman dressed in black, "the way these cabbies drive. Wild, they are, just wild."

"That's not the case here," Vasiliev said edging toward a gap in the crowd.

"Well, now, we'll see about that, sir. Just hand me your papers."

The policeman had unbuttoned his holster.

"This is absurd, officer. Are you threatening me?"

The crowd pressed in closer anticipating a lively scene.

"Look, here are my documents. I'm a barrister."

The policeman scrutinized Vasiliev's passport.

"Ah ha, a foreigner, I see."

"Where there's foreigners there's trouble," said a voice from the crowd. A group of young men started whistling.

"Now we'll have none of that," cried the policeman.

"Officer, I am late for an important appointment. I was just a passenger in the cab, not involved at all. I am staying at the European Hotel and my papers as you see are in order. So I would be grateful if you would clear the crowd and let me pass."

"Well, now, I'll be deciding the proper procedure here. What we need is a bit of order here." More whistling. The old lady in black had gone over to the boy, opened her purse, taken out a vial of eau de cologne, poured some on her handkerchief and applied it to the boy's temple. There was applause from the crowd. The boy seemed to enjoy the attention. He was smiling now and making motions to the crowd behind the policeman's back. This touched off laughter and more applause.

The policeman was copying down something from Vasiliev's passport. It was clear he thought his authority was being challenged by the crowd. "Now let's have your statement, sir."

Vasiliev kept his voice even, but he felt trapped by his own disguise and exposed to ridicule by speaking with a German accent. The crowd kept mocking him and the officer kept repeating. "What was that, sir. Can't you speak a proper Russian?"

Vasiliev quickly finished speaking. But the crowd did not disperse.

"Now, where is the cabby? He'll need to confirm what you say."

"But isn't it the other way around?"

"Well, we'll see about that, sir."

The cabby told his story in a confused way while the boy kept shaking his head.

"It wasn't that way at all."

"Give the lad a chance," a shout went up.

Vasiliev's impatience was giving way to panic. There was no way for him to intimidate the policeman, or bribe him with the crowd looking on. Would they let him through no matter what he said or did? For most of them street entertainment was all they had.

Suddenly, there was a commotion from the rear of the crowd. The traffic jam had attracted the attention of the Gendarmes. A blue uniform pushed into the circle.

"What's going on here, constable?"

"An accident, sir. I'm interrogating witnesses."

"Well, for God's sake break up the crowd and get that likhach off the street." The boy scrambled to his feet and dodged under the legs of one of the whistlers who slapped him on his rump to push him through.

"And who are you?" the officer demanded, turning to Vasiliev.

"A passenger."

"Well, no need for you to stand around here. Constable, bring the cabby over here and disperse the crowd, I say. Don't you read your daily security bulletin? No crowds allowed to congregate within the city limits. And you've backed up traffic for blocks. Now get a move on!"

The constable pulled out his whistle and gave a series of short blasts. People slowly gave way as he and the officer waved them back. More whistle blasts. Another officer arrived. Vasiliev slipped away, walking briskly back toward the center, cursing the street urchin, the policeman, and the crowd. It was insane. He would never find a likhach out here. Then a regular cab came out of a side street and he waved it down. They drove up to the terminus on Izmailovsky Regiment Street ten minutes before the last omnibus was scheduled to arrive.

He could see to the end of the line of street lamps where Smolensk Field began. It was a poor quarter and deserted at this time of night. Could Irina's source have been wrong? He started walking along the pavement when he heard the rumble of the omnibus. It was arriving early. He moved into the shadow of an archway opening into a courtyard. The omnibus discharged only one passenger, an old man carrying a canvas bag. He limped heavily as he made his way down the street toward the Field. A figure in workman's clothes came out of a basement traktir and fell into step about twenty meters behind the old man, clearly having mistaken him for Vasiliev in disguise. Vasiliev gave them a good head start before following. Beyond the last street lamp where the pavement ended, the Smolensk Field was in darkness. A shutter clattered and a dog barked. Vasiliev passed through a shadow under a broken street lamp. He glanced behind him. The street was empty.

Vasiliev slowed his pace, tense with anticipation. Two men stepped out of a doorway on the sidewalk ahead of him. They were dressed in civilian clothes but carried themselves with a distinctive military bearing. Vasiliev smiled to himself. It was another case of the tail following the tail. The trap was closing. But the Gendarme agents were too confident, arrogant, as Irina had observed. They never checked behind them. They had put all their faith in the informer. Vasiliev was safe for the moment but he felt exposed and helpless. There was no way to alert Zheliabov. In a few minutes he would lose his last chance to get hold of the letters and with it his only hope of bringing down Van der Fleet. Now he had to concentrate on saving his own skin. Just then the old man turned into a courtyard and the worker stopped in his tracks, obviously confused by the behavior of the man he believed to be Vasiliev.

"Keep going, you idiot," Vasiliev muttered to himself. But the worker must have been a recent recruit. He was just following instructions, to trail the last man off the omnibus who was heading toward Smolensk Field and catch him up at the safe house. He had already failed to take elementary precautions, not once having looked over his shoulder. Not arrogant like the Gendarmes, just inexperienced.

The worker finally turned around, but the two agents had disappeared in a shallow doorway. Vasiliev wanted to cry out as he watched the workman make his second mistake. Instead of aborting the operation, he made for the safe house. Even from where Vasiliev stood he could see how rattled the man was; now he was fumbling at the door latch. Had he forgotten the code or was he unable to fit the key in the lock? Vasiliev was only a few steps from the courtyard where the old man had disappeared. If the agents were distracted, he thought, he could dodge in there without being spotted.

Suddenly, a police cab shot out of the darkness of Smolensk

Field and hurtled toward the safe house. The two plain-clothes men closed in from the other side, drawing their revolvers as they ran towards the house. Vasiliev slipped into the doorway where the agents had hidden. The worker managed to get the door open, but then staggered and fell across the threshold. Had he been hit? Shots rang out inside the house. One of the agents threw up his arms and slumped to the pavement. The other went down on his knees and kept shooting. The police cab discharged four more Gendarmes with rifles. Two of them provided covering fire while the others charged the house, firing as they ran. The body of the fallen worker blocked the doorway. Those inside couldn't drag away his body without exposing themselves to the fusillade from the street. The façade of the safe house seemed to explode, riddled with bullets, chips of brick flying into the street, the windows blown in. Vasiliev broke cover, edging his way along the wall of the building toward the archway of the courtyard.

A second police cab rolled out of a side street. Vasiliev heard shots from the rear of the house and the splintering of wood. More shouts, the screaming of wounded men. Lights began to go on up and down the street. Vasiliev stood motionless in the dark court-yard. Somewhere he had lost his pince-nez.

He was startled by a voice behind him. "Quick, Inspector, back here, watch your step, chicken crates." Magician grasped him by the sleeve and pulled him into a stairwell. "We have our own place. Up these stairs. Careful, missing planks." Vasiliev lost his footing. Magician caught hold of his arm and pulled him into a darkened room. Outside the shooting had stopped. Magician released his hold.

"Don't worry Inspector. It's our place, a spy hole. Swan's idea, for keeping watch on the People's Will." He was breathing hard, but there was excitement in his voice. "It looks as though you'll have to spend the night on the floor, against the far wall, a mattress." The next thing he was gone.

It was an inside room. Vasiliev could see nothing of the street. There were steps overhead, then silence. He leaned up against the wall and cursed silently. A great tiredness came over him. He knelt down on the floor. He could smell the mattress before he felt it, filled with straw, thin and rough to the touch. There was no cover. It was cold. He wrapped his frock coat tightly around him but it gave little warmth. What did it matter? He had slept in worse places, on the Danube, in the Ural forests, at Osholovo. Before he fell into a fitful sleep his thoughts went back to Dominique's, the white table cloths and the raspberry ice melting in her dish; "so strange a taste," she had said, "after all these years."

Chapter
Thirty-Four

The early morning omnibus from Izmailovsky Regiment Street was crowded with passengers talking quietly about the raid.

"They say they've taken Zheliabov himself," a man in an old army coat muttered, glancing around furtively.

The dawn seemed reluctant to break over the city. It was still half-light when the omnibus reached Nevsky Prospekt. It slowed to pass a string of horse carts where the night before the landaus, barouches and troikas had lined the thoroughfare. Vasiliev gazed vacantly at the city streets beginning to come awake. Porters who had spent the night wrapped in their sheepskins at the entrances to courtyards brushed the frost from their beards and went inside to seek the warmth of the stove. Peasant servants, dressed in scarlet cotton blouses and trousers of black velveteen tucked inside the wrinkled leather boots, darted from shop to shop buying fresh rolls and cream for their masters' morning tea.

The omnibus stopped across the boulevard from Dominique's, now dim and shuttered. Above Plavilchikov's the facsimile of a book swayed in the breeze from the Neva. Vasiliev got off and walked down to the European Hotel. Serov was waiting in the lobby looking bleary eyed and rumpled as if he had camped out all night. The bright smile on his face froze as he saw the defeated look on Vasiliev's face. Together they mounted the red carpeted stairs.

"We'll rest for a few hours," Vasiliev touched Serov on the shoulder and they parted without another word.

Vasiliev slumped down in a chair, his eyes resting on the bucolic landscape hanging over the bed. What a bad painting, he thought.

The Vasilievsky Island Omnibus

In a few minutes he had fallen asleep. It seemed only a few minutes when a knock on the door woke him up.

"Good morning, Your Honor. The Colonel sends his respects and asks you to accompany me."

"Give me a moment to shave and change into my uniform."

A new spirit seemed to have invaded the Winter Palace. Couriers were arriving and departing at a gallop. Cossack patrols grouped together in threes and fours, were chatting animatedly. The sentries stood at parade rest, the lines of tension gone from their faces. They joked as they glanced at Vasiliev's documents. In the corridors he caught the same excited mood. Adjutants hurried from office to office. Two Gendarme officers approached, nudging one another as they brushed past Vasiliev. The courier left Vasiliev with Ivan's orderly who was wreathed in smiles. After a minute Vasiliev was ushered into an unfamiliar office, more like a lounge, with a samovar and empty glasses on a table in the center. A full-length portrait of the tsar in the uniform of the Semenovsky Guards hung between the long windows; even he looked pleased. A low hum of voices came from an adjoining room. Vasiliev prepared himself a glass of tea, added a slice of lemon and a few cubes of sugar, hoping to revive his flagging spirits. No apple jelly here, he noted ruefully. He anticipated another stressful interview.

Ivan strode in wearing a freshly pressed uniform and all his medals, extending both hands to Vasiliev.

"Vasili, dear fellow, I wanted to be the first to inform you of the good news. Russia is saved. By God, we've done it at last. The terrorists are done for. The People's Will has been smashed. We've rounded up the entire executive committee. Do you hear, *mon vieux!*" Ivan rubbed his hands in glee

"It is the greatest day in the reign since the emancipation."

Vasiliev seemed preoccupied with his tea, stirring mechanically as he watched the cubes of sugar slowly disintegrate.

"Do you understand what I am saying? You look bewildered. Well, I can't blame you. Whatever you may think of Van der Fleet, he carried it off. Swooped down on them like an avenging angel. A brilliant stroke. Imagine. They nabbed Zheliabov, the ring leader, the real brains behind the whole terrorist network. We've been tracking him for years. The People's Will has been decapitated; no one left now, no one of consequence, no one who can mastermind the assassination of the tsar, our beloved Alexander Nikolaevich."

"Yes, Ivan, I already know about it."

"Do you now! What a pity that I didn't have the pleasure of being the first to tell you. Who was it? One of those chatterboxes in the corridor? An old friend from the Page Corps, eh? Not my courier, I'll wager. I told him to say nothing and my adjutant wouldn't have dared..."

"None of them, Ivan. I knew before your courier arrived this morning."

"What! Come now, Vasili, don't tease me. Take your setback like a man. It's all right. We'll get Bagration. I'm sure that Van der Fleet will hand him over now or else provide us with an explanation. Though I must say he hardly needs to. You've done a splendid job, Vasili. I don't mean to take any credit from you. Thanks to you we can reassure the panic-mongers among the nobility and that rascal

Katkov that there are no mad dog terrorists out to bomb them into oblivion. Your work just completes the circle."

"I saw them take Zheliabov, Ivan. I was there, an eye witness, you might say."

"What are you saying, Vasili? You...no you couldn't have be part of the raid. It's unthinkable. How strange you look, today. This whole thing..."

"No one told me about the raid, not your courier or adjutant, or any chance meeting in the corridor and I wasn't part of it. No, I was in a courtyard on Izmailovsky Regiment Street last night at eleven o'clock. I saw the Gendarmes spring the trap, the agent shot down in the street, the three police cabs, the storming of the house, number 94 if you want the address."

"How did you know where it was?" Ivan's jubilant expression crumbled.

"I had a rendezvous with the Exec-Com at that precise hour."

"For the love of God, Vasili, are you mad?"

"That is possible, Ivan. I am beginning to wonder. But not your ordinary madness, not unreason. Oh, forget that. If I had met my appointment I would have been swept up in the raid, arrested and accused of being a double agent. The plan was ingenious, just a shade too ingenious. Still, one must admire the finesse, the timing. Van der Fleet does have style."

"I don't understand, there is no way you could have obtained these details..."

"...except to have been there. This is what I am telling you. Now, as to why I was meeting Zheliabov and company, let me explain."

Vasiliev pulled out Bagration's letter from his breast pocket and laid it on the table. "This is one of a dozen letters that proves Usha-kova was blackmailing Bagration. It was given to me by members of the Peoples Will as a handwriting sample so I could verify its authenticity. No question, it's Bagration's hand. I read eleven other letters. They looked genuine to me. But the terrorists insisted on keeping them until I arranged to have them all published in a daily newspaper. I agreed. Everything was set. Last night I was to pick up the remaining letters. I didn't get there in time. One of those little accidents of history. I don't suppose Van der Fleet reported having found them?"

Ivan was drumming his fingers on the table. He was annoyed that Vasiliev was trying to tarnish another victory by the Gendarmes over the terrorists. He had become dangerously single-minded in this case. There was even the danger that his eccentricity was giving way to perversity. He picked up the letter.

"This implies much but proves little."

"The others leave no doubt."

"Do you really think, Vasili, that Van der Fleet organized the entire operation just in order to confiscate the letters and save his friend's skin..."

"Of course not, it was just a bonus."

"...or to nail yours to the wall?"

"Another bonus, if you don't mind my saying so, rather more important to him and even more carefully planned."

"But what in the name of everything that's holy do you think Van der Fleet is up to? You can't impugn his loyalty, his devotion to the crown. Think of the work he has done—Goldenberg, Kletochnikov, Mikhailov and now Zheliabov. We may owe the stability of the empire to him more than any other man."

"That is what worries me, Ivan."

"Stop speaking in riddles, man. Look, I have a minister, two privy counselors and three department heads waiting in my office. Tell me in plain words what is bothering you now."

"Have you lifted the surveillance, Ivan?"

"Come now, Vasili, under the circumstances what else could we do?"

"Of course, what else?"

"Vasili, listen to me. There is an explanation that makes sense, much as you might not like it. It fits the evidence though not always your interpretation of it. Let's assume that Ushakova was blackmailing Bagration, but that the Prince did not kill her, as you suppose. Let's assume it was his son, in a fit of madness or rage. You said he as much as admitted it. The Prince tried to cover up his son's crime. So he was crazed with fear when you confronted him with the evidence. He attacked you—a folly for which he must pay. Van der Fleet intervened, disarmed you and ordered you detained. Why? That is the crucial question. He claimed that he was going to decide the fate of the empire and that you would be in the way.

There is only one logical way to explain this. The Prince's letters had fallen into the hands of the terrorists. That is a known fact, correct? My instinct tells me they were going to use the letters for the same purpose as Ushakova, to blackmail Bagration. This would provide them with the money they needed to keep their rag tail army in the field, purchase explosives, bribe guards or whatever they needed to do in order to carry out their murderous plans. The executive committee intended to use you as an instrument in their blackmail by getting you to publish the letters if the Prince did not pay. Van der Fleet had to accomplish two things at once. He had to keep the Prince under his surveillance so that the man did not cave in. You know how volatile he is. And he had to eliminate you temporarily from the case in order to prevent the terrorists from using you or to prevent you from disrupting his plans to spring the trap.

"Let's admit too the presence of an informer among the terrorists who kept Van der Fleet apprised of their activities. They knew you were coming for the letters last night. Bagration was desperate. Van der Fleet assured him the letters would never be handed over. He intended to sweep you up in the raid. All right he was a shade too clever, but it may have been the only way to prevent you from committing a folly, don't you see? Now that he has decided the fate of the empire, he may be in a generous mood. It's time I arranged a meeting between the two of you, possibly in Count Ushakov's office to tie up loose ends."

"And the letters?"

"Quite possible destroyed, to save Bagration. Perhaps the son will be quietly put away in an monastery. Bagration should be made to apologize to you. The incident might be brought to a satisfactory end."

"Your explanation is plausible."

"So you agree?"

"Except for Petya's attempts to kill me, the killing of Nasya, the maid, and of my great friend, the Komi guide, Borka."

"Exactly the reason for the little meeting I suggested. It may be Petya was a double agent, or acting on his own or...well, Vasili I can't solve all the mysteries in this tangled affair. I'm sure Van der Fleet also has questions about your ties to the revolutionaries. If you could prove to me that Van der Fleet's behavior masks a more sinister motive—and I admit it is out of the ordinary – I'm prepared to act. But what is this monstrous conspiracy of his you keep alluding to?"

Vasiliev had gone over Ivan's interpretations a dozen times. They fit some of the facts but not all of them; there were still loose ends. Vasiliev had questioned his own motives in drawing conclusions. He had tried to discount his love for Irina, his dislike of Magician, his hatred of Van der Fleet. But when all was said and done he still believed that his explanation was the one closest to the truth. It was not just a matter of guessing. He had examined every piece of the puzzle from all sides and strung them together in a logical sequence. Yet even now, he thought, the temptation was great to join the victors. Perhaps Serov's folk wisdom was right; the mind of another was like a dark forest. Did he really understand what was behind the strange behavior of Bagration and Van der Fleet? In all his cases there were moments like this, when he doubted his own conclusions. How certain was he now? Chalk it up to intuition, he reflected, but intuition guided by facts; he would prove he was right. But he also realized that this was a time to be cautious.

"There is much in what you say, Ivan. Yes, a meeting with Van der Fleet might well clear the air. No sense working at cross-purposes any more. Who knows, perhaps we should have joined forces at the beginning. But indulge me once more. Give me a few days to lick my wounds, put my life in order."

Ivan had expected more resistance. Had his explanation been so convincing? He was not so sure himself and he was skeptical of his apparent victory. Vasili does not surrender so easily, he thought. But he was not asking for anything unreasonable. Ivan nodded in agreement and they shook hands. Vasiliev left the building wondering what his next move would be.

Chapter
Thirty-Five

Vasiliev returned to the European Hotel in the police sleigh Ivan had ordered for him. Bundled in fur blankets he felt nothing but pain and exhaustion. A fine snow was falling steadily. The legendary Petersburg dampness had lodged in his bruised arm and sprained ankle. His thoughts kept jumping from one thing to another. He took little pleasure from the fact that the revolutionaries had given him more help than his own side. But what was his side? He kept asking himself. Perhaps a message from Irina would be waiting at the Hotel. There wasn't much else to hope for at this point. He thought of Serov combing the streets. Had he set the good Sergeant a fruitless task? He ought to have joined him but he hadn't the strength. Not now at least.

Finding no message at the desk, he dragged himself up to his room. He pulled off his uniform, took a sedative and fell into a dreamless sleep. The sound of rapping on wood came from far away. He opened his eyes to the drumming on his door. He swung his legs down from the bed, the pain coming back like a curse. Outside it was dark. Had he slept through another day or were the snow clouds gathering again? The rapping was insistent and he heard Serov calling his name.

"A message, Sergeant?"

"No, sorry, nothin' of that sort, Vasili Vasilievich."

"Come in Serov. I hardly expected any good news on the Ides of March."

"Beggin' your pardon, Vasili Vasilievich?"

"Today is March 13 according to the Gregorian calendar in use in the rest of Europe. It is a dangerous time for heads of state."

Serov gave him a puzzled look.

"Sorry, it was a poor joke. Now what sights and sounds of our haughty Petersburg beauty have brought back that sparkle to your eyes."

"It's that for sure, haughty I mean. Not your warm and friendly Moscow people. But there's plenty of goin's on here, yes plenty. One odd bit caught my eye, beggin' your pardon. Might have an interest for you."

Vasiliev thrust both hands in his dressing gown and resigned himself to one of Serov's tale telling sessions. All indications were that this one would be well worth listening to.

"Just down on Malaya Sadovaya, not a pebble's throw from where it crosses Nevsky, you know, they're tearin' up the street. Heaps of cobblestones, mud, some heavy timber lying about here 'n there. I was takin' in the scene as you said I should, just leanin' against a wooden trestle munchin' on a *pirozhok* when along comes a wagon. There's big letters on the side. The color is peelin' a bit, but you can make them out all right. Says Kobozev Cheeses. Now that doesn't mean much by itself. I'm watchin' closely, mind you, to see how he gets around all the stones and timber, stickin' right out there in the street. Well, the driver isn't the best I've ever seen, handled the horses sort of roughly, almost got 'em tangled up somethin' awful. But he manages to make his way. Just as he's about clear, why the rear wheel jumps the curb. The wagon tips like a drunken peasant. Two caskets roll out the back pretty as you please, one chasin' the other. Made quite a racket. The driver gets out fast like, and runs back. Short, thin fellow he was. Spectacles bouncin' around on his nose. Grabs hold of the casket. It's a mite too heavy for him. He's wrestlin' with it to get it back in. I was about to give him a hand, but then I thought to myself, now Serov, just sit tight and watch. That's your job, to watch. One of these big fellers diggin' up the road went right over and gives him a hand. Nothing to it for him, whereas the driver was puffin' and red faced. He tries to press a copper into the big feller's hand. But the other won't have none of it.

"Then the little feller climbs back on his wagon and drives off. The worker's still standin' there scratchin' his head, like he's wonderin' about one thing and another. The others call him back. They're sayin' 'brother, you've done enough charitable work for the day'. He shrugs and goes back to his diggin'. I bolts the rest of my *pirozhok* and strolls over, seein' as you told me to take care as to anythin' that was a wee bit different. I look down and sees for myself what made the worker scratch a bit. Now can you guess, Vasili Vasilievich, seein' how you likes to do that, what it was?"

Vasiliev was beginning to chuckle as Serov exaggerated his village speech and his drawl as if he wanted to have some fun at the expense of the Petersburg accent with its exaggerated lisp. There was little enough in this case that had given either one of them much to laugh about.

"So one of the barrels had cracked, eh Sergeant? And there was something that spilled out, and it was lying there right in front of your eyes."

"Now I couldn't say it better, Vasili Vasilievich. Now you'd expect cheese, wouldn't you?"

"I most certainly would , Sergeant. But it wasn't cheese was it?"

"No sir, it most certainly was not."

"Then what was it?"

"Dirt, not mud, mind you, but dirt."

"Dirt?" Vasiliev looked blankly at Serov for an instant. He was not playing Serov's game any more. He didn't see the point, at least not right away. Then it came to him.

"Tunneling? Of course, tunneling!" Vasiliev cried out. "Did you check Kobozev's?"

"I can recommend their Yaroslavsky cheese. The owners speak like they're from the provinces, Orel I'd say. They look the part of petty trades people. He's a fat, bearded feller and she's a nice young thing with dimples and a pug nose. Nobody takin' much notice of them. A couple of plain clothes types up the street. It's one of those shops below street level. And there's more than one room, though they're only sellin' in the front. A door leads to the back, I guess. But more interestin' is the sackcloth on the wall. Right behind the counter it is. I'm wagerin' that it's hidin' another door. But I had no claim to go in there. The main thing, Vasili Vasilievich, is that Kobozev's Cheese Shop lies smack in middle of the crossroads of Malaya Sadovaya and Nevsky."

"In other words, at the center of the route the tsar normally takes on his way to the Riding Academy." Vasiliev threw off his dressing gown and reached for his jacket.

"Let's go, Sergeant, but this time, we play strictly by the rules."

It took them an hour to get through to Ivan who was tied up in a high level meeting.

"You have no idea, Serov, what pleasure this meeting is going to give me," Vasiliev said as he paced the anteroom of Ivan's office.

"Vasili! Ah, and Sergeant. Why you look like a new man. Always had great powers of recuperation didn't you? But I believe our good news has finally caught hold of you as well, isn't that so?"

Through the windows of the office they could see the amphitheater of the Palace Square where the lanterns had just been lit. The excitement of the morning had dissipated and only a few couriers cantered across the vast open space.

"Ivan, I need your help. It looks as though we might be able to land a rather big fish. I want you to be in on the catch. I've been converted; no more masquerades, no more one-man performances. What we need is a legitimate police operation, an impeccable witness—that's you—and I promise you the outcome will be different. No one is going to doubt your word."

"A big catch, eh? I didn't think any were left in the sea. But I see you are taking after our Gendarmes." Ivan felt he could afford to chafe Vasiliev a bit. "You're in luck. I've just finished up here and no dinners tonight, thank God. You have the hunter's look. So what is your surprise?"

"First, I'd like to pay a visit to police headquarters. Now don't worry I'm not about to cause a scandal. I've learned my lesson. There are just a few things to clear up, all connected to ensuring the Emperor's security. And then I'll spring my surprise on you, Ivan, not the kind you like, but one you'll appreciate."

They took a cab. Vasiliev refused to say anything further. Ivan did not press him. Let him have his fun, he thought. The St. Petersburg Chief of Police, Colonel Adrian Dvorzhitsky, was about to leave his office, but greeted them with enthusiasm. "Vasili Vasilievich, how many years has it been? I must say I expected to see you before this. Now that the excitement is all over you show up on my doorstep and in such excellent company."

"Adrian Sergeevich. it has been too long. I accept your scolding with a bad conscience. But you've had your hands full without having to entertain an old friend. I've just been poking around on my own. Nothing of importance turned up until today. Quite by accident my assistant, Sergeant Serov here, observed some suspicious activity. As we are all concerned over the safety of the Emperor, we thought it best to consult you and ask for your help."

"Of course, Vasili Vasilievich, you acted correctly. We have the city blanketed with plain clothes men and police, but it is always conceivable that they may have overlooked something. I'm a great believer in the old saying that you can't be too careful."

"May we see the reports of police surveillance covering the past week or so in the Malaya Sadovaya—Nevsky area."

"Right away." Dvorzhitsky rang the brass bell on his desk and gave an order to his assistant.

"Interesting you should ask about it. The area is of particular concern to us. It is heavily patrolled by Cossacks. The Gendarmes have detached a few men to help us make spot checks."

The assistant returned within minutes and handed Dvorzhitsky a thick dossier.

"Perhaps we could start with a few shops. Let me see now." He hesitated and then to Serov's great delight he raised his eyes to the ceiling. "How about Kobozev's Cheese Shop."

Ivan was seated next to the Chief, swinging one leg over the other and smoking a long Turkish cigarette. He wore an amused look on his face. His old friend simply could not resist a theatrical gesture. Serov stood at rigid attention behind Vasiliev.

Dvorzhitsky flipped through the reports, his head bent low over the desk." Hmm, the latest one is dated three days ago, March 10. Just a moment. A Gendarme surveillance party dressed in uniforms of the sanitary commission paid a visit, questioned the owner, searched the place thoroughly." The Chief raised his head. "There had been some reports from my plain clothes detectives that a number of young men had been observed entering and leaving the place at irregular intervals. Let's see now." His eyes ran down the page. "But there is a note at the end saying, 'Nothing suspicious to report.'"

"May I ask, Adrian Sergeevich, who signed the report?"

Dvorzhitsky removed his pince-nez and brought the paper close to his face. "Looks like Colonel Van der Fleet's signature, if I'm not mistaken."

"I'm sure you are not," said Vasiliev.

A long ash from Ivan's cigarette fell onto his tunic.

"I have a favor to ask," Vasiliev went on. "Might we have the use of four of your men for an hour or so?"

Dvorzhitsky raised his eyebrows. He did not understand the connection between the report and Vasiliev's request. "We are stretched thin right now..."

"It is vital, Adrian Sergeevich."

Ivan leaned over and asked Dvorzhitsky for the dossier. He studied it for a minute in silence, then placed it on the table. "It is important, Adrian, as Vasili says."

Dvorzhitsky shrugged. "Of course, I have some men coming off duty right now. They'll be a bit weary, but it won't be the first time to send them back on the street." Being a cautious and thorough man, Dvorzhitsky assigned six detectives. "You will take your orders from the Colonel."

Fifteen minutes later three police sleighs drew up in front of Kobozev's Cheese Shop. Three detectives went down a side street and took up positions in the rear courtyard of the shop. Three more remained in a sleigh stationed on Malaya Sadovaya. Vasiliev, Ivan and Serov descended the narrow stone steps and pushed open the door. The only customer in the store, an old crone, scurried outside when she saw the uniforms. The detectives stopped and questioned her, then let her go.

The man behind the counter was thick set, bearded with a face the color of a brass samovar, just as Serov had described him. His eyes were fixed on their epaulets. "Yes, gentlemen, can I be of service?"

A younger woman with a snub nose meeting Serov's description peered out of the back room. Had something in her husband's voice alerted her? She closed the door softly.

"Several days ago a sanitary commission paid you a visit. They registered a complaint about your storage facilities. We wish to examine them again."

The bearded man pursed his lips and shuffled his feet. "The

sanitary commission appeared to be satisfied. I heard no complaints. These visits are ruining my business, gentlemen. People are afraid these days when they see the police entering a place of business."

"Please stand aside," Ivan ordered.

"But the storage facilities are in the back room," the man replied, edging his way toward the rear of the shop. Vasiliev nodded to Serov who vaulted the counter and pulled the canvas away from the wall, disclosing a crude door of wooden planks nailed together and padlocked.

"Open it up," Ivan gestured.

The man hesitated, then pulled a ring of keys out of his pocket and fumbled at the lock. Ivan waved him ahead into an unheated, windowless room. The walls had been freshly whitewashed and the floor swept. Bales of straw were piled on one side. Large cakes of ice were packed around a dozen sealed casks standing against the opposite wall. A crowbar was standing in the corner.

"You seem to have misplaced your storage facilities," said Vasiliev. "Isn't that what you use this room for?"

"Yes, yes. But we keep only a few cheeses here, the most perishable ones from abroad. You see?" He leaned forward and pointed to the faded Latin letters on a cask that read "D'Ardèche."

"Open the casks, please." Ivan was growing impatient.

"But Your Excellency, the cheeses have been carefully packed to resist spoilage. If they are opened and not sold at once I'll suffer a huge loss."

Vasiliev picked up the crowbar and drove it with all his strength into one of the casks. He felt a ripple of pain shoot through his sore arm. The staves gave way and dirt trickled out onto the floor.

"Isn't it an extravagance to pack and ice freshly dug soil?"

The man was now sweating profusely in spite of the cold. "We have been doing some repair work on the foundations," he stammered. "This cask must have gotten mixed in with those packed with cheese."

Vasiliev handed the crowbar to Serov. "Sergeant, it's your turn to test the man's theory." Serov made a little too much of selecting his target, but his blow was well aimed and dirt poured out of the second cask.

"Show us where you made the repairs."

The bearded man bolted for the door shouting, "Anna save yourself, police!" Serov quickly subdued him. The man spat mother curses at them as he lay pinned to the ground, tears of rage streaming down his cheeks.

"Take him out to the courtyard, Sergeant. The detectives have probably already intercepted the girl. Tell them to stay put and make certain that the prisoners don't cry out or, God forbid, slip away. I suspect this couple are alone right now. The terrorists wouldn't risk digging while the shop is open. But we don't want to take any chances on someone returning early."

They hung a closed sign on the front door, drew the curtains and went into the back of the shop where they found two rooms. One contained boxes of Yaroslav and Krasnodar cheeses. The other was the couple's living space, sparsely furnished, giving off the faint but unmistakable odor of sewage. In the corner straw matting covered mounds of earth. Vasiliev pulled them off and threw them into the center of the room. Under one of the mats wooden planks had been laid. Serov lifted them with the crowbar releasing a powerful stench.

"They must have dug into a sewer by mistake," said Vasiliev covering his face with his neck cloth.

"Look, Vasili Vasilievich, under the bed—picks, a shovel and a kerosene lantern." Serov was down on his knees holding his nose.

"Crude, but effective. Sergeant are you willing to chance it? You'll ruin your uniform for sure." It was then that Ivan noticed for the first time that Vasiliev never gave Serov a direct order.

Without a word Serov scrambled through the opening into the tunnel. Several minutes passed while Vasiliev and Ivan listened to the dull echo of heavy carts on Malaya Sadovaya rumbling over the tunnel. From inside the tunnel came the sounds of earth falling in clumps. Then Serov emerged, his face, hands and uniform soiled with dirt and offal. One sleeve of his tunic was torn from wrist to elbow. In his hand he held a dynamite fuse.

"They built well. Timbers holdin' up a roof, about two meters high; the whole thing around fifteen meters long. I crawled to the end. Lots of dynamite, enough to blow up the road and what's on it. Fuses attached. Here they are, I pulled them out. The mine is disarmed." With Ivan present Serov had dropped his homey manner.

Ivan's face was grim. "Well done, Sergeant. You'll want to wash up. There must be a pump in the courtyard." He turned to Vasiliev. "Fifteen meters brings the tunnel right under the center of Malaya Sadovaya. Tomorrow the tsar was to pass over the very spot on his way to a review at the Riding Academy. We'll make certain that doesn't happen."

"On the contrary, Ivan. We must make certain that it does happen. With the mine disarmed there is no safer route for the tsar than to go down Malaya Sadovaya. Wait a moment. We must think clearly. The main thing is to set a trap for the terrorists. I don't think our bearded friend could have squeezed himself into the tunnel. There will be others to set the fuses and explode the mine, probably coming tomorrow, the day of the tsar's ride down the boulevard. But they might show up tonight to make a last minute check. We have to be ready for them. And we must prevent the People's Will from finding out what has happened here. That means extra precautions, Ivan. I trust no one now except for you, Adrian and Serov. We don't know any more who is in on the plot. We'll instruct Dvorzhitsky's men to keep the prisoners here for the night. The detectives will have to stay as well. No one leaves, I don't give a damn how uncomfortable they'll be. We will get the police sleighs out of sight and bring in the detectives waiting in front. Assign some of your best men to surround the place with orders to shoot on sight anyone trying to leave, including the detectives. Don't worry we'll warn Dvorzhitsky's men. I want this shop sealed off from the outer world."

Ivan was staring down the hole to the tunnel. "I'll pick the men myself, and bring them back with me. It's hard to believe that the Gendarmes could have overlooked the tunnel when they made their search. I can't understand it. Why did Van der Fleet take the risk? Why delay breaking up the operation? Just to make another spectacular arrest? Has become so obsessed with his reputation as a savior?" Ivan shook his head as they walked back into the shop. "I owe you an apology, Vasili, I misjudged him seriously."

"On the contrary, Ivan, I don't think you are giving Van der Fleet his proper due."

Ivan regarded Vasiliev with astonishment. They left the shop together to instruct the detectives waiting in the courtyard.

Chapter
Thirty-Six

Before Ivan's picked detachment arrived Serov had gone off to buy fresh rolls and enough tea to keep the samovar in the shop bubbling all night. He added two bottles of pepper vodka to the package, knowing that Vasiliev would not have approved. But two liters were not going to reduce the efficiency of six men. For this service he earned the gratitude of the Petersburg detectives for years to come. As for the cheese, there was an ample supply to last them for a long siege.

After having posted his men, Ivan went off reluctantly to a reception in the Ministry for the Gendarmes. Vasiliev had persuaded him how important it was to avoid arousing suspicions that they were on to Van der Fleet's game. Vasiliev and Serov rode back to the European Hotel where they had a late supper of blini and crab salad. "It will all be decided tomorrow," said Vasiliev. They went to their separate rooms.

Vasiliev went round early to rouse Ivan from his bed. The first feeble rays of the sun had just touched the needle tower of the Admiralty. Ivan was more subdued than Vasiliev had ever seen him. The reception had proved to be an ordeal and he had slept only a few hours. He hardly remembered his jubilant mood of the day before. Instead he recalled a half-forgotten incident from two years ago that further darkened his mood. He began to explain when the cab swerved sharply and he seized Vasiliev's arm to keep from pitching forward. Vasiliev winced in pain. Ivan was too deep in his black hole to notice, and Vasiliev did not want to break his train of thought.

Ivan said he had been working late when a secret message had arrived from General Todtleben, then Governor General in Odessa. His men had tapped a leak in the southern organization of the People's Will. A plot to kill the tsar. The plan was to dig a tunnel under one of Petersburg's main thoroughfares at a spot where the imperial coach frequently passed on the way to the Palace. It was only the visit to Kobozev's that jogged his memory; there had been something in Todtleben's report about a cheese shop. The report went through the normal channels, further inquiries were made, the investigation placed in the hands of the Gendarmes. Then— nothing. The trail went cold.

Vasiliev thought for a moment. "We have to work along two lines, Ivan, and we have to move fast. What you say about Todtleben's report is crucial evidence. We have to locate it. Adrian Sergeevich can be trusted to run it down. But I have to interrogate Zheliabov. He is the only person who can tell us what happened to the letters. You see how your good influence has changed me?" He smiled his crooked smile. "You insisted on hard evidence and now we have it, the sanitary commission report, the mine under Malaya Sadovaya and the information from Odessa. The final nail in Van der Fleet's coffin will be the letters. Then we can go to Loris Melikov with an impressive dossier. There will be no further question of the ravings of an eccentric detective."

"Vasili…"

"My apologies, Ivan for exacting petty revenge. Forgive me. Let me be serious. Do you have the tsar's itinerary for today and tomorrow?"

"There will be no difficulty in getting it to you."

Snow was falling more thickly now, promising an accumulation. Under the grey sky the pedestrians dressed in black, bundled up and hurrying along the Nevsky looked like phantoms. In the open sleigh under heavy furs they were not cold but Ivan felt a inner chill. He remembered how he had patronized Vasiliev in Nizhnyi Novgorod, and dismissed his theories in Piter. Now the distance between them had closed up again. But he was terrified at the consequences of his lapse in trusting the one man who had never disappointed him.

"As you say, Vasili, headquarters and then the Peter and Paul Fortress."

It seemed that everything conspired to delay them. The snow squall slowed the heavy traffic on Nevsky to a crawl. When they arrived at headquarters, Dvorzhitsky had already left, and the clerks were in no hurry to recover Todtleben's correspondence. At first it seemed it had been transferred to another building. Ivan made a fuss and the dossier finally arrived.

"Worse than I remembered," said Ivan handing over a letter and an attached memo. Todtleben's information was graphically precise. The terrorists had planned as far back as a year and a half before to buy a cheese-shop and mine Malaya Sadovaya. They had intended to blow up the tsar during one of his scheduled daily trips to the Riding Academy.

"We've got to get the reports of Todtleben and the Sanitary Commission into the hands of Loris-Melikov at once. This should give him pause about Van der Fleet's zeal."

Ivan gave his orders with characteristic precision but his whole manner had changed. His voice was low and hoarse, his face ashen. The clerk noticed too. He bent his head to hear every syllable and to avoid the eyes of the iron colonel. Like a stricken man Ivan led the way to the cab. "The military commandant of the Peter and Paul Fortress," he called out to the cabby who by this time looked like a snowman perched on his box.

In silence they crossed the Chain Bridge, past the parade grounds and along the canals, avoiding the main thoroughfare. They traversed the river over the Palace Bridge, turned to the left and entered a narrow passage. In the past five years over two thousand politicals had passed under the high arch on which Dante's inscription over the gates of Hell might well have been inscribed: '"Abandon ye all hope who enter here." No prisoner had ever escaped from Peter and Paul and few had left it alive. The cab rolled to a stop at the office of the commandant, General Korsakov. All along the approaches to the fortress Gendarmes had been posted. Not even the Winter Palace was so heavily guarded.

General Korsakov was in no mood to satisfy Ivan's request. He made it clear that he was not obliged to take orders from a colonel. Ivan produced a general letter of authorization from the Minister of Interior. Korsakov took his time extracting his reading spectacles from his breast pocket before reading the letter with deliberation.

St. Peter and Paul Fortress, St. Petersburg

He appeared reluctant to hand it back to Ivan.

"You will have to see prisoner Zheliabov in his cell. He has been placed under maximum security. I must request that you leave your side arms in this office. Please wait here and I shall see to it that you are escorted." Korsakov bowed icily and left them alone.

"I'm still in the dark, Vasili. I must admit I can't figure it out..." Ivan's voice trailed off.

"The pieces are not all in place but I'll tell you what I know and what I guess to be true. You know that when Loris-Melikov antagonized the Gendarmes when he reorganized the security forces. They lost a good deal of status. Their precious Third Section was abolished. They resented being transferred from His Majesty's Chancellery and placed directly under the Minister of Interior, that is to say, Loris-Melikov himself. It is no secret that they found him personally objectionable. After all he is Armenian and not Russian. They also identified him with reform, a word and an idea they associate with treason."

"But Loris-Melikov has bent over backwards to smooth their ruffled feathers. He gave Ushakov full authority over them and the Count was a great friend of Shuev."

"True enough. Still, they regard Loris-Melikov as an opportunist. Van der Fleet called him a chameleon to my face. As for Ushakov, they never took him seriously. The main point, though, is their fear of reform. You yourself told me how widespread the opposition is within the government. The heir is against it. So are some of the leading ministers, many high ranking officials, Katkov and other press lords. I'm not a political animal, Ivan, but even I understand one thing. A mortal struggle for the soul of Russia is going on behind all the paper shuffling. Yesterday you were jubilant. Loris-Melikov, you said, was on the verge of victory. You remember how that piece of intelligence touched off my outbreak of madness."

"I'll never forgive myself."

Vasiliev smiled his crooked smile and put his hand on Ivan's shoulder.

"I'll tease you for the rest of your life, Ivan, so be prepared. But, yes, you were shocked that I should have exploded that way. I know I acted like a madman. Too bad I was so excited. I lost a chance to explain things to you rationally. But what you said made me realize what Van der Fleet meant when he spoke of deciding the fate of empire. He was determined at all costs to block the reform, some kind of assembly as I understand it, not even a constitution. They used every trick to try to head it off. They didn't plan the Ushakova killing; it fell into their lap. They used it in their campaign to frighten the nobility and isolate the tsar. But there was a problem. Van der Fleet now had to protect Bagration who was the link to the heir.

"Van der Fleet made a mistake in telling me so much. He couldn't resist boasting. He sees himself and Bagration as the saviors of Holy Russia, though there is nothing holy about either one of them. They hate the tsar. They also despise Princess Yurovskaya, something else they share with the courtiers and the heir. Perhaps they have good reason to despise her. It's none of my business."

"But surely you are not implying that the Grand Duke is involved, that he is a party to the conspiracy?"

"No. Not at all. But Bagration and Van der Fleet benefit from the heir's patronage. It doesn't matter that he has no idea of their murderous plans. They believe he is a sworn enemy of reform. Are they right?"

"I fear so. Alexander Alexandrovich has become a bitter man. He was never his father's favorite. And he adored his mother; he sees Yurovskaya as a usurper taking his mother's place. As for his politics, I'm less sure. I'm not part of his inner circle. But he has made one thing clear; he regards any elected representatives of the nation, even to a consultative assembly, as a threat to the autocratic power of the tsar."

"That's all the plotters need. They won't make the same mistake as the assassins of Paul I. They won't take the heir into their confidence. Alexander Alexandrovich will never know that he came to the throne because his closest friends and allies killed his father."

"It sounds logical and all the evidence fits. Yet I still find it hard to believe that they would go this far...to kill the tsar! If true then how do you explain Van der Fleet's relentless pursuit of the terrorists? Why should he destroy the one group that has the best chance of carrying out his dirty work without soiling his own hands?"

"Therein lies the genius of Van der Fleet."

The clang of the iron door announced the arrival of a Gendarme officer and a detail of fortress troops in their soft felt boots. Vasiliev and Ivan followed them to a cab where the officer gave orders to the driver and climbed up onto the box. The escort mounted their horses and trotted alongside the cab as it crossed the snow covered courtyard.

"You see, Ivan," Vasiliev was now whispering, "if our friend did not show results he might have been removed from his command. Someone more loyal to the tsar would have replaced him. What he wanted was to become indispensable."

"So he could get all the credit for saving the man whose death he was plotting."

"Exactly. Once he was above suspicion, he could play a leading role in the new reign. Who knows where his ambition might have taken him."

"But how could he be so certain that the People's Will would succeed?"

"Remember the sequence of events. The arrest of Goldenberg placed all the threads of the organization in his hands. The next move was to take Kletochnikov, the master double agent inside the Department of State Police. Once that was done, Van der Fleet could orchestrate the movements of both the police and the terrorists. And you have seen the results with your own eyes. The executive committee was decimated. But the mine under Malaya Sadovaya was allowed to go undetected."

The cab slowed and the Gendarme officer jumped to the ground and signaled them to wait. He spoke a few words through an iron grill. He returned to the cab. "My apologies, your Excellencies, I must ask you for your documents." The guard behind the grill was proving stubborn. He wanted General Korsakov's written permission. He did not know these men. They were not in the chain of command. The argument became heated. Ivan called out and produced his letter from the Minister of Interior. The guard took time to study it.

"But why did they try to have you killed? Then later at Bagration's Van der Fleet had his best chance to get rid of you. Why didn't he do it?"

"I don't think Van der fleet was responsible for Petya. My hunch is that Petya was taking orders from Bagration. He came from a village on the Prince's estate. Bagration is not an easy man to control. I suspect he was simply acting on his own once he had learned from a leak in the Ministry that I was being called in on the case. He knew that I would discover the cover up right away. But Van der Fleet is a professional. He put me under surveillance, but just to find out what I knew. He saved my life at Bagration's because he knew how you would react. You'd launch a real investigation. You would have torn apart Bagration's explanations. Clever man, Kostya Van der Fleet. All he had to do was to keep me out of the picture for a few days, until there was a new tsar. Then he and Bagration, the two king makers, would be unassailable. They could release me and laugh at my wild story. What evidence did I have except a blood stain and a torn curtain?"

"I never should have doubted you. But why did Van der Fleet supply Petya with Berdan rifles?"

"I'm not sure he did. Bagration had plenty of contacts in the police and army. It was another of his mistakes."

"So the murder of Ushakova had nothing to do with the political conspiracy?"

"None at all, except for Van der Fleet's need to protect Bagration who was link to the heir and the guarantee of future access to the throne. But the only way we can prove that is by getting the letters. Here comes our escort to the man who can provide them."

"We are ready, your Excellencies."

The gate swung open admitting them to a narrow passageway. They passed through a second iron gate into a stone corridor which sloped downward to the cells. The officer unlocked a small room, lit two candles and asked them to wait. It was so damp that Vasiliev wondered whether they were beneath the level of the river. In the distance they heard the muffled sound of a metal door, then the clang of chains. A moment later two guards entered flanking a towering figure with red hair falling to his shoulders and a full reddish beard. His hands and feet were manacled. Even in the dim light his eyes appeared to flash defiantly. It was Zheliabov.

Chapter Thirty-Seven

"I would like to interrogate the prisoner alone?" Vasiliev asked.
Ivan raised his eyebrows but said nothing.

The Gendarme officer frowned. "My orders are to remain with the prisoner."

"No need to worry, he's in chains. He can't attack me. There is no chance of his escaping. Your men will be right outside the door. I have good reasons for making this request. It's a matter of protecting state secrets. The Colonel can vouch for me."

The officer had recently been transferred to the fortress. He was uncertain how to respond. These two men were obviously important. Otherwise they wouldn't have been allowed to meet a state prisoner of Zheliabov's importance.

Ivan stepped forward. "I can obtain a special order from Count Ushakov, if you oblige me to do so."

"With all due respect, Colonel, Count Ushakov has no jurisdiction here."

"The Minister of Interior, General Loris-Melikov, then."

The officer was unprepared for this. What harm could there be in permitting the interview? Besides, why run the risk of offending the dictator of the heart?

"Surely you have confidence in your own security arrangements," Ivan added. The officer nodded to his men and they filed out. Ivan followed them.

Zheliabov watched with wry amusement. How comic these people are, always obsessed with their rules and ranks, he thought. But when the door shut his smile faded quickly.

"Our last meeting was forestalled by some ambitious police-man," Vasiliev began, noticing that Zheliabov's eyes really did appear incandescent. "So we have unfinished business."

Zheliabov spat on the floor. "I do not deal with police stoolies."

"No one could mistake that voice of yours, Zheliabov. If I was uncertain before, I am sure now. You were the one who negotiated with me about publishing the letters."

Zheliabov remained silent, his watchful stare unwavering.

"I'm not here to interrogate you. It's not my purpose to get you to betray the last of your comrades at large. I suspect it would be useless to try. Perhaps when you have heard me out, you will give me what I want on the agreed upon terms."

Zheliabov gave no sign that he had heard or understood Vasiliev.

"My part of the bargain was to get Bagration's letters published. It's been arranged with Lanin of *The Russian Courier*. I was on my way to tell you when the Gendarmes sprung their trap. Perhaps you think I betrayed you. Not a chance. That's not my style. Think about it for a moment. You were the one who trusted me enough to make contact in the first place. How could I have engineered your arrest? I didn't even know where the second meeting would take place. Yes, I had instructions to get off at the last stop on Izmailovsky Regiment Street. But you always take precautions. You might have had another message waiting for me there. The Gendarmes had set up everything beforehand."

"There are half a dozen explanations of how you could have arranged it. I have never underestimated the police. I made a mistake in trusting you."

"I was not in on your arrest; I took no part in it. You know that. Why didn't I share in the glory of capturing the head of the People's Will?"

"So you could arrange this interview."

"For what reason? Your suspicion has no basis; it makes no sense. I need the letters, and now they have disappeared. Why not have you arrested after you handed them over?"

"The letters are secondary, we are primary."

"In your scheme of things, yes, but not necessarily in mine."

Zheliabov curled his lips into a sneer but did not reply.

"Listen, we can still come to terms. Even though you are a prisoner, the publication of the letters still has value for your organization, doesn't it? What possible motive could I have for coming to you now except to see justice done, to prove who killed Ushakova.?"

"Another police trap. No thanks."

Vasiliev felt a growing sense of desperation. He felt Van der Fleet's evil genius blocking him at every turn.

"All right Zheliabov, Listen carefully. I need the letters to convict Bagration of murder or to being an accessory to his son's murder of Ushakova. But there is something more important involved here. Bagration is being protected by a high ranking police officer who has infiltrated your organization, placed an agent in your Exec-Com. That's how they knew about the plan to meet me. But they did not know the exact address on Izmailovsky. Your man led them there. That should give you a clue as to who the double agent may be."

"You must be crazy," Zheliabov laughed for the first time.

"Think back, Zheliabov, think back. It has been two years since they took Goldenberg. Surely you remember him, how reliable, tough-minded and self-sacrificing he was. How did they get him to talk? His lips were sealed against threats, beatings, torture. Someone convinced him that it was in the interest of the revolutionary cause to unburden his heart. You found out about it from someone on the inside, the double agent. Didn't you suspect the source?"

Zheliabov's face remained stony.

"Listen to me. Do you recall how they took Kletochnikov? He had access to everything at police headquarters, all the coded messages, all the double agents, all the safe houses. He knew when the police raids were planned down to the minute. How was it possible to catch him? The Gendarmes floated a story that he left the office too early to intercept a message from a confederate. It would have warned him of a police raid on the apartment where he had a rendezvous. Who do you think got Kletochnikov out of the office? You must remember him too, the master spy, fiendishly clever, naturally secretive, a loner who trusted no one and never made a mistake."

Vasiliev thought he was having an effect. Zheliabov's contemptuous smile had vanished; he licked his lips which had gone dry; his shoulders had tensed up.

"Once they removed Kletochnikov you had no one else on the inside. You were at the mercy of the master counter-spy. He turned one or two of your people. I admit I don't know their names. But he got to them somehow — the psychological method I've heard about, or bribery, threats to family — I don't know. But they began to feed you false information. Last night's trap was set up through this weak link. Someone at our first meeting on the Vyborg Side is a traitor. But I have given you enough for you to figure out who it is."

Vasiliev decided to play his trump card, but he had to be careful. He could not lie to Zheliabov.

"Yesterday we discovered the mine under Malaya Sadovaya." Would Zheliabov draw the logical conclusion that this too had been the work of the double agent?

Vasiliev paused. He caught the change of expression that passed over Zheliabov's features. He seemed to be weighing his choices. Was he going back over the incidents in his mind? Had he already decided who the traitor was? Studying him Vasiliev understood the power Zheliabov exercised over the movement.

"Come back in two days. I'll have an answer for you then. I have nothing more to say now." Zheliabov turned his back on Vasiliev and faced the wall glistening with moisture. A tiny rivulet of water trickled down from the ceiling.

Vasiliev had known what it meant to fail, but this time success seemed so close. He was overcome by despair. In two days it would be too late. One way or the other it would all be over. There was still an outside chance that the reform would be signed, the revolutionaries rounded up and the tsar saved. But Van der Fleet was in a powerful position to change all that. Zheliabov's closest collaborator, Sophia Perovskaya, was still at large. He would have to outwit them both, an unholy alliance if there ever was one.

Vasiliev called the duty officer. "You may return the prisoner to his cell."

Ivan pressed him for details, and Vasiliev gave him a word for word account. "Zheliabov was wary of another police trap. He was not even shaken by my telling him we had discovered the Malaya Sadovaya mine. He is counting on Sophia Perovskaya to carry off a last attack."

"We'll redouble surveillance on the streets. Perhaps Loris-Melikov can persuade the tsar to stay inside the Winter Palace, at least for the next forty-eight hours, until the reform bill has been signed."

"What are the chances of that happening?"

"I'd be fooling you if I said they were good. The tsar is not easily intimidated. He has survived seven attempts. He's convinced the danger is past."

"How many people were arrested in Van der Fleet's last sweep?"

"Only two, Zheliabov and another executive committee member. Two others were killed in the gunfight. The initial reports were exaggerated."

"God almighty! Van der Fleet is a genius at manipulation. He's created the impression that the organization has been crippled. That means that the security people will relax. He doesn't make many mistakes."

When they entered the Palace Square there were fewer check points; the Cossack patrols appeared less frequently.

"It will take a miracle to instill a sense of urgency again," Ivan muttered.

Vasiliev took hold of Ivan's arm as he tried to leave the cab. "Listen, Ivan, I want to be assigned to the tsar's bodyguard."

"I'm not sure I can manage that. There are limits to my influence you know. Besides, the bodyguard is loyal. I can vouch for every man. Van der Fleet has no influence with them. Dvorzhitsky will also be with the tsar at all times. He has plenty of plainclothes men on the street. All right, I grant you they are no longer in a high state of alert. But what good can one man do at this point?"

"You may be right, Ivan. But remember you are the only senior officer who is convinced that Van der Fleet is part of the conspiracy. He is resourceful. We're agreed on that. The security people could be fooled. I have to be close to the tsar at all times."

Ivan sank back against the cushions, his fingers forming a tent. He thought about how to introduce Vasiliev, a stranger to the tsar, into his bodyguard. An unlikely prospect at best. Vasiliev pressed ahead.

"Serov and I have a special kind of street knowledge. He was the one who led us to the cheese shop though the police have had it under surveillance for weeks. We can spot disguises, believe me, like spotted deer in a shady glen. I know your men are good, Ivan. But the revolutionaries are clever too. They probably know every police agent by sight, especially the plainclothes men you've posted along the tsar's normal travel routes. It's not difficult to pick them out of a crowd. Serov and I are wild cards. No one expects us to turn up. At this point routine is our greatest enemy. Surely it's not asking too much at this stage."

"Vasili, the problem is not in convincing me or probably not even Loris-Melikov, though that may not be easy. It is the tsar. He may know you by reputation. But that isn't the same as being an intimate, someone who has been with him during this whole ordeal. He is a brave man but he's also stubborn. We have very little time to persuade him. I'll do my best, but if I fail it is not due to any lack of trust in you."

As they left the cab they saw a lone horseman ride across the Square. A Cossack patrol intercepted him and examined his papers briefly. Vasiliev recognized Serov, and they waited for him to approach.

"Van der Fleet's flown the coop, Vasili Vasilievich. The Gendarme guards have pulled out. The place is deserted. I couldn't find out where he's gone."

"What does this mean?" asked Ivan.

"That we have very little time. The last act of the manhunt has begun." muttered Vasiliev.

Chapter
Thirty-Eight

The sky over St. Petersburg had lowered under the weight of leaden clouds. The city itself had a devitalized appearance. Piles of snow heaped high along the embankments were lumpy and discolored. The Sunday crowds seemed sullen and lifeless. Even the blackbirds were subdued. They huddled together in broken ranks on the gutters of the Winter Palace.

Vasiliev drank Turkish coffee alone in his room, memorizing the tsar's daily schedule, the details of the route he would take, calculating the potential danger points where the crowds might thin out offering a better chance for an attack. He kept returning to the easy solution. If only the tsar could be persuaded to hold off his ceremonial visit to the Riding Academy for a day. He wanted to plea with the tsar himself; just give us twenty hours, and we can make the streets safe for you. But there seemed little chance that he would give in.

Serov was polishing his buckle when Vasiliev entered his room. They regarded one another for a quiet moment.

"Is the arm better?" He had decided not to ask about the ankle. No sense in treating Vasiliev like an invalid. He could see for himself that Vasiliev was still limping.

Vasiliev nodded, moved to the window and parted the lace curtains. Perhaps it was the softness of the material that made him wonder where Irina was at that moment. Why had there been no message? He was suddenly afraid for her, playing the role of Shuev's mistress and uncovering the secrets of the last conspiracy. One side or the other was bound to destroy her.

"Let's make our tour, Sergeant. It's all we can do now. God damn it, I have never felt so useless."

As they crossed the foyer of the hotel the night concierge was just going off duty.

"A message, sir, left for you early this morning. I didn't want to disturb you."

Vasiliev almost tore the cream colored envelope out of his hand. Foreign made, of high quality bond, addressed to Inspector Vasiliev. He instantly recognized the handwriting. He loosened the flap and took out a single sheet of expensive bond paper that matched the envelope. Its edges were slightly discolored as if it had lain for years in a desk drawer. A few words printed in block letters stared at him.

"The signal will be give by a white handkerchief."

He held the message up to the light, expecting to see a watermark of the Davidov family crest.

"What does it mean, do you think?" Serov was peering over Vasiliev's shoulder.

"A warning from a trusted source," Vasiliev said, turning to the concierge who was already thinking about his coffee and fresh cream.

"Were you on duty when this was delivered?"

"Yes, sir, but it was handed to the doorman outside. He's gone home now, but he'll be back tonight."

"Do you have his address?"

"Ah. No sir. I think he lives on the Vyborg side."

Vasiliev crumpled the paper and stuffed it into his pocket, muttering, "the location, Irisha, the location, couldn't you get me the location?"

They walked their horses over the scheduled route of the tsar, scanning the shops, the courtyards, alleys and side streets, committing every detail to memory. Later, when the imperial coach went by they would have a mental picture of the route in their minds, watching for a face they had seen before, a person loitering, a vehicle standing in an odd spot, an open window, a break in the pattern of traffic. From time to time one of them would point out an individual, a pie seller standing on a corner, or a porter lolling against the wall of a house.

Cossack Patrol

"What do you think?"

"He looks genuine enough. Keep him in mind, though."

Just before noon they rode back to the Winter Palace through streets crowded with large four wheeled carriages and fashionable traps mixed with drays and peasant carts. Breaking away from the press, they galloped down Malaya Sadovaya past the cheese shop where all was quiet. They turned into Italianskaya and followed it until they reached the Catherine Canal, then rode along its frozen course past the Mikhailovsky Gardens until the great facade of the Winter Palace loomed before them. A Cossack patrol stopped them on the way. "At least, they haven't completely relaxed," said Vasiliev." Perhaps Ivan has sent out a message restoring some discipline."

A group of officers stood on the lower steps of the Palace. Vasiliev dismounted, leaving Serov with the horses. He went up to Ivan who was chatting with Count Ushakov.

"Ah, here is Vasiliev now."

Count Ushakov inclined his head and smiled, extending his hand. Vasiliev noticed the changes in his face, deeper lines around the mouth, a weary almost haggard look. "I find your discoveries fascinating," he said. Vasiliev bowed.

"General Loris-Melikov has been trying all morning to persuade His Majesty to forego the cavalry review at the Riding Academy today."

"God grant that he is successful", said Vasiliev.

"Unfortunately, the Emperor was reassured by the arrest of Zheliabov," said Ivan. "He was in excellent spirits this morning. He believes the danger is over."

"Ivan is correct, Inspector. Even the security forces are euphoric, though I have done my best along with the Colonel to remind them that there are still important members of the People's Will at large. Unfortunately, your friend Dvorzhitsky has been telling his men that the terrorist pack is leaderless and scattered. He mentioned your splendid work in eliminating the last danger spot."

Vasiliev wondered whether it had not been a mistake to have kept Dvorzhitsky in the dark about Van der Fleet. He trusted the chief of police but there was always the chance of a slip of the tongue.

"Is there any news of Van der Fleet?"

"General Shuev tells us that Van der Fleet is 'eternally vigilant' his very words. You heard him, Ivan. Yes, very touching this devotion of his." The Count kept raising his hand to his mouth in a nervous gesture.

Just then there was a stir among the officers nearest the entrance to the Palace. The Emperor, Alexander Nikolaevich, emerged wearing the uniform of the Guards Regiment of Sappers. His wife, Princess Yurovskaya, was clinging to his arm. General Loris-Melikov was a step behind him. Vasiliev was shocked at the tsar's appearance. His face had become fleshy, his eyes sunk in deep shadows. He held himself erect but he moved with a slight hitch in his stride. Ekaterina Dolgorukaya, as Vasiliev had known her when she was still a giggling adolescent at the Smolny Girls Schools, had matured into a stunning woman. But she cultivated an aloof manner, treating everyone but her husband with a shade of condescension; quite different from the former Empress. No wonder she was so unpopular, he thought. Loris-Melikov had moved to the side of the tsar and was speaking urgently in a low voice. Alexander II was smiling at his wife. Vasiliev just caught the last few words.

"...but Zheliabov still had time before the arrest to plan another operation and put his people in place, Your Majesty."

The officers drew aside and bowed. Alexander nodded graciously as he passed. He paused on the bottom step, gazing up at the granite column of his namesake and uncle, Alexander I.

"My dear Mikhail Tarielovich," he turned his head to address the General. "I believe you, but I do not intend to be kept a prisoner in my own home."

"Of course not, Your Majesty. That would be an admission of weakness that Your Majesty is incapable of showing. I only ask you to consider, Sire, the wisdom of waiting a day or two until the last of these vermin are wiped out."

"And what shall I say to *ma chère cousine*, Catherine? She reproaches me for having neglected her. She sends messages that she has made unusual preparations for my visit. General, we have weathered the worst of the storm. I think you have not given yourself the credit you deserve. Your arrests must have completely disoriented the terrorists. Now they have lost their leader. You know how it is with bandits. Remove the head and the body scatters to the four winds. Don't worry, Mikhail Tarielovich, I will be in capable hands," he gestured grandly in the direction of Dvorzhitsky who stood at attention by his sleigh.

"Isn't that true Colonel?" he said addressing Ivan. "I'm certain the only people we see on the street will be your men." There was an appreciative ripple of laughter from the group of officers. Alexander embraced his wife who clung to his sleeve.

"Sasha, you promised me you would take the prescribed route. Please tell me again that you will follow the safe way home." Princess Yurovskaya's eyes were moist.

"My darling, this will be another good day in our lives."

The tsar climbed into his closed, bulletproof carriage, a present from the former Emperor Napoleon III. It was drawn by two superb grays from the Orlov stud. Six mounted Terek Cossacks with carbines slung over their shoulders and lances held at the ready moved into position on the flanks of the carriage. Dvorzhitsky leapt into his open sleigh, which wheeled quickly into line behind the carriage. A second sleigh followed carrying Captain Koch and another Gendarme officer whom Vasiliev did not know. He looked at Ivan skeptically. "I made sure the officer was an ambitious rival of Van der Fleet," Count Ushakov grinned. The Princess waved a limp hand until the convoy passed under the Alexander Arch.

Ushakov stepped to Loris-Melikov's side. The General too looked exhausted and the tic in his cheek had become constant and more prominent. He made no effort to conceal his nervousness, striking his thigh with a riding crop, staring at the disappearing carriage.

"Your Excellency...?" Count Ushakov had been waiting for months to hear the answer to his unfinished question.

"His Majesty signed the draft manifesto this morning," Loris-Melikov said.

"Congratulations, Your Excellency. Russia owes you a great debt."

Loris-Melikov's eyes remained fixed on the point where he had seen the last of the convoy. "I could have forbidden him from going today. It is within my power." He spoke as if the Count were not there.

Ushakov dropped back. For once in his life he was at a loss for words.

The wind was coming off the Gulf of Finland, blowing the snow up into a myriad of tiny swirls all over the Square. A few lazy flakes drifted down from the bank of clouds. In the distance they could hear the booming of the church bells from the Kazan Cathedral. It was one o'clock in the afternoon.

The animation had gone out of the group. The Princess had turned to go inside without acknowledging the bows of the officers. Each man seemed cut off from the rest, frozen in position, as if he had lost the power of speech and motion. Vasiliev struck his spurs against the stone steps. That seemed to break the spell. Ushakov started out of his reverie and glanced at Vasiliev who shot him an unmistakable look.

Is everyone paralyzed? Vasiliev wondered. He had the same feeling once before when his commanding officer had lost his nerve in the trenches facing Plevna.

The Count approached Loris-Melikov with what seemed to Vasiliev excruciating deliberation. For a moment Ushakov stood beside the General as if waiting for a sign that he could speak. Vasiliev could hardly restrain himself, wanting to shout at them all. For God's sake this is not the time for your damned deference to rank. Out of the corner of his eye he spotted Serov holding the horses.

Ushakov cleared his throat. "Then you have no objection Your Excellency to taking additional precautions?"

Loris-Melikov shook his head. The tsar had been out of sight for a few, at most five minutes, and Loris-Melikov had already changed his mind twice about sending a messenger to call him back. He looked around for a rider and caught sight of Vasiliev for the first time. A question suddenly came to him. What had the man been up to for the past six months? It didn't matter now. He felt he had gambled and won. The court was restless but no longer rebellious. He had witnessed the tsar's signature, the affixing of the official seal on the manifesto. It would not be a constitution as they all feared. But at least they could now appoint a group of public-spirited men to advise the tsar and break the strangle hold of the old guard. So let the poor man enjoy his one pleasure as emperor, reviewing his beloved cavalry. Let him go to his cousin. They had him tightly wrapped in a security blanket that no one could penetrate.

"Yes, yes," he said, but the Count had already turned back. He signaled Ivan with a wave of his hand.

"Listen, *mon vieux*, we got the General to agree. You may follow the convoy, But we have to consider the Emperor's sensitivities. You have to keep well out of sight, say no closer than a hundred meters." Ivan hurried on, ignoring Vasiliev's look of astonishment. "Here are papers identifying you as a special emissary of the Director of the Department of State Police. They grant you extraordinary authority."

Vasiliev stuffed the papers in his tunic and ran down the steps to join Serov. General Loris-Melikov watched them mount, still debating whether or not to have them recall the tsar. In the end he said nothing. Vasiliev and Serov galloped across the Square and under the arch in pursuit of the tsar's convoy.

Loris-Melikov had given orders to the driver of the tsar's

carriage to move at top speed through the streets of the city. The Cossacks were forced to gallop to keep up. Vasiliev and Serov pressed their mounts hard until they caught sight of the convoy. Several plainclothes men watched them carefully; they had not been informed of a special detail. But they had received no orders to intercept couriers. At the Riding Academy Alexander descended from the carriage and strode briskly toward the main entrance. He was immediately surrounded by guards and cavalry officers.

Vasiliev turned in his saddle. "Serov, this isn't working. We're too far behind to be of any use. When the tsar leaves the Academy we'll ride ahead of the convoy. That will give us a chance to scan the crowd. Remember, no hesitation. If you spot anyone moving toward the carriage with a bundle or package, or raising his arm, ride him down.If necessary shoot. I'll let Dvorzhitsky know what we are doing. While the tsar is reviewing the troops we'll go over the whole route to the Grand Duchess' Palace. The tsar will pay her a brief visit. He plans to return to the Palace at three o'clock."

Dvorzhitsky nodded his approval as Vasiliev outlined his plan, then settled back under the heavy furs that covered him. Vasiliev felt everything come into sharper focus. It was as if all his senses had suddenly become keener. Little things caught his attention: a thin rim of snow clinging to the Chief's fur hat, clouds of steam rising from the sleigh horses' flanks like the smoke of cannon. The smell of wet leather harness stung his nostrils. His ankle began to ache. He removed his glove and reached down to massage it. Serov's mount stamped impatiently.

The review took forty minutes. The tsar emerged to the traditional cry of "Hurrah" from the guards and quickly entered the carriage. The convoy was moving again toward the palace of the Grand Duchess. Vasiliev and Serov rode ahead, picking out the plainclothes men who lounged conspicuously at intervals along the street. The two riders turned to watch the tsar step out of his armored carriage for the second time that day. The Terek Cossacks formed a protective shield around him as he unhurriedly mounted the staircase to his cousin's palace. On the porch a large group of people waited bareheaded, enfolding him as he passed under the portico.

Vasiliev and Serov went back over the tsar's prescribed route.

They followed "the safe way to return"—even Princess Yurovskaya had called it that—down Malaya Sadovaya where the tunnel had been cleared of dynamite and the detectives still held their prisoners in the back of the cheese shop. Vasiliev and Serov exchanged glances, as if they agreed that the moment of greatest danger appeared to have passed. It would only be a matter of travelling the short distance back the Winter Palace. It would take no more than fifteen minutes. One thought comforted Vasiliev. The terrorists would be counting on their confederates in the cheese shop to explode the mine. Why would they station additional bomb throwers along the route?

But there was still a nagging doubt in his mind. Irina's message had read, "The signal will be a white handkerchief." She must have been sure about it. This was no time to relax his guard. He and Serov rode back to the palace. They scanned the crowds of pedestrians that were beginning to thin out.

St. Isaac's Cathedral, St. Petersburg

They sat in their saddles waiting. Vasiliev timed the tsar's visit. Exactly thirty minutes had passed when he came out on the porch with his cousin on his arm. She was wrapped in furs. He embraced her. Vasiliev counted the steps as he descended all the way down to the street where the wall of men and horses closed around him. When the tsar took his place inside the carriage, Vasiliev breathed easily. The revolutionaries had lost their best chance.

There were only two possible dangers now, a well-coordinated attack by several men supplied with hand bombs or an explosive charge too heavy to be thrown by a single man. They should be able to disrupt the first and they had already averted the second. The bells of St. Isaac's Cathedral began to ring. Vasiliev took it as a sign of celebration.

From his vantage point he watched the Cossacks move into a new position on all sides of the coach, two in front, one on each side and two in back. He felt reassured. This made it even more difficult for potential bomb throwers to score a direct hit on their main target. He signaled Serov to follow. He eased his mount into a slow trot. They passed several storefronts on Malaya Sadovaya where small groups of people had gathered. The snow was blowing lightly into their faces. The two horsemen hardly noticed the gap opening up between them and the convoy. It was still parked in front of the palace. As the Cossack screen formed around the coach, two uniformed horsemen rode out of a side street and reined in beside Dvorzhitsky's sleigh. One pointed with a gloved hand back down Engineering Street toward the canal. Vasiliev never knew what made him turn in the saddle at that moment and look back. What he saw made his blood run cold. The Chief of Police, Adrian Dvorzhitsky, was standing in his sleigh, having thrown off his furs, and was shouting an order to the tsar's coachman. Vasiliev could not make out the words. They were muffled by the sounds of traffic but he sensed danger. He reined in and stood in the stirrups trying to make out what was happening. One of the uniformed riders who had been speaking to Dvorzhitsky swung out of his saddle and tossed the reins of his horse to his companion. Then he jumped into the second sleigh with Captain Koch, displacing the Gendarme officer who had climbed out on the other side.

The convoy remained stationary. The Cossacks appeared to be

milling around the coach, but they had not broken their formation. Then, the coachman waved his hand and turned the Orlov bays. The Cossacks wheeled their mounts. The carriage moved off in the direction of Engineering Street. It was moving away from Vasiliev and Serov, leaving Malaya Sadovaya, "the safe way to the palace" where the mine had been disarmed. As the second sleigh made its sharp turn to bring up the rear of the convoy, Vasiliev recognized the man sitting next to Captain Koch. It was Van der Fleet.

"Quick, it's a trap." He shouted as he spurred his horse forward, Serov closely behind him.

The convoy was moving fast down Engineering Street, where the traffic was light, toward the Catherine Canal. Vasiliev and Serov were held up behind vehicles that had been waved over to the curb by the Cossack outriders and were now moving back into the center of the thoroughfare.

Vasiliev was shouting at the top of his lungs to clear a passage. They swerved to avoid two peddlers who dashed out in the street ahead of them and they barely avoided a collision with a barouche. They broke free of the congestion on Malaya Sadovaya and galloped at full tilt down Engineering Street. It was a short stretch of roadway ending in a T at the Catherine Canal. Vasiliev saw the tail end of Koch's sleigh carrying Van der Fleet swing round the corner to the right onto the embankment of the Catherine Canal. The convoy was moving away from the heavily patrolled areas of Malaya Sadovaya and Nevsky Prospekt toward the Mikhailovsky Gardens. Vasiliev recalled there were no police agents posted along the Canal. Within a few minutes the curtain of security around the tsar was melting away. Outside his armored box, only the Cossack outriders shielded him. Vasiliev reached the corner at a dead gallop and turning sharply felt his mount slip on the slippery cobblestones; her rear legs gave way. He was almost pitched backwards. With an effort that sent a spasm of pain shooting up his leg, he flung himself forward on the horse's neck. Serov had slowed at the turn and closed in to help, but the mare recovered her balance. Vasiliev righted himself in the saddle. But they had lost ground. The convoy was several hundred meters ahead of them and widening the gap. Vasiliev plunged his spurs deeply into the mare's flank and she responded with a burst of speed.

His eyes swept the nearly deserted embankment. Which one was the assassin? On one side of the street an errand boy hurried along the sidewalk, a wicker basket under his arm. Some distance behind him a man wearing the greatcoat of an artillery officer was strolling and gazing at the house numbers, hands clasped behind his back. On the other side a man in a tall fur hat was peering across the Canal, leaning his elbows against the railing of the embankment. The convoy had gone about half way down the block when Vasiliev saw a woman at the far end step off the curbstone and pause in the middle of the street. She pulled a large white handkerchief out of her bag and let it flutter in the breeze before pressing it to her face.

Vasiliev drew his revolver as the man at the railing whirled and ran into the street. Vasiliev gripped the revolver with both hands, leaned over the neck of his horse and fired twice at the very moment when the man raised his arm. One bullet grazed his thigh; the other struck him in the chest. He staggered and fell to his knees in the snow. Before collapsing he hurled an object into the air as the tsar's carriage drew parallel. It looked to Vasiliev like a dirty snowball as it landed and rolled under the legs of the Orlov grays. In the rear sleigh Captain Koch twisted around to determine the source of the shots. An explosion sent a shower of snow into the air.

A cloud of blue smoke blotted out the carriage. Vasiliev heard the screams of the horses, their bellies eviscerated by the blast. A wave of fear and rage broke over him. The wheels of the carriage were blown off; the rear end was scorched and scarred; shards of glass covered the writhing bodies of the Orlov grays. One of the Cossack escorts lay face down, pinned under his dead horse. The snow around him was tinted red. A second Cossack struggled to rise, having been thrown from his horse a dozen meters across the street. The errand boy was lying on his side, blood pouring out of his chest and neck.

Dvorzhitsky's sleigh had skidded to a stop behind the wrecked carriage. The Chief flung off his furs and jumped down, shouting orders to the Cossacks who had drawn their sabers and surrounded the bomb thrower. Blood was streaming from flank wounds on several of their horses. Captain Koch was standing in his sleigh blowing short blasts from his police whistle. People were running in from the side streets. Vasiliev and Serov reined in. Tears were streaming down Serov's cheeks.

"My God, my God, what have they done? Have they killed him?" Serov blurted out. The carriage was tilted but had remained upright. They watched with disbelief as the tsar forced open the damaged door and stepped out into the reddening snow, a stunned look on his face. Dvorzhitsky, indifferent to the gash in his forehead from a flying splinter, shielded the tsar with his body.

"Your Majesty, are you hurt?"

"No, thank God, but look at those poor devils." The boy was dying. The Cossack crushed under his horse lay motionless. The Cossack who had been blown across the street was badly wounded. He was crawling towards them on all fours, shaking his head and sending spurts of blood into the snow. Vasiliev tore his eyes away from the tsar. Koch's sleigh had skidded to a stop, narrowly averting a collision with Dvorzhitsky's. The Captain had jumped down and was hurrying toward them, the whistle still in his mouth. Van der Fleet had disappeared. Police and plain clothes men came running from an adjoining street, responding to Koch's whistle. The Cossacks were holding back the growing crowd.

Vasiliev grabbed hold of Koch's shoulder. "Where is Van der Fleet?" he demanded. Koch looked bewildered. "What?" He gasped. It took a moment for Vasiliev to realize what had happened.

"Serov, listen, the tsar is saved by a miracle. But Van der Fleet has gotten away. He must have taken a Cossack's mount. Quick, after him. Get him Sergeant. I don't care how, but get him." He pointed through the rising smoke where they could see a rider disappearing at the end of the street. Serov whirled and leaped into the saddle, shouting as he charged through the crowd. Vasiliev stepped forward to cover the tsar on the Canal side; Dvorzhitsky was begging him to get into his sleigh.

"My poor Cossacks," Alexander murmured. His fleshy face was ashen, the features of a man suddenly grown old.

Vasiliev touched Dvorzhitsky's sleeve. "Adrian Sergeevich! We must get the tsar out of here. There may be others... and in this crowd...he is defenseless...quick."

The tsar looked past Vasiliev, a dazed look on his face, and turned to the Police Chief. "I want to see this man, Colonel." The tsar spoke as if in a state of shock, "this man who would kill me."

Vasiliev was ready to seize the tsar in his arms and carry him away. But Dvorzhitsky signaled the Cossacks and they led their horses up to form a wall around Alexander. Dvorzhitsky walked beside him as they approached the bomber whose fur hat lay trampled under the horses' hooves. Four soldiers had pinned him against the railings.

"Who are you?" asked the tsar.

"Rysakov of the People's Will." The man coughed up blood, and there was a dark stain on his side where his coat had been ripped to shreds by the blast. He was dying.

"Your Majesty, I implore you to return to the sleigh. There may be more assassins here. The Princess is waiting." Dvorzhitsky's voice was shaking. He raised his hand to wipe the trickle of blood running down his cheek.

"You are right, Adrian Sergeevich, of course. But I want to remember this terrible scene for the rest of my life. I want to see the very spot where the explosion occurred." He shook his head as he stepped around the dying boy. For a moment he stared at the blackened funnel in the street and then allowed Dvorzhitsky to guide him toward the sleigh. Vasiliev stood with his back to the tsar, scrutinizing the shocked faces of the crowd. There were no hurrahs now, just the whimpering of the errand boy and the neighing of the wounded horses. Two shots rang out. The onlookers scattered in all directions, some hurling themselves to the ground. But it was only the Cossacks destroying the Orlov bays that had been writhing in agony in their traces.

The tsar was only a few steps from the sleigh when a man who had not moved when the shots were fired left the railing where he had been leaning and threw his arms into the air over the heads of the people kneeling around him. Vasiliev distracted by the shots saw him too late. He reached for his revolver. A second explosion knocked him off his feet. Darkness closed over him. He recovered consciousness almost immediately, the acrid smoke forcing him to gasp for breath. He raised himself on his elbows. His right leg felt numb and blood was coming from wounds in his shoulder and neck and from shreds of human flesh that adhered to his face. All around him he heard screams, the moaning and the thrashing of dying men and horses. He counted a dozen bodies sprawled in the black and red snow. One of them, thrown back against the railings by the force of the blast, was Alexander Nikolaevich, tsar of all Russia. He was bareheaded. His fur-trimmed cloak was ripped apart, the brilliant green Sapper's uniform torn and shredded, his legs shattered. A pool of blood spread evenly around him. The man who had thrown the bomb lay crumpled lifeless beside him. Dvorzhitsky was crawling toward the tsar, blood spurting from half a dozen wounds. Vasiliev staggered to his feet, extended a hand to Dvorzhitsky and pulled him upright. They heard faint cries from the tsar.

"Help me, Adrian Sergeevich," Vasiliev groaned, "we must get him into the sleigh."

Vasiliev sank down on his knees beside the tsar. He barely heard a hoarse murmur. "So cold...quick, home to die."

Chapter
Thirty-Nine

The porter at 88 Izmailovsky Regiment Street waited until he was sure that the shooting had stopped before he stuck his head out of the yard. He watched the Gendarmes loading bodies onto their sleighs. When they drove off he was one of the first to rush into the street. He commandeered a strategic position between the two large pools of blood on the sidewalk in front of the house that had once been safe.

"Never heard anything like it, a real battle it was." He addressed a small crowd gathering around him. "Sat out here all night, I did; something was going on over there; didn't smell right." He pointed toward the shattered facade of the safe house. "You have to be vigilant these days." His stocky figure, short bristling hair and loud, hoarse voice gave him a faintly military air, as if he had once been a sergeant-major in the imperial army. Because the Gendarmes had sealed the house, the curious had to be satisfied with peering through shattered ground floor windows into a dark interior or poking their fingers into the many bullet holes that scarred the facade in hopes of retrieving a souvenir.

The porter embroidered his story with each retelling, adding details supplied more by his imagination than the facts of the matter would warrant, just to spice things up, he reassured himself. When the last of his audience had departed, he reluctantly returned to his room, to be greeted by a large gray cat who rubbed against his leg, reminding him that supper was long overdue. The porter sat with his cat, stroking its back as it consumed its plate of bread soaked in fish oil and thinking about strangers who came and went at odd hours of the day and night.

Porter at Izmailovsky Regiment Street, St Petersburg

Letchik had some trouble finding the safe room. Magician had been vague about the address. He had mentioned a street name, Izmailovsky Regiment, without providing a number. It had not been a trip Letchik intended or wanted to take. A friend had warned him that the police were rounding up and interrogating all students who had not been attending lectures. He had barely managed to scrape together the third class train fare to Piter from his tutoring fees. The capital was no safer, but it was close to the border with the Grand Duchy of Finland. Letchik had convinced himself that life as an émigré was preferable to life as a fugitive. Magician greeted him warmly but could not conceal his exhausted state.

"You see how I live," he gestured at the mattress lying in the corner of an otherwise bare room. "Think of it, you just missed Vasiliev. He was my guest for the night, *tout confort*. He barely escaped a police trap down the street. Christ, what a fight. They took Zheliabov. I can't stay here much longer. You say Moscow is no longer possible. What's to be done?"

"Listen I've just about made up my mind to leave Russia."

"Really!"

"Think about it. They've killed Norka and Marko, I just made it out of Moscow and I find you eking out an existence here. And where is Swan?"

"Still with Shuev."

"God Almighty, do you think she has been turned?"

"Never. But she can't keep it up much longer. He's bound to find out."

"So, it's time to leave. The reforms are not going to save us. I've still a few rubles." Letchik took out of his pocket a rag tied at the ends and jingled some coins. "Enough to get me across the border into Finland. The Gendarmes have no authority there. Just have to get past the frontier post. It's the best way out. The Gulf is still frozen. We have to go overland. Others have done it. How about you?"

"Where? To do what?"

"If we can get to Germany I have friends studying at Leipzig, the medical faculty, two Russians who left a year ago. They'll help."

"It's amazing how we've been thinking the same way. But let's get some tea. It's freezing in here. You must be starving."

They left together. Did the prospect of a new future opening up before them lull them into a false sense of security? Perhaps they had already left Russia in spirit. The yard porter was sitting at his window and saw them. "More of the same," he muttered to the gray cat in his lap as he scratched the back of her neck.

The traktir around the corner was crowded, but Magician was known. A place was found for them by the kitchen door. The proprietor's wife brought tea and hot rolls. She ruffled Magician's hair as she left them.

"Now let me tell you what I've been up to," said Magician. He broke a cube of sugar between his teeth and dropped half of it into a glass of tea. "This is really amazing, you coming here just now with your plan for Leipzig. Well, the thing is I've been earning a few kopecks myself, helping an old fellow, name of Evsei, to do translations from the German. I wish you could meet him, but he sees no one but me these days. That reminds me, I have to buy him some bread and sausage. He's a veteran of forty-eight, fought on the barricades in Dresden with Bakunin. Imagine! Incredible life he's led. Renounced anarchism in prison and began reading political economy, Ricardo, Mill, Roscher. Dry stuff, you say. Nothing of the sort. He understands that the factory is taking over the world. The peasant cottage will soon be a relic of the past. Bakunin is wrong. The peasant will never rise, not by himself at least. Don't you see? We've been banging our heads against a wall of indifference. Christ, I remember the summer of seventy four. I was eighteen trying to preach socialism to them. They took one look at my soft hands and laughed. I thought it was me. But it was they who did not get it, and they never will, God bless them."

Magician broke a hot roll in half and waved it around before popping it into his mouth. The man sitting next to him, bundled up in a sheepskin and smelling of earth and dung, had fallen asleep, chin on his chest and was snoring. Magician smiled. "You see, talk political economy and you put them to sleep."

"You seem a different person," said Letchik.

"Listen, old Evsei talks to me after we spend a few hours working together. He's even more persuasive than the books. And he says to me ' Iuri, Russia is too much in a hurry. Always catch up, catch up.' Yes, sure some day, but you can't skip stages. You see, Letchik, where we've made our mistake."

"So, we wait for the factories?"

"They're coming. Well, listen, I'm not going to lecture you. You have your medicine. I'll have my political economy. Evsei says, 'Get out, Russia is moving like an ox cart.' No, he's not contradicting himself. History is one thing, the individual another. So what's good for you and me is — well, listen to what Evsei told me. He says you can't preach or bomb your way to a revolution. It has to come by itself, of its own momentum. It will take a generation of preparing. And you, meaning us, need to be prepared. So go to Germany, study, learn from the social democrats."

"But Bismarck has cracked down on them, too."

"Right, but that can't last. Germany is like a cauldron, ready to bubble over. Listen. We'll go together. That's it. In a few days, Evsei will get paid for the first part of the translation. I'll get enough to get us both to Leipzig or wherever."

"Sounds like a new partnership. You'd better change your nom de guerre, to *Rabochii*, the Worker." They laughed and clasped hands. The sleeping peasant kept snoring.

As they left Letchik asked, "By the way what are you translating?"

"Karl Marx, *The Critique of Political Economy*. It's dynamite. But not like Khalturin's. This charge will blow up more than the imperial dining room."

The knocking woke them at the same time. They had been stretched out, fully clothed on the mattress. It was still dark, but that could have meant any hour until mid-morning in the winter gloom of Piter. The old fear sprang up in Magician's chest. He vowed they would not take him again. Trembling he crept on all fours toward the door. The rapping came again. This time he was fully awake and recognized the signal, three loud, two soft. Still, who could tell any more what had remained secret. Safe houses were raided, revolutionaries turned into double agents. But there was no other exit. The drop from the window would have broken his legs. He lifted the latch and peered into the dark corridor. It was Swan.

She pushed her way past him and let a small bag slide to the floor. Letchik was pulling on his boots. He could hardly make out her features. Magician had closed the door and was leaning against it, his heart still pounding.

"The tsar is dead," she said in a dead tone. "A bomb on the Catherine Canal. Rysakov and the others. A carnage."

Magician gasped and stepped forward seizing her by the arms. Letchik cursed under his breath. "We'll never get out now." He struck the mattress with his fist, raising a cloud of dust.

"I've left Shuev. No more can be accomplished there. I tried to warn Vasiliev. I don't know what happened to him. There were two explosions. Perovskaya organized it. We've lost." She turned away from them, tears streaming down her cheeks.

Magician spun her around. "Irina, you did everything humanly possible, more than that. You led us from the beginning, inspired us. You were strong when some of us wavered. Now, listen to me. The police will redouble their efforts. Letchik has just come from Moscow where they are arresting everyone. We've got to get out now. What did you tell Shuev?"

She was leaning against the wall, holding her throat as if to steady her voice. "I left a message. Said that mama was ill and I had to rush off to Como."

"Will he believe you?"

"For a while. But too many people have seen me at his house. Yesterday Colonel Van der Fleet arrived unexpectedly. I was in the drawing room with Gri...Shuev when he came in. I excused myself, but he had a good look at me."

"All right. Do you have any roubles? Never mind. We have to wait two days. I'm owed some money. We've been talking, Irina, Letchik and I. You are right, we've lost. It's time to get out. There is nothing more to do here. The new tsar is an enemy of reform. He is surrounded by reactionaries. It will be a new reign of Arakcheev."

The name was like a galvanic shock to Swan. It was what they had called her father. Everything was confused, the past catching up, repeating itself only now at the very center of Russian life. She could not follow what Magician was saying. He seemed to have acquired new energy. She had never seen him so decisive.

"...and we'll get to Germany and start a new life, but always keeping Russia in mind, preparing for the future when we can return and..."

"I cannot leave." Swan spoke almost without thinking.

"What are you saying, Irina?" Letchik intervened. "If we stay we'll be hunted down. We have no money. The People's Will has been decimated. You remember how they used to provide us with money. And I hated it. It was dirty money, stolen. No, this is no way to live."

"I cannot leave Russia," Swan repeated.

"All right, you haven't thought about it. You've been living in Hell. It will take time. But Irina, you have to think hard for we only have a few days. You can rest here. I'll find you a blanket and buy you some food. You should stay in hiding. I'll stay with Evsei. How about you Letchik?"

"Don't worry. A friend can smuggle me into the university dormitory for one, two nights. Then we bolt."

"Good." Magician gestured grandly. "It's not a palace," he tried to laugh but produced only a gurgling sound. "But you will be alone and safe. I'll bring some food," he repeated.

Swan sat down on the mattress. "I'm very tired."

Van der Fleet sat at his desk, toying with a bronze letter opener. He was putting together all the pieces. When he finished, he saw that they all fit. He was very pleased with himself The porter on Izmailovsky Regiment Street had reported to the local constable that several suspicious characters had been hiding out at number 88. The constable had dutifully notified the Gendarmes. Van der Fleet had assumed personal command of the raiding party. They had arrested three suspects and to his astonishment one of them, the girl, had been in Grisha Shuev's apartment the night before. He had heard rumors about Shuev's new mistress. Confirmation came from Grisha's housekeeper who regularly received payments from Van der Fleet's special fund. Up to now there had been little return on his money. But now he had received a rich dividend. Grisha had been losing his grip lately; he should have retired in favor of more energetic men, like himself. Everything was clear. He pushed back his chair, buckled on his holster and strode down the hall to Shuev's office.

The headmaster was seated at his desk staring out the window. He hardly noticed that Van der Fleet had entered without knocking. Above him hung a portrait of the imperial family in happier days, as Shuev used to say. The Emperor, Alexander Nikolaevich, and his Empress, Maria Fedorovna, stood proudly behind their two sons, the heir and bright hope for the future, Nikolai Alexandrovich, now dead these ten years and more, and his younger brother, Alexander Alexandrovich, the second son who never should have been the heir. Now he was the new tsar. Shuev regarded him as a man of limited intelligence, a view he had never shared with anyone. At least he would get rid of the reformers and might restore Russia's greatness.

"I've failed, Kolya, I failed to protect him. I thought we had destroyed the vipers' nest. How did they survive? After all your successes, now this."

Van der Fleet studied Shuev's face. Flabby and discolored, diseased perhaps. God only knew what sleeping with one of those nihilists might do to you. He glanced around the office. It was neat, even sterile, no files cluttering his desk, the fine grained wood polished to a high gloss.

"Yes, Grisha, I'm afraid I must agree with you. You have failed badly."

The headmaster was startled. Subordinates did not address him in that accusatory tone; it came like a judgment from a higher authority. Van der Fleet caught the look of puzzlement and then of alarm that flitted in quick succession over Shuev's features.

"I beg your pardon, Kolya, were you addressing me?"

"Grisha, we have just arrested three of your revolutionaries in their hideaway, a safe room they mistakenly call it, on Izmailovsky Regiment Street. It was just a few doors down from Zheliabov's lair. One was shot attempting to escape; in this case, not a euphemism. His attempt—and I was there to witness it—was so foolhardy and hopeless that I am tempted to call it a form of suicide. More to the point, the young woman who was arrested is quite well known to you. I last saw her in your drawing room, yesterday evening. She is Irina Borisovna Davidova, alias Lebedeva, Swan.

Shuev stood up, gripping the edge of his desk. "You must be mistaken. Yes, a case of mistaken identity. The young woman of that name—you can forget that ridiculous alias—is on her way to Lake Como to rejoin her parents. Her mother has been taken seriously ill."

"No, Grisha, you have been duped by a very clever woman. She admits to her real identity. We did not apply any physical or psychological pressure, by the way. She states of her own free will that she was living with you for the past two months."

"This is impossible. I demand that you bring this imposter here, to my office."

"Let me continue, Grisha. There is more. She refuses to give any further information. But I do not need her testimony to puzzle out the rest. She and her confederates were using this safe room to spy on a rival organization, the People's Will. We have also arrested in a separate operation another young fool, a clerk at Plavilshchikov's Book Emporium. We have long suspected the place of serving as a mail box for the People's Will. He was most accommodating, unlike the misnamed Swan, who is really a hard case. He assures us that the Davidova woman obtained information from him about Inspector Vasiliev's plan to make contact with Zheliabov on Vasilievsky Island. Now the question remains; how did she also find out that we were planning to raid their safe house on the date of that meeting? You remember how carefully we planned it—to arrest him along with the terrorists."

The headmaster sagged visibly and slumped back into his chair, holding his head in both hands.

"I think we can safely assume that she warned Vasiliev so he was able to escape our little trap," Van der Fleet continued relentlessly.

"My God, my God," Shuev groaned repeatedly.

Van der Fleet rested his closed fists on the headmaster's desk. He leaned forward and hissed: "Grisha, you were a good policeman. You protected the tsar as long as your strength held out. I do not know, perhaps no one will ever know, whether this lapse on your part contributed to the tragedy on Catherine Canal. I am about to see our new tsar, Alexander Alexandrovich. If I were to take with me your letter of resignation, then..." He stood straight again and walked to the window.

"The Davidova girl will be given an administrative sentence of ten years, and that is the last we shall see of her."

When Van der Fleet left the office he carried with him Shuev's letter of resignation in his breast pocket and Shuev's service revolver in its holster, having persuaded the headmaster not to do anything foolish. It could only create a scandal, destroy his reputation and undermine confidence in the new reign. Van der Fleet promised to see to it that the resignation was accepted. He would recommend to the new tsar that Shuev be decorated for his service to the state with a St. Vladimir, second class.

As he stepped into the fast police cab waiting to take him to the Anichkov Palace and his meeting with Alexander Alexandrovich and Prince Bagration, he was heard to remark to no one in particular, "Headmaster, indeed!"

Chapter Forty

Vasiliev was dreaming of lying in the leather couch in his father's library, his nanny reading stories from Grimm's fairy tales about giants and dwarfs. Irina came into the room her hair braided in pigtails but wearing a ball dress and they waltzed around old Count Vorontsov's desk, faster and faster until she spun off into space. He opened his eyes and focused on a hairline crack in the ceiling, following it down the wall until it terminated above a white cap worn by a nurse. She smiled at him. He closed his eyes and slept again. When he woke she was still there. His throat was parched; he wondered if he would ever be able to speak again.

"Water, please." He was surprised to hear his voice sound normal.

She lifted a glass to his lips and let him drink as much as he wanted. Then she patted his mouth with a damp cloth. "You have a visitor. He has been waiting a long time." She moved out of his line of vision and he was able to see how the hairline crack continued down to the floor. He recognized the wall paper; then a familiar figure came into view.

Serov stood looking down at him. "I took the liberty, Vasili Vasilievich. I know you have a horror of hospitals. So we've rigged up your hotel room."

"Good man, Sergeant."

Vasiliev closed his eyes again and listened to the chair creak. Has Serov replaced the nurse? His mind wandered back to the Palace Square as if he were seeing it from a great distance, the enormous crowd of people, perhaps thousands, sinking to their knees as the sleigh glided past them. It seemed to him like a vast open-air cathedral. What had brought them there? The sound of the explosions or a general alarm? The *nabat*, of the church bells as in the days of the Tatar raids? Or just the tolling of the great bells of St. Isaac's Cathedral? He had been looking back over his shoulder, despite the pain, to watch the long trail of blood extending behind the sleigh as far as he could see, his blood, Dvorzhitsky's and the Emperor's mixed together. He kept losing consciousness as he tried to staunch the tsar's terrible injuries. Dvorzhitsky's bloodied head bounced against his shoulder all the way back from the Canal.

The dryness constricted his throat again and he began to cough, sending spasm of pain through his body and right leg. Serov was at his side raising the glass to his lips.

"No internal injuries, Vasili Vasilievich. The doctor said you could drink."

"The water dribbled over his chin. He sank back on the pillow. He had been so thirsty in the sleigh. His tongue had cleaved to the roof of his mouth and his lips had felt parched. Like the summer heat of the Balkan highlands. He remembered the tsar reviewing Russian troops on the Danube. When was it? Three short years ago when the Bulgarians had hailed Alexander as their liberator from the Turks. And now his own people had turned against him. Those terrible wounds, the red trail behind the sleigh. How had they let it happen? He dozed off again.

When he woke up , the images were sharper. He and Dvorzhitsky somehow had managed to carry the tsar's body into the Palace. How could they have allowed that? Ushakov had been there, Adlerberg, the Court Chamberlain, guards, servants all of them had shrunk back from them, he and Dvorzhitsky covered with blood, staggering under their burden, the tsar, his legs so mangled there was nothing human about them, pieces of flesh falling away from his shattered trunk.

He remembered Serov rushing up to help, pushing aside senior officers, seizing Vasiliev by the arm as he stumbled at the threshold to the antechamber. How had he gotten there? He must have ridden back when he heard the second explosion, disobeying his order to pursue Van der Fleet, fearing for Vasiliev. Loyal Serov, always making the wrong choice, choosing his Vasya over the fate of the

empire. What did it matter now? He heard the rustling of a newspaper.

"They write so badly about him. It's all so stupid."

"You were there in the antechamber, weren't you Serov? You
saw the Princess throw herself on him, embrace that horror."

"Yes, Vasili Vasilievich, I saw."

"Whatever they say about her, she loved him."

Vasiliev asked for tea. He sipped it slowly recalling the final
scene in the Winter Palace anteroom. They had covered the lower
part of the tsar's body, and the doctors had moved over to bind
Dvorzhitsky's wounds and then his. The double doors had opened
and the heir came in. Now he was tsar wasn't he? Alexander, the
third to bear that ill-fated name, had entered with tears streaming
down his face. He had gone down on his knees beside his father's
body begging his forgiveness and blessing. Had Alexander II heard
him, or was the slight movement of his hand just the last flicker of
life?

Vasiliev had shifted his gaze to the doorway where Van der
Fleet and Bagration were standing like guardian angels. Their man
was now tsar. Van der Fleet must have ridden straight to the Anichkov Palace bringing the news, or his version of it, which would now
become official. How would he explain the change in the route? He
could invent a dozen plausible excuses. After all he was the arch enemy of terrorists. Who would now contradict him? Vasiliev? With a
story of a white handkerchief? He would not even be allowed near
the new tsar. Who else would risk it? The tsar is dead long live the
tsar! He remembered having tried to shake off the doctor and...
what? Denounce Van der Fleet over the dying body of Alexander?
Fortunately for him, gentle hands had restrained him. It was then
he must have collapsed.

"You did everything you could," said Serov. "It was not to be."

A knock at the outer door. The nurse came from the vestibule,
carrying a tray. She placed it on the table next to Vasiliev's bed and
murmured, "Chicken bouillon with dumplings, Your Honor. You
need some nourishment. You've lost a lot of blood." She smiled
pleasantly and left.

"No food, Serov, not now."

"It's not right to punish the body for the grief in our souls."

Serov lifted the white linen napkin that covered the tray and then, cursing wildly, flung it on the floor. "What is this shit? My God, the filthy swine" Serov was wavering a hectograph sheet that had been placed over the bowl of soup.

"Workers of Russia!" it began. "Today, March 1, Alexander the Tyrant has been killed by us Socialists. He was killed because he did not care for his people."

"This is trash, this is shit, the bastards," Serov raged.

But Vasiliev was not paying attention to Serov or the revolutionary proclamation. His eyes were riveted on the tray where between the soup and a basket of toast lay a small packet tied in a white ribbon.

"Sergeant, hand me the letters." Serov stared at the packet stupefied. He balled the hectograph sheet in his fist and hurled it into the corner. He picked up the letters.

Vasiliev sniffed and counted them. There were twelve. He had already taken one away with him. Another letter had been added. It was at the bottom of the packet. He had not seen it before. He unfolded and read it. Written in a feminine hand it was signed with the letter E.

Dear A.
You will invite Van der Fleet. He is in this filthy business up to his neck. It will be a pleasure to watch him squirm.
P.S. Need I say whose little boy told me?

Vasiliev passed the letter to Serov. "Bring me a fresh uniform, Sergeant."

"What does mean, Vasili Vasilievich? Did they know? Did the People's Will know?"

"We'll talk on the way, Sergeant."

Vasiliev was already sitting on the edge of the bed, having thrown off the covers. The pain was excruciating. He was afraid he would pass out from nausea and dizziness For the first time he saw his bandages. He kept repeating, "My uniform, Serov."

"Vasili Vasilievich, listen, we can send for the Iron Colonel. You're not fit, not yet, wait a day." Serov was moving to the wardrobe knowing he could not win the argument. He laid out fresh linen and a dress uniform.

"At least take some nourishment."

"All right, Sergeant, just to satisfy you. Well, yes, I don't want to pass out at the wrong moment, not today." Vasiliev raised the bowl to his lips. The broth was excellent. He bit into a dumpling as Serov helped him dress, but he nearly fainted when he put on his tunic. Serov had ammonia salt ready, saying nothing. Vasiliev stood up, leaning on Serov's shoulder.

"My compliments to the chef. But how about a brandy to cap it off? Call the nurse. I'm going to need her to help you walk me downstairs and into a cab. What a wreck I am."

Between the two of them they managed to get Vasiliev down to the lobby. The concierge had come out from his place behind the registration desk and was standing by the entrance. The doorman had hailed a likhach and was holding the cab door. Vasiliev freed his arms. He walked unaided into the street, swaying from side to side. Inside the cab he fell back against the cushions, his face wet from perspiration. A reddish stain was spreading on his head bandage. The nurse had Serov hold him while she dressed the wound again.

"I don't think they found out until I told Zheliabov that there was a double agent in the Exec-Com. Then he knew right away what the Countess meant by 'this filthy business.' He must have smuggled out a message. Incredible. The fortress is hermetically sealed off. Zheliabov knew his own people would get to the tsar. He leaves it up to me to get Van der Fleet, our mutual enemy."

They passed through the Senate Square. Fashionable ladies were out for a stroll as if nothing had happened to shake their world. Looming in the distance was Falconnet's statute of the Bronze Horseman, Peter the Great astride his great charger hurtling westward. Vasiliev caught his mind wandering. Had he led them too far too fast? Or had they moved too slowly to finish his work? The image faded.

The cab pulled up at Ivan's residence on the Fontanka Canal. Ivan rushed out. He and Serov half carried Vasiliev in the house, Ivan holding him up on one side.

"Vasili, what in God's name? You'll kill yourself, *mon vieux*. You've done everything humanly possible."

"I'll live, Ivan, with the help of your excellent brandy. Still serving the Armenian stuff or have you changed the brand already?"

The Bronze Horseman, St. Petersburg

"You are impossible. My God, how can you joke?"

They lay him on the couch. Vasiliev took the packet of letters out of his tunic and placed it on the table. "Fair exchange," he said as he gulped the brandy.

"The letters?"

Vasiliev nodded and closed his eyes while Ivan read them through without a word.

"This will finish both of them. Why didn't you tell me about this one?" He held up Ushakova's note.

"I just saw it for the first time. I'm not sure that the People's Will had it when I first met them." Vasiliev thought for a moment. Where did they get it, then? Another unsolved mystery. He would never know who had ambushed Borka, though he held Bagration and Van der Fleet jointly responsible. In the end the loose ends do not get tied up neatly, *pace* Gaboriau and Poe.

"If only we'd had them two days ago, we could have saved the tsar. But we can still use them to save the reform. Loris-Melikov is fighting for his political life. The letters prove that the police alone cannot protect the throne. We have to win over the public. That's what the whole Ushakova case was about from the beginning."

"You are willing to take on the new tsar's favorites?"

"Vasili, have you ever doubted me?"

Vasiliev gave a gallant imitation of his famous crooked smile. "Yes, Ivan, I did. But that wasn't the only mistake I made in this case."

Ivan sat down on the couch by Vasiliev's legs. "Christ, man, you've had a rough time of it. Are you in shape for the biggest test yet? They are going to try to make you back down on this one."

It was decided to leave the nurse and Serov behind.

"I'm sorry you won't be in on the kill," said Vasiliev as Serov helped him into the cab.

"I hope that's what it is," said Serov.

Vasiliev dreaded the return to the Palace. It was not the physical pain of the cab ride over uneven cobblestones, but the memory of the trail of blood. Hundreds of people were still gathered around the Alexander Column, kneeling in prayer for the new tsar. A cordon of regular army men had sealed off the Palace grounds, but Ivan and Vasiliev had no trouble getting through to Count Ushakov.

Vasiliev had never seen such confusion in the corridors of the Palace, secretaries and clerks moving in and out of offices, collecting in small groups and breaking off to hurry somewhere else. Security was tight but chaotic. They showed their documents a dozen times but no one seemed to understand who they were or where they were going.

Ushakov appeared to be nervous and distracted. He read the letters hastily, murmuring, "unbelievable" as he put them down. He played with the white silk ribbon for a moment and then as if addressing an unseen presence murmured, "Elena, Elena, you betrayed your country as well as me." Then he turned to Ivan and Vasiliev. "If only we'd had the letters a week ago. Now we have to move carefully. The tsar, Alexander Alexandrovich, is still undecided about issuing Loris-Melikov's manifesto. Van der Fleet and Bagration are sitting on the tsar's inner council. There is a rumor that Van der Fleet will be appointed governor-general of St. Petersburg. Bagration may get a ministerial post. The Council of

Ministers is meeting at this moment. Let me think. We may have to reveal the source of the letters. Can you tell me?"

Vasiliev had asked permission to sit. He was facing the angry Tibetan god suspended over the Count's desk. "They were delivered at the European Hotel this morning, placed on my breakfast tray. I have no idea who put them there. I first read them at a secret meeting with the executive committee of the People's Will."

Vasiliev caught the change in the Count's expression, like a faint shadow had passed over his face. "I see. That creates fresh problems." Vasiliev guessed what was going through Ushakov's mind. If the letters were made public it might mean the end of his career; on the other hand if Bagration emerged unscathed it surely would.

"I think it's necessary to consult General Loris-Melikov," Ivan said.

"All in good time, Colonel. It might be best if I smoothed the way. I could show him the letters. With the documents you sent me, the report of the sanitary commission, General Todtleben's memo from Odessa, all this make a strong case." The Count wondered whether he could hold back Elena's note. Wouldn't the others be enough?

An orderly interrupted them with papers for the Count to sign. They walked to the door together. The Count gave instructions in an inaudible voice. Ivan also seemed to be absorbed by the angry Tibetan god over Ushakov's desk. No one noticed Vasiliev pocket the letters.

"Count, could you tell me where Van der Fleet and Bagration are?"

"What? You mean right now? Let me see. They should be on their way to a meeting of a special investigating commission. It begins at five o'clock."

"In the Palace?"

"Of course, a small reception room in the west wing."

"Who is presiding?"

"General Obruchev, the Chief of Staff."

"Ah, yes, Nikolai Nikolaevich. We were together in the Caucasus. A patriot and an honest man. Count, I would like to appear before the commission at once." Vasiliev felt a dizziness come over him but he forced himself to sit upright in his chair. The angry god looked down on him; he seemed unforgiving.

"Yes, well, Vasiliev, let's not be too hasty. We have to plan our timing. You could walk into a hornet's nest. Ivan, please convince your friend that timing is everything now."

"I don't see that we have much to lose by moving expeditiously."

The Count walked across the room until he stood close enough for Ivan to smell his sour breath. "We do not know the tsar's pleasure," he said.

Ivan hesitated for a moment. The door opened again and a white head bowed. "All right, I'm on my way. Come Ivan, the Council of Ministers is breaking up. I need your advice." He turned to Vasiliev. "You've done heroic work, Inspector. I have already recommended you for the cross of St. Stanislaus, first class. But you should not exert yourself now. We are still in need of your services. Your wounds are severe. My personal orderly will serve you tea. And then we'll see to it that a special cab takes you back to your quarters. Later we will speak again."

Ushakov had taken Ivan by the arm and was propelling him forward. "Really Ivan, the demands you place on your subordinates." The door closed quietly behind them.

Vasiliev sat slumped in his chair, feeling nothing but pain and a great weariness. He closed his eyes and dozed off for a few minutes. He started awake when the orderly wheeled in a table bearing a samovar and a plate of poppy seed cakes. "Make it strong, will you please?"

The orderly filled the glass three quarters with *zavarka* and added hot water so that the tea was almost black.

"If you need anything, Your Honor just ring the bell. I've left it on the table."

Vasiliev gulped down the tea as fast as he could without scalding his tongue. He bit off a piece of poppy seed cake and rang the bell.

"Listen, my dear fellow, I'm all done in. Is there a place I can stretch out? Couldn't make it to a cab, need to rest."

"Certainly, sir. The Minister has put his entire suite at your disposal. If you give me your arm, well just go through here. You can stay as long as you wish. I'll put the bell right here on the table. I'm in the adjoining office."

Vasiliev thanked him, sat down heavily on a leather sofa and fell back. The orderly lifted his legs gently onto the sofa and covered them with a fur-lined pelisse.

"Where does that door lead? No one will come barging in here, will they?" Vasiliev pointed to a door at the opposite end of the room.

"No, it is a door to the corridor, but I'll make sure by locking it from the inside.

"Good, but leave a key. I have a phobia about being trapped in locked rooms. And one more thing. Could you roll in the samovar? I might need some tea after my nap. There's a good fellow."

When the orderly returned Vasiliev was snoring quietly. The orderly left the rolling table and tiptoed out of the room, after having made sure that the corridor door was locked and the key left lying next to the samovar.

At precisely five o'clock General Obruchev, freshly arrived from his post in Warsaw, called to order a meeting of the special investigating commission. A dozen officers and high ranking officials took their places around a circular table. Obruchev ran his eyes over the agenda. He was about to read it aloud when his aide-de-camp entered with a note and a sheaf of papers. Obruchev looked inquiringly at the young officer before reading the note. He set it aside and examined the papers carefully. When he finished he scribbled a few words on the back of the note and handed it to the aide-de-camp. Then he leaned back in his chair, removed his spectacles and placed the tips of his fingers together.

"Gentlemen, these are extraordinary times. They require, I think you will agree, unusual measures. Occasionally, in the field it is necessary to alter the order of battle at the very last moment when fresh intelligence has clarified the enemy's intentions." He paused. A low murmur spread around the table as members of the commission exchanged bewildered looks. "Now is such a moment. Will you please admit our guest."

The double doors swung open. "Inspector, Major Vasili Vasilievich Vasiliev of the Department of State Police."

Heads turned toward the door, faces registered annoyance and surprise. Prince Bagration who was sitting to General Obruchev's left half rose from his place. Van der Fleet, in the chair beside him, gripped his arm tightly and forced him back into his chair. Obruchev observed the pantomime with satisfaction and folded his hands on his stomach.

"You wish to make a statement, Vasili Vasilievich?"

"Your Excellencies, my apologies for interupting you. My deepest thanks to you, Nikolai Nikolaevich, for permission to speak outside the agenda. Gentlemen, the documents in the hands of General Obruchev include letters from a member of this commission to Countess Ushakova. With the testimony I am about to give they will prove his guilt in her murder."

A stunned silence was followed by a babble of voices. General Obruchev raised his hand for silence. He noted with satisfaction that the color had drained from Prince Bagration's face.

"You may proceed, Vasili Vasilievich."

"What's more important to the purpose of this meeting, I shall also show with the help of other documents in General Obruchev's possession that this same criminal together with a second member of this commission were directly responsible for the assassination of our beloved tsar, Alexander Nikolaevich, the Emancipator."

Vasiliev's last words were drowned out in the uproar. Several members sprang to their feet and began shouting at him. Others looked to General Obruchev, crying out, "Can this be true?"

Bagration shook off Van der Fleet and hurled himself on the table, grasping for the letters. He seized them before Obruchev could stop him and tore them into pieces which he began to stuff into his mouth, uttering guttural cries and choking as he tried to swallow them.

Van der Fleet calmly got to his feet, and for an instant stared at Vasiliev with bitter hatred. Then he turned smartly on his heel and left the room by the door behind General Obruchev. Vasiliev pushed aside two members of the commission who stood in his way. General Obruchev stood up to block him.

"It's not necessary, Vasili Vasilievich. There is no exit from that room."

A shot rang out. The shouting stopped at once and a hush fell over the room. The only sound that could be heard was the babbling of Prince Alexei Bagration as he sprawled half-conscious on the table, his hand clutching a white silk ribbon.

Epilogue

Excerpt from the Society Page of the *Duluth Post Dispatch*, October 3, 1916.

The twenty-fifth anniversary of the wedding and the arrival in Duluth of Basil and Irene Vas was celebrated last Saturday at the grand ballroom of the Midlands Hotel in downtown Duluth. Among the one hundred guests were many leading personalities from the political and cultural world of the city and state, as well as the Vas' twin sons, Thomas and Edward, graduates of the University of Minnesota in Law and Engineering. Basil and Irene were jointly honored with a presentation of the city's annual award for outstanding citizenship in recognition of their long and valued contribution to the life of our community.

Basil and Irene arrived in Duluth from Russia. Although descendants of noble families, they devoted their lives to the pursuit of justice and liberty for the downtrodden. Irene Vas had suffered exile in the cruel Siberian camp system for her political beliefs. Basil, known locally as the Major, enjoyed a reputation as a famous detective in Russia. His talents were immediately recognized in Duluth where he was elected sheriff for three consecutive terms without opposition. He was often heard to quip that he would have preferred to have had to run against an opponent; it was "more democratic" he said. He was known throughout the state for having introduced modern crime detection techniques.

Irene Vas became active in politics after having taught for ten years in the Duluth public school system, rising to the rank of principal and member of the city and then state education commission. She has been a strong supporter of woman's suffrage and an adviser to the state committee of the Farmer-Labor Party on that issue.

Basil and Irene founded two orphanages, the Alexander Boys Refuge and the Lincoln Girls Refuge, both, they told this reporter, to honor the men who freed the serfs and Russia and the slaves in our country. Basil was known as an avid hunter, always in the company of a native guide from the Ojibwa tribe. He and Irene established a medical point for the tribe and sponsored several Indian children in trade schools in Duluth. Basil was elected an honorary member of the tribe in 1910.

The concluding remarks at the banquet preceding the ball were delivered by Dr. John Letchik, an old friend and Chief of Surgery at the Duluth Medical Center.

THE REAL AND THE IMAGINARY

In 1874 after more than a decade of reforms, a number of idealistic students fan out into the Russian countryside preaching socialism to the peasants. They are met with indifference or hostility. Many are arrested. This was the "mad summer of '74." Five years later an underground organization called Land and Liberty dedicated to the same goals splits into two wings. The advocates of spreading socialism through propaganda take the name Black Repartition meaning the redistribution of the Russian land among the land-hungry peasantry. The other wing, the People's Will, embraces terror. Their goal is to kill the tsar, thereby removing the lynchpin that holds together the autocratic government and opening the way for socialism. While they hunt the tsar, the tsar's secret police, the Gendarmes, hunt them. The terrorists penetrate the police and the police turn them into double agents. Spectacular attempts like the bombing of the Winter Palace by Stefan Khalturin persuade the tsar to adopt counter measures. He appoints General Loris-Melikov, hero of the Russo-Turkish War of 1877-78, as a reforming Minister of Interior. Called the dictator of the heart Loris-Melikov institutes tight security measures but also seeks to rally public opinion against the terrorists by creating an elected advisory body to the tsar. The Gendarmes arrest the leader of the People's Will, Zheliabov; the tunnel under the cheese shop is discovered. But the tsar is killed by the bombs of the remaining members of the People's Will. These events provide the historical background for the novel. The conspiracy of Van der Fleet and Bagration is invented. So are most of the characters in the novel though they represent real historical types. The novel was inspired by a lingering question about the tsar's last ride. Why did his coach not follow the prescribed "safe way home?"

CAST OF CHARACTERS

Many historical characters are merely mentioned but do not appear in person including the radical critic Nikolai Chernyshevsky whose picture adorns the safe room, Mikhail Katkov, the conservative editor, and revolutionaries captured by the Gendarmes: Goldenberg, Kletochnikov, Mikhailov.

Other historical figures who do appear are as follows:

Alexander Nikolaevich (Emperor or Tsar Alexander II)
Alexander Alexandrovich (his son, heir to the throne and later Alexander III)
Ekaterina Dolgorukaya, Princess Yurovskaia (the tsar's morganatic wife)
Lt. General Loris-Melikov, Minister of Interior
Colonel Adrian Dvorzhitsky, commander of the tsar's bodyguard
General Nikolai Obruchev, chair of the special committee on the assassination
Stepan Khalturin, member of the People's Will
Andrei Zheliabov, member of the People's Will

Imaginary characters

Major, Inspector Vasili (Vasya) Vasilievich Vasiliev
Sergeant Serov
Borka
Ivan, the Iron Colonel
Count Dmitri Ushakov
Countess Elena Ushakova
General Gregory (Grisha) Shuev

Colonel Nikolai (Kolya) Van der Fleet
Prince Bagration (a real name but here a fictional person)
Princess Tamara Bagration
Young Prince Bagration
Irina (Irisha) Davidova (Swan)
Iuri Tarashkin (Magician)
Letchik (Healer)
Norka (Minx)
Marko
Petya
Nasya

All the minor characters are also imagined.

Readers who wish to pursue an interest in the terrorist plots to assassinate the tsar might begin with a new edition of an older classic, Avrahm Yarmolinsky, *Road to Revolution: A Century of Russian Radicalism.*

CPSIA information can be obtained at www.ICGtesting.com
Printed in the USA
BVOW03s1713041113

335317BV00001B/223/P